IN THE HOUSE
OF THE WICKED

A REMY CHANDLER NOVEL

THOMAS E. SNIEGOSKI

A ROC BOOK

ROC
Published by the Penguin Group
Penguin Group (USA) Inc., 375 Hudson Street,
New York, New York 10014, USA

USA | Canada | UK | Ireland | Australia | New Zealand | India | South Africa | China

Penguin Books Ltd., Registered Offices: 80 Strand, London WC2R 0RL, England
For more information about the Penguin Group visit penguin.com.

Published by Roc, an imprint of New American Library, a division of Penguin
Group (USA) Inc. Previously published in a Roc trade paperback edition.

First Roc Mass Market Printing, August 2013
10 9 8 7 6 5 4 3 2 1

 REGISTERED TRADEMARK—MARCA REGISTRADA

ISBN 978-0-451-41544-8

Printed in the United States of America

PUBLISHER'S NOTE
This is a work of fiction. Names, characters, places, and incidents either are the product of the author's imagination or are used fictitiously, and any resemblance to actual persons, living or dead, business establishments, events, or locales is entirely coincidental.

The publisher does not have any control over and does not assume any responsibility for author or third-party Web sites or their content.

For Hurricane Irene . . . thanks for nothing. . . .
And for Pat and Bob Dexter, thanks for the juice.

ACKNOWLEDGMENTS

For LeeAnne, as always, for all that you do, and Kirby for making me smile.

Thanks also to Christopher Golden, Ginjer Buchanan, Katherine Sherbo, Liesa Abrams, James Mignogna, Dave "Who Threw the Pies?" Kraus, Kathy Kraus, Pam Daley, Mom & Dad Sniegoski, Mom & Dad Fogg, Pete Donaldson, Kenn Gold, Erek Vachne, Garrett Jones, and Timothy Cole and the Morlocks down at Cole's Comics in Lynn.

Farewell and adieu to my dear Spanish Lady . . .

—Tom

PROLOGUE

Occupied Poland, Dachau
1943

It was cold in the interrogation hut, and Konrad Deacon wondered how much longer it would be.

For a moment he considered that the man he wished to speak with had already met his fate in the chambers, that the invaluable information he held in his mind was lost to the ages as suffocating gas filled his lungs, and all that he had been was turned to smoke and ash within the fires of the crematorium.

It was a disturbing thought, and one that Deacon did not wish to dwell upon as he sat in the wooden chair behind the simple desk, clutching his leather satchel to his chest, waiting for the man promised by Reichsführer Himmler himself.

The information Deacon hoped to receive from this man was priceless, and should be more than enough to finally allow him membership in the cabal. He'd been trying to gain a seat for years, but now he believed he had found something that would finally force the gathering of the world's most powerful sorcerers to recognize him.

He squirmed impatiently in the chair, then pulled up the edge of his purple leather glove to check the time. He'd been waiting twenty minutes, but it might as well have been twenty hours, as far as he was concerned.

Konrad Deacon was not accustomed to waiting, and contemplated voicing his displeasure to der Führer when next they met to review Adolf Hitler's astrological chart.

Yes, Hitler was indeed a madman, but even madmen were useful. Let him have the world if it would reveal to Konrad the mysteries of the universe beyond the pale.

The sudden sound of heavy-booted feet made him gasp, and Deacon looked toward the door in anticipation. He stood, satchel still clutched to his chest, watching as the door swung open and armed soldiers roughly pushed a tattered old man inside.

Deacon studied the hunched figure. He was clothed only in the filthy, shapeless, striped uniform of the concentration camp; worn leather shoes missing their laces were on his feet. His hair had been shorn to the skull, his once-impressive beard cut away. But even in this desolate state the old man radiated something special.

It was a power passed down from the ages, a power that would be no more once this vessel met its inevitable end. Which was why Deacon had come to this godforsaken place, to speak with this godforsaken man.

The old man shivered as he gazed about the interrogation shed, his dark, sunken eyes clearly wondering why he had been brought here, what new horrors awaited him.

"Rabbi Eshed," Deacon acknowledged the man, unable to suppress a smile.

Eshed stumbled back, as if repelled by Deacon's joy in such a loathsome environment. The holy man turned his gaze toward the guards who still waited at the door, then back to Deacon.

"You may wait outside," Deacon told the pair.

They hesitated, giving each other a worried look.

"I take full responsibility for the prisoner," Deacon reassured them. "And I will be sure that Reichsführer Himmler hears of your excellent service." He lifted a gloved hand and motioned them out.

"Much better," Deacon said, as the guards stepped outside and closed the door. Then he gestured at the chair positioned directly in front of the desk. "Please sit," he said to Eshed, and he sat again, the wooden chair creaking under his weight.

Eshed didn't move.

"Sit," Deacon repeated, an edge to his voice. "I insist."

"Why have I been brought here?" Eshed asked, moving slowly toward the chair.

Deacon did not answer, silently watching the old rabbi as he carefully lowered himself into the chair.

"Thank you," Deacon finally said. He placed his leather satchel down upon the desk and reached inside to remove a leather-bound journal. "You wouldn't believe the pest I made of myself trying to locate you, Rabbi."

"Locate me?" the old man asked. He sat stiffly, eyes darting warily about. "For what reason?"

Deacon placed the satchel on the floor against the chair leg, then centered the journal on the table in front of him. He removed his gloves and put them in the pockets of his coat. Then he opened the journal to where a pen had marked his place.

"At first I believed the stories to be nonsense," Deacon said as he removed the pen's cover and placed it on the table beside the book. "But then I continued to hear them, and I began to wonder if they might, after all, be true."

Deacon looked up, running his bare hand over the creamy white surface of the blank page.

"Stories," the old man repeated. "What stories have you heard?"

Deacon smiled again.

"One about a battalion of fine German soldiers assigned to purge a tiny Polish village of its Jewish influence, only to be ruthlessly killed by a monster."

He watched the old man's eyes, searching for a hint.

"A monster made of clay."

Still the old Jew showed nothing.

"A monster brought to life using ancient magicks long believed lost with the passage of time," Deacon continued.

"Fairy tales," Eshed grunted.

"Excuse me?"

"You have brought me here to discuss fanciful tales told to children to make them behave—to eat their vegetables and to go to sleep when they are told. Yes, of course I know these stories well. I heard them from my own parents and told them to my—"

"You misunderstand me, Rabbi," Deacon interrupted, feeling his ire begin to rise. "I talk not of fairy tales, but of actual eyewitness reports that—"

"Drunks and fools," Rabbi Eshed spat. He managed what appeared to be a smile, though it could very well have been a grimace of pain.

"Let me be certain that I understand. You are calling soldiers of the Third Reich drunks and fools?"

"Perhaps they concoct such fantastic stories to deflect the truth that a village of farmers and craftsmen were able to defeat so many of their number. Of course it was a golem that stopped them. . . . What else could possibly have stopped the führer's expert soldiers?"

The old Jew actually laughed then, a horrible sound that said so much of how the holy man felt about his captors.

"I said nothing about a golem, Rabbi Eshed," Deacon said.

"Everyone knows the tales," the rabbi countered. "A man of clay brought to life by supernatural means to avenge the offended."

Deacon slowly nodded. "Of course, of course," he murmured, running the smooth part of his thumb up and down the shaft of his pen. "But what of those from your village? Those who, to spare their own lives, swore that the golem was indeed real and that it was you who brought it to life."

"Many would swear to almost anything if they believed it would grant them another few moments of life," Eshed said.

"Do you honestly believe that's true, Rabbi?" Deacon asked, feigning a sad smile. "That your people would swear to a lie before meeting their maker?"

"We believe in the afterlife, but doubt of its existence is never stronger than when we are faced with death. Some cling desperately to what they already know rather than face the uncertainty of the unknown."

"How about you?" Deacon asked. "Do you fear the unknown?"

The old Jew shook his shaggy head. "I do not," he said. "For I know that Paradise is waiting."

"Then all of this"—Deacon lifted his hand, gesturing to indicate the world outside the shack, the concentration camp—"it means nothing."

The old man did not answer, but his eyes were intense as they bored into Deacon's.

"And what of your family?" Deacon asked. "Do they believe as you?"

There. Deacon saw the slight flicker in the holy man's gaze.

"My family is . . ."

"Your daughter-in-law," Deacon continued. "And two grandchildren, if I'm not mistaken." He reached into the pocket of his coat and removed a folded piece of paper. "Jacob and Hannah," he said, looking up from the names. "Perhaps I shouldn't have stopped their executions . . . perhaps I should have allowed them to feel the embrace of your God."

"They are alive?" the old man asked.

Is that a spark of hope in his ancient eyes? Deacon certainly hoped so.

"Jacob is quite proud of his grandpa," he said. "The stories he told me . . . and little Hannah, as well."

The rabbi looked down at the floor.

"But, of course, they're just children," Deacon said. "Repeating fairy stories told to make them eat and go to bed."

"Exactly," Rabbi Eshed said, his gaze still on the floor.

"But what if their stories were true?" Deacon mused. "How wonderful would it be if Jacob and Hannah's beloved grandpa could create a man made from clay and bring it to life, to thwart their enemies? What a world this would be, eh?" He placed his hands on either side of the open journal. "It would be a world that Jacob and Hannah could live in for quite some time, a world filled with magick."

The old man finally met Deacon's gaze.

"I could give them that world," Deacon pressed. "I could see that they were taken from this place."

It was indeed hope that he had seen in the holy man's eyes, and now it burned out of control.

Deacon knew that he was close and carefully reached for his pen. "For the sake of Jacob and Hannah—"

"What . . . what do you wish to know?" Eshed asked, defeated.

Deacon set pen to paper.

"Tell me everything."

Eshed spoke for hours.

Once the words began, there was no holding them back. Some of what he had to say was already familiar to Deacon, but there was much that wasn't, so many details . . . multifaceted pieces of information that finally revealed the magnitude of it all.

They were at it for hours: spells, diagrams, formulas, and words. The rabbi gave him everything Deacon would need to create his own man of clay and to improve upon it.

When they had begun, the journal was empty, and now it was nearly filled. Deacon felt an overwhelming sense of joy and accomplishment as he flipped through the pages. There was so much work to be done now that he had all the missing pieces.

He'd become so engrossed with what he had collected that the sudden appearance of the two guards surprised him. But then he remembered where he was and who had helped to fill the sucking void of arcane knowledge that had eluded him for so long.

Rabbi Eshed still sat across from him, looking far smaller than when he'd first entered the room. It was as if all the knowledge he had revealed had somehow caused him to diminish in size.

The guards stared from the open door, the cold, Polish winter flowing into the confines of the tiny room. Deacon's time with Rabbi Eshed was at an end.

He pulled his purple gloves from his coat pockets and jammed his freezing hands into them. Then he closed his burgeoning journal, retrieved his leather satchel, and slid his prize inside.

The old man watched his every action with growing anticipation.

Deacon stood and, clutching the satchel protectively to his chest, walked around the desk and past the old rabbi. Eshed turned in his chair and reached out to grab the sleeve of his cashmere coat.

The guards moved, but Deacon stopped them with a glance. He turned his gaze to the old man.

"My grandchildren," the rabbi said hesitantly. "You . . . you said that if I were to tell you . . . that they would be safe."

Deacon pulled his arm from the old man's desperate clutches.

"Rest assured, they are in a better place," Deacon said coldly, watching as the realization sank in and the light of hope that had been in the old rabbi's eyes was extinguished.

"They . . . they are already dead," Eshed proclaimed, the weight of the words seeming to crush him down even farther into the chair.

"Freed from the horrors of this world, so they can find peace in the next," Deacon said, feeling no shame. "I will be sure to tell Reichsführer Himmler of your excellent service to me," he again praised the guards as he passed between them on his way out the door.

"Herr Deacon," boomed the rabbi's voice from the cold space behind him. It was as if he'd been grabbed by the shoulder and spun around to face the old Jew, who still had not risen from his chair.

"Another piece of information I give to you of my own

free will." A new fired burned in Rabbi Eshed's eyes. "There will be a special darkness for you," he proclaimed, as if knowing the words he spoke were undeniably true. "For you and all who would dare to love you."

Then the rabbi abruptly turned his back to Deacon.

Finished with him.

Finished with this world.

Waiting for Heaven.

CHAPTER ONE

It had been quite some time since Remy had last listened.

That was why he was here, standing before the high front gates of the New Hampshire Correctional Facility, staring at the harsh angles of the prison beyond.

He had come because he had listened again.

Thunder crashed, lightning pulsed across the nighttime sky, and rain fell in straight sheets to the earth. Remy was soaked to the skin, but he didn't give it a thought, his mind occupied with the reason for his being in this inhospitable place on this most inclement of evenings.

He had come in answer to a prayer.

A prayer that he, a former emissary of Heaven, had overheard as someone had pleaded for God's attention. And although Remy had struggled to block out those prayers in his quest to be human, tonight he had heard and was compelled to act.

Invisible to the video cameras that watched the comings and goings from the prison, Remy spread his powerful wings to their full span and, with a single mighty thrust, lifted himself up and over the fence to the open yard beyond.

The world was changing. He could smell it in the air, taste it on the tip of his tongue, feel it like a faint electric current on the surface of his skin. Remy knew it had to do with how close the earth had come to the Apocalypse a year or two back, a catastrophe that he had had a major role in averting. Ever since then, life had been growing stranger, deadlier, with every passing day—as if being that close to the end had set the world on a different path.

Stirred things up like silt from the bottom of a lake.

Remy had changed, as well, for the love of his life had died, and without her strength, he'd found himself fighting to hold on to the humanity that he'd worked so hard to fabricate. His human nature had begun to tatter, his angelic essence trying to assert itself as he drifted further away from the mundane existence he had created as a private investigator—and husband.

But as the world that he loved—and fought for—continued to transform, Remy had to face the fact that the warlike nature of the Seraphim was needed. If he was going to continue to protect this changing world and all he loved from the rapidly escalating supernatural threats, the two warring natures at the core of his being would have to unite.

Finally, with the help of the memory of his beloved Madeline, Remy had embraced a side of his nature that he had been attempting to stifle for thousands of years. Remy Chandler was transformed.

Whole.

The human and the angelic were one. He was a creature of both Earth and Heaven, and tonight he had chanced a listen to the prayers of humanity. It was a mother's plea that had touched him tonight, compelling both the human and the Seraphim to action.

Remy walked across the puddle-covered blacktop of the prison yard and stopped beside a guard who stood outside the main entrance, smoking a cigarette beneath an overhang. Patiently, he waited in the steady fall downpour as the man finished his smoke, then followed him into the brightly lit building, the heavy metal door slamming closed behind them.

Remy had been relaxing on the roof of his Beacon Hill

brownstone, sipping a glass of Scotch as his canine friend, Marlowe, snored loudly at his feet. The rain hadn't started, but the dampness permeated the air, and he'd known that it was only a matter of time before it did.

He had seen the glow of the lights at Fenway Park and absently wondered if the Sox would be able to get their game in before the deluge. He had allowed the effects of the alcohol to wash over him. His psychic connection to the world's inhabitants danced in the corners of his perception. Normally he would have blotted it out, not wanting to eavesdrop on the pleas of the needy and devout, but something about this particular night had encouraged him to open himself up to the cacophony of prayers.

It had been like being in a sea of sound, a multitude of voices in every worldly dialect, all speaking at the same time.

Remy had been tempted to pull back from the deafening roar but forced himself to concentrate, whittling down the sounds of many to a select few, until he was focusing on only one, the strongest and most plaintive of them all.

The prayers of Catherine Perlas.

Remy was deep inside the prison now. The noxious smell of violence and desperation hung stagnant in the air, despite the nearly overwhelming stink of industrial cleaner. He'd left his escort to wander on his own and was passing the prison infirmary when his acute hearing picked up the sound of heavy breathing—someone fast asleep.

He stepped inside a darkened office to find an older man sleeping at his desk, file folders spread out before him as if sleep had claimed him in the midst of work. Silently, Remy approached the man.

"Robert Denning," he said softly in the voice of an angel.

The man twitched with a grunt and slowly raised his head, leaving a small puddle of drool on one of the folders. He looked around the room, bleary-eyed and still mostly asleep, searching for the source of the voice.

"Where can I find him?" Remy whispered into the man's other ear.

The man could barely keep his eyes open. His head bobbed up and down as sleep tried to pull him into its embrace once more.

"Where is Robert Denning?" Remy repeated.

"Maximum Security," the man mumbled. "Special Housing, Unit Six."

His eyes closed again, and this time they did not open. His breathing grew deeper as he laid his head back down on his pillow of folders. He was snoring as Remy looked around the office, searching for some kind of floor plan. On the back of the door he found an emergency map of the facility and quickly located the maximum-security wing.

Catherine Perlas had lost her daughter and twin grandchildren to murder, and prayed with all she had that God would punish their killer.

The story had been all over the local news. Charlotte Marsh, a thirty-three-year-old single mother, and her six-year-old daughters had been found brutally murdered in their Camden, New Hampshire, home. They had been together, maimed to render them unable to escape, and Charlotte had been the last to die.

Who could do such a thing and why? asked everyone who heard the tale of horror. The answer was far from satisfying, and more disturbing than most could bear.

Robert Denning was a twenty-year-old college dropout and, according to the testimony at his trial, had always been curious about how it would feel to take a life. After a particularly taxing day when he'd fought with his girlfriend, Robert had felt the overwhelming desire to satisfy that murderous curiosity.

He'd seen Charlotte and her daughters, Amanda and Emily, at a local supermarket and followed them home. He had parked his car and waited, unnoticed, until the house grew dark. Then he'd entered through an unlocked door in the garage. Details were sketchy, but they said he'd taken his time with them.

Remy found his way into Maximum Security, transporting himself through the locked doors by wrapping his wings about his body and picturing the other side.

It was as if the prisoners asleep behind the doors of the cells could sense his divine presence; many of them cried out pathetically as he strolled past. Most simply returned to a restless sleep when he paid them no mind—the prowling Seraphim on the hunt for a specific prey.

Denning had tried to escape human justice by declaring that he was insane at the time of the murders, but the jury hadn't bought it, agreeing with the prosecutor, who had portrayed the man as a cold, calculating killer.

Remy stopped before a white metal door, the number 6 stenciled large and black above the single Plexiglas window. He stood for a moment staring at the door, imagining what was on the other side. A part of him—*his human side*—yearned to sense some unspeakable evil emanating from the cell, something beyond the norm that would explain why Robert Denning had done what he had.

A form of demonic possession or some such manifestation of evil.

A way to make some strange kind of sense from the senseless.

But Remy felt nothing out of the ordinary, and that just made it all the more maddening.

The angel stepped closer to the cell, peering into the small, darkened space, seeing a shape huddled beneath a blanket on the bed.

He opened his wings, wrapped them about himself once again, and he was there on the other side of the door, beside the bed, watching the figure in the embrace of a seemingly peaceful sleep. Remy wondered briefly about Catherine Perlas, wondered if it was possible for the poor woman to sleep peacefully again. Or would she be forever haunted by the memories of her murdered family?

His emotions had never been more acute as they had since embracing his angelic side once more. Even the most mundane feelings affected him with startling acuity. Never had he experienced love so strongly, or, as in this particular instant—

Hate.

"Robert Denning," Remy said into the darkness, his voice resonating with divine presence. "Awaken."

Denning stirred on the bed, the angel's command pulling him into the waking world.

"What? Who's there?" the young man asked sleepily, pushing himself up on his elbows, squinting into the shadows.

Remy chose to remain visible this time and had not hidden his wings. The brilliant white of their feathers cast an unearthly radiance about the cramped cell.

And Robert Denning saw what had come into his room. He sat up with a sucking gasp, throwing himself back against the wall, clutching his blanket tightly beneath his chin.

His eyes were wide and filled with fear, and Remy wondered if the young man was thinking of Charlotte, Amanda, and Emily then . . . thinking of how afraid they had been in his presence that night he had yearned for and sampled the act of murder.

Remy hoped that he was.

"What the fuck?" Denning screamed.

"Keep your voice down," Remy commanded, not wanting the murderer's cries to summon any of the prison staff.

Denning opened his mouth to cry out again, but Remy was across the small room with the speed of thought, snatching up the prisoner by the front of his jumpsuit. "You will not cry out again," Remy ordered, his face mere inches from that of the young man.

He had taken on the full guise of the Seraphim warrior, his body adorned in golden armor, stained with the blood of recent battles, of which there had been many.

Denning's mouth moved like that of a dying fish desperate to feel the flow of water over its gills again.

Remy looked into his eyes . . . *really* looked into his eyes. They were welling up with tears, but there was little else there; no sign of some otherworldly evil that might have taken up residence in a frail human shell.

All Remy saw was a terrified human being.

"I . . ." Denning was trying to speak but was having difficulty forcing the words from his gaping mouth. "I . . . I'm . . ."

"What?" Remy snarled. "What do you have to say for yourself?"

"I'm . . . sorry," Denning managed, and then fell limp, sobbing uncontrollably in Remy's grasp.

"You're sorry?" Remy asked incredulously, barely able to control the anger in his voice. "You took the life of a mother and her two children in cold blood, and you're sorry?"

Remy could feel the divine fire building up inside him, traveling through his body as he remembered the prayers of a mother who had lost so much. It took a mighty effort not to allow the hungry flame to emerge, to consume the flesh of the lowly human he held, to award him an excruciatingly painful death.

It would be the closet thing to Hell that Remy could manage.

The fire . . . the fire of Heaven would start with the soul first, burning it away before moving on to the physical . . . the flesh and blood, organs and bones. It would happen quickly, but a pain like that would seem to last forever.

And it couldn't happen to a nicer guy.

The flames moved down Remy's arm toward his hand, and he struggled to hold it back, trying to convince himself that this wasn't want he wanted to do.

But it was what he wanted . . . what the Seraphim wanted.

He heard Catherine's plaintive prayers again echoing inside his skull, begging the Almighty to punish the man who had taken her loved ones.

And wasn't that what the angel Remiel had been created to do? To carry out God's will? To be His divine messenger?

Denning was looking up at him, tears streaming down a face flushed with emotion as he jabbered on.

"I never believed in you . . . I never knew. . . . So sorry for what I did . . . sorry that I didn't believe . . . so, so sorry . . ."

Remy could feel the fire at his fingertips now, straining to be released.

Hungry to feed on the flesh of the sinner. To return this one to the dust from whence he had come.

Suddenly his fingers began to glow, and Remy knew he could no longer hold it back.

With a growl, he roughly tossed the young man away, back onto the bed. Then Remy threw his wings about himself like a cloak of feathers and was transported high above the prison into the storm-swept sky, where he released the fire of Heaven into the night, his own furious screams drowned out by the roar of thunder.

His rage temporarily spent, Remy returned to the prison cell to find Denning kneeling, his face pressed to the floor, his body trembling uncontrollably and stinking of urine, as he prayed for forgiveness to a God who was not listening.

Denning slowly raised his head, and Remy felt a certain satisfaction when he spotted five circular burns on the man's face where he'd gripped him with a hand engorged with Heavenly fire. And in the young murderer's eyes was terror, a terror that had taken him beyond the brink.

It had been a struggle not to kill him, but Remy had come to the realization that it wasn't his place. Human justice had prevailed here, and now, for as long as he lived, Robert Denning would never know another moment without fear.

Fear of living, and what awaited him beyond.

For now that would have to be enough.

Spain
1945

The magick was killing him.

But it was also keeping him alive.

Algernon Stearns clutched the knife in his hand all the tighter as black spots blossomed before his eyes.

The irony of the situation was not lost to him as he stumbled forward, grabbing hold of one of the child's spindly legs in an attempt to keep from falling. The boy tried to scream, but the gag in his mouth stopped the sound. His body, hanging upside down from a thick metal hook in the stone ceiling of the basement chamber, began to swing like a pendulum.

Algernon's old flesh tingled and he sweated profusely beneath his scarlet robes, despite the chill temperatures in the secret room beneath the Spanish castle. He opened his mouth and took in large gulps of air, trying to keep from losing consciousness.

The preparations for the spell had taken more out of him this time than they usually did—another sign that his time was growing short. How many times had he performed this very ritual? A parade of young faces coursed past his mind's eye, reminding him of those he had sacrificed to extend his life over the past twenty years or so.

And he needed to perform the ritual more frequently.

The dizziness finally passed, and Stearns reached out to steady the struggling child.

"That'll be enough of that," he said in the boy's own tongue, but it did nothing to calm the youth, for he knew that his life would soon be forfeit.

But better the child's life be extinguished than Stearns' own. There was much he still desired from the living world, and he meant to have it all.

Stearns gazed down at the circle drawn on the floor beneath the youth's head, wanting to be certain that the sigils were intact. They had been meticulously drawn in chalk molded from the bones of a Catholic nun impregnated by a demon conjured from the region of the seventh veil. To have even a single line out of place meant certain death for the conjurer.

And this conjuring was all about keeping himself very much alive.

He slid the knife through the belt of his robes and turned toward the altar, where he'd arranged the items he would need. Grabbing the copper bowl, he carefully bent down and placed it in the center of the mystic circle, directly beneath the child's head. Then he retrieved the ancient tome from its place on the altar, opening to the page that held the spell to prolong his life. He hoped he had enough strength left to see it through.

The old man began to read ancient words of power transcribed when humanity was still very young. The words flowed from his mouth, and the power they carried chipped away at his life force. His eyesight began to blur, and tufts of hair, once a golden yellow, fell from his dry scalp to obscure the arcane words on the page from which he struggled to read.

Every time he performed this spell, Stearns had to wonder if this would be the time he expired before he could finish.

The air was suddenly charged with arcane energies as the last words of the spell slipped from lips numbed by age and weakness. The boy hanging from the ceiling began to spin slowly above the circle, moved by the powers that had answered the sorcerer's summons.

Stearns let the book fall from his grasp, not having the strength to return it to its place upon the altar. He lurched toward the spinning youth, plucking the sacrificial knife from beneath his belt.

The child spun round and round, and Stearns waited for his opportunity. He had to strike at precisely the right moment, severing the jugular exactly as it presented itself.

To miss would be disastrous.

Through eyes failing by the moment, Stearns watched as the boy's throat came round once more, the vein that carried the source of life—*his continued life*—pulsing beneath the thin covering of tanned flesh.

And he struck, almost missing the mark, but still managing to puncture the skin and nick the vein. It meant that the child would die more slowly, but Stearns didn't care, as long as he got what he needed.

Blood poured from the child's throat into the copper bowl beneath his head. Weakness drove Stearns to his knees upon the cold stone floor as he waited for the bowl to fill, his hands ready to snatch it up.

"Come on," he growled, surprised by the sound of his own voice, his vocal cords ancient and dry, the image of a mummified corpse struggling to speak filling his fevered thoughts.

He pitched forward, unable to stop himself from falling, but at least still having the dexterity to avoid disturbing the chalk circle. He lay on his side, eyes transfixed by the thread of scarlet raining down from the dying child's throat.

Maybe it's enough, he thought, willing his hands to reach into the circle, but then reminding himself that all the blood must be within the bowl to have any lasting effect on him. Slowly, he withdrew his withered hands.

And still the blood continued to drain.

The vision of red had turned to black, and Stearns did not even realize that he had lost consciousness. He struggled in the pitch darkness, feeling the pull of death upon him and hearing the unfamiliar sound of wings flapping in the chamber around him.

Was this the angel of death arriving at last to claim the prize that had evaded him for so very long?

And then there came the taste of revitalizing blood on his lips.

The warm fluid flowed into his mouth, and Stearns immediately felt its rejuvenating effects—the horrible burning pain as his body began to repair itself.

Stearns gulped the blood; the faster the magically enhanced life stuff entered his system, the quicker he could reclaim the vitality almost permanently leeched from him.

Returning from the brink of death, the old sorcerer finally opened his eyes.

"What madness is this?" he asked at the sight of a small, gargoylelike creature drawing back the nearly empty bowl of blood from his lips.

The creature did not appear to be of flesh but of some kind of stone, and it stared at Stearns with eyes that were no more than pinpricks of light in the craggy makeup of its face.

"What are you?" Stearns asked, more fascinated now than anything else. This strange thing had saved him. But why?

The stone creature lurched toward him, bowl in its three-fingered hands, offering its contents once more. Stearns took it and drained the remainder of the blood in one mighty gulp.

His skin tingled as the cells repaired themselves; the burning on his scalp told him that his blond hair was again starting to grow.

The gargoyle watched intently as Stearns carefully placed the empty bowl on the ground beside him.

"Did someone send you?" he asked the creature, wiping the blood from his lips with the sleeve of his scarlet robe.

He stood easily, the movement sending the beast into the air, fluttering impossibly on wings of stone before landing atop the sorcerer's altar.

"You must have come here for a reason," Stearns continued. "Tell me why you have saved my life. Show me why you are here."

The gargoyle stared silently at him for a moment, then sat down on the altar, wrapping its spindly arms around its knees and opening its mouth.

Stearns watched in awe as the creature's mouth opened wider and wider still, and then a voice emanated from the darkness within.

A voice shockingly familiar.

"Greetings, Algernon. So happy to be of assistance."

"Deacon?" Algernon questioned, drawing closer to the creature. "Is that you?"

"It is, my friend," the voice of Konrad Deacon replied. "It has been too long."

Deacon spoke the truth. It had indeed been a very long time since Stearns had last seen him, or any other member of their sorcerers' guild, for that matter. The members of the cabal had become more concerned with pursuits of an individual nature, amassing power and building their own personal empires.

"To what do I owe your timely visit?" Stearns asked.

"I come bearing a gift." Deacon's excited voice drifted out from the mouth of the gargoyle. "The gift of life."

"Life? What do you mean?"

"Exactly that. Life, my brother. More life than you could possibly imagine."

Stearns was intrigued, for life was something that the sorcerer could always use more of.

In fact, he was quite greedy in his desire of it.

One could say he was insatiable.

The air warped and rippled just above the road outside the New Hampshire Correctional Facility. There was a brief flash of white and the sound of wings beating the air as a rend in the fabric of time and space appeared to disgorge Remy Chandler.

The Seraphim stumbled as he came forth, folding away his appendages of flight as he caught his balance and began to walk.

Remy knew that he'd done the right thing in leaving the young murderer alone with his fear, but a part of him still wasn't satisfied, and if he'd stayed any longer, Denning would have been dead.

That was what he'd always been wary of, why he'd pushed the angelic essence of the Seraphim deeper and deeper inside himself, locking it away. It had always been wild, always reacting on instinct only.

It was what Remy feared.

What if he continued to think more like an angel? What if the more rational, human side of his dual nature hadn't won this time?

The urge was still there, like an itch at the center of his spine, taunting him to scratch.

A vibrating sensation from the pocket of his jacket suddenly, thankfully, distracted him from his troubling thoughts, and Remy pulled out his phone and saw that Linda was calling.

He guessed that he would call her his girlfriend, but something still didn't feel quite right about that. It was odd talking with another woman after having been with Madeline for so long; even odder to know that he was beginning to develop feelings for Linda. He still felt guilty at times that he was somehow cheating on his dead wife. His issue, of course, and something else that he would have to deal with.

"Hey," he answered.

"Hey yourself," Linda replied. "What's going on?"

"Nothing much," Remy lied, as he continued to walk down the center of the deserted road. The rain had temporarily ceased, but the air was still saturated, causing a writhing mist to snake up from the ground as the evening temperature gradually cooled. "Just wrapping up some stuff for work. What's going on with you?"

"I got out of class early," she said. "I'm planning a date with some lounging clothes, a bottle of Merlot, and the *Real Housewives of New Jersey.*"

"Sure one bottle will be enough for all of you?" Remy joked. "I hear those housewives can really put it away."

She laughed, and he was reminded again of how much he liked the sound—and her.

"I miss you," she said.

Remy stopped walking, experiencing that moment of electricity that proved he wasn't the only one starting to have those kinds of feelings.

"I miss you, too."

"So, what are you doing now?" Linda asked again.

He was about to suggest that he join her and the house-wives when he remembered that he still had something left to do.

"I was planning on stopping by Steven Mulvehill's," he said.

"Has he returned any of your calls?" she asked, concern in her voice.

Linda was aware that a rift had formed between the two friends, but she hadn't been made privy to the specifics. The homicide detective had become involved in one of Remy's recent cases and had received a full dose of the kind of world that Remy often walked in.

A kind of world that Steven would have preferred never to have seen.

"No, he hasn't," Remy admitted. "But I'm thinking of dropping by his place, anyway, to try to straighten this business out face-to-face."

"Good luck with that," she wished him.

"Thanks. I think he just needed some time to himself. Things should be fine once we've had a chance to talk. No worries."

"Do you want to stop by after?" she asked.

"I'd love to, but Marlowe's been alone for most of the day, and—"

"Bring him with you," she interrupted.

Remy felt himself smiling at the suggestion. It had been a few days since the dog had seen Linda, and Remy knew he'd jump at the chance to go for a ride in the car, especially if it meant seeing his new friend. It would definitely make up for having been left alone for most of the day.

"Let me see how late it is once Steven and I get finished."

"No pressure," Linda said. "Just thought it would be nice to see you."

"And Marlowe?"

"And Marlowe." She laughed. "I've been missing him, too."

"I'll give you a call when I leave Steven's, okay?"

"I'll be here."

"Talk to you later."

"Bye."

Remy put his phone back in his pocket and looked around, surprised to see how far he'd wandered while chatting. The prison was off in the distance now, practically hidden by the thickening fog.

Far enough away that he was able to resist the temptation to go back.

CHAPTER TWO

The Catskill Mountains
The Deacon Estate
February 1945

Deacon's hands trembled as he tried to knot the silk bow tie about his throat.

He admitted to himself that he was indeed nervous about the night to come, but the tremor through his once-surgeon-steady hands and the painful ache deep in his joints were what made this evening crucial.

"Damn it," he hissed, ripping the failed attempt from about his white-collared throat.

He gazed at the angry image of himself in the mirror on the armoire door, seeing a man much older than his forty years. The skin around his eyes had begun to dry and wrinkle; lines and age spots showed on his once-smooth brow. Hair that had been jet-black, like a raven's feathers, was now streaked with gray, and his hairline was starting to recede.

The magick had done this to him; every time he called on the dark arts, it took a little bit more of his life.

It was a fair price to pay for immortality, but was there enough currency remaining to achieve such lofty goals? Deacon was not sure, which was why he had called for the gathering this fateful evening.

He placed the black silk around his neck again, willing his fingers to do as he instructed, but the stiffness . . .

"Here, let me," Veronica said, coming up behind him.

His wife took control of the tie, as he watched their reflection in the mirror.

"I can't believe you didn't ask me to do this," she said, the smell of alcohol on her breath. "You've never been able to manage one of these."

Deacon's reflection smiled. "Still not used to having you here, I guess."

Veronica's face grew sour as she continued to manipulate the silk around his throat, transforming it into a perfect bow tie. She started to move away, but he turned and grabbed her arm in one of his aching hands.

"Don't be mad at me," he said.

She stared glacially at him, pulling her arm from his grasp.

"I didn't want to come here," she said, returning to the table where she'd left her latest drink. "I told you that, but still you insisted that Teddy and I come."

"You're my family," Deacon said. "Of course I want you here."

"But *we* don't want to be here," Veronica said, her words dripping with scorn.

"This is *my* home," Deacon said forcefully. "And I want it to be yours and Teddy's, as well."

"But we already had a home," she told him.

"Without me."

"You made your choice." The ice tinkled merrily as she brought the glass to her mouth and drained its contents.

"What can I do to make you understand?" Deacon asked. "Everything I've been working toward is for you and Teddy."

Veronica smiled with little warmth or humor. Then she turned away and walked to the portable bar in the corner of the room.

"All for Teddy and me," she repeated, dropping some ice cubes in her glass before filling it to the brim with bourbon. "And here I thought it was all about your little play-mates joining us this evening."

She leaned her hip against the cart, waiting for his response.

"They're important to the future . . . our future," he tried to explain.

"They're monsters," she snarled. "I would say they'd sell their souls for some arcane piece of knowledge that would put them a step above their fellow man, but I'm guessing they already did that some time ago."

She took a long pull from her drink.

"The members of the cabal are extremely powerful individually, but together, I doubt there's anything they couldn't do," Deacon stated. All had come from vast family fortunes that they had used to become masters of industry, as well as masters of the dark arts.

And joined together, they had the power to shape the world.

"But they hate each other," Veronica retorted. "None of them trust each other. You've told me as much."

And therein lay the rub. The mistrust the members had for one another was monumental, hindering any greatness their powerful gathering could muster.

"It is the nature of powerful men and magick users," Deacon excused with a shrug.

"And you still hunger for their acceptance."

"Only for *our* benefit. If I can get them to come together, to join our powers . . ."

Veronica only laughed and shook her head. "The great Konrad Deacon will change them," she scoffed.

"If I can convince Algernon Stearns, the others will follow suit," he told her. "If he believes in what I have to show them . . ."

"They'll give you a special place in their club," she finished scornfully.

Deacon couldn't stand it anymore. He charged across the room, slapping the drink from her hand, and grabbed her roughly by the shoulders. "Listen to me," he roared, trying to hold back the violence he wished to unleash upon her. "I'm doing this for you and the boy!"

"You're doing it for power," she spat, squirming to escape his grasp, but he held her arms tightly in spite of the agony he felt in his hands.

"Yes, I'm doing it for the power . . . the power to keep you safe . . . the power I need to fight. Germany? Japan? They're just the tip of the iceberg waiting on the horizon."

Veronica closed her eyes, refusing to look at him . . . refusing to see what he was trying to do.

"There are dark times approaching," Deacon hissed, squeezing his wife's arms all the tighter, hurting her so that she might listen. "And the world will need men like me . . . like Stearns and the other members of the cabal . . . those who can lead the world from the shadows that will threaten to overtake it."

The door to the bedroom swung open, and Deacon immediately released his grip on his wife. Both of them looked to the doorway as their son entered, holding the hand of one of Deacon's magickal creations.

"Hello, Daddy. . . . Hello, Mommy," Teddy greeted them, a hint of a British accent in his speech, an accent that Deacon was sure would fade now that the boy was in his proper home.

"Hello there, Teddy," Deacon said, shaking off the terrible mood his drunken wife had put him in. He opened his arms, inviting the boy to run to him.

Teddy released the hand of the large and powerful golem and jumped into his father's arms.

"What are you still doing awake? You were supposed to be tucked in and fast asleep hours ago."

Deacon looked to the golem for answers, admiring his handiwork. What he had done with the information from the rabbi at Dachau was quite impressive, and he had perfected the magick with magick of his own.

"The child summoned me to his room," the pale-skinned being explained. His stark faux flesh was adorned with black tattoos, making the name that the artificial life-form had given himself—Scrimshaw—fabulously appropriate.

"Is that so?" Deacon asked the boy.

"I couldn't sleep," Teddy said. "I heard cars coming up the drive. I didn't know we were having company."

"In fact, we are," Deacon said, holding his son close as he turned to his wife. Veronica rubbed the reddened places on her arms where bruises would surely form. "Some very important friends of your daddy will be here this evening."

"Can I meet them?" Teddy asked.

"Not right now," Deacon said, bringing Teddy over to Veronica. "Perhaps another time." He placed his son in the arms of his wife and looked back to the creature that still waited obediently.

"Have all my guests arrived yet, Scrimshaw?" he asked, humoring his creation by addressing him with the name he'd given himself.

The artificial being beamed, his chest swelling with pride.

"Yes, master. All of the cabal have arrived, except for Algernon Stearns."

Deacon's stomach clenched. If Stearns did not show, there would be no point to this evening. The cabal would do nothing without first seeing what the oldest and most powerful of the sorcerers would do.

"Fine," Deacon said. "Tell our guests that I will be there shortly."

The tall, pale figure bowed at the waist and promptly exited the room.

"What if he doesn't show?" Veronica asked.

Deacon looked at her, at his son in her arms, and said nothing, imagining a world where the cabal did not act together.

A world not guided by their combined power.

He could not bear to think of such a thing.

As luck would have it, there was an empty parking space in front of Steven Mulvehill's apartment building, and Remy pulled in close to the curb.

Marlowe began to whine and pant from the backseat.

"What are you going on about?" Remy asked as he put the car in park.

"No going on. Excited," Marlowe expressed, drool starting to leak from the sides of his jowls.

"Yeah, we haven't seen our buddy Steven in a while," Remy agreed, glancing up at the second floor and seeing one light on. He retrieved the brown paper bag with his liquor-store purchase from the passenger's seat and got out of the car, opening the rear door to let the dog out.

"Excited to see Steven," Marlowe said, darting across the narrow street and lifting his leg to urinate on a telephone pole.

"I can tell," Remy said, watching as the dog finished and began to sniff around. "You done?"

"Yes," Marlowe said, running back to join Remy on the steps to the front porch of the building.

The doorbell was busted, but the front door was always unlocked, so Remy pushed it open and Marlowe immediately began the trek up two flights of stairs to Steven's apartment. The angel followed, feeling a sense of trepidation.

He hadn't seen Steven in a couple of weeks, not since that nasty bit of business with the shape-shifting Shaitan.

Remy had asked Steven to check in on an elderly friend of his, not realizing the connection to the case he was working on or the danger he was putting his friend in. The homicide cop had nearly been killed, and had gotten a full taste of the weird shit that Remy often dealt with. Since then, Steven had avoided Remy and hadn't answered any of his calls.

Marlowe's whining interrupted Remy's thoughts, and he reached the second-floor landing to find the Lab sitting outside Mulvehill's door, wagging his tail.

"Did you knock?" Remy asked.

Marlowe looked at him indignantly. *"No knock. No hands."*

"Well, you could scratch," Remy suggested.

Marlowe just looked back at the door and cried as Remy reached out, rapping his knuckles on the heavy wood.

He waited, listening for sounds of life from the other side, but heard nothing.

"Steven," Remy called out, knocking again. "I've got a bottle of Glenlivet here with your name on it. . . . Open the door and it's all yours."

He tilted his head, listening all the more intently, but still he heard nothing. "Is he in there?" he asked the Labrador.

Marlowe pushed his snout into the crack beneath the door and began to sniff. *"Smell him."* He began to bark pathetically.

Remy closed his eyes and reached out with his senses. He could hear everything in the building and even some of what was going on in the houses next door and across the street. He pulled back and focused on Steven's place, the hum of the refrigerator, the whirr of the clock over the stove, the hiss and gurgle of the hot-water heater in the far corner of the kitchen.

And the sound of someone breathing nervously—someone who did not want to open the door no matter who was on the other side.

Or because of who was on the other side.

"He must be out," Remy said to Marlowe.

The dog looked at him. *"Smell him,"* he growled.

"Of course you do. It's his apartment." Remy turned and headed for the stairs as Marlowe continued to sniff beneath the door. "C'mon, buddy. We'll come back another time."

Marlowe offered one more pathetic-sounding bark.

But still the door did not open.

The Labrador started down the stairs as Remy momentarily paused. He looked at the paper bag that held the bottle of fifteen-year-old Scotch and returned to the apartment door.

"A peace offering," he said, placing the bag with the bottle in front of the door before following Marlowe downstairs and back out into the night.

Steven Mulvehill sat perfectly still, waiting for his friend to leave.

He'd known it would be only a matter of time before Remy showed up; Steven had lost count of how many times Remy had called since—

The images flooded his mind again: a beast whose flesh shifted and changed like smoke that had shown him the dangers of a hidden world.

Of monsters and angels.

The physical injuries Steven had sustained in his encounter with the Shaitan were healing well. But the mental ones were deep and still ragged, so much so that he was surprised when he actually had the courage to get out of bed these days.

Seeing Remy Chandler right now wasn't in the cards. As much as Steven hated to blame him, Remy was, after all, responsible for exposing him to things he never should have known about.

A Boston homicide cop for more than fifteen years, and he'd never known this kind of fear before. He was reminded of his early childhood and how he'd gone through a phase when he'd been terrified to go to bed at night.

And now he understood what he had known in those early years: that there really were good reasons to be afraid of the dark.

The Catskill Mountains
In a Subterranean Chamber Beneath the Deacon Estate
August 6, 1945

And to think, I wasn't going to attend Konrad's little soiree, Algernon Stearns thought as he watched one of Deacon's golem servants finish attaching the last of the numerous coils and wires to a heavy metal harness the sorcerer wore on his naked body.

The artificial man tugged on the vest to be sure it was secure and accidently pinched Stearns' left nipple.

"Damn you!" Stearns hissed. Supernatural energies that could easily have reduced the being to dust danced at his fingertips.

"Is everything all right, Algernon?" Deacon asked as he checked the connections on his own vest.

Stearns managed to suppress his anger, offering a tight smile. "Everything is fine, Deacon. Just a little pinch is all."

"Well, if everything goes according to plan, you'll be experiencing far more than a pinch shortly," Deacon warned. "But what you will gain from this temporary discomfort . . ."

"Is power," Stearns finished.

He glanced around at the other four members of the cabal. They were all there: Daphene Molaar, Robert Desplat, Eugene Montecello, and Angus Heath—some of the world's wealthiest and most powerful magick users. And they all appeared nervous, their eyes darting about the room.

They stood in a circle in a subterranean room beneath Deacon's estate, all naked except for the same metal vest that Stearns and Deacon wore. Cables trailed across the cold stone floor, connecting the vests to a series of complex machines that, in turn, were attached to an impressively large device that had been erected in the room's center. Stearns understood that the device was a kind of antenna— an antenna that would attract vast amounts of life energies and distribute the raw power among those who wore the vests. If Deacon was right, his machine would transform the cabal forever.

Konrad Deacon, the hero of the day.

Stearns knew what the man was up to. Deacon coveted his position as leader of the cabal, and now the upstart believed that he had what was needed to steal away Stearns' authority.

Well, Stearns wasn't about to let it go so easily.

He thought about the night that had led to this. He had been tempted to stay in Spain and skip Deacon's little party, but curiosity had made him change his mind. Even still, he had arrived late to Deacon's mansion, and was amused by the relief he saw on his host's face. In fact, the whole cabal shared the expression, for an affair of sorcerers could never convene without the presence of Algernon Stearns.

It had been some time since they had last gathered, and Stearns was taken aback by how old and frail they all appeared. He wasn't alone, after all; the use of magick was taking its toll on all of them.

Then, as if on cue, Konrad Deacon had tapped the side of his crystal champagne flute with his knife, and all eyes were on him. He began his speech, and Stearns quickly grew impatient as Deacon welcomed them to his home, then launched into a dissertation on their responsibility to a world on the brink. The war in the Pacific lingered on and the instability in the world meant that nobody noticed the rise in supernatural activity, except for those in tune with the ways of the weird.

These were all things that Stearns knew well, and he was considering walking out when the youngest member of the cabal made his daring pronouncement. He could give them back their vitality.

Stearns was distracted from the memory of what had brought him back to the Deacon mansion for a party of a different sort. He watched as Deacon checked his machines once more. This was to be their rebirth—their bodies healed, transformed, and filled with the power to guide the world through troubled times.

At first Deacon's proposal had sounded like lunacy. Of course it had been a theory among the brotherhood of magick users that life energies could be used to restore the human form. Blood sacrifice had always been the method of choice within the cabal, but no one had ever been able to make the process work correctly, for the collected energies were expended far too quickly. They were having less and less effect, and the years of magickal abuse were quickly catching up to all of them.

But if what they were up to tonight worked . . .

"How much longer must we endure this discomfort?" Angus Heath grumbled. He shifted his great weight, threatening to disconnect himself from the machines.

"Afraid you might miss a meal, Angus?" Stearns taunted.

"The machine cannot be activated until the precise moment," Deacon explained, hurriedly approaching the large man to make sure that his connections were still intact.

"Patience, Angus," Stearns said. "I hear it's a virtue."

"Something that I never knew you to have, Algernon," Daphene intoned, the crooked smile on her aged face hinting at their dalliances throughout the years.

Stearns ignored her and returned to thoughts of Deacon's plan. Over dinner that night, he had explained his advancements in the collection of life energies. The moment of death was when those energies were most powerful, he theorized, but multiple deaths were required if the energy was to have any prolonged effect.

So, what are we to do—murder entire cities in order to collect the proper amount of energy?" the oil baron Eugene Montecello had asked.

Deacon's answer had been startling and quite exciting.

"We don't have to murder anybody," he had said. *"We just have to be in the right place when somebody else carries it out."*

Deacon returned to his space in the circle and glanced up at the clock hanging on the stone wall. "Our time is near," he stated. "Prepare yourselves."

Evidently, this young upstart's connections within the United States government ran deep, and those connections had given Deacon the answer to his—and the cabal's—prayers. The military, growing weary of the seemingly never-ending war with the Land of the Rising Sun, had created a weapon, a bomb so terrible that it was guaranteed to bring Japan to its knees. They planned to drop it on a Japanese city, and Deacon had found a way to harness the energies of the many who would die as a result.

"Ready in five . . ." Deacon began the countdown, eyes riveted to the clock.

Stearns watched as well, as the second hand made its inexorable pass around the clock's face.

"Four . . ."

He again wondered about this bomb.

"Three . . ."

Deacon said that they had nicknamed it Little Boy.

"Two . . ."

Certainly not a name that struck fear in the hearts of men.

"One."

How powerful can it really be? Stearns wondered as the machine in the center of the room came suddenly to life with the most cacophonous of sounds.

And the life energies of those instantly slain when the atomic bomb detonated over the Japanese city of Hiroshima were collected.

And delivered unto them.

CHAPTER THREE

Remy was surrounded by sleep.

He sat on the red couch in Linda's apartment, his girl-friend curled up on one side of him and Marlowe, lying flat on his side as if he'd taken a bullet, snoring at his feet.

The Housewives was over by the time Remy had ar-rived, but Linda had saved him some wine and they'd cud-dled until sleep had claimed her. Shortly afterward, Marlowe had succumbed, as well, leaving Remy alone with the television.

But mostly it had left him alone with his thoughts, and there was much to think about this night.

Like what he had been doing traveling to New Hamp-shire to confront the murderer of Charlotte Marsh and her daughters. At the time it had felt like a completely rational thing to do, and that scared him.

He wasn't thinking like himself. And what about the next time? Would the angelic side of his nature persuade him that it was perfectly all right to mete out God's justice on the wicked?

It was only a matter of time before he started burning people who were double-parked with the flames of Heaven. That was what he had been afraid of, why it had taken him so long to allow his angelic essence to meld with his human persona. He would have to be careful in the coming days;

obviously, there were still some bugs to be worked out in the unification of his two sides.

And then there was Steven. Remy could fully understand his friend's anger, but there was very little that he could do to make things right. The snake had been let out of the box, so to speak, and there was nothing Remy could do to put it back. Steven had gotten dangerously up close and personal with an aspect of the world not usually seen by humanity, and for that Remy was sorry, but that was really all he could be.

It wasn't as if he had some magical way to take away the memory of the experience. Besides, if that were the case, their whole friendship might as well be excised from Mulvehill's mind. Remy remembered the night that Steven had lain dying at his feet, afraid of what awaited him. Wanting to offer him some peace, some certainty of what was on the other side, Remy had revealed his true face to the homicide detective.

He'd never expected Mulvehill to survive, but he had, and they had been close friends ever since.

But now he had seen too much of Remy's world and nothing could change that.

Remy had no choice but to let things be as they were, to give Steven the space that he needed to process his experience. And maybe, with time, they could once again be friends.

"I think that's sad." Linda's sleepy voice spoke, as if commenting on Remy's thoughts.

"Excuse me?" he asked, startled, looking down at the top of Linda's head as she snuggled up tightly beside him.

"The little girl," she said.

"I have no idea what you're . . ."

"On the news," Linda said groggily, and Remy looked at the television to see that the local news was on, and there was, in fact, a little girl on the screen.

The child, no older than six or seven, lay in her bed surrounded by dolls and stuffed animals. People stood around her as reporters yelled out questions and pictures flashed.

"What's her story?" Remy asked.

"Guess she's been in a coma for a few years—some kind of accident. They never expected her to wake up."

Linda stretched, her arms reaching up over her head as she yawned.

"And now she's awake," Remy said, still watching the TV. The cameras pulled in close to the child's face as she peeked out from beneath her covers. There was something haunting about her eyes.

"Awake and talking about all kinds of stuff."

"All kinds of stuff?"

"Yeah, religious stuff. She says she has a message from God."

The station cut to a commercial break, leaving a bad taste in Remy's mouth. He had little patience for supposed prophets proclaiming a direct line to Heaven.

"What's the message?" he asked, trying to hide his distaste.

"No idea," Linda said, sliding to the other side of the couch for her wineglass atop a side table. "She says He hasn't told her yet, that it isn't time or the world isn't ready, or something like that."

Remy doubted very much that the child was responsible for the proclamation, guessing that an ambitious family member was likely to blame. He wondered how long it would be before they were selling vials of the little girl's tears and displaying her features on special healing pillowcases or some such nonsense.

"I find it very sad," Linda was saying as she sipped the last of the wine from her glass. "A sick child being exploited like that."

The Seraphim stirred in agreement. Ever since the earth had been saved from the Apocalypse, more and more of these diviners, seers, and soothsayers had been crawling out of the woodwork with some vision of the future. The world was indeed in flux, but Remy seriously doubted that any of these people had the inside track on anything worth paying attention to.

Linda set down her empty glass and yawned loudly. Marlowe sat up and yawned, as well, as if in solidarity.

"Sleepy?" Remy asked her.

"Yeah," she answered with a nod. "You two want to stay over?"

"Nah." Remy stood. "I want to get to the office early tomorrow, and you're a very bad influence on my work ethic."

"Your loss," she said, shrugging. "But since I'm working both lunch and dinner shifts, we probably won't see each other tomorrow."

Linda was a waitress at Piazza, a restaurant on the trendy Newbury Street. She also attended school, working toward her teaching degree. Sometimes it was a bit tough to see each other.

"See what a bad influence you are? I'm not even out of your apartment, and already you're working your wiles on me," Remy said as he bent toward her.

He kissed her noisily on the lips and she reached up, gently holding the back of his head, making him kiss her more.

Bad influence or not.

Remy didn't mind in the least.

The Catskill Mountains
The Deacon Estate
August 8, 1945

Deacon had no idea if his mad plan would work.

He had learned from a trusted, high-ranking source in the Pentagon where the first of the bombs was to be dropped, and had prepared to collect the energies that would be released when that bomb detonated.

Using less-than-legal channels, he had managed to dispatch the most sophisticated golem he had ever created to the island of Japan, where it traveled to the target city to await the inevitable. This golem would be the receiver for the death energies, collecting the vast amounts of power and transmitting it back to the receiver in the Catskills and into the members of the cabal.

At least, that was the plan. Whether or not it worked had yet to be determined.

Hundreds of thousands of people had died when the atomic bomb exploded over Hiroshima, and as their life energies were transferred to Deacon, he experienced the life of each and every one of them. A mad rush of images, feelings, and sensations poured into him, threatening to drown him in their intensity.

He awakened with the screams of thousands upon his lips. He saw as they saw, their final memory of the fiery conflagration burned into his own.

Quickly he touched his own flesh, needing to prove to himself that he had not been reduced to ash. His flesh was damp with sweat, but it also tingled with vitality.

He sat up and held his hands out before him, flexing his fingers, feeling none of the aching pain that he'd been suffering. He felt his heart begin to beat faster, a pleasurable rush of blood to his head.

Did it work?

Deacon threw back the covers, exposing his nakedness. There was something different . . . the way he felt.

I think it did.

He swung his bare feet over the edge of the bed and touched the cold hardwood of the floor. Then he stood, experiencing a moment of stiffness as he lurched across the bedroom to his wife's vanity. Deacon's eyes widened as he caught his image in the large mirror that hung above it.

It was as if the hands of time had been turned back and he was looking at a photograph of himself from when he was barely in his twenties.

"It did work," he whispered with wonder, bringing his fingers to his face to touch the healthy, taut flesh no longer ravaged by the passage of time and the use of corrosive magicks.

He smiled a perfect, healthy smile and stepped back to admire his youthful body.

"It worked!" he yelled, pointing at his magnificent reflection. It was then that he remembered the others . . . the
cabal. If it had worked for him, then . . .

He bolted toward the door, remembering his nudity only
as his strong, healthy hands closed on the crystal knob. He
went to his wardrobe and removed a silk dressing gown,
marveling at the sensation of the material on his rejuvenated flesh.

Then he dashed to the door and threw it open, tying the
belt around his waist as he stepped out into the hall.

"It worked!" he bellowed once again with a laugh as he
proceeded down the darkened hallway toward the stairs.

It was there that he discovered the first of his golems. It
was one of his earlier, less-human-appearing designs, lying
on the stairs on its stomach, as if it had fallen while ascending and was unable to rise.

Still barefooted, Deacon started down the steps past the
prone form, noticing the circular burn mark in the center
of its back. His mind raced. He quickened his pace to the
lobby, where more of his creations lay, limbs akimbo, their
artificial lives stolen from them.

Deacon immediately thought of his wife and son. "Veronica!" he cried, stepping over a fallen golem. "Teddy!"

The large house was eerily still as he rushed through the
many rooms, finding more of his inhuman servants struck
down by some destructive magickal force.

*Were we attacked by the forces we plan to confront with
our newly acquired life?* he wondered as he passed through
the kitchen and headed down another winding set of stairs
toward his study.

"Veronica!" he called out again, moving down the corridor to the heavy wooden door at its end.

The door was ajar, something he never would have allowed, but before he could consider it, he heard the cry of
his son.

"Teddy," Deacon called out, pushing open the door and
storming into the study.

Where he froze, stunned by the sight before him.

Teddy was struggling in the arms of Angus Heath, while the other members of the cabal pored through his belongings.

"Ah, you're awake," a far-younger-appearing Stearns said from where he stood beside a file cabinet, one of its drawers wide open to expose all the secrets contained within.

"What is the meaning of . . . ," Deacon began, but never finished.

Stearns moved like quicksilver, his hand extended, a spell of violence on his lips. A bolt of magickal energy shot out from his fingertips, striking Deacon square in the chest, sending him across the length of room, where he smashed into a bookcase filled with scientific journals and fell to the floor.

"Do you understand the meaning now?" Stearns asked, removing a handful of files from the cabinet drawer and sliding it closed. "Or would you like another example?"

Deacon was flat on his belly, his entire body numb. As he fought to stand, he tilted his head to one side, catching sight of a body on the floor behind the great expanse of his desk. It was his wife, crumpled on her side, eyes wide in obvious death.

"Veronica!" he cried out.

He managed to get to his hands and knees, crawling toward her body.

"I wouldn't waste too much emotion on that one, Konrad," Stearns said, coming to sit on the corner of the desk. "She was all too happy to show us your study." He hefted the files he had removed from the cabinet, then tossed them on the desktop.

Deacon reached his wife, gently pulling her limp body into his arms. "What . . . what have you done?"

"Isn't it obvious, man?" Stearns asked. "I struck her down."

The other members of the cabal laughed.

"Daddy!" Teddy cried out. "They hurt Mommy!"

"Evidently, she had second thoughts once we began our

search," Stearns said. "She tried to stop us." He laughed. "But I wasn't about to leave until I got what I came for."

"What do you want?" Deacon asked, looking up from Veronica's body cradled in his arms. "All you had to do was ask me and—"

"I want it all, Konrad," Stearns said. He waved his hands. "Everything you've done . . . everything responsible for this."

He slid from the desk to show off his rejuvenated form.

"This was something, sir," Stearns sneered. "Something to be truly proud of. You actually did it. You made me . . ." He looked quickly about the room at the others. "You made *us* strong again . . . stronger than we've ever been."

Deacon could feel the anger at his core . . . the rage starting to grow.

"You killed my wife," he said, his voice rising.

"I did," Stearns said. "And I'm going to kill you, too, and take everything that belongs to you."

"I'll kill you first," Deacon cried out, his own spell of destruction leaving his lips as he raised his hands and unleashed pure magickal force from his fingertips.

"You'll try," Stearns responded casually, erecting a shield of his own magickal force to deflect the attack. The blast went wild, blowing a burning hole in a nearby wall.

Deacon released his wife's corpse, scrambling to his feet as his child cried out, "Daddy! Daddy!"

He wanted to go to his child, but he had to save himself first.

Stearns was unstoppable. Fiery blasts of arcane force rained down on Deacon. He did his best to shield himself, but the cabal leader had been made too strong, and each blow made it more difficult for Deacon to concentrate.

Deacon lay crumpled in a smoldering heap on the floor of his study. He could hear Stearns approaching, the fall of his shoes on the litter-strewn floor, and he prepared himself. He could not lose; everything that he was, everything he had done, depended on it.

The sound of the sorcerer calling forth a spell that would

end his life flowed through the air, and Deacon sprang up, unleashing a blast of supernatural power summoned from the very core of his being. He watched as Stearns was engulfed in preternatural force, then turned his attention to the other members of the cabal.

"How dare you?" Deacon roared, enraged by the cabal's betrayal.

Spells of violence started to fly; they were all so much stronger now. Deacon locked his eyes on his son as Angus Heath dragged the boy about the room, using his small body as a shield. The little boy twitched and writhed as magickal bolts of arcane energy struck him.

"No!" Deacon cried out in horror, throwing all caution to the wind as he hurled himself across the study.

Heath tried to strike him down, but the spell just missed its mark, nicking Deacon's shoulder as he grabbed for his son. The three of them fell to the floor in a thrashing heap.

"Pig!" Deacon screamed, his fist landing heavily on Heath's ruddy face, drawing a spray of blood. He punched again and again, the urge to reduce this vile creature's face to so much pulp bringing him nearly to the brink of madness.

But then he heard the sound of his son calling his name, barely audible through his rage. He let Heath drop to the floor and turned to take his son into his arms.

"Teddy," Deacon said, looking into the boy's eyes, seeing that they had already begun to glaze. The magick was already going to work on him, like a powerful poison coursing through his young veins. It had been cast to kill Deacon; he could only imagine what it was doing to his child.

He searched his mind for spells—something, anything—that could stop it. Some were even more dangerous than what the child was experiencing, but what choice did he have?

Deacon leaned in close to the dying boy, lovingly stroking his cheek, and he began to utter the ancient words of a spell that might save his dwindling life. . . .

But Deacon's enemies would not have it.

A bolt of humming black energy struck him hard, hurling him to the floor atop his child. He tried to continue the spell, but the words would not come and his child's life slowly ticked away.

He rolled over, gazing up into the sneering face of Algernon Stearns. It was bright red and blistered from the magick that had struck him, but Deacon could see that he was already healing.

The life energies from Hiroshima had made the sorcerer strong . . . had made them all strong.

"Please," Deacon begged. "Let me save my son. Then everything I have . . . everything I know . . . it's yours."

The other members of the cabal came to stand beside their leader, all of them staring at Deacon with utter contempt in their eyes.

"Let me kill the boy," Heath slurred through swollen lips and broken teeth.

Stearns ignored the fat sorcerer, his gaze fixed on Deacon.

"Please," Deacon tried again, feeling his child's life continue to slip away.

"It already belongs to me," Stearns said, and he smiled as his hand began to pulse with an unearthly glow.

Still looking into Deacon's eyes, Stearns thrust his hand downward, a flash of light leaving the tips of his fingers to strike the child laboring to breathe—fighting to remain alive.

And the child breathed no more.

Deacon lost all connection to the world with his son's dying gasp. "Why?" he cried over and over again as he cradled his son tightly in his arms. "Why? Why? Why?"

"Because you gave me the power to do so," Stearns said, leaning in close to whisper in his ear.

Deacon felt himself start to slip away, Stearns' malignant words echoing down the lengthening corridor of his approaching unconsciousness.

He knew that he had the power to strike one last time,

but also knew that it would be for naught; Stearns and the others would only strike him dead and take everything that he had worked so hard to achieve.

Though the darkness tugged at him, Deacon managed to wrest himself from its grip, forcing his way up through the ocean of oblivion, back to the realm of consciousness. Through bleary eyes he watched as they pillaged his study, as from deep within the recesses of his memory a spell slowly bubbled upward like a bloated, gas-filled corpse rising from the bottom of a murky lake.

And as he uttered the arcane words and the magick began to flow, the mansion started to shake—a slight tremor, barely noticeable at first—but growing in intensity and strength. Stearns stumbled as the floor beneath his feet bucked and heaved.

"You did this," the sorcerer snarled, trying to keep his footing as he turned back to where Deacon still lay across the body of his son.

"Because I can," Deacon echoed mockingly, trying with all his might to stay alive and to see the magickal manifestation of his power through.

The mansion began to creak and moan as its structure was challenged, and the shadows within became like a hungry thing, bottomless and black.

Drawing the house into its maw.

The Deacon estate, consumed by darkness.

CHAPTER FOUR

The vessel had to be filled before he could return to his creator.

Zeroing in on the collective pulse of multiple life energies, the vessel strolled down the quiet city street until he came upon the nightclub. He moved toward the door, drawn to the hum of vitality within, but he was blocked by a large, bearded man whose own body vibrated with excess vim and vigor.

"Fifty-dollar cover," the man announced.

The vessel stepped back to assess the situation. He appeared human, although was far from it, and had the strength to easily snap this man's neck and simply walk into the bar brimming with life. But his creator had also given him far less destructive means of getting what he required. He reached into the back pocket of his trousers and removed a wallet filled with several types of currency.

"Fifty-dollar cover," the vessel repeated as he held out a fifty-dollar bill.

The bouncer's hand closed around the cash, snatching it from the vessel's grasp. Their fingers touched briefly as the exchange was made, and the vessel sampled some of the large man's energy. It was relatively healthy, clean of any terminal disease. The selection was accepted, and now the vessel was that much closer to being full.

The big man swayed ever so slightly, then seemed to shake it off as he pulled open the door for the club's newest guest.

"Enjoy yourself," he said, as the vessel passed by him on his way inside.

The vibrancy of life emanating from within nearly pulled the vessel down a red-lit corridor, electronic music growing louder, beating like a strong, healthy heart. The hallway ended at the top of a metal staircase and the vessel stopped for a moment to watch the activity on the dance floor below him—bodies overflowing with an abundance of vivacity, their exuberant gyrations beckoning him, calling him to walk among them.

To sample the vitality they radiated.

The vessel descended to the dance floor. With hands outstretched, he waded into the sea of bodies, and everyone he passed, everyone he casually brushed up against, filled him with their life.

The Shadow Lands
Sixty-seven Years Ago

It was dark in the Shadow Lands, but then again, when wasn't it? That was probably one of the things Squire liked most about the place: It didn't pretend to be anything other than what it was.

The hobgoblin pulled his tattered cloak about his squat, muscular body as a freezing wind from another time and place found its way into the repository of shadows to caress him.

It was a realm of perpetual darkness, a place connected to all the shadows that ever existed—then, now, and even into the future. Traveling the Shadow Paths could take him just about anywhere, but for right now, the hobgoblin was content where he was.

Squire sat, reveling in the quiet. He couldn't recall how long he had been here this time but knew that this was where he needed to be . . . where he belonged.

The long hairs on the back of his thick neck suddenly came to attention, and the hobgoblin was in motion, pulling the concealed machete from inside his cloak to meet the attack from one of the myriad life-forms that called this black realm its home. Shades of darkness writhed about him, and he narrowed his vision to see the beastie that used the shifting colors of black and gray for cover.

It was insectoid in its basic design, and he had run into one or two before. Squire also recalled that its meat was quite tasty, if one enjoyed the flavor of rotting meat soaked in Listerine, which he did.

The creature attacked high, and Squire went low, slicing the blade that he had sharpened that very morning across the exoskeletoned belly of the large bug. Its innards spilled out onto the ground, its life ended before it could even complete its leap.

Squire was used to such things, always waiting, always ready for that next attack. For as long as he could remember, somebody or something was trying to kill him.

The hobgoblin figured that it probably all started with his birth, when his kicking and screaming from his mother's womb resulted in her death. That didn't go over well with his father, to say the least. And from that day forward it seemed as though someone had pinned a sign on his back saying KILL ME, and that's what everybody had been trying to do since.

Of course, it hadn't helped that he'd gotten himself mixed up with a band of would-be heroes—monsters, ghosts, and magick users trying to save from various supernatural threats a version of the Earth that he had made his home. At first that had seemed like a really good idea, but in the end . . .

Not so much.

The hobgoblin hated for his thoughts to go there; he'd spent too long remembering what had happened to his friends and the world that they had been trying to save. Emphasis on *trying*.

But failing miserably.

He'd used the Shadow Paths to travel to other worlds just like the one he had lost. Though details varied, he found them all on the verge of heading down that same road his world had gone, or, worse, having already succumbed to the planet-devouring threat.

No, he would just stay here in the realm of darkness. It was simpler here, and the things that tried to kill him were only doing it because they loved the taste of hobgoblin meat.

Nothing more complicated than that.

Squire dug into the insect's carcass with his knife, breaking the thick shell to get at the soft insides. *Just like lobster, but different,* he thought as he cut away the foul-smelling meat and shoved it into the lined leather bag that he always carried.

He felt the disturbance in the air behind him and readied himself for another attack, but as he turned, he realized that it came not from an imminent threat but something off in the distance. The sky in this place was like a black velvet curtain, and as he gazed across the plain of shadow, it looked as though something was moving behind that curtain, punching and pushing on it.

Stretching it.

He'd never seen anything quite like it, and got that nasty feeling in the pit of his belly that told him it couldn't be anything good.

Leaving his kill, he trudged closer. The phenomena intensified, the sky writhing like the belly of a shadow snake after swallowing its prey alive. Squire suddenly knew that something was about to happen—he could feel it on his skin like pinpricks of electricity—and he raised his cloak to cover his face just as the explosion came.

The sound was deafening in the dark and quiet world. The force of the blast tossed him across the blackened landscape, tumbling like a pile of dry fall leaves, until he managed to sink his fingers into the solidified shadow that comprised the ground of this place, stopping his progress.

As the winds died down, he carefully climbed to his feet

and could not believe what lay before him. Where there had once been only rolling plains of shadow, there now stood a house . . . a mansion, really.

It sat there, squatting in the perpetual gloom like some gigantic prehistoric toad.

The air was tinged with the stink of ancient magicks, and he knew that the dangerous environment that he had come to embrace had now been changed forever.

"Fuck me," the hobgoblin grumbled before spitting a wad of something hard and green onto the ground. "There goes the neighborhood."

The Deacon Estate
The Shadow Lands
Sixty-seven Years Ago

Deacon had wished them all dead, using every ounce of power his body had stored.

He had never expected to awaken, but his eyes did open and the nightmare that his world had become was reintroduced to him. His wife and son were still dead, his research ransacked. The bodies of his enemies were nowhere to be found, and he had to believe that the spell he had cast had failed.

Weak beyond words, he dragged himself from the basement study, leaving behind the remains of his family.

He hauled himself up the stairs to the first floor, remembering how the estate had moaned and groaned as he'd unleashed his spell, as if being torn asunder in the grip of a powerful storm. He was surprised to see that the old manse had managed to stay in one piece. Although as he lurched through the door and rebounded off the wall, he realized that the house was strangely askew. He was reminded of a family trip to a Coney Island fun house, and almost heard the shrieks of laughter from his son as they made their way through the distorted amusement.

But there was nothing amusing about this.

The ancient spell had come from someplace deep within his memory, something discerned from an arcane tome, deciphered and memorized in the effort to acquire as much ancient arcana as he could store in his human brain.

He passed a mirror that had fallen from the wall and caught a glimpse of himself in the shattered fragments. It appeared that his home was not the only thing changed by the spell. The magick had taken much from his human form, leaving behind not the visage of a man rejuvenated by the life forces of thousands, but an old man in the twilight of his existence.

The spell has taken much, but did it succeed?

Deacon thought he'd had an understanding of what the spell would do, but realized that his translation of the scroll may have been . . .

Lacking.

The house creaked as he struggled through it. He hoped to see the bodies of the members of the cabal along the way, but found only those of his golem staff, left by his former partners in their assault upon his home.

Did they manage to escape? he wondered. *Were my efforts wasted?*

Deacon struggled to maintain his footing on floors that bulged upward and then slanted precariously to one side, as he fought to reach the foyer of the grand old home. On aching hands and knees, he crawled up a section of marble floor, then slid down the other side to reach the front doors, now skewed drunkenly to the right.

He reached up, grasped one of the doorknobs, and pulled himself to his feet, the bones in his spine popping loudly as he righted himself. The brass knob was incredibly cold in his gnarled fingers, but, surprisingly, it turned. He tugged on the door and it swung heavily open.

At first his mind rationalized what he saw outside his door as only nighttime in the Catskills, but then he noticed the lack of stars in the sky. And where were the verdant forests just beyond the front gate?

There was only darkness, the blackest he had ever seen.

Slowly it dawned on him. This wasn't the night at all; he—*his entire home*—had been transported to somewhere else.

And it didn't appear to be anyplace on Earth.

The call of inky shadows drew him outside the safety of his home. Deacon squinted into the pitch-black, trying to see beyond the ocean of darkness, but there was nothing.

Suddenly, there came the slightest of sounds, and at first he believed he had imagined it, that his mind was attempting to fill the vacuous void that now surrounded him. But then he heard it again: the soft expulsion of breath, like a sigh.

Deacon moved farther from the front door and was about to descend the steps to the stone path that led from the front doors to the gate when he thought he saw movement.

Something darker than the blackness around him.

And then it rushed at him, swimming through the ocean of dark, mouth agape, ready to claim its prey. Even in his prime, Deacon wasn't sure he would have been fast enough to escape it. The only thought in the magick user's brain was the hope that the other members of the cabal had met with a similar fate. If that was the case, Deacon would go to his death happily.

A hand fell hard upon his scrawny neck, and Deacon felt himself yanked roughly backward toward the still-open door. A powerful figure now stood where he had been, the sounds of gunfire echoing strangely in the world of shadows.

The attacking beast emitted a high-pitched shriek that caused the hair on Deacon's body to rise, but the rifle fire was enough to drive it away.

He blinked wildly as he stared at the broad back of the one who had saved him. Slowly the figure turned, and he looked into the pale, tattooed face of the golem Scrimshaw.

"It is dangerous here," the golem said, moving to his master and pulling him to his feet. "We will need to be careful if we are to venture outside."

"You should have let the damnable thing take me," Deacon spat. "There is nothing left to live for."

"What of your son?" Scrimshaw asked, shouldering the rifle.

"My son?" Deacon asked angrily, looking at the tattooed face of his creation. "My son is dead."

Scrimshaw slowly shook his head.

"No, master. Your son still lives."

CHAPTER FIVE

Remy didn't immediately recognize the woman as she entered his office. Even though he had known her for years, Carol Berg had never been to his office, and it threw him off a bit to see her there.

"Carol," he began, a smile making its way across his face as he realized who she was.

"She's missing, Remy," Carol said quickly, and it was then that Remy noticed her troubled expression, the lines of worry that had already etched their way into the skin of her face.

She looked ten years older.

"What are you talking about?" he questioned as he stood and moved around his desk toward her. "Who's missing?"

Carol's shoulders sagged, and he was afraid that she might fall down. He helped her to the chair in front of his desk and knelt beside her, a comforting hand on her arm.

"What's happened?" Remy asked gently, trying to remain calm even though his heart was now hammering in his chest in anticipation of what was to come.

"It's Ashley . . . We've been calling her for days and she hasn't answered," Carol said, reaching into her purse to get her phone on some off chance that a call had come in and she hadn't noticed. "We've left message after message . . . begging her to call us . . ."

The woman's voice cracked and she started to cry as she slid her phone back into her purse.

Remy sat back on his haunches, allowing the information to sink in. Ashley Berg was Carol's daughter. She was also a good friend of Remy's—more than a friend, really—and had proven herself the most reliable babysitter Marlowe had ever had. He stood and grabbed a box of tissues from his desk, holding it out to Carol.

"Have you called the school?"

Ashley had gone off to Ashmore College in Brattleboro, Vermont, not three weeks ago. They had talked last week, and she was very excited about her classes, living in her own apartment, and finding a part-time job.

Carol nodded as she took the Kleenex and dabbed at her eyes. "They said she hasn't shown up for classes in three days. We called the police and they're working with the college, but we don't know what to do."

Carol fell eerily silent, staring ahead as if seeing a glimpse of something right around the corner. "Oh, my God, Remy," she gasped, emotion dripping from every word. "Oh, my God. What if somebody has hurt her?"

Remy reached out to put his arms around her, to lend her some of his strength. "It's going to be all right," he tried to soothe her, as she sobbed into the collar of his button-down shirt.

"Where is she, Remy?" Carol asked between sobs. "Why isn't she answering our calls? Why hasn't she been to school or her apartment?"

"I don't know," Remy said, holding her tighter, afraid that she might disintegrate in his arms. "But I'm going to find out."

She pulled away from him then, her wide, wet eyes staring into his.

"I'm going to find out," he repeated with a nod of promise.

"I knew that's what you'd say." Carol's lips trembled as she tried to pull herself together. "She loves you and Marlowe so much. . . ." And then she closed her eyes, rivulets of tears running down her face. She crammed the tissues against them.

"Carol, where's Karl?" Remy asked about her husband, Ashley's father.

She looked at him again, appearing to think a moment before answering. "He's at the house . . . just in case she . . . just in case somebody calls and . . ."

"That's good," Remy said, standing beside her chair. "I think you should go there, as well . . . be with Karl. Support each other."

"We're going up to Brattleboro as soon as I get home."

Remy had no doubt that that's where they would be heading.

"Keep me in the loop," he said. "Give me a call if you hear anything at all, no matter how insignificant it might seem."

She got up from the chair. Remy held her by the elbow just to be sure she was steady enough on her feet.

"I will," she said, sniffling. "I'm so sorry that I broke down like that. . . . I . . ."

"No worries," Remy said to her.

She managed a halfhearted smile and walked toward the door.

"What are you going to do?" she then asked.

The Seraphim nature was fully aware and listening, sensing that what it could do—what it existed for—would soon be called upon and put to use.

"I'm going to start my own investigation," Remy told her.

She nodded, opening the door, and was about to step out into the hall when she stopped and turned.

"Promise me that you'll find her," Carol said. "That no matter what, you'll bring my little girl back to me."

"I promise," Remy told her.

And he'd never meant anything more.

Beacon Hill
Summer 1996

Remy trekked up the hill from Charles Street carrying a bag of groceries, odds and ends Madeline had asked him to pick up for supper.

It was a blazingly hot day on the Hill, but Remy didn't allow himself to feel it. He enjoyed being human and all that it entailed, but if he could tweak his body temperature during the hot-and-humid Boston summers, he could see no problem in acknowledging what he truly was from time to time.

An angel of the Heavenly host Seraphim could be comfortable at the North Pole, on the surface of the sun, or even Beacon Hill in the middle of August.

As he headed up Mount Vernon Street, he noticed a Gentle Giant movers' truck double-parked in front of one of the brownstones. The back of the truck was wide open to reveal a jam-packed trailer filled with a combination of covered furniture and multiple boxes. The movers were just starting to unload and were already soaked with sweat.

Bet they wish they were of the Heavenly host Seraphim, Remy thought as he drew closer.

The sidewalk in front of the brownstone was crowded with items unloaded from the truck, so he stepped into the street to get around it.

And that was when he noticed the little girl.

She couldn't have been any older than five, and was crouched down outside a black, wrought-iron fence in front of a house across the street on Louisburg Square. He could hear her little voice, talking away as he drew nearer. *Where are her parents, and who the hell is she talking to?* he wondered.

He could now see a frazzled-looking woman giving instructions to the movers from the steps of the brownstone, and a man on a cell phone pacing back in forth in the midst of a heated conversation with what sounded like the cable company.

Remy guessed that the little girl belonged to them.

She had stuck one of her small arms through the rungs of the wrought-iron fence and was making little smacking sounds.

Remy couldn't help but slow down to see what she was up to.

On the other side of the fence was a small garden, a cherry blossom tree in the center surrounded by an assortment of wildflowers and some tall grass. Remy could just about make out the shape of a little black-and-white cat, hunkered down, trying desperately to hide in what grass there was.

The child must have sensed Remy's presence behind her and turned her adorable gaze up to him.

"My kitty got out of her box and ran across the street into the grass," she informed him. "Can you help me get her out?"

Remy stepped over to the fence, setting his bag of groceries down as he squatted beside her. "What's your cat's name?"

"Spooky. She's a girl."

"That's a very nice name for a girl," Remy said.

"Mine is Ashley."

"Well, it's nice to meet you, Ashley. I'm Remy."

"Remy, can you get Spooky out of there?"

"Let me see what I can do," Remy replied.

"Don't be a-scared, Spooky." Ashley turned her attention back to the cat still cowering under the cover of the tall green blades of grass. "Remy is gonna get you out."

Spooky began to growl, backing farther away as Remy made eye contact.

"Hey there, Spooky," he said, so the cat could understand him. "Why don't you come out of there, and we'll get you back into your box. . . ."

"No," the cat hissed, followed by an even more ferocious growl. *"No box . . . no car . . . no."*

"What's she sayin'?" Ashley asked.

"I don't think she liked being in the box or going in the car."

"She makes weird noises in the car," Ashley agreed with a nod.

"That's 'cause she's upset," Remy explained. "The car scares her."

"I'm a-scared of ghosts," Ashley said matter-of-factly.

"Really?" Remy asked. "Well, it's a good thing there aren't any ghosts in your new house."

"There isn't?" the little girl asked, looking across the street. Her mother was helping the movers with some of the smaller boxes, but Dad continued his argument on the cell phone.

"Nope, I checked it out before you moved in. Perfectly ghost-free."

"Thanks, Remy," the little girl said, and he felt her tiny hand slip into his.

He turned his head slightly to look at the five-year-old, who was staring fixedly at her cat, still hiding in the garden grass.

"You think Spooky is ever gonna come out of there?"

"Yeah, I think she will," Remy said. "Just let me talk to her a little more."

"Okay."

"Hey, Spooky." Remy again spoke so the cat could hear him in her feline tongue. "You might want to think about coming out of there before it's too late."

The cat glared at him, her green eyes nearly matching the color of her grassy cover. *"Why?"*

"Doone lives in this house."

"What's Doone?"

"Doone is a very large dog." Remy glanced at his watch. "And if I'm not mistaken, he should be leaving for his afternoon walk any minute now."

Remy could see panic flicker in the cat's eyes. She became even more skittish, glancing from where she hid up toward the front stairs to the building and the front door.

"Dog?" Spooky asked. *"Dog here?"*

"He's right inside there," Remy said, pointing to the house. "And I know for a fact he doesn't care for cats."

"You better come out of there, Spooky," Ashley coaxed. "Doone don't sound very nice."

"Hey, Ashley?" Remy asked. The little girl looked at him. "Would you get me Spooky's box?"

"Sure, Remy." She turned toward the street.

"Be careful of cars," Remy cautioned.

She stopped and looked both ways before darting across the street.

"Okay, then," Remy said, turning back to Spooky. "Ashley is going to get your box, and that's where you're going to go. All right?"

"Doone dog," the cat whined nervously. *"Where?"*

"Doone is inside the house," Remy explained. "If you get back into your box and let Ashley take you inside the new house, you two will never even make eye contact. Do we have a deal?"

Remy looked away to see Ashley on the other side with the cardboard pet carrier. He checked for traffic and then motioned her across once the coast was clear.

"Here's her box," Ashley said, handing it to him.

"Thanks." He took the box and opened the cover, then placed it just outside the wrought-iron fence, between two of the posts.

"C'mon, Spooky," Remy urged the cat. "Let's shake that tail."

"No shake tail," the cat snarled, her tail whipping angrily from side to side.

"All right, then," Remy said, as he stood up. "Maybe Doone can get you to move." He looked at the stairs and the door above, as if expecting the dog to emerge at any moment.

Spooky bounded out of the grass, through the wrought-iron bars, and jumped into her cardboard carrier.

"Yay!" Ashley shrieked, doing the cutest dance while clapping her chubby hands.

"Good job, Spooky," Remy said. He reached out to close the lid on the carrier, and Spooky's paw shot out, raking bloody tracks across the back of Remy's hand.

"*Scared*," she hissed, letting him know that there was nothing to cheer about as far as she was concerned.

Remy nearly dropped the carrier, but managed to balance it on his knee as he finally got the lid closed.

"Did she get ya?" Ashley asked as Remy set the carrier down on the sidewalk.

"Yeah, but that's all right." The gashes stung like crazy, but he could feel his flesh already beginning to heal. "It's not too bad."

Ashley pulled his hand down so she could see the wounds.

"Your mother should wash that up and put a Band-Aid on it," she said. "Don't want it to get defected."

Remy chuckled. "I'll get right on that." Then he reached down and picked up the carrier, handing it to Ashley. "You should probably get Spooky in the new house so she can get used to it and not be afraid anymore."

"Okay," Ashley said, moving toward the street. "C'mon, Spooky. You don't have to be afraid; there isn't any ghosts inside. Remy said he checked."

She crossed the street and headed up the walkway toward the brownstone, passing her father, who was still pacing and on the phone. He reached out and patted her head as she went by and started up the stairs, hauling the cat carrier.

Halfway up the steps, Ashley stopped and turned, her gaze searching. "See ya tomorrow, Remy," she called out, waving with her free hand before continuing on into her new home.

Ashley's father waved at him also, mouthing the words *thank you* as he continued with his call.

Remy retrieved his bag of groceries and walked around the corner to Pinckney Street and the brownstone he shared with his wife. He was certain she'd be wondering where he had been all this time.

And he would tell her about the little girl who now lived in their neighborhood, who had troubles with her cat.

A little girl named Ashley.

*   *   *

Remy was at Piazza, writing a note for Linda, when she showed up for her lunch shift.

"Hey, you," she said, warming him with her smile and then a kiss on the lips. "What are you doing here?"

"I tried to call but couldn't reach you," Remy said. "I was leaving you a note."

"Phone died," she told him. "I forgot to charge it. What's wrong?"

"I've got to take off for a bit," he replied, watching the expression on her face change—partially annoyance and maybe a little sadness. "Ashley might be missing, and I'm going to poke around, see what I can do to help."

"Oh, my God." Linda moved closer, taking his hands and looking deeply into his eyes. "Are you all right?"

"I'm fine," he said, not really telling the truth. Remy felt like a caged animal, eager to get out . . . eager to hunt. "But I need to get up there, flip over some rocks to see for myself."

Linda hadn't met Ashley, the right time not having presented itself, especially with Ash getting ready to leave for school. Although she certainly knew how important the girl was to Remy.

"This isn't like her, is it?" she asked.

"No, not at all."

"Anything I can do?"

He held up the note he had been writing. "I was wondering if you could look after . . ."

"Besides Marlowe," she said. "That's a given. I'll zip over after lunch and take him for a walk; then I'll pick him up once I'm done here for the night."

Remy reached into his pocket and removed a key, placing it in the palm of her hand. "Just in case you don't feel like driving him back to your place."

She stared at the key for a moment, and then closed her fingers around it. "Hopefully you put all your valuables away," she said, trying to lighten the mood just a little.

"My stamp collection is locked up tight," Remy confirmed.

They smiled at each other then, but the intensity of the situation was too great, and he felt the oppressive weight of what he still had to do pushing down on him, his entire focus on finding that little girl who'd had problems with Spooky the cat just yesterday, it seemed.

"Go on. Get out of here," Linda prodded, as if reading his thoughts.

"I don't know how long I'll be," Remy said.

"Long enough to find her."

And Linda released her grip on his hands, letting him go to work.

CHAPTER SIX

Remy opened his wings in the backyard of the building where Ashley and a friend from high school had rented an apartment. He wanted to be certain that no one was home before going in and poking around.

He glanced toward the driveway and saw that the space reserved for the first-floor tenants was empty. All clear. He closed his eyes, summoned his wings again, and took himself into the apartment.

The familiar smell of put-together furniture permeated the air as he unfurled his wings in the living room. He had taken Ashley to IKEA, just south of Boston in Stoughton, to get bookcases for her apartment, and had helped her put them together the day she'd moved up here.

His eyes scanned the room, looking for anything unusual. The area still had that unfinished look to it, with boxes stacked up against the wall.

Remy walked into the kitchen. A dirty frying pan filled with soapy water rested on one of the stove burners. The tiny kitchen table held several opened boxes of sugary cereals. He already knew about Ashley's obsession with Apple Jacks, and gathered from the boxes of Honey Smacks and Cap'n Crunch that her roommate had similar tastes.

He drifted down the short, dark hallway toward the bedrooms. Ashley's was the first on the right. The door was partially closed and Remy reached out, pushing it open with a creak. The shades were drawn, but there was enough natural light shining through that he could see perfectly well. He was surprised to find Ashley's bed made and the room tidy, having been privy to a few of her mother's rants about what a slob she was. Maybe she was turning over a new leaf now that she was out on her own.

Ashley's desk was what interested him now. He pulled out the wooden chair and sat down, turning on her laptop. As he waited for it to boot up, he looked over the surface of the desk. On the corner was a framed picture of Marlowe, and he felt a lump start to form in his throat.

Where did you go, Ash?

He found a notepad with some names and addresses written on it and jotted them down on a pad he took from his jacket pocket. He had no idea if they were significant, but wanted to leave no stones unturned.

The computer was ready, but just as he was attempting to get into Ashley's e-mail account, the sound of a car door closing stopped him. He went to the window overlooking the driveway and saw a short, dark-haired young woman heading toward the door. Ashley's roommate was home, and it probably wouldn't have been good for her to find Remy inside.

He summoned his wings again, closed his eyes, and was back outside in a rush of air. Then, after waiting a moment, he climbed the front steps and knocked.

The girl appeared at the door, pulling aside a sheer curtain to peer cautiously out at him.

"Hi. Melissa, isn't it?" Remy said loud enough to be heard through the glass. "We met a few weeks ago. I'm Ashley's friend," he reminded her.

It took a minute or two, but finally Remy saw recognition dawn in Melissa's eyes, and she turned the lock.

"Ashley's missing," were the first words she said as she opened the door.

"I know," Remy answered. "But I'd like to talk to you for a minute, if that's all right."

"I've already talked to the police . . . both of them, campus and regular."

"I'm sure you have," Remy agreed. "I have just a few questions of my own. I'm a private investigator and figured I'd do some poking around myself."

"Right," she said. "Ash told me about that." Melissa opened the door wider and motioned Remy inside.

"Thanks. When was the last time you saw Ashley?" Remy asked, as she closed the door behind him and then led the way to the living room.

"About four days ago. I was driving back to Melrose for the weekend, but she was staying here. She was hanging around, working on her computer."

"Do you know what she was doing?"

Melissa shrugged. "Checking e-mail and stuff, I guess. I know she'd been looking for a part-time job and was making a list of places in the downtown area to try."

The mystery of the list was solved.

"Had she been on any interviews?" Remy asked.

"No, she was just getting together a list of places to apply. I think she was planning on starting to fill out applications last Friday, after classes . . . that last day I saw her."

"Did she talk about meeting anybody?" Remy chanced. "A new acquaintance . . . a guy, maybe?"

Melissa smiled sadly and shook her head. "No . . . That was one of the last things we talked about. We both thought we were gonna meet all these cute guys up here, but we've been so busy, we haven't even had a chance to notice anybody, never mind meet anyone."

Tears began to fill her eyes and she looked down at her feet.

"You've been a great help," Remy said quickly, trying to take the attention away from her emotion.

"Thanks." She sniffed loudly and ran the back of her hand under her nose. "Are you really a detective?" she asked.

"Yeah, I really am," Remy answered.

"Ash used to talk about you a lot," Melissa continued.

"She always said that if she flunked out of school, she was going back to Boston to work for you . . . be your assistant or secretary or something."

Remy smiled. Ashley had never shown much interest in what he did. "Let's hope she doesn't flunk out."

"Where do you think she is?" Melissa suddenly asked. "You don't think somebody took her or anything like that, do you?"

It was obvious that the girl was frightened.

"I really don't know," Remy answered quietly. "But the police are looking into it, and so am I."

"You're gonna find her, right?"

"I'm certainly going to try."

"She said you were, like, the best private eye in Boston," Melissa said. "I guess now's the time to prove it."

Remy nodded slowly.

"You're right," he said. "Now is the time."

Remy had already been to three of the addresses on Ashley's list. She had indeed dropped off copies of her résumé on Friday. Most of the people he'd spoken with had remembered her, and all said that economic times were tough and they had nothing for her. A few were curious as to why he was asking about her, and when he'd told them that she was missing, they suddenly had so much more to say—how polite she had been, what an impression she had made.

They all hoped that she was all right, and so did Remy.

The fourth address on the list was to the Junk Drawer, a consignment/antique store minus the snootiness. The aisles of shelves were stacked high with used books and *National Geographic* magazines, old toys, and dishes and glassware, and multiple racks were hung with vintage clothing. Madeline had loved stores like this, referring to them as a walk down memory lane, a place where the hunger for nostalgia could be fed.

A yellowed, original movie poster for *The Magnificent Seven* hung crookedly on a wall, and Remy considered asking the price. He knew the film to be one of Francis' favorites, although he hadn't seen his friend since that business with the Garden of Eden. Remy had thought him killed in the Hell realm of Tartarus, but Francis had lived, although he was definitely different. Something had happened to him, but Remy hadn't been able to find out exactly what that was.

The Junk Drawer's single proprietor was busy at the front of the store, discussing the value of some *Star Wars* action figures with a customer. As he waited, Remy caught the swish of a puffy brown tail as it quickly disappeared toward the back of the store.

Figuring there was no harm in trying, he walked to the back, where he found a few overstuffed couches, a set of rattan chairs, a glass-topped coffee table, and one extremely large Maine Coon cat nestled inside a wicker hamper atop a folded red blanket.

Remy stood very close to the basket and looked down at the cat, whose eyes remained tightly shut.

"Hey," Remy addressed the animal.

The cat did not respond in any way.

"Hey, I'm talking to you." Remy poked the base of the hamper with the toe of his shoe.

The cat's eyes shot open, staring intensely ahead, but not at him.

"Would you mind if I asked you a couple of questions?"

"Leave me," the cat growled.

"Sorry to disturb you, but I really need to ask you a few questions," Remy told the annoyed feline. "Then I promise I'll leave you alone. All right?"

The cat slowly lifted its furry head to glare at Remy with eyes the color of jade.

"There was a girl in here a few days ago," Remy began. "She came in to ask for a job, but I can't imagine that she wouldn't have seen you and tried to make friends."

"No girl," the cat said, closing its eyes.

Remy kicked the base of the hamper again.

"She would have been really nice, and probably would have scratched behind your ears and told you what a pretty cat you were, or something like that."

The cat raised its furry bulk, arching its back with a hiss; then it paused, seeming to think about what Remy had just said.

"Nice girl," the cat said after a moment. *"Did scratch . . . felt good."*

The Maine Coon sat and turned its face up to him. *"Yes,"* it said.

"So you remember her?"

"Didn't hear?"

"Yeah, I heard," Remy said, trying to keep the annoyance out of his voice, reminding himself why he thought that most cats were assholes. "Do you remember if anything out of the ordinary happened while she was here? Anything that you might've noticed?"

"No," the big cat said, standing up and moving in a circle as it prepared to again curl up on the blanket. *"Scratched and stroked . . . then gone."*

"That was it?"

The cat didn't answer as it snuggled back down and closed its eyes, finished with Remy. Well, he had said he would leave the cat alone if it answered his questions.

He was turning to leave when the cat's voice stopped him.

"Strange man," it said.

"Excuse me?" Remy turned back and peered down into the hamper.

The cat was looking up at him.

"Strange man in store," the cat said. *"Followed nice girl."*

"A strange man followed her out of the store?"

The cat made a face, as if something disturbed it.

"What do you mean by strange man?" Remy wanted to know. "What was strange?"

"Smell," the cat explained.

And the cat's ample fur puffed out on its body as if the threat was still there.

"Smell wrong."

*   *   *

Remy grabbed a coffee from a pizza shop on the corner and stood at the window counter, gazing out at the people walking by on their daily grind. He imagined Ashley doing the same, moving from one store on her list to the next.

A strange man following.

He sipped the hot black coffee, letting it burn the inside of his mouth. He wanted to feel something other than the growing sense of dread in his belly.

The cat had said that the man smelled wrong—strange. Animals were extremely sensitive to the unusual, the bizarre, and Remy was forced to wonder if Ashley's disappearance could have had something to do with him.

And what he actually was.

He'd tried as hard as he could to keep the more unusual aspects of his existence separate from his human life, but, as of late, it was becoming increasingly difficult. And what if someone—*something*—with a grudge against the angel Remiel had decided to get even by striking against those about whom he cared the most?

Remy drank from his cup again, scalding the inside of his mouth. He didn't care for that thought, not one little bit. Briefly he imagined what he would do to anything or anyone that tried to hurt him through his friends. All he could see was fire; all he could hear was the screams of whoever or whatever might be stupid enough to dare.

The imaginary screams were suddenly drowned out by the sound of his phone ringing. He reached into his pocket and checked to see who it was.

Carol Berg.

"Carol?" Remy answered, feeling his body immediately tense.

"Remy," she said. "They just called . . . the police . . . They found her car."

His heart began to race faster and faster, and he thought it might explode.

"They found Ashley's car."

CHAPTER SEVEN

The police had found Ashley's car not five miles from her new apartment.

It was in the parking lot of a small strip mall, where they'd gone for a quick cup of coffee when Remy had helped her move.

He wished himself invisible and approached the car, watching as the local police swarmed about the Honda, searching for clues.

Remy could feel his anxiety growing, and then he heard the words he dreaded most.

"I've got blood in here."

He quickly stepped up behind an officer who was leaning into the vehicle, shining a flashlight on the passenger's seat. He forced himself to remain calm as he waited for the officer to withdraw. It seemed to take forever, but finally the policeman stepped back and Remy was able to take a look, relieved to find only a few spatters of blood on the passenger's seat.

Images of Ashley fighting an attacker flashed before his mind's eye. He saw her scratching the assailant and drawing blood; he saw her being struck, the blood upon the cloth seat from her nose.

He shook his head and moved away from the car as more detectives approached to gather their evidence. The scent of Ashley's blood lingered in his nostrils, and he cursed senses that had become stronger since embracing his true nature.

He had hoped that this was all some sort of enormous mistake, that he would arrive in Brattleboro to find Ashley at her apartment, wondering why everyone was so upset when she had simply gone to visit a friend at another campus, lost track of time, and her phone had gone dead.

But that wasn't her. . . . Ashley wasn't wired that way.

Remy looked to the car again . . . the empty car where spatters of blood had been found. He watched the policemen doing their job. He wanted to do something, too. But what?

Frustration roiled within him. An angel of the Heavenly host Seraphim was not accustomed to standing idle. He was a creature of action, of battle, of war . . . but there was nothing to lash out at with his sword of fire.

He was helpless, the only clue he had coming from a cat that happened to notice a strange-smelling man follow Ashley from a store.

He was considering going back to the store to question the Maine Coon some more when his cell phone began to ring. The officers around him immediately reacted, checking their own phones as Remy walked away from the scene, taking the phone from his pocket. He expected it to be Carol, but instead saw a number that he immediately recognized.

"Ashley?" he cried into the phone, desperate to hear her voice, desperate to know that she was all right.

There was an odd silence from the other end, reminding him of the roaring sound he and Madeline had heard when they'd pressed seashells to their ears at the beach on the Cape.

"Hello?" Remy prodded. "Ashley, is that you?"

"Remy Chandler," said a voice as dry as the grave. "Is that what you call yourself, angel?"

"Excuse me?" Remy asked, stunned. "Who is this?"

"Never mind that," the voice croaked. "I have the girl. . . . I have Ashley."

Remy was silent, waiting for what was to follow.

"Go someplace quiet and wait for me to contact you again."

"If you've hurt her . . . ," Remy began.

"Now, why would I want to hurt the darling who has given me you?" interrupted the voice, sounding jubilant. "Go and wait for my call."

The line went dead, and Remy stood there, too stunned to move. It was exactly as he feared. Not only had Ashley been forcibly taken.

It *did* have something to do with him.

Remy took a room at the Simons Motor Lodge.

He sat in the semidarkness, cell phone on the circular tabletop beside him, waiting for it to ring.

He'd put the television on, hoping for a distraction, but it did little more than annoy him.

Lucky him, there was another story about the little girl who'd awakened from a coma with a message from Heaven. He saw pretty much the same footage he'd seen the other night at Linda's, but this time he learned the young child's name.

Angelina Hayward.

She'd suffered massive head trauma after falling off the back deck of her home, putting her into a coma from which no one ever expected her to awaken. But little Angelina had surprised everybody, saying that the angels had brought her back and that the Almighty had a message.

Remy could not help but feel contempt for the media and how they played up the story. He knew that angels had nothing to do with the girl's awakening. As far as he knew, they were far too busy dealing with the return of Lucifer Morningstar. And as far as getting a message from God? Well, suffice it to say that Remy doubted the validity of that claim.

Angelina was just a very lucky little girl who had managed to beat the odds and come out on the other side reasonably unscathed.

The screen showed a close-up of the child in her bed, clutching a stuffed bear, the reporter asking her if she had anything to say to all the people watching her.

"Talk to you soon," she squeaked, then smiled, hugging the bear.

The anchors gushed about how inspirational the child was, and Remy was about to change the channel when his cell phone began to ring. He snatched it from the table and saw that it was Ashley's number. But instead of relief, it now filled him with dread.

"Remy," he said.

There was that pause again, that hollow rushing sound before the old voice began to speak.

"There's a farm on the outskirts of town. Used to belong to the Deacon family . . . Do you remember them?"

"Can't say that I do," Remy answered truthfully.

The voice went silent, and Remy wasn't sure if the line was still open.

"Hello? Are you—"

"Never mind," the voice interrupted. "They haven't been in the public eye for quite some time. They were once like royalty, you know."

"And what does that have to do with—"

"You will go to that farm and wait," the voice instructed.

"Wait for what?"

"I need to be sure of you, Remy Chandler," the voice said. "I need to be sure that you are what the girl showed me."

"Ashley has no idea what I am . . . and neither do you."

The voice laughed, a sound like old, dried leaves being crushed.

"I know exactly what you are, angel."

"Why are you doing this?" Remy asked.

"Because I can, angel," the voice said. "Because I can."

Beacon Hill
Fall 2008

Remy found Ashley sitting on the steps of her brownstone, staring straight ahead at nothing. Madeline had given him the news: Spooky had died that morning.

"Hey," he said, sitting down beside the teenager. He handed her a Dunkin' Donuts coffee.

"Hey," she said back, carefully taking the cup.

"Two creams, one Sweet'N Low?" he asked.

She nodded, peeling away that little piece of plastic on the lid so she could sip the hot drink. "Right. Thanks."

"Are you all right?" Remy asked, taking the cover off his own cup of strong black coffee.

"Did you hear?" she asked.

"Yeah, Maddie told me. I'm really sorry, kiddo."

She nodded quickly, and he could see a fresh tear spill down her cheek. She had some more of her coffee.

"She stopped eating yesterday," Ashley said. "Didn't matter what we gave her. We even tried sliced turkey. She loved sliced turkey, but she wouldn't even take that."

"I guess it was just time," Remy said.

"Yeah," Ashley agreed. "She was pretty old."

"Had a good life, though," Remy assured her.

"Ya think?" she asked. She turned her head to look at him, and Remy was surprised to see not the little girl he'd first met on that hot summer's day in '96, but a young woman dealing with one of the sad facts of life.

Everything eventually died.

It was something that he still wrestled with in his own immortal existence, one of the difficult truths of being human.

"Sure," Remy said. He drank some more of his coffee, thinking about what he was going to say. "She had somebody who loved and cared for her, who gave her a safe place to live. I really don't think a cat could want for anything else. Do you?"

She thought about it for a moment, taking a long sip from her drink.

"You're probably right," she finally agreed.

They were both quiet for a bit. He could tell that she was still thinking, working things out. Remy was glad that he was sitting with her, wanting to do everything he could to help ease the pain.

"Spooky slept with me last night," Ashley said. "She

never slept with me. I think it was because she wanted to sleep exactly in the center, and that's where I would be. . . . But last night she came into my room and meowed for me, and I had to help her up onto the bed. . . ." She sniffled as more tears began to fall.

"She got onto the bed and sat down . . . and looked at me. It was kinda giving me the creeps, so I asked her what her problem was, and she just gave me one of those disgusted-Spooky looks and lay down right beside me."

Ashley began to cry, and Remy moved closer, putting his arm around her.

"She started to purr, Remy," she continued. "Spooky never purred . . . but last night, she started to purr and then she went to sleep."

She cried some more, and he said nothing, choosing instead to just hold her.

"She . . . she was . . . gone when I woke up," Ashley said, struggling to get the words out. "She must've died sometime in the night."

"A nice way to go," Remy said. "Sleeping beside the one you love."

They sat like that for quite some time, the sun slowly setting, the warmth of it gradually overcome by the evening's chill.

"Did you ever have to deal with this kind of thing, Remy?" Ashley asked him.

"Sure," he said, remembering without regret the pets and the acquaintances he had lost in his seemingly endless existence. How empty his life would have been without them. They had helped him to be what he was today. "It never gets any easier."

"Didn't think it would," she said, tipping the cup back and finishing the last of her coffee.

"Don't let this experience spoil it for you," he said.

"What do you mean?" Ashley asked, looking at him.

"What you're feeling now, the sadness . . . don't let it take away from all the happiness that you had with Spooky. . . . It's too special to be spoiled by a sad fact of life."

"Everything dies," Ashley said.

"Afraid so." Remy nodded.

They sat for a bit longer, and finally she had had enough of the fall chill in the air and stood.

"I'm getting cold. I think I'll head in now."

"You gonna be all right?" he asked her, standing up from the steps.

"I'm good," she said. "Sad . . . but good."

Remy understood perfectly. "You hang in there, all right?" he told her.

"Yeah, it'll probably take a little time, but I'm sure I'll be fine."

"Good to hear." He headed down the steps. "If you need anything, give me a call."

"Will do," Ashley said, climbing the stairs to the building's front door. "Thanks, Remy."

"You're welcome," he said, already on his way when he stopped. "Oh, Ash?" he called to her.

She was halfway in the door but turned back to see what he wanted.

He'd been thinking about this for a while, and he and Madeline had pretty much decided that they would do it.

"We're thinking about getting a dog," he told Ashley. "How would you feel about that?"

He could see the beginning of a smile at the corners of her mouth.

"A dog? Really? What kind?"

"Maybe a Labrador or a golden retriever."

"Labs are awesome," she said. "I think that would be pretty cool, especially if you let me babysit."

"It's a deal," Remy said, waving as he turned the corner. *A Lab it is.*

CHAPTER EIGHT

It hadn't taken Remy long to find the Deacon farm. It had been pretty much where the voice on his phone had told him it would be.

The dilapidated main house and the skeletal remains of a barn next door were at the end of an unkempt dirt road that Remy had found behind a rusted chain-link fence topped with barbed wire. As he moved closer to the old farmhouse, he could see the wide expanse of weed-covered fields beyond. It had been a long time since anything of use was taken from this land.

From what he understood, the Deacons were once one of the country's wealthiest families, starting out in farming but then branching off into gunpowder during the Civil War. It wasn't long before they were producing virtually all American gunpowder. The family was wiped out after a tragic accident claimed the last Deacon and his heir sometime during the forties.

Remy stood before the front porch, wondering if he was alone. Perhaps Ashley's kidnapper wanted to make him squirm a bit, or maybe he had no intention whatsoever of showing up.

Remy didn't even want to consider the latter.

He decided to explore the farmhouse, and his foot had just landed on the first creaking step to the porch when he

sensed that he was no longer alone. He turned to see a smiling man standing behind him. There was nothing unusual
about his appearance—middle-aged, average height and
build—and Remy wouldn't have thought twice about him
if he'd passed him on the street.

"Are you the one who called me?" Remy asked.

But the man simply stood there, smiling strangely.

Two more men and a woman stepped out from the over-
grown bushes hiding the house from the road and joined
the first of them.

Then there came the creaking of a door, and Remy
turned to see yet another man coming out of the farmhouse.

"Are you really an angel?" he asked as he pulled the
door closed behind him. "Give us a taste."

Remy heard the sound of movement and spun around
as the four figures in the yard rushed at him. The men
grabbed at his arms and the woman fell to her knees, taking hold of his left leg.

Remy gathered his strength and managed to shake them
off, kneeing the woman backward into the dirt.

And that was when he realized how weak he was feeling,
how his head had started to swim.

"Tasty," the man on the porch said as he slowly descended the rickety steps. "But nothing too out of the ordinary."

The three men and the woman were on their feet and
heading, arms outstretched, for Remy again. He reacted
purely on instinct, shedding his human guise and assuming
the form of the Seraphim. Wings the color of gold exploded
from his back, and his human garments were replaced with
the armored raiment forged in the divine fires of Heaven's
armory.

"Keep back," he warned, his body radiating a heat so
intense that it warped the air around him.

Remy's attackers hesitated but only for a moment, and
then they were on him again, grabbing hold of his holy visage even as their bodies burst into flames. The angel tried

to rip them away, but they continued to cling to him like thirsty ticks, and he felt himself grow steadily weaker. Somehow the mere touch of these creatures was draining his strength.

He had to get away. He stretched out his wings and crouched down, preparing to take flight, but there was a sudden weight on his back and he realized that the man from the porch had joined the fray. The combined weights of the five attackers brought him to his knees on the dusty ground as even more of his energy was siphoned away. Remy fought to stand, but was finding it hard to even remain conscious.

Then one by one the creatures released their grips. Remy watched as they absorbed the flames of Heaven, leaving behind creatures burned and blackened, with not even a hint of the mask of humanity they'd once worn.

The one from the porch was the least damaged of the five, his clothing singed and his flesh burned a red so deep that it was almost purple.

"Vessels, return home with what you've collected," he instructed, and the charred creatures immediately formed a line and marched toward what was left of the old barn, and disappeared inside.

Remy looked away from the barn and focused on the man who still loomed above him. "What are you?" he managed.

"Very, very hungry," the creature said, reaching down to take the angel's face in his hands.

The pain was incredible, but Remy was too weak to cry out as his life force was slowly drained away.

For as far as he could see, the golden fields of Heaven were buried beneath the bodies of his fallen brethren.

Yet still they came at him.

He was tired and did not want to fight anymore, but the angel Remiel continued to defend his Lord God against those who had chosen to stand with the Morningstar.

Not long ago they had been one family, and now they

were enemies. They descended upon him, wings pounding the air as they screamed for his death, their fiery blades eager to drink deeply of his Seraphim blood. Remiel tried not to look at them, tried not to see which former brother desired to take his life.

But it was an impossible task. The art of warfare, of violence and death, was such a personal thing.

He struck them down, his brothers, one after another. And as each body fell, its blood seeping into the rich soil of Heaven, tainting with a hint of scarlet the few yellow blades of grass that managed to reach up from between the corpses of the vanquished, Remiel of the Heavenly host Seraphim cried out to his Lord God that he could do this no more.

Yet still they came.

And still he fought.

Remy awoke to the sounds of clattering dishware.

Cautiously, he opened his eyes, not wanting to make it known that he had returned from unconsciousness as he gathered his strength and surveyed his surroundings.

He was inside the farmhouse, lying in the center of a wooden table. The creature that only wore the guise of a man moved around the table, setting out dust-covered plates and cups, muttering to himself.

"It'll be just like old times," he said, placing a broken cup next to the jagged half of a plate. "A real family dinner. Just like I remember." He stopped, his bulging eyes scanning the settings. "But . . . what do I remember?" He rubbed a burned hand across his forehead, as if he had an excruciating headache.

"They're not yours," he said bitterly. "They belong to somebody else."

"They are mine!" he screamed, grabbing a coffee cup and smashing it to the floor. "I collected them and now they belong to me!"

He leaned against the table, breathing heavily.

"All right, then." He took a deep breath and stood

straight, adjusting the neck of his shirt as if he were wearing a tie. "Let's just sit down and have a nice dinner, without the drama."

Pulling out a chair, the man sat down and made himself comfortable. "Fine by me," he muttered. He picked up an oily rag and laid it across his lap. "I'm absolutely famished."

He reached across the table to lay his hand upon Remy.

"Enough," Remy cried, coming suddenly to life. He captured the man's wrist in one hand and with the other grabbed a knife from the table, infusing it with the intensity of Heaven's fire. He pulled the man closer and plunged the glowing blade squarely into his captor's chest.

The man yanked his hand from Remy's grasp, stumbling backward, gazing with disbelieving eyes at the metal instrument protruding from his chest. "Now, is that any way for dinner to act?" he asked.

Remy sprang from the table as tongues of divine flame began to consume the man from within.

The creature stumbled about the room, fire leaking from his burning form, igniting the ragged curtains. "All I wanted . . . ," he screamed. "All I wanted was to have them for my own . . . memories of my own . . ."

The farmhouse was primed to burn, and in a matter of seconds, the entire house was engulfed. Flames swirled hungrily around Remy like eager dogs anxious for play, but they did not try to touch him, for they knew he was their master. He spread his wings and leapt through the burning ceiling and into the smoke-filled second floor before ripping through the roof to the clear air outside.

Remy hovered above the farmhouse, watching as it collapsed in upon itself with a forsaken moan of weakened timbers. Then, as if satisfied, the flames began to dwindle until only ribbons of thick, gray smoke remained.

His mind was filled with questions. What were these human-shaped creatures that could drain away his life energy with just a touch? He'd never seen their like before, so why had they targeted him? And why through Ashley?

He lowered himself to the ground in front of the rickety

old barn and assumed his human guise. Since he'd allowed his first opportunity for answers to burn in a fire of his own making, maybe he could find something in the barn where four of his attackers had disappeared.

The barn was empty, nothing but the lingering aroma of magick in the dusty air, too faint to track. "Damn it," he snarled in frustration.

He walked toward the smoldering wreckage of the farmhouse and surveyed the remains. Something wedged beneath a section of wall caught his attention. He reached down and pulled away plaster that disintegrated in his grasp, to reveal a charred skull nestled in a pile of ash. Pulling the remains from the rubble, he gave the skull a shake, loosening the soot that clung to it. The skull was far heavier than it should have been, and as Remy ran a finger along the jawline, he came to the realization that it was not composed of bone, but from some sort of stone.

Or clay.

He gazed at the grinning skull for a moment, then pulled his cell phone from his pocket and placed a call.

"Yeah, it's me," he said into the phone. "I'm sorry to bother you, but I think I might need some help."

CHAPTER NINE

The jet-black limousine cut through the rainy Detroit night, tires hissing as they rolled across the water-covered blacktop.

From the backseat, Algernon Stearns gazed out at the dilapidated ruins that had once housed businesses but now were just empty shells, reminders of what had been.

Shadowy figures watched from doorways as the luxurious vehicle drove past. Stearns could feel their eyes, their hungry eyes, starving for just a morsel of what he had.

With that thought, his own body began to ache. Every part of him, right down to the individual cells, was suddenly awake, demanding to be fed. Calling it hunger did no justice to the agony; it was so much more than that. He had learned to live with the pain but not to ignore it, for to do so was to suffer beyond words.

Stearns looked at the crumpled piece of paper in his hand, then leaned his head against the cool, tinted glass of the window, allowing his eyes to follow the ascending numbers on the storefronts.

"Right here, Aubrey," he announced, tapping the glass with the diamond ring he wore.

The driver obeyed at once, slowing the car and pulling over to the curb in front of a particularly dismal-appearing structure. The driver exited the vehicle and moved around to the rear passenger's door, holding an umbrella in one hand as he opened the door with the other.

"Thank you, Aubrey," Stearns said as he stood and breathed in the humid air of the nearly deceased city.

"Shall I go with you?" Aubrey asked, closing the door.

"No need." Stearns eyed the building before him. "I should be fine." He felt a tremor in his legs brought on by the hunger, and hoped that he had the strength he would need to accomplish what had brought him to Michigan on such an ungodly night.

"Very good, sir," the driver said. He shielded Stearns from the rain as they walked toward the front entrance of the building, then promptly turned back to the limousine when Stearns gestured him away.

There was a filth-encrusted buzzer on the side of the metal door, and Stearns tentatively raised a finger. Deciding that he wouldn't be making contact with it long enough to catch something contagious, he quickly pressed the button.

How many of these kinds of visits have I made over the years? he pondered as he waited. He looked back to the car and saw that Aubrey still stood with the umbrella, observing his progress. His driver was one of a kind. He had actually passed away from pancreatic cancer a year ago, but Stearns wasn't about to let death stand in the way of twenty-five years of excellent service. Good help was so hard to find; a simple spell of resurrection had saved Stearns the trouble.

A sharp click interrupted his musings as the door popped open about a half inch. Stearns gave his driver a nod as he pulled open the door and slipped inside the building.

It was dark in the entryway, lit by only a single bulb from an emergency light; its partner had burned out. There was a door below the emergency light, and Stearns moved toward it, careful to avoid the dust-covered pieces of office furniture that had been left in the hallway.

Is that where Daphene is waiting?

Stearns had been searching for his former lover for quite some time and had begun to believe that she had met an untimely end, when she had reached out to him. She had learned of the murders of Desplat and Montecello and feared the future for herself. They had arranged a meeting, and here he was.

Stearns stopped short just before the door, encountering one of the largest rats he had ever seen. He considered grabbing something from the floor to throw at it, but the way it looked at him—unwavering as it balanced on its thick, gray haunches—was almost as if it were studying him.

Verifying him.

Seemingly satisfied, the rat turned its large, hairy body toward the door that opened with an offending buzz.

Stearns stepped through the heavy door and began to follow the rat down a series of concrete steps. Wall-mounted emergency lights tinted the stairway an arterial red. They descended three levels, the already damp air growing more fetid with the nearly choking smell of urine.

As he reached the last step, the rodent darted quickly away into a patch of darkness. Stearns could not see what waited beyond it, but knew that was where he needed to go.

Cautiously, he entered the shadow. Something smelling of mildew brushed against his cheek, and he recoiled, then carefully reached out to touch what seemed to be velvet curtains. He pushed them roughly aside and entered another passageway. The rat was waiting for him and turned to scamper through an open doorway at the far end of the short corridor, where a flickering light in the room beyond beckoned.

A sudden spasm of pain nearly sent Stearns to his knees, reminding him of what he needed. He took a deep breath and managed to right himself, using the damp cinder-block wall to steady himself as he made his way toward the room at the end of the hall.

The air grew heavier with the stench of mold and piss, and there was also a sound. He could not place it at first, but when he was finally able to discern the squeaks and growls of multiple rats, an image started to form inside his head.

An image that became reality as he stepped into the large, underground storage room.

The floor was a sea of writhing, furry bodies. Everywhere he looked there were rats, thousands of them, crawling atop one another, some lashing out with snarls and hisses, some busily grooming themselves as if wanting to impress a suitor, some just attempting to scurry from one area of the floor to another, others simply waiting for who knew what.

Stearns was both disgusted and fascinated.

"Is that you, Algernon?" a woman's voice asked from somewhere in the room.

"Daphene?" he called out, moving farther into the room, trying not to step on the living carpet at his feet.

"I'm so glad you were able to come," the woman said.

And with those words, the rats seemed to part like the Red Sea before Moses, revealing a hunched figure sitting in a wheelchair at the far end of the space.

Stearns had expected to see the same vivacious woman with whom he'd shared numerous sexual liaisons over the many years they had been alive, perhaps a bit older, given the time that had passed since last they'd seen each other, but still with the same hungry vitality for life she had always possessed.

But the closer he got, the more disturbed he became.

For sitting in the wheelchair was a swollen wreck of a woman, her obscenely fat body straining against the material of the drab, short-sleeved dress she wore. Her arms were pale and flabby, like unbaked dough; her legs were a mess of blue veins crisscrossing beneath mottled, ulcerated skin. Her slippers were split at the sides, unable to contain the flesh of her puffy feet.

"Have I changed that much, my love?" she asked in a wheezy, congested voice.

And to think she once made her fortune in fashion design.

Stearns was repulsed by what he saw. He stared at her bloated face, looking for some trace of the woman he had once lusted after hiding beneath layers of pale, sickly flesh.

"It has been too long, darling," he finally said, watching as the rats crawled upon her chair and her person. She stroked them lovingly as they came within reach, and then he saw the oddest thing. As Daphene laid her hands upon them, the rodents became suddenly still, falling limply onto their sides.

"Even though we've been given more life than the average person, time still marches on at an alarming clip," Daphene answered, brushing still bodies of rats from her expansive lap.

"And what have you been doing with that additional life?" Stearns asked, fighting to hide his revulsion.

"What haven't I done?" she exclaimed with a laugh, causing her ample flesh to undulate. "I made the world my lover. . . . I had whatever I wanted, whenever I wanted it. It was good for a time," she said, gazing off into the distance. "Quite good. But then it all went wrong when the dreams started."

She turned her glassy-eyed stare to Stearns.

"Do you know what I'm talking about, Algernon?"

He knew exactly what she meant: the memories of all those killed in Hiroshima coming to him when his mind was at rest, desperate to be claimed as his own. "The dreams," he said, reaching down to swat a rat beginning its ascent up his trouser leg. "They can be quite . . . overpowering at times."

"Yes," Daphene agreed. "They can be, but once I adjusted to them . . . the hunger came."

Just the mention of the word made every muscle in Stearns' body contract painfully. He hid his body's response with a casual cough.

"At first I had no idea what was happening, but then I realized that Deacon's experiment that night had changed me. I hungered for the energies of living things."

She continued to stare at him, petting rats two at a time, draining their life forces before moving on to the next.

Insatiable.

He could have sworn she was growing larger before his eyes.

"Which explains your little friends," Stearns said, still in awe of the multitude of vermin that surrounded them.

"They breed very quickly, and are quite nutritious as far as life energies go," she explained. "They're also very easily manipulated with magick."

The rats were climbing up, then dropping off, her body in droves now, their conversation obviously making her anxious—and hungry.

"What about you, Algernon?"

Stearns stared at her, pretending he didn't know what she was getting at.

"Were you changed, too?" she asked, a trace of desperation in her voice.

Stearns finally nodded. "Yes, Daphene. Deacon's damnable contraption changed all of us."

She picked up a squirming rat and squeezed the life from it like the juice from a lemon.

"Have you talked with the others?" she asked.

He nodded and began to shuffle closer to the wheelchair, the rats at his feet shrieking with protest as he stepped on their tails.

"Robert and Eugene, yes. I tried to find Angus, but have had little success. You were quite difficult, too, but then you found me."

He was standing behind her now. He took a deep breath, then placed his hands on her shoulders, gently massaging the soft, pliant flesh beneath the cotton dress. It felt disgusting, but it was necessary.

Daphene had stopped feeding.

"How long was it after you spoke to Eugene and Robert that they . . . they . . . ?" She had problems with the next word.

"That they died?" Stearns asked, kneading the flesh of her shoulders, barely able to feel the tender muscle beneath the layers of fat. "Let's not mince words, my dear. They were murdered."

The rats suddenly became more agitated, snapping, hissing, and biting any other that was close by.

"All right." She swallowed noisily. "How long was it after you spoke to them that they were murdered?"

"Actually, I spoke to them just before they died." Stearns knew that he shouldn't, but he couldn't help himself. He leaned close to his former lover's ear and whispered, "Right before I killed them."

The rats were going wild now, and Stearns actually felt a hint of tension through the flab. Daphene tried to turn her bulk in the chair, but he held her tightly, feeling the tiny mouths that had formed on the palms of his hands less than a year after being hooked up to Konrad Deacon's machine eagerly opening and closing.

"What are you doing?" Daphene screamed.

"What I need to do." He gripped her flesh all the tighter, allowing the mouths to take hold. "Nothing else was enough. It was like Chinese food; I'd always be hungry again in a matter of days."

"Algernon, please," Daphene begged. She was struggling to wheel herself away. The rats that continued to climb upon her body were biting at each other as well as at her.

Stearns held her fast, feasting on the unique life force of another cabal member.

"And then I started to think about all my good friends and what we'd been through together, and I became soooooooooooo hungry."

Daphene thrashed but could not escape his grip as Stearns continued to feed, making his pain go away. Satisfying the hunger.

"Something deep inside told me that my friends were the answer, that they would be the ones to save me . . . to feed me. . . . And it was right."

He could feel the flesh beneath his hands starting to wither.

The rats were in a panic as Daphene lost her grip on their tiny minds. They darted this way and that, frantic to flee the basement.

His former lover no longer fought him. She leaned back in the wheelchair, her eyes now a milky white, looking up at him, begging him to stop before it was too late for her. But he would not. He had to take it all and leave nothing behind.

The mouths on his hands eagerly sucked at the remaining life stuff, hungrily taking in energy. She would be dead soon; he could feel its approach.

The cherry atop the sundae.

As her life ended, he saw her memories, staccato flashes of a life of privilege, magick, and decadence. A life leading to this one spectacular moment when it would all be given up.

For him.

And then it was over. That last bit of delicious life clinging to the shriveled carcass in his hands broke free of its mooring and flowed into the mouths of his hands and into his newly enlivened form.

Stearns shuddered with obscene pleasure, tossing his head back as he experienced the sensations of his revitalized body. It was like that morning in the Catskills all over again, when hundreds of thousands of people died to give him life.

To make him strong.

He released Daphene's decaying remains, wisps of lingering life force, like smoke, trailing from her body to the sucking mouths still visible on his hands. The corpse pitched forward, tumbling from the chair to land upon the multitude of dead rats she had drained for sustenance.

His entire body hummed with life—with power. He looked at his hands, watching as the writhing mouths receded back into his flesh. Then he moved swiftly through the shadows and out of the building.

There was only one member of the cabal remaining, but Stearns had already set plans in motion for the future. Plans that, if carried out precisely, would sustain him long after the final cabalist had withered beneath his hands.

It was a changing world, and Algernon Stearns was starving to be part of it.

*   *   *

Remy returned to his room at the farthest end of the motor lodge with the clay skull beneath his arm, wrapped in his jacket.

He was just about to slip the key attached to a green plastic pine tree into the lock when he sensed it.

Danger.

He hesitated a moment. He was still weak from his encounter at the farm. But, then, even though every preternatural sense screamed in warning, he unlocked and pushed open the door.

A serious sense of menace rolled from the room like a thick fog as he stood in the doorway. The shades were drawn, but his eyes quickly scanned the dimness, searching for the cause of his overwhelming unease. His gaze fell on a shadowy shape sitting in the chair wedged into the corner of the room beside a floor lamp, and watched as the figure reached up to switch on the light, expelling the unknown.

"What took you?" Francis asked. "I almost dozed off."

Remy forced himself to calm down, even though his senses continued to warn him of danger. He found that odd, for he and the former Guardian angel had been friends for quite a long time. He wondered if it had something to do with the fallen angel's stay in the Hell dimension known as Tartarus. Something had happened to Francis there. Something he had not yet shared with Remy.

"You got here fast," Remy said, closing the door behind him. "I appreciate it." He set his jacket-wrapped bundle on the end of the bed and sat down across from his friend.

"What's the story?" Francis asked, casually crossing his legs.

The former Guardian angel and part-time assassin was dressed in his usual attire: two-piece suit, dark socks, dress shoes. He looked more like a certified public accountant than a fallen angel of Heaven serving out his sentence on Earth. Francis knew he had made the wrong decision when he chose the Morningstar over God, and had begged for forgiveness from the Almighty. For penance, he wound up as a guard at one of the passages between the hellish Tartarus and Earth.

A job that had come to an end with the return of Lucifer Morningstar.

"Somebody's taken Ashley," Remy blurted out, the words stirring the destructive power of Heaven that churned inside him, still waiting for its opportunity.

Francis said nothing, which surprised Remy, but he continued anyway.

"I wasn't sure at first if it had anything to do with me, but—"

"But it does," Francis interrupted without emotion. He reached into his suit-coat pocket and removed a pack of cigarettes, tapped it against the side of his hand, and slid one from the package.

"Yeah, it does," Remy admitted, the very words painful.

"Any idea who's responsible?" Francis put the pack away and lit the smoke with a metal lighter that he took from another pocket of his suit coat.

"I've talked to the guy. He called me with Ashley's cell phone, but I haven't a clue as to who he is. Seems to have a hard-on with the notion that I'm an angel."

Francis puffed on his smoke.

"And how does he know that?"

Remy shrugged. "Maybe from Ashley."

"But she doesn't know, unless . . ."

"No, I haven't told her," Remy said quickly, starting to think.

"Never can tell," Francis said. "Every now and then, you seem to get the urge to unburden yourself."

Remy wasn't listening to Francis' jab; instead he was focusing on the mysterious voice at the other end of his cell phone. He had specifically said that Ashley had told him, but if Ashley didn't know, then how . . .

And then he remembered the creature at the farmhouse, seemingly struggling with memories that did not belong to it. Could one of these creatures have taken some of Ashley's life force, and, in doing so, somehow figured out what Remy was?

There was still so much that he didn't know, and it made his Seraphim nature want to destroy something. But Remy managed to keep a level head, which reminded him . . .

He turned on the bed and grabbed the object wrapped in his coat.

"The last time the guy called, he told me go out to an abandoned farm for a meeting," Remy said as he carefully unwrapped the clay skull.

"What've you got there?" Francis finished his smoke, and, not finding an ashtray, pinched the tip and dropped the remains on the carpeted floor.

"I was attacked by these artificial beings," Remy explained as he showed the skull to his friend. "They appeared to be human, but when they got their hands on me, they began to siphon off my life energies."

"And this head belongs to one of them?"

"Yeah. Most of them left after nearly draining me dry. This one stayed behind to finish me off."

"So you were set up," Francis commented, taking the skull from Remy for a closer look.

"Looks like it."

"So how do you know that Ashley is still alive?"

"Don't even think that," Remy snapped.

"I know it's tough to hear, but you've got to think of this from all the angles. If one of this guy's creature flunkies tried to kill you—or drain you dry, or whatever the fuck it was doing—then your contact could already have gotten rid of her."

"No. He wants something from me," Remy said firmly.

"Then why try to off you?"

"I don't get it, either. But there was something he said in our last conversation about needing to know that I was actually what he thought I was. Why the need to verify if he just wanted me dead?"

Francis was still holding the skull, but stared at Remy. "You know you're clutching at straws."

"It's all I've got right now, which is why I gave you a call. Any idea what that thing is?" Remy nodded toward the skull.

"Some kind of artificial life-form—a homunculus or golem—likely created by a pretty powerful magick user, but that's all I've got to contribute." Francis hefted the skull. "What the fuck is it made out of, anyway?"

"I think it's clay."

"Wonder if it has a brain, or something that functions like one," Francis mused.

"I have no idea," Remy answered. "Why would you . . ."

Francis reached into his jacket pocket to remove what looked to be a glowing scalpel, its blade seemingly made from light.

"Did you get that from . . . ," Remy began.

"Yeah, took it from Malachi," Francis said casually. "Right after I put a bullet in his head."

Malachi had been one of the first angels created by the Lord God and had helped the Creator design many of the forms of life that had first appeared on the earth. The blade was his most prized tool.

"What are you going to do with it?" Remy asked Francis.

"If there's a brain, or something like it, inside this skull, I'm going to use the scalpel to see what I can find out. You'd be amazed at what an all-purpose tool this is. I can see any memories stored inside there, and, if I want to, I can cut them out. You watch: All the kids will be screaming for one of these this Christmas."

Francis plunged the blade down into the hardened clay of the cranium and closed his eyes as he took a deep breath. "Oh yeah," he said. "No brain, per se, but there is information stored here."

The jaw of the skull suddenly sprang open, and Francis pulled back the scalpel, dropping the skull to the floor.

"Shit," he exclaimed, as a thick, black smoke billowed from the mouth.

Remy quickly stood, but the smoke didn't spread. Instead, it formed a writhing cloud in the air before them.

"That's different," Francis said.

Remy saw that his friend had put away the scalpel and had now drawn a gun from inside his jacket, a gun that Remy had seen before—a gun that had once belonged to the Morningstar.

"Remy Chandler," said the gravelly voice that he recognized as the one he had heard over his cell phone.

"I'm here," Remy said, looking from his friend to the undulating mass of gray.

"If you wish to see the girl alive . . ."

"One of your . . . things already tried to kill me," Remy interrupted. "Why should I trust anything you have to say now?"

"An unplanned misfortune," the voice explained. "My creations sometimes have strong attachments to memories that do not belong to them, which in turn cause problems with their function. That was the case in your situation, and I apologize."

Remy glanced at Francis to find him staring at the cloud, his finger twitching on the trigger of the gun that was once named the Pitiless.

"In any case, you will do as I instruct, or the girl—beautiful, vivacious Ashley—will meet a fate that I wouldn't wish on your dog."

Remy was taken aback by the acknowledgment of Marlowe.

"Get on with it," he snarled, angered that the voice knew so much, and he so little.

"You will come when you are called," the voice said. "And you will come alone."

Remy waited for more, but there was nothing. The roiling smoke collapsed in on itself, gradually receding back into the open mouth of the skull like some enormously long tongue.

"I guess it told you," Francis said, putting the gun away.

"It did, at that." Remy's eyes were still on the skull as Francis bent to retrieve it.

"So, what are you going to do?"

"I really don't have a choice," Remy replied. "I wait until I'm called."

"Figured that'd be your answer." Francis pushed past him into the bathroom, returning with a towel in which he wrapped the skull.

"And what are you going to do with that?" Remy asked.

"I'm gonna take it to somebody who knows about these things," Francis answered. "I doubt that making something like this is easy. Maybe someone in the know might be able to narrow down the playing field."

Remy nodded, liking what he was hearing. "Thanks. I appreciate it."

"Yeah, thought you would." Francis put the towel-wrapped skull under his arm. "Even though it's probably a waste of time."

"Don't say it," Remy said firmly.

"Hey, you know me," Francis said. "Always the voice of reason. Guys that can do shit like this usually play by their own rules."

"So I'll play by his rules until . . . ," Remy said.

"Until?"

"Until it's time to play by mine."

Francis nodded slowly as he turned his back on Remy. A section of air in front of him started to shimmer, like the reflective surface of a pond caressed by the wind. "I'll give you a call if I learn anything," he shot over his shoulder. Then he reached out with his free hand to tear away the vibrating section of air, ripping a hole in the very fabric of reality.

Remy could only stare as his friend entered the passage he'd summoned, and the wound in time and space quickly healed behind him.

Francis had never been able to do that before.

Remy was aware of the passage of time by the movement of the shadows beneath the drawn window shades. He watched the shadows grow stronger, bolder, pooling in patches around the room, growing in strength as the daylight surrendered its supremacy once again to the inevitable night.

He had switched off the lamp after Francis had departed, preferring the solitude of darkness. Carol Berg had called repeatedly, but he did not pick up. He couldn't bear to speak with her now.

He couldn't let her know that this was all because of him. All he could do now was sit and wait.

And do everything in his power to make things right.

Remy's eyes fell on a deepening stain of black on the closet door. There was something about the shadow and the swiftness with which it seemed to move across the wooden surface, blotting out the slats as it flowed down to the floor like dripping ink.

Remy stood and cautiously approached the door, feeling the cold radiating from the area. *This is it,* he thought as he reached out for the door, not surprised to feel nothing beneath his fingertips but cool air. A passage had been opened for him, and he did as he was expected to do, stepping into the blackness.

The entrance gradually constricted and closed behind him, leaving him standing alone in a world composed entirely of shades of darkness. He turned slowly, attempting to get his bearings. Every one of his senses was alive, searching for something, anything, to take hold of. The place smelled of cool dampness, like an old basement, and that strange hollow sound he had heard over the phone was carried in the air.

He raised his hand, willing it to be filled with the divine light of Heaven, and his fingers started to glow, dispelling the shadows. Holding his burning hand aloft, he walked farther into the shadowy world. There was a bizarre landscape beneath the cover of darkness, and Remy thought he might have seen movement among the inhospitable terrain.

There was a sudden flash of brilliance, followed closely by what sounded like a clap of thunder, and Remy experienced an intense pain in his burning hand, and quickly pulled it to him.

There was no doubt about it; he'd been shot.

"Extinguish your damnable light, you fool," boomed a voice from somewhere in the gloom.

Remy fell to his knees, clutching his bleeding hand against his chest, waves of pain coursing through his body with each beat of his heart. He could feel his rage growing, eclipsing any logical thought. The pressure of Ashley being taken coupled with the shrieking pain in his injured hand made it difficult for him to see beyond the violence that the Seraphim could unleash.

But he managed to hold it together, watching as a pair of muted green lights like cat's eyes grew steadily closer, as did an engine's roar. And then a vintage limousine stopped just inches from him with a squeal of brakes. Remy stood as the driver's-side door swung open and a powerful figure unfolded itself from within, rifle by its side.

"Sorry for shooting you," the man said. "But your fire would have drawn the beasts in droves."

He stepped into the green light thrown by the vehicle's headlights, and Remy could see that the pale skin of his face was adorned with swirling, patterned tattoos. He slung his weapon over his shoulder and smiled.

"Besides, what harm could a little gunshot do to an angel of Heaven?"

Remy's anger was about to be unleashed when a horrible roar echoed through the endless night surrounding them.

"They've seen your light after all," the pale man said. "We should get to the house quickly." He turned and strode back to the car, pausing as he opened the driver's-side door. "Are you coming, or do you plan to acquaint yourself with one of the hungry beasts that call the Shadow Lands home? It's really up to you."

Remy hesitated, but then the roar came again, this time much closer, and he climbed into the passenger's side of the limousine beside the tattooed figure.

"Thought you'd change your mind," the man said, putting the car in drive, turning it around, and stomping on the accelerator.

Remy had no idea how he could tell where he was going in the inky darkness, but it was obvious that he could.

"Shit," the pale man hissed as he glanced into the rear-view mirror.

Remy turned to look out through the back window, and was shocked to see something quickly coming up behind them, its monstrous shape faintly illuminated in the greenish glow thrown by the vehicle's taillights. Then it fell back, once again lost in the swirling darkness. And just as he was about to look away, Remy thought he saw something else: a small humanoid figure wearing a hooded cloak and peering out from the shadows, before disappearing in the blink of an eye.

"Hold the wheel," the driver bellowed, releasing his grip before Remy could even reach across. The car began to swerve, but Remy managed to take hold of the wheel and control of the vehicle.

The tattooed man had rolled down the window and was hanging out with his rifle, taking aim at whatever it was that pursued them.

Remy gazed up into the mirror just as the beast surged out from the darkness, its flesh blacker than the shadows surrounding it. It had no eyes, but its mouth was enormous and round and ringed with multiple rows of saw blade–like teeth. It galloped on all fours, its powerful limbs tight with muscle. It stretched its neck and was just about to take the bumper in its open maw when the rifleman fired.

The creature reared back with a pain-filled shriek. For a moment it was lost in the shadows, but it emerged at an even faster clip, enraged by its injury. The tattooed man did not hesitate, firing three more times in rapid succession. With the last of the shots, the great beast pitched forward in a tumble, and Remy caught a glimpse of other, smaller monsters of shadow pouncing on their dead pursuer before there was once again only blackness in the rear window.

The driver drew himself back inside, placing his rifle on the seat between them.

"That should distract them," he said, relieving Remy of

his steering duties. "They'd just as soon eat one of their own as chase us."

"Good shooting," Remy said.

"Living here in the Shadow Lands, you can't afford to be anything but."

Remy was about to ask some questions when he thought he saw something through the ebony pitch ahead. At first he didn't believe his eyes, but then realized that, in fact, what he saw was real.

A mansion sat in the midst of the darkness, its every window alive with light, tinted the same unearthly green of the car's headlights.

"Welcome to the Deacon estate," the driver said, as he blew the car's horn.

And the wrought-iron gates across the driveway slowly parted wide to receive them.

CHAPTER TEN

"Get out," the tattooed man ordered, bringing the vintage car to a stop in front of the steps of the elaborate home.

Remy gave him a quick glance before doing as he was told. He had barely closed the door again before the limousine sped off around the side of house, leaving him at the bottom of the stairs, bathed in the green glow of the house lights. He briefly stared off into the pitch darkness of the shadows beyond, imagining what nightmares waited there.

The sound of someone clearing his throat startled Remy, and he turned quickly to see a shape standing in the entryway to the house.

Remy began to climb the stairs as the figure beckoned for him to enter, and then came to realize that it wasn't a *someone* who had cleared his throat, but a *something*.

It was dressed in the classic tuxedo of a butler, but the creature appeared anything but human; in fact, it seemed to be crudely sculpted from clay. It was featureless except for the most rudimentary details—deep, shadow-filled indentations for eyes, two holes in the flat of its face for nostrils, and a crooked slash for a mouth.

Remy carefully watched the clay figure for any sign of hostility, but it remained perfectly still as he passed it and stepped inside the house.

He stopped and gazed about the foyer in amazement. Everywhere there could possibly be a source of illumination, there it was: electric lights, candelabra, candlesticks dripping thick trails of wax on just about every flat surface. The floor itself was strangely uneven, the large windows were askew in their frames, and a nearby staircase canted upward at an odd angle. It was as if the home had been disassembled and put back together by someone who had had one too many cocktails.

The door closed behind him, and Remy turned to see the clay butler standing there, waiting. The creature motioned toward a nearby corridor, and Remy followed it from the foyer, doing as the creature did—bracing one hand against the wall to navigate the strangely slanted floor.

They reached the doors at the end of the hall and the butler pushed them open to reveal an elaborate library inside. It too appeared to have suffered the strange, distorting effects that plagued the rest of the house: books piled on the floor in multiple stacks, unable to sit on the slanted shelves.

The butler started to leave.

"I guess I'm supposed to wait?" Remy asked.

The butler paused briefly, nodding its great clay head as it pulled the heavy wooden doors of the library closed behind it.

"Great," Remy said, struggling with the urge to leave the library, clad in the armor of war, to tear apart the estate as he searched for Ashley. That was what the Seraphim would do, but in this particular instance, Remy believed that a cooler head would prevail.

Everything had to be right with this one. No risks taken unless necessary. He could not allow Ashley to be harmed in any way. He could not give in to the Seraphim's penchant for violence.

He had to find out more—about Ashley's captor and about what he wanted from Remy. He had to bring Ashley home safe and sound.

The door opened, and the tattooed man entered.

"Mr. Deacon is getting dressed for dinner. He'll join us

shortly," the man said. He crossed the library to a large decorative wooden globe suspended within the framework of a stand.

"Drink?" he asked, opening the globe to reveal crystal decanters of liquor sequestered inside.

"No, thanks," Remy said. "I'm not feeling all that social at the moment."

The man chuckled, taking a tumbler for himself. "Don't tell me you're still upset that one of Mr. Deacon's vessels tried to kill you."

"That and the abduction of one of my friends. Yeah, I guess you could say I'm still upset."

The pale man poured what looked to be some good Scotch into the glass and returned the decanter to the globe, closing the lid. "That was all a mistake," he said, taking a sip of his drink as he strolled about the room.

"A mistake," Remy repeated with a nod. "Sure, it was. Who are you again?"

"Me? Let's just say I'm Mr. Deacon's right hand."

"Deacon," Remy repeated the name thoughtfully. "Wasn't that the name of the family that owned the farm where that little mistake occurred?"

The man sat down in a leather chair and crossed his legs. "Yes, it was," he said. "The farm belonged to the Deacon family for a very long time. As a matter of fact, my master was born there."

"Your master?" Remy asked, surprised at the moniker. "That's a little dramatic, don't you think?"

"No, not really. He created me from nothing and gave me life. I really should be calling him my god."

Remy started to look at the figure in a different light.

"Created you?"

The man had some more to drink. "He certainly did, just as he created that monkey-suited slab of clay that showed you in, and all the others."

"You're one of those . . . vessels?"

"Same basic design, but different function," the man explained. "I'm not sent out for collection."

"And what do these vessels collect?" Remy asked, recalling his experience with the creatures. "Energy? Life forces?"

The tattooed man smiled, the dark lines on his pale face taking on an entirely new configuration. "Aren't you the smart one? You must be a detective."

Remy felt the urge to wipe the smile from the artificial life-form's face. "So how about filling me in on the rest?" he suggested instead. "Start with why these energies are being collected."

The creature was about to answer when there came the tinkling of a bell. "That would be for us," he said, draining his glass and leaving it on the tilted surface of a table beside his chair as he stood.

"So you're not going to answer my question?" Remy asked, following him to the door.

"I'm sure Mr. Deacon will be more than happy to answer your questions," the man said, letting Remy step out into the tilting hall. "But right now, dinner is served."

The dining room was elaborate and sloped to one side, although the dining table had been modified so that it sat level on the uneven floor.

Remy saw that he wasn't the first to arrive. A female figure sat alone at the end of the table. He was just about to introduce himself when he realized that she was dead— long dead, from the looks of her mummified flesh.

He turned to the tattooed man for explanation.

"The master's wife," he said. "He doesn't have the heart to put her in the ground."

The woman's body was propped stiffly in the chair. She was wearing a powder blue dress, and the shriveled flesh about her neck was adorned with fine pearls. Her hair was freshly set.

A huge, crystal chandelier hung above the table, making the fine dinnerware sparkle in its green-tinted light. Remy counted the place settings: five.

A faint, high-pitched whine filled the air outside the dining room, growing louder as it slowly approached. Eventually an elaborate electric wheelchair appeared in the doorway, the clay butler walking stiffly behind it. The chair carried the hunched and shriveled body of an old man, his formal tuxedo hanging from his skeletal frame.

The chair stopped just inside the double doors, and slowly the old man gripped the arms of the wheelchair and stood with a grunt and the hum of machinery. It was then that Remy noticed the man wore some kind of body brace, an exoskeleton clamped around his withered limbs to aid him in his movement.

The old man briefly teetered, and the tattooed man was quickly beside him.

"I've got this, Scrimshaw," the man snapped, and Remy recognized the voice from his cell phone.

Scrimshaw, Remy thought upon hearing the artificial man's name. *It fits.*

Scrimshaw stepped back obediently as the old man gained his balance and proceeded toward the table, the motors on his elaborate brace whining with each step.

He stopped next to the chair at the head of the table, motioning for the butler to take away the wheelchair, before nodding toward his wife. "My dear," he said.

Then he turned his deep, sunken eyes on Remy.

Remy was silent as he stared at the man who had dared to take his friend.

"Remy Chandler," the old man said, looking him up and down. "You're not at all what I expected."

"Sorry to disappoint you," Remy replied. "Maybe you'd like to see my wings?"

The old man grunted. Remy thought that it might have been a laugh.

"I am Konrad Deacon," the man said, watching Remy carefully, searching for a sign of recognition on Remy's face, but finding none.

"A name lost to the ages, I'm afraid."

There was activity at the door again, and the old man turned with a mechanical whir. "Ah, the rest of our dinner guests."

Remy stiffened at the sight of Ashley Berg in a fancy dinner dress being led into the dining room by a little boy holding a leash attached to a collar about her throat.

"This is my son, Teddy. And you of course know his playmate."

It took all of Remy's strength not to unleash the full fury of the Seraphim.

But he managed to behave, telling himself that this was all for Ashley's safety.

"Please be seated." Deacon motioned Remy toward the chair on his left as he lowered himself into the chair that Scrimshaw held out for him at the head of the table.

Ashley and the young boy sat across the table. She made eye contact with Remy as she sat.

"Are you all right?" he asked, pulling his chair in closer to the table.

His heart sank as she looked away, staring blankly at the reflective surface of her china plate.

"Of course she's all right," Deacon answered for her. "A minor spell of obedience and some laudanum to calm her has transformed her into the perfect houseguest."

"She was a little wild when she first got here, but she's adjusted quite nicely," Scrimshaw agreed, standing attentively against the wall.

Remy looked at her again, seeing the dullness in eyes that usually twinkled with vitality. It was as if she weren't even there, which was probably a good thing.

He turned his attention squarely on Deacon and leaned in close to the old man. "If you've harmed her in any way," he said calmly, quietly, "there will be a tremendous price to pay."

Scrimshaw moved closer to the table, but Deacon gestured him away. "I assure you, Mr. Chandler, Miss Berg has been treated with the utmost care, and will continue to be treated so as long as she remains with us."

"As long as I decide to play along," Remy stated.

Deacon smiled as he reached for a silver bell to the right of his plate. "Exactly."

He rang the bell, and the doors into the dining room swiftly opened. Servants of clay filed into the room, pushing various carts that Remy guessed were carrying dinner.

Deacon's son stood up in his seat, watching with wild eyes as the clay servant placed a silver-lidded tray in the center of the table. The boy began to grunt and howl.

There was something not quite right about this child.

"Sit, Teddy," Deacon commanded, and the child squatted atop his seat, eyes still fixed on the covered tray.

A tureen of soup was placed on the table next, followed by smaller trays of what Remy thought might be steaming vegetables. He'd never seen anything quite like them before.

"Harvested on the land outside the estate," Deacon commented. "My recollection is that they taste a bit like mushrooms, but it has been quite some time since solid food has entered my system."

One of the clay servants reached across the table, removing the silver cover over the main course. Remy had no idea what he was looking at. It resembled a turkey, but he'd never seen any form of fowl that sported six limbs.

"Also from the property surrounding the estate?" he asked, knowing what the answer would be.

"Shot it myself," Scrimshaw said proudly. "One of the few critters here that I can kill with a single shot."

Teddy sprang up and lunged across the table, tearing off one of the animal's limbs and jamming it into his mouth.

"Manners, Teddy. Manners," Deacon reminded.

A servant began cutting away slices of the strange gray meat and placing them on a serving tray.

"Help yourself, Mr. Chandler," Deacon offered.

"I'm afraid I'm not very hungry at the moment, Mr. Deacon." Remy looked from the meal to his host. "I believe we have business to discuss."

Deacon continued to watch as the slices of meat were cut from the beast.

"Give the young lady a slice, Godfrey," Deacon instructed the clay man.

IN THE HOUSE OF THE WICKED

Godfrey used the knife and a large fork to place a slice of the meat upon Ashley's plate. Remy was surprised to see her pick up her knife and fork and begin to eat. She'd recently forgone most meat in favor of a predominantly vegetarian diet. His concern for her was growing.

The doors swung open again, and two normal-looking people, a man and a woman, came into the room. There was nothing odd about them at first, but Remy was quickly reminded of the five that had attacked him at the farm.

"I do not partake of solid foods, although I do still require sustenance," Deacon explained as the two people stood beside him. "Do you mind?"

"Go right ahead," Remy said, curious as to what would follow.

The pair began to unbutton their shirts. Scrimshaw moved up behind his master's chair and reached down to the back of the exoskeleton, pulling up two long, black cords, each with a very long, very sharp-looking needle attached. Without any hesitation, he turned and plunged one of the needles into the man's chest; the other into the woman's.

"Bon appétit," Scrimshaw muttered, fiddling with something on the back of Deacon's brace.

A hum began to resonate through the room, growing steadily louder.

"Ahhhhh," Deacon groaned, eyes partially closed. "These are particularly ripe."

The humming sound continued as Deacon opened his eyes and turned his attention to his guest.

"You're probably as curious about me as I am of you," the old man began. "My condition, as you see it here, is a result of my experimentation with life energies, specifically a test where I tried—and succeeded—in collecting the life force of the thousands slain by the atomic bombing of Hiroshima. Unfortunately, it left my body dramatically altered and it didn't take me long to realize that I needed the energy of living things to continue my own life."

Deacon nodded toward the pair standing beside him,

steel needles protruding from their bare chests. "This is how I harvest the energy I need to survive," he explained. "They are an advanced version of golem I have managed to perfect over the years. I bundled both science and sorcery to create artificial beings—vessels, if you will—that can walk among the citizenry, able to collect and store samples of people's life energies without their notice. Once they are filled, they return here and allow me to dine upon their bounty."

Deacon leaned his head back against the chair. Although the brace around his neck prevented his body from totally relaxing, the pleasure of feeding was clear on his face. Remy watched him for a moment, then realized that he appeared healthier, his cheeks flushed with a new vitality.

Younger.

"How does all of this explain why you took Ashley?" he asked.

The old man opened his eyes to slits. "With life energies also come residual memories—emotions, tastes, smells."

The humming of the machine began to quiet, and Scrimshaw was again attentive. He approached the vessels and pulled the needles from their chests.

"About a week ago, there was a street festival in Brattleboro, Vermont," Deacon continued as Scrimshaw carefully returned the needles and cords back to the housing compartment on the back of Deacon's brace. "One of my vessels was there, walking among the teeming crowd, gently brushing against those who had come to enjoy the fair. These events are always my particular favorites—so filled with life and happiness. I was eager to sample the energies and dug in, so to speak, as soon as the vessel returned."

Deacon looked at Remy with calculating eyes.

"Imagine my surprise as I feasted, bombarded by the memories of those whose energies sustained me . . . and I saw you, Remy Chandler. I saw you with this lovely young lady and received the slightest taste of the residual energy you left behind."

The old man paused, his stare becoming even more intense.

"I was able to read that energy, Mr. Chandler. And I saw you for what you truly are."

"You saw that I'm Seraphim."

"I saw exactly that," Deacon agreed, nodding slowly. "Through Ashley's memories I could see the fire that lives inside you . . . but I also saw you had the potential to be so much more."

He leaned forward as if to share a special secret with his guest.

"I saw you as a weapon, Remy Chandler," Deacon said, eyes no longer dulled with age, but twinkling with life.

"An instrument for revenge to be turned on my betrayers."

CHAPTER ELEVEN

Francis no longer carried the special key to Methuselah's. He'd left it to Remy Chandler while he was vacationing in Hell.

But his current employer, one Lucifer Morningstar, had a unique relationship with the owner of the otherworldly gin mill, so it was never too far from where Francis needed it to be.

Still clutching the towel-wrapped skull beneath his arm, Francis walked across the weed-covered parking lot to what had been the Rubber Ducky Car Wash until the current recession had made people realize that their mileage was just as good with a dirty car. He approached the open concrete bay where filthy cars had had their offending grime washed away and peered inside.

He could feel that this was the right place and walked farther into the bay. Inside the cool space, he found a door, its glass window covered with cardboard. It had probably led to the manager's office, but Francis sensed that at this particular moment there was something far different on the other side.

He tried the handle and found it locked. He gave it a bit of a jiggle and waited a few seconds before trying it again. The second time was a charm. The door opened with an ear-piercing squeak, and Francis found himself looking down a long, stone corridor, at the end of which was another heavy wooden door with a red neon sign announcing METHUSE-LAH'S.

Francis strode down the hallway as the door to the car wash slammed closed behind him and was replaced by a wall of moist-looking rock. But he wasn't looking at where he had been; he was thinking about where he was going. If there was any place where he could learn more about the creation whose head he carried, it would be Methuselah's.

Placing a hand on the cold metal handle, he squeezed the latch and pushed the heavy wooden door open into the warmth of the bar. It was dark inside. It took a moment for his eyes to adjust, and when they did, he found himself looking into the not-so-friendly face of the minotaur bouncer who charged toward him on cloven feet, horned head lowered menacingly.

"Phil, you ugly son of a bitch," Francis exclaimed, reaching up to slap the creature's thick skull between his ears and horns. "How the hell have you been?"

"You've got a lot of fucking nerve walking through that door like you own the place," Phil said, getting so close to Francis' face that he could have easily reached up to give the gold ring hanging from the beast's flaring nostrils a good yank.

The minotaur's dark, animal eyes bored into the fallen Guardian's, and Francis began to think that maybe he had made a mistake when the bull-man let out a barking laugh and pulled the fallen angel up into his thick, muscular arms.

"We all thought you were dead," Phil cried, practically squeezing the life from Francis as he spun him around. "Hey, boss," he called out, dropping Francis and turning toward the wooden bar across the room. "Look who it is."

Francis watched the large stone man behind the bar drying a beer mug with a filthy rag.

"Well, I'll be a son of a bitch," Methuselah said. The expression on his stone face changed ever so slightly, but Francis knew he was smiling. "How are you, Francis?"

"I'm good," the former Guardian said, strolling across the floor to the bar, Phil at his side.

"Didn't I say he was still alive?" the minotaur said, throwing his powerful arm around Francis' shoulders. "I said it would take a lot more than Tartarus going ass end over teakettle to put Francis down for the count."

"You did say that," Methuselah agreed, still drying the inside of the heavy glass mug.

"Nice to know that somebody's got a little faith in me," Francis said as he grabbed a stool and took a seat, placing the towel-wrapped skull atop the bar.

There were some strange-looking folks sitting on either side, and as he made brief eye contact with them, they decided they no longer wanted to sit at the bar and slunk off for the privacy of one of the many tables that littered the floor.

"Great to have you back, Francis." Phil gave him one last hard slap on the shoulder before returning to his post at the front door.

"I never even knew he liked me," Francis said to the stone man.

"He just about broke down in tears when he heard the rumors of your untimely demise," Methuselah said, slinging the dirty towel over a broad shoulder. "What can I get you?"

"The usual would be nice."

"Your buddy was in here not too long ago," the bar's owner said as he picked up a glass tumbler from beneath the bar and turned to a display of dusty old bottles behind him.

"Chandler?" Francis asked. "Yeah, he's still got my key."

"You don't need a key." Methuselah shook his head as he poured a drink for Francis. "You've got the all-access pass now."

"And Phil loves me."

"And Phil loves you," Methuselah agreed, placing the

drink in front of him. "Think that gets you a free appetizer once a month or something."

"Sweet." Francis took a large swig of the ancient Scotch. "Remind me of that the next time I'm in."

"Yeah, I'll do that."

They were silent then, the sounds of the bar—multiple voices conversing softly in myriad languages, forked tongues lapping eagerly at libations, the ghost of Roy Orbison singing from the vintage Wurlitzer jukebox at the far end of the establishment—reminding Francis that he'd been away for a while.

And how good it was to be back.

"More?" Methuselah held up the old bottle.

"You twisted my arm," Francis said, pushing the tumbler toward him.

"So, you on the clock?" Methuselah asked, tipping the bottle's golden contents into the empty glass.

"Not right now."

"Looking for work? I got a few freelance gigs that could provide you with some nice shekels for one or two of those medieval playthings you like to collect," the stone man said as he placed the glass stopper back into the bottle and passed the tumbler to Francis.

"Actually, I'm poking around for Chandler," Francis said. "Got something I want to show you."

"A free appetizer doesn't make us *that* intimate," Methuselah joked.

Francis smirked, sliding the wrapped skull toward the bartender. "I thought you might be able to tell me something about this."

"What's the Seraphim gotten himself involved with this time?" Methuselah asked, unwrapping the towel with thick stone fingers. "Holy shit," he exclaimed, staring at the skull.

"Were my suspicions right?" Francis asked, taking a drink.

Methuselah picked up the skull and carefully ran his

fingers over its rough surface. "Whoever's responsible does exceptional work," the barkeep said, his stone eyes scrutinizing the object in his great hands. "I'd love to see the rest of it."

"Yeah, too bad it was destroyed in a fire of divine reckoning."

"Hate when that happens," Methuselah said, setting the skull down on the bar, gaze still riveted to it. "Where did you say it came from?"

"I didn't," Francis replied. "When it was whole, it and a few others attacked Chandler, but that's pretty much all I know. It's got something to do with a case he's working on."

"Doesn't it always?"

"From your mouth to my ears." Francis held up his glass in a toast. "From what I was told, it looked completely human."

"You don't say," the stone man said. "If I had known this level of golem quality was out there somewhere, I'd have seriously been thinking of an upgrade."

Methuselah was one of the oldest original human beings on the planet, but far too many years of wear and tear had caused his body to break down. Wanting to continue with the long-lived existence he'd grown accustomed to, the old man had decided to transplant his life force into the body of a golem.

He was the first person Francis had thought of upon seeing the stone skull Remy found.

"So it is a golem?" Francis asked.

"It's a golem, all right," Methuselah confirmed. "But it's top-of-the-line."

"I don't suppose you have any idea who might be responsible for this little creation."

Methuselah's head and neck made a harsh grinding sound as he shook it. "I'd love to meet him, though," he said. "Having my soul transferred into something like this would be like going from an Edsel to a Ferrari."

"Know anybody who might be able to tell me more?"

Francis asked. He swiveled on the barstool, looking out over the tables. "Anybody in here, maybe?"

"Nah, just the usual bunch of reprobates right now, I'm afraid," Methuselah said as he wiped down the bar with his towel. Then he stopped, as if he'd suddenly gotten an idea. "Wait a minute. Give me a second, will ya?"

"Sure," Francis said, continuing to enjoy his Scotch as the stone man lumbered off through a set of double doors near the bar.

It wasn't long before he was back, a fat guy wearing a stained apron and a paper hat in tow.

"This is Angus, my cook," Methuselah told Francis. "Makes an excellent meat loaf, but he also knows a few things about magick."

Angus pushed past his boss, his rounded belly leading the way as he approached the bar. He was carrying a large glass of ice water and was about to take a drink when the motion stopped.

His eyes were transfixed by the golem skull.

"Look familiar to you?" Francis asked, closely watching the big man.

Angus finally took his drink, and Francis noticed a slight tremble in his hand, one that he didn't think was there before.

"Nope," Angus said, turning quickly toward his boss. "That it?"

"Nothing?" Methuselah asked.

"Nope, it's nothing I've ever seen before," Angus answered. "I gotta get back to the kitchen. . . . Tonight's haggis special isn't gonna make itself."

Methuselah waved the man past, and Francis watched him head quickly back through the double doors, sure the cook knew more than he was letting on.

"Sorry about that." The stone man shrugged. "Thought he might've been able to help you." He reached for the bottle of Scotch. "Hit you again?"

"No, I'm good," Francis said, although he was sorely tempted.

He climbed off the stool, reaching into his back pocket for his wallet.

"No worries," Methuselah said, shaking his stone hand in front of Francis as he retrieved the empty tumbler with the other. "Your boss has an open line of credit here."

"But this isn't my boss's case," Francis told him.

The stone man laughed, dunking the dirty glass into a sink of soapy water beneath the bar.

"It always starts off that way, doesn't it?" Methuselah said as he started to rinse the glasses from the sink.

"Be seeing you, Francis. Nice to know that the rumors of your demise were greatly exaggerated."

Francis knew that it was only a matter of time before Methuselah's cook would step out back for a smoke. His fingernails, stained brown with nicotine, had been the dead giveaway.

He had been waiting in the shadows for more than an hour, the golem skull on the ground at his feet, observing the comings and goings of the strange, insectlike creatures that were Methuselah's busboys as they took their breaks. He was fascinated by the odd game they played, similar to dice but with two small, hairless rodents that screamed like the dickens when they were rolled.

The screen door opened again with a creak, and this time Angus the cook finally stepped out. He was already lighting up as the screen door slammed closed behind him.

Francis noticed that he'd removed his paper cap and was no longer wearing his filthy apron. It looked as though the cook's shift was finished. How opportune; now Francis could have him all to himself.

Angus took a long, deep pull on the cigarette. And Francis took the opportunity to kick the golem skull toward him. It rolled awkwardly across the pavement and stopped directly in front of the cook, staring at his feet.

Francis couldn't have asked for a better kick.

Angus was so startled that he leapt backward, dropping his cigarette and muttering something beneath his breath.

In a matter of seconds, his fingers were crackling with a spell of defense.

Methuselah had been right about the large man's magickal background.

"See, this is why I decided to hang around," Francis said as he stepped from the shadows. He lit up his own smoke, casually puffing away as the cigarette dangled from the corner of his mouth. "That reaction to the golem skull tells me you do know something about it."

Angus unleashed a blast of supernatural energy that arced through the air like lightning. Francis ducked, and the destructive magick struck an overflowing Dumpster, flipping it over and sending foul-smelling refuse across the alley.

The cook was gearing up to let loose another volley, but Francis was already on the move, darting across the alley to place the blade of the divine scalpel beneath the fat man's throat.

"I don't think we need any more spells. Do you?"

"What do you want from me?" Angus asked, eyes wide as the blade dimpled the flabby flesh beneath his chin.

"I want to know the truth about that skull," Francis said.

Angus squeezed his eyes shut. "I told you I don't know anything about—"

"And I'm telling you that you're lying," Francis interrupted coolly, pushing ever so slightly on the scalpel so that its tip entered the flesh no more than a millimeter.

Angus hissed, pulling away, but Francis and his blade followed.

"Look, I used to be an angel of the Heavenly host Guardian, and we can totally tell when somebody is lying, which you are."

Some of the insect busboys had come outside for another round of their game. They caught sight of Francis and Angus and immediately crouched lower to the ground, clicking and buzzing, watching with their segmented eyes.

"Everything's fine here," Francis announced. "Go on and play your game. And watch out for that one." He nodded toward the bug standing closest to the building. "I think he's cheating."

The insects reacted, as the accused bug attempted to defend himself.

"Let's go someplace less crowded and talk," Francis said quietly to Angus. He withdrew the blade and placed it inside the pocket of his suit coat.

Angus stumbled back with a gasp, the fat fingers of his right hand wiping at the bead of blood that seeped from the wound in his chin, while the left started to radiate with excess magickal energy.

Francis just stood there, staring at the man with unblinking eyes.

"You're . . . you're not going to kill me?" Angus wheezed.

What remained of his cigarette still dangled at the corner of his mouth, and Francis let it drop to the ground. "No, as long as you take that glowing hand you're sporting and stick it in your pocket."

Angus seemed to think about that for a moment, then brought the hand shining with destructive potential to his mouth and blew on it, snuffing out the power.

Francis nodded.

"I didn't know that about Guardians," Angus said.

Francis wasn't sure what the man was talking about, and his confusion must have shown on his face.

"That you could tell when somebody is lying," Angus elaborated.

Francis laughed.

"We can't," he said, turning to leave Methuselah's back lot. "I lied."

Francis marched Angus into Methuselah's, taking a table in the far back of the tavern, the single candle in the table's center barely keeping the encroaching shadows at bay.

A waitress with skin so pale that Francis could actually see her entire circulatory system brought them drinks.

Both were having Scotch, neat. No surprise there. What else would a guy named Angus drink?

"So tell me about it," Francis said, puffing on another cigarette.

Angus was holding the skull in his chubby, nicotine-stained fingers, staring into the dark recesses of its eye sockets.

"There's no doubting the craftsmanship," he replied, turning the skull around. "I didn't want it to be so, but it all makes a twisted kind of sense now."

He set the skull on the table and grabbed his drink, pouring it down his gullet in one gulp. Then he smacked his lips and breathed heavily, his massive chest heaving up and down.

Francis caught the translucent waitress's eye and motioned for another round.

"So I'm guessing you do know who made this," Francis said, finishing his own libation.

Angus nodded, his round face glistening with perspiration in the feeble light of the candle. "Knew him, and believed myself partially responsible for his death." He picked up his empty glass and tipped it back, as if hoping for one last drop. "Myself and the cabal.

"But this," he said, eyeing the golem skull again, "tells me that he still lives."

"Let's start with *who*," Francis prodded. "Who's still alive?"

"Konrad Deacon," Angus answered. "He was a member of a sorcerous cabal that included me and four others."

See-through Sally returned to the table with their drinks, and Angus eagerly grabbed at his.

"Why don't you drink that one a little slower," Francis suggested. "I don't want you forgetting anything important."

The sorcerer glared, but did sip at his drink.

"There ya go," Francis said. "Lasts longer that way, anyhow. So, tell me about this Deacon."

"He was the youngest, and the last to be accepted into our exclusive club," Angus recalled. "He had a gift for creating artificial life. . . . Golems were his specialty. In fact, he gave us the knowledge to create our own. We all used them. They were great for walking the dog, doing yard work, taking out nosy reporters doing a tell-all story on one's family."

Francis placed his hand atop the clay skull and turned it to face him. "And you can tell that this is one of his?"

Angus nodded. "He had quite a knack. Nobody I've encountered since has been able to make them so realistic . . . so human."

"And this somehow led to his supposed death?"

Angus paused for a moment, his drink partway to his mouth again. "In a way, perhaps," he finally stated. "He showed great promise as a leader . . . until Stearns decided that he was too dangerous to live."

"Stearns?"

"Algernon Stearns. Newspaper family. Very influential politically; has branched off into electronic media, television, and Internet. He's extremely reclusive."

"Oh yeah," Francis said, vaguely familiar with the name. He remembered that one of Boston's newer skyscrapers was owned by the family.

"At that point, Stearns was the leader of the cabal."

"Ah," Francis said. "Should have figured that one out."

"Stearns convinced us that Deacon was dangerous, that he would try to usurp our power, so we did to him what we believed he would do to us: We attacked first, taking his magickal knowledge to split up among us."

"But Deacon didn't die."

"We thought he had. In fact, the rest of us barely escaped with our lives that night." Angus was staring wide-eyed into the darkness, reliving the moment. "Deacon unleashed a terrible spell. His entire home seemed to collapse in on itself and was sucked into the unholy abyss of nothingness."

"This Deacon sounds like one powerful magick user," Francis commented.

"We all were . . . and we owed it to Deacon. He showed us how to tap into the power of life . . . how we could use the universal force of existence to make us the most powerful magick wielders upon the planet."

"And you tried to kill him for it," Francis said.

"We thought we'd succeeded, but now . . ." Angus gazed at the skull. "The cabal eventually disbanded; petty squabbling caused us to go our separate ways . . . and we lost track of one another."

Angus' eyes shifted uneasily to Francis.

"But then I heard murmurings in the magickal community that members of the old cabal . . . our cabal . . . were turning up dead. I decided to make myself scarce, just in case."

"Which explains why you're cooking at Methuselah's."

Angus shrugged. "I've always liked to cook, and I needed something to do with my spare time."

"So, you think Deacon is still alive and is hunting for you?"

"I wasn't sure at first, but now . . . seeing this." Angus gestured toward the skull with his chin, the thick wattle around his throat vibrating. "I'm convinced it's him."

"So I'm thinking you haven't a clue as to where I can find this Deacon?"

Angus raised what remained of his drink. "If I knew that, he'd already be dead." Then he downed the last of his Scotch.

Francis stood. "See? That wasn't so bad."

Angus was eyeing the Scotch left in Francis's glass, so he slid it across the table to him.

"Help yourself. And thanks for the information."

As Francis started for the door, Translucent Tricia moved to intercept him with the bill.

"Put it on my tab," he said. "And be sure to give yourself a good tip."

*   *   *

Angus Heath, fortified with twenty-five-year-old Scotch, ventured out into the night, weaving a shroud of enchantment to distort his appearance and warn him of magickal attack.

He had no desire to end up like the others, whatever their fates may have been.

Passing through the heavy wooden door at the end of the path from Methuselah's, he entered a maintenance closet in one of New Orleans' finest restaurants. The smells of the place made him remember what it was like to eat. He breathed in the delicious aroma of gumbo and shrimp rémoulade, a specialty of the house. But no matter how much he wanted to indulge, he dared not.

His body craved a different sustenance.

He had been sorely tempted by the life energy emanating from the fallen angel and had almost reached out to sample his tainted divinity. But something had stopped him, telling him it wouldn't be wise. He remembered the scalpel of light and how easily the angel had wielded it, as if it were an extension of his body. No, he was glad he had shown restraint.

He left the restaurant and began wandering the nearly vacant, rain-swept streets of the French Quarter. His home was located on Royal Street. A big, old, three-story American town house he'd converted to his needs over the many years he'd lived there. To the average eye, the place appeared unlived-in, but looks could be deceiving. Angus couldn't count the number of times he'd glanced out the window of his second-floor bedroom to see people crossing themselves as they passed.

Angus climbed the steps to his front door, waved a hand before the lock, and listened as the mechanisms within changed their configuration and slowly the door swung open to grant him entrance.

It was dark inside, so he clapped his hands together, igniting the lamps that hung from the walls—lamps that contained the nearly developed souls of the aborted. It was surprising how much light they could generate.

That special hunger was gnawing at him now and he could think of nothing other than sustenance. He hauled his bulk up the stairs to his second-floor living quarters, but he did not stop there, continuing on to the third level, where he stored his food.

The hunger grew with the exertion of the climb, and he was nearly beyond insatiable as he let himself into his larder. He liked to keep it full, receiving frequent shipments of teenage boys and girls from a special supplier. The cost was outrageous, but on nights such as this, when the hunger was like a thing alive inside him, screaming to be satisfied, it was worth double the price.

He rushed inside the room and froze.

Nothing could have prepared him for this.

They were all dead, his beautiful young adults, strewn haphazardly about the room, their life forces silenced, leaving behind nothing but empty husks.

Something moved, and Angus immediately began to summon a spell of combat. But then a familiar voice called out to him.

"Angus. Is that you?"

"Algernon?" Angus lowered his guard. "What on earth are you doing here?"

"I've been looking for you," the onetime leader of the cabal stated. "To warn you . . ."

"It's Deacon," Angus said excitedly. "Konrad Deacon is alive and seeking revenge."

"Deacon, you say?"

Angus nodded eagerly. "I've seen proof that he still lives."

He looked sadly at his food, spoiling on the floor. "Is this how you found them?" he asked.

Stearns was gazing at the bodies, but Angus could tell that his former leader's thoughts were far away.

"Algernon?" Angus approached his comrade.

"No," Stearns said suddenly. "They were all quite alive when I arrived."

Angus was startled but had no time to react, for it was then that Stearns struck. His arm shot out, his hand grabbing Angus' corpulent face, fingers splayed.

"I had no idea how long you would be, and I was famished."

Angus tried to pull away, but found his strength sapped. He could feel movement against his face, small openings—like eager mouths—on the palms of Stearns' hand attaching themselves to his face.

Hungry mouths feeding upon him.

CHAPTER TWELVE

The idea of being used as some kind of weapon felt like the point of a spear being jammed into Remy's belly and slowly twisted.

"You look uncomfortable, Mr. Chandler," Deacon said.

"I don't care for the idea of being used," Remy replied quietly, rearranging his silverware. "In fact, it makes me quite angry."

Deacon leaned back in his chair, as much as the exoskeleton would allow him. "Would it help if I apologized?" he asked, his tone lacking all sincerity. "I'll do so if it will clear the air."

"I doubt it would matter." Remy could feel his true nature attempting to assert itself, but he forced it back. It wasn't yet time to call on its talents.

The old man seemed to think about that for a moment. "I guess you're right," he said finally. "Abducting the girl does set a bit of a tone."

The silver knife was cold in Remy's hand, and he imagined it hot, radiating with the divinity of Heaven.

But his concern was for Ashley. If there was any risk that she could be harmed . . .

"I took the girl to prove how serious the situation is, Mr. Chandler." Deacon leaned forward again. "That I would be willing to take the chance of arousing the ire of a being as powerful as yourself to finally get what I have craved for so long." He paused.

"Revenge, Mr. Chandler," he continued. "Revenge against those who betrayed me . . . who harmed my beautiful wife and child . . . and were responsible for my time here in a land of darkness."

Teddy jumped up from his seat and crawled across the table, grabbing at the food, tearing off chunks of strangely colored meat and shoving them into his mouth.

Deacon closed his eyes with a sigh, lifting an arm to address one of the golem butlers, but Scrimshaw was already on the move. He dragged the growling child from the table and sat him back in his chair.

"In exchange for Ashley's safety," Deacon began again, "I would like you to consider me your god, for the time we are together."

"Don't do this," Remy warned, fire in his eyes.

"And as your god, you will do as I tell you."

"Don't," Remy warned again, his anger nearly blinding.

"You will rain holy vengeance down upon my enemies," the old man continued, ignoring his guest. "And you will show them no mercy, for you wouldn't want to upset your god."

Remy jumped up, sending his chair tumbling backward.

"I warned you," he said, and he could feel the fire starting to crackle from the tips of his fingers, his wings starting to press against the flesh of his back.

Scrimshaw was suddenly standing behind Ashley's chair, holding her knife, still stained with the blood of her meal, against her tender throat.

"And I warned *you*," Deacon stressed.

The tension in the room was escalating.

"Stand down, Mr. Chandler," Deacon snarled. "Your god commands you."

Remy could hold it in no longer. But as his wings exploded from his back and the fires of Heaven swirled around his head, the blaring sound of an alarm distracted everybody in the dining room. Using the distraction, he sprang into the air and, flying across the table, landed in a crouch before the addled Ashley. He lashed out with a wing, swatting at Scrimshaw, sending him crashing across the room.

"I'm getting us out of here," Remy told Ashley as he pulled her from the chair and into his arms.

Teddy began to howl, tugging on the leash still attached to the collar around Ashley's neck. Remy yanked the leash from the boy's grasp, driving the wild child back with a ferocious glare.

Ashley in his arms, Remy was about to take flight when Scrimshaw made his move. Remy hadn't heard his approach over the clanging alarms, and suddenly the artificial man was on his back, throwing his powerful arms around him, constricting his wings. Remy roared with unbridled fury as the three of them fell atop the table, then crashed to the floor with the dishes.

Remy recovered quickly, wanting to burn the life from this mockery of a man, but Ashley was too close.

Scrimshaw took advantage of that, inhumanly powerful blows striking relentlessly at Remy. The Seraphim spread wide his wings and lashed out at his attacker. Scrimshaw rolled back and away, then leapt to his feet, ready to attack again. But he hesitated.

And Remy saw a smile creep across his face.

The angel began to turn, his senses on full alert, but he wasn't fast enough.

Steel needles were thrust into his back, just beneath his wings. He cried out, wings flailing, as the metal rods scraped along his rib cage.

But that was nothing in comparison to the pain of the needles being activated. Remy spun around, reaching out for the trailing wires, but the infernal feeding device had already started its work.

He could feel his strength waning as the fury and the fire that was the essence of the Seraphim was drawn from his body. He crashed to the floor as if a rug had been pulled from beneath his feet. He tried to summon the fires of divinity, but all he could produce were small bursts of flame that quickly flickered and died.

Remy could feel himself dying, everything that he was being drained away. He fought to his feet, calling on every ounce of strength he had left, but Scrimshaw was suddenly there, a savage kick sending Remy back to the floor to writhe in the grip of agony.

From where he lay, he could see Deacon, an expression of euphoria on his face as he tasted divinity, even as the old man's mechanical skeleton began to smoke. The sorcerer had no idea of the power he was playing with. Remy tried to warn him, but Scrimshaw kicked him again.

He rolled onto his side, trying to protect himself, and caught a glimpse of Ashley cowering in the corner of the room, Teddy jumping up and down beside her. Remy didn't want her to see this, as all that he was was taken into Deacon's infernal machine.

But it would not go quietly.

It would not go without a fight.

He rose to his knees, his body a quivering mess. Scrimshaw came at him again, but the Seraphim, desperate to live, was now in charge. As Scrimshaw's foot descended for another kick, Remy lashed out, grabbing the ankle with a twist, and hurled the artificial man away.

Remy stood on shaking legs. His wings, his glorious wings, were fading. Feathers fell to the floor like autumn leaves. He was dying. . . . This man . . . this sorcerer was killing him. He looked at Deacon, crackling wires still trailing from the external skeleton that he wore over an ancient tuxedo and into Remy's back.

The Seraphim grabbed at the wires, wrapping them about his fingers. They burned his hands, and the stink of his melting flesh wafted into the air as he savagely pulled. Deacon lurched toward him, but the wires held. With smoldering hands, Remy dragged the sorcerer closer. The old man struggled with surprising strength, trying to plant his feet, but the soles of his black dress shoes were smooth, sliding across the wooden floor.

Remy was weak, weaker than he could ever remember being.

Would this be the time? Would this be what finally ended his existence? This pathetic old man ravenous for revenge. He thought of Francis, what his friend would think, and managed to be embarrassed.

The struggling Deacon was closer. The man appeared younger, his flesh healthy, flushed tight with blood. The mechanical skeleton he wore had started to spark, to whine in protest, for the supernatural energy that filled it was too much.

Too powerful.

Something designed and created by humans was not meant to contain the power of Heaven.

"Is this what it feels like?" Deacon gasped, his voice little more than a breathless whisper above the still blaring alarms. "To be this close to God?"

Remy caught a glimpse of something from the corner of his eye. At first he thought it was the artificial man—Scrimshaw—coming back to help his master, but then he realized who it was who stood in a patch of shadow, and wasn't surprised at all.

Israfil was there, watching, waiting.

The Angel of Death had come for Remy Chandler.

But Remy wasn't ready.

He looked away from the death specter and his eyes fell on the cowering form of Ashley Berg, whose life had been transformed into a living nightmare because of her association with him.

Remy had to fix that; he had to make it right. Then death could come for him, as it had for his beloved Madeline.

But not right now.

The angel that he was rallied from the brink of surrender, like one of the great fishes of the ocean being drawn in on a line and finding that deep, hidden reserve of strength for one final attempt at freedom.

"Give it to me," Deacon hissed, his face obscured by smoke and the stink of ozone. "Give it all to me."

And as crazy as it seemed, Remy did just that.

A flash of brilliance exploded from his body, a flash so bright that it chased away all the darkness in the room.

So bright that it chased away Death's angel.

Deacon's scream joined with Remy's as the room was consumed in light.

There was a moment of nothing, of sweet oblivion, but it didn't last long before the chaos returned. Alarms wailed, growing steadily louder as Remy regained his awareness.

He was lying flat on his back, a cracked and seared ceiling coming into focus above him. He sat up and surveyed his surroundings. The room had been obliterated by the release of energy. What appeared to be the broken shape of Deacon was lying among the wreckage of the heavy dining room table, and Scrimshaw was furiously working to uncover his master's remains. Ashley still cowered in the far corner of the room, the animalistic Teddy crouched beside her.

Remy rose unsteadily to his feet, incredible pain in his back causing explosions of color to detonate before his eyes. Reaching awkwardly behind him, he found the metal spines of Deacon's feeding apparatus and tore them from his back. It was an agony the likes of which he'd only experienced a few times, agony that should have had a special place in the pain hall of fame. He started to drop to his knees again as his body rebelled against the damage being heaped upon it, but he fought on.

It was what he did. What he always did.

He focused on Ashley. He'd made a promise to her mother to find her, to bring her home, and that was what he was going to do.

"Ashley," he said, as he stumbled across the room. His voice sounded weak, rough, as if he'd just woken from a long slumber.

Teddy reacted with a hiss, springing at Remy, teeth bared.

And pure instinct powered Remy's response. He slapped the child roughly to the ground, and, like a dog struck with a newspaper, the boy fled across the room to glare at him from a distance.

"We have to go now," Remy said, reaching for Ashley.

She pulled away, putting her face against the wall, her eyes tightly closed.

"Please, Ash," he said, firmly gripping her arm.

She turned from the wall to look at him. What he saw—or didn't—in her gaze disturbed him greatly, but he couldn't let it deter him. He lifted her to her feet and pulled her to the entrance of the dining room, its double doors blown from their hinges by the release of his angelic might.

They walked across the fallen doors, into the corridor. The sound of alarms still filled the air, and as they turned the corner to the passage that would bring them to the large foyer, Remy saw what had triggered the security system.

Deacon's golems, some dressed as household staff, others just human-shaped pieces of clay, fought against multiple attackers. Things with skin blacker than total darkness were attempting to gain access to the home, things that slithered, flew, and crawled were being held at bay by Deacon's supernatural creations.

Ashley hesitated at the sight of an ebony serpent that surged through the open front door to grab up a golem in its cavernous maw. The artificial man struggled as it was dragged into the darkness outside.

Which, if they had any intention of escaping, was where Remy and Ashley needed to go.

Remy gave Ashley's arm a yank, and they ran down the short hall toward the still-open door.

The darkness beyond the pale green lights of the Deacon estate beckoned, promising them one of two things.

A chance at freedom.

Or a fate worse than death.

Scrimshaw watched the angel escape the dining room. He was tempted to go in pursuit, but he had to know if his master had survived.

The explosion of energy was like nothing the golem had

ever experienced before. He doubted there was any way
that Deacon could have lived through it, but he had to be
sure.

The dining table had been shattered, and Scrimshaw
carefully pulled away the broken sections to get to his
fallen master's remains.

He sensed that he was being watched, and stopped for a
moment to find Teddy staring at him, concern in his semi-
human eyes. The boy had seriously deteriorated since sur-
viving the attack by the traitorous Algernon Stearns. It was
Deacon who had truly saved him—if that's what he called
it—using arcane magicks to retrieve him from the brink of
death. But something had been lost in the process. It was
as if the child's humanity had been damaged by Stearns'
assault, and even though Teddy's body had been restored
to life, his soul had continued to die.

Even still, Scrimshaw could see that Teddy feared for
the one who sired him. Normally he would have reassured
the boy, telling him that everything would be all right, but
Scrimshaw did none of that now.

Instead, he carefully picked through the rubble, gradually exposing the tuxedoed body of the man he called master trapped beneath the wreckage. He gently uncovered the
man's head and face and was shocked by what he found.

Konrad Deacon as Scrimshaw remembered him more
than fifty years ago: hair a stark black, skin free of wrinkles, unblemished and taut.

Scrimshaw reached out to check for a pulse, and Deacon's eyes opened wide as his hand shot out and grabbed
the golem's wrist.

"The angel?" Deacon asked excitedly. Golden energy,
like liquid fire, drifted from his eyes.

"He's escaped," Scrimshaw managed, completely taken
aback. "He took the girl, as well."

Deacon seemed to consider this a moment, then released his hold upon Scrimshaw's wrist. The golem gazed
at the burns left by his master's touch.

Teddy howled his pleasure, crawling across the rubble

to get to his father. But as Deacon rose, he extended his arm and a wall of flame roared from his fingertips, driving back the screaming young boy.

Deacon shrugged off the broken pieces of table and dinnerware, and Scrimshaw saw that he no longer wore the exoskeleton that had helped his fragile body to move. It was as if he'd somehow shed his old form to reveal something shiny and new beneath. Tears in the dusty old tuxedo revealed new muscle and flesh beneath. His master had somehow been transformed into a perfect specimen.

But a perfect specimen of what?

The alarms still assaulted their senses as Deacon turned and walked from the dining room. Scrimshaw took the frightened Teddy's hand, and, with a little urging, the two followed into the melee outside.

The golem was about to drag Teddy to someplace safe when he saw his master walk dangerously close to an open window. There was a flurry of movement on the other side of the broken glass, and Scrimshaw pushed the wild child away as he darted to intercept his master, who seemed totally oblivious to the potential harm.

A tentacle as black as ink flowed in through the broken window, ready to embrace the man. Scrimshaw grabbed a jagged piece of wood from the floor just as the muscular appendage wrapped about the transformed Deacon.

There was a searing flash of white.

Scrimshaw shielded his eyes from the sudden brilliance, then dropped his hands to see the stump of the tentacled monstrosity withdrawing through the broken window, the wail of the injured beast ear piercing over the still-insistent alarms.

The release of divine light had driven not only Deacon's attacker away, but all the mansion's attackers. Scrimshaw watched as the golem staff gradually began to recover.

Deacon turned his glowing gaze to Scrimshaw. "Turn that off, will you?" he said, hand indicating the blaring alarm around them.

Scrimshaw called to one of the other stone men to shut

down the alarm, and in a matter of seconds, it was quiet in the house again. He watched as his master strolled to the door, peering outside at the now-still shadow place.

"Do you want me to go after them?" Scrimshaw asked, and Deacon turned his attention to him.

"The angel and the girl . . . do you want me to go after them?"

Deacon began to smile as he looked back through the open doors. "No need." He held up his hands, tongues of divine fire leaping from the tips of his fingers. "I've already gotten far more than I could ever have hoped."

Angelina Hayward did not want to go to sleep.

If the little girl could have had her way, she would never go to sleep . . . never ever, for she believed that she had already spent way too much of her time unconscious to the excitement going on around her.

Since awakening from a coma that the doctors swore she would never recover from, the girl had become the center of a maelstrom. Not only was her return to consciousness considered a minor miracle, but she had also awakened with the promise of a very important message for the world.

A message from God.

The little girl sat in her bed, propped up by multiple pillows. She was trying to put the pretty new dress that her uncle had bought on her favorite baby doll. She was supposed to be resting, but how could she do that when her mind was racing round and round?

Angelina's life was now filled with excitement. Everybody wanted to speak to her. She'd been afraid of the television people at first, with their cameras and the pretty ladies who never stopped talking and smiling, but she had grown used to their visits and their questions.

The same questions, over and over.

When is God going to deliver His message?

And Angelina would just smile at them and tell them that God was very busy, although as soon as He contacted her, they'd be the first to know.

Her parents mostly made the TV people stay outside the home her uncle had provided for them while she recovered, but every morning Angelina would ask her father to carry her to the window so she could wave to those who were camped on the front lawn. This morning she had been especially excited to see them, for she had something she wanted so badly to share with them.

The most beautiful angels had come to her in a dream that night, but she had been so excited to see them that she had woken up. She had nearly burst into tears, until she realized that the angels had followed her. They had worn shimmering robes and golden armor in her dream, but now, as they stood around her bed, she saw that they were dressed in handsome suits and ties. They were still quite beautiful, even without their special angel costumes.

She had been so excited to see them, asking if God had sent them . . . if it was time for her to give His message to the world.

The angels had smiled at her then, and it was like being out in the sunshine, it was so bright and warm.

And they had told her in pretty voices that sounded like music that they had come to help her prepare for what she was going to do. One of the angels, whose name was Armaros, sat down on the side of her bed and took her hand in his. He told her that it would soon be time for her to speak to the world . . . although not quite yet.

"Will you be ready, child?" Armaros had asked her.

And Angelina had answered yes, meaning it with all her heart and soul.

It was no wonder that she didn't want to sleep. What if God and the angels came again? What if they found her asleep and decided to pick some other little girl?

She'd voiced these concerns to Armaros and the other angels as they'd prepared to leave her. They had laughed at her, and it had sounded like church bells on Sunday morning. Then Armaros had told her that no one else could do what she had been created for.

That she was so very special.

Angelina smiled as she remembered the angel's words.

"Did you hear that, Dolly?" she asked the baby doll that was her favorite toy and confidant. "They said I was special."

And she hugged her doll to her chest, secure in the idea that no one could replace her—the angels had confirmed what her favorite Uncle Algernon had always told her.

No one else could do what she was created for.

CHAPTER THIRTEEN

Francis had no desire to be back in Louisiana so soon after laying his wife to rest.

His wife.

The words still felt wrong in his mind, but so much had been wrong there already. He figured he should be grateful for remembering Eliza Swan at all.

The former Guardian had decided that it might be wise to follow Angus Heath. He'd watched from the shadows as the fat sorcerer let himself into his New Orleans home, and was considering making a call to Remy when anguished cries from somewhere inside cut through the silence of the Louisiana night.

Francis studied the old home for a moment, then closed his eyes and imagined what it would look like on the inside. It was a talent that he'd once put to much use while serving the angelic Thrones, but it was a muscle that he'd allowed to wither—until now, in his service to the Morningstar.

The house had three stories, so he imagined a passage opening before him that would place him at the foot of the stairs on the second floor. The air rippled and the existing reality grew thinner, weaker, until Francis tore it apart and stepped through to the darkened house.

The passage closed with a whoosh of air behind him.

He drew his pistol, listening for any sound that would tell him where he needed to go.

Then, as if in answer to a prayer—*fat chance of that*—another, weaker cry echoed from upstairs. Francis took the steps, two at a time, bounding onto the third-floor landing. He paused again, the few angelic senses he had left since the fall searching for clues.

There.

There was no mistaking the smell of death and magick wafting out from the behind the wooden door to his left. It was like dirty socks and gasoline, only not as pleasant.

Francis charged straight for the door, putting all his weight into it as he slammed his shoulder against the wood. He could feel the resistance as he struck, then bounced back into the hall—*magick.*

He aimed the Pitiless pistol and fired at the lock. Bullets made from the divine energies of the Morningstar tore into the enchanted wood, obliterating the magick, and a solid kick gave him access to the room. Francis stormed inside, eyes darting from left to right, searching for Angus.

He didn't have to look far at all.

Angus was standing in the center of the room. A yellow-haired man with dark, bottomless eyes stood before him, holding Angus' fat face his hands.

"Drop him," Francis cried out, firing a single shot from the Pitiless pistol, striking the blond man in the shoulder. The attacker stumbled back, a look of shock on his face, as Angus slumped to the floor like a sack of dirty laundry.

"Who the fuck are you?" the man snarled.

But before Francis could even come back with a pithy retort, the man unleashed a blast of magickal force that screamed like a banshee as it traversed the room toward him. Francis dove from the path of the wailing supernatural energy, tripping over a naked leg sticking out from beneath a pile of dead bodies. Falling atop the fleshy mound, he turned to see the power arcing to the left, coming around in search of him.

Like a heat-seeking missile, he thought, scrambling to his feet.

The magickal spell was louder now as it zeroed in on him. He didn't see much of a chance of outrunning it. Instead he reached down and hauled up the naked body of a woman, tossing it into the path of the oncoming magickal force. The body exploded, and the spell dissipated as Francis again withdrew his weapon to fire on Angus' attacker.

The offending sorcerer was quick, however, erecting magickal shields that absorbed the impact of the bullets, sending the kinetic force of the shots back toward Francis. The floor and wall around him were chewed into splinters as he ducked for cover behind a threadbare chaise longue.

The shriek of another magickal spell filled the air, and Francis was on the move again, crawling across the floor just as the longue that he had been hiding behind went up in flames.

Scrambling to his feet, he saw that Angus was staring at him through hooded eyes.

"A little help here?" he suggested, firing his weapon on the off chance that he might hit his target.

"I doubt you'll be receiving much help from him," the sorcerer said with a snarl, as a magickal construct of pure energy resembling an enormous hand snatched Francis up from the floor, lifting him into the air.

The sorcerer then lifted his own hand, clenching it into a trembling fist. The magickal fist holding Francis squeezed, as well, and he felt the air forced from his lungs. Hungry darkness began dancing on the periphery of his fleeing consciousness.

"So, who might you be?" the sorcerer asked, striding closer as the Guardian fought to breathe.

"That . . . would . . . be   telling . . . Deacon," Francis grunted as the giant hand continued to squeeze.

The sorcerer seemed startled. "Deacon? You have me confused with someone I killed a very long time ago," he said.

The sorcerer was looking up at him now, studying Francis' gasping face as the grip intensified. Slowly the man raised a hand toward him, and that was when Francis saw what looked like tiny mouths on the flesh of his exposed palm, opening and closing hungrily.

Who the fuck is this guy?

Francis tried to avoid the sorcerer's approaching hand, but it was soon clamped on his face, the eager mouths attaching themselves to his flesh.

The mouths started to feed, suckling on Francis' life force.

The fallen angel moaned aloud, thrashing in the grip of the giant hand of magick.

"Oh, my," the sorcerer said as the life energies of the angel flowed into him.

Francis' question of the powerful magick user's identity was suddenly answered with a scream. "Stearns!"

Francis forced his eyes open to see Angus swaying on weakened legs, and a large ball of flesh hurtling toward the sorcerer standing below him. He fell to the floor as Stearns let go of him, the magickal hand that had held him high dissipating in a sizzling flash.

Stearns turned to defend himself and was struck squarely in the chest by the ball of dead. He was hurled backward and pinned to the wall on the other side of the room.

Getting quickly to his feet, Francis ran toward Angus. "We're getting out of here," he told him, already beginning the process of weakening a space between here and somewhere else.

There was a deafening clap of thunder, and a gory rain of torn flesh and body parts fell down on them.

"If we're leaving, it might be a good idea to do it now," Angus suggested, eyes widening with terror as Stearns headed toward them, hands crackling with unbridled power, some of which had come from Francis himself.

"Give me a fucking second, will you?" Francis said, realizing that he was much weaker than he thought.

He had to think quickly, and the first place that popped into his mind appeared before them through the gossamer curtain separating one location from the next.

"Jump," Francis said, grabbing Angus by a flabby arm and pushing him through the curtain.

Francis glanced over his shoulder to see Stearns raising his hands to unleash another blast of magickal force. But this time, Francis was faster. He flipped the sorcerer the bird, then fell backward through the curtain, firing the Pitiless pistol to cover their escape.

The doorway from one place slammed closed as he tumbled through to the next.

Stearns could still taste the interloper's essence coursing through his body.

And it filled him with rage and concern.

The magickal force flowed from his splayed hand, passing harmlessly through where the passage had been to strike at the wall behind it, blasting away ancient plaster and wooden slats.

Stearns gazed down at his hand. The mouths were still there, yearning for another taste of their last prey.

What *he* was distressed the sorcerer. The piquancy of Angus' rescuer was still fresh within him. He could taste a trace of divinity but the flavor was muted, tainted.

Even still, there was no mistaking what he was.

Stearns spun on his heel, walking through expanding puddles of gore as he left the room, wondering if his partners were aware of this wrinkle. The idea of his plans being disturbed was like a kernel of sand stuck in his eye: merely a bother, but irritating nonetheless.

Almost as annoying as being mistaken for Konrad Deacon. Nearly seventy years dead, and still his old adversary haunted him. The thought of Heath believing that it was Deacon who was stalking the cabal forced the hint of a smile to appear at the corner of Algernon's mouth, but it was quickly gone as he recalled the origin of the one who had attacked him.

He threw open the door to Heath's home, descending the steps to the limousine now waiting at the curb. He did not speak to Aubrey as he got in; his living-dead driver already knew that a private flight awaited them at the airport.

Stearns remained lost in his thoughts throughout the entire flight to Boston and the short drive from Logan International Airport to Back Bay. Carefully, he reviewed every detail of the plan he had formulated over the years, a plan that had not been fully realized until he had met his new business associates.

They had made his plans a reality with their knowledge of arcane magicks . . . magicks that they had, in fact, been responsible for introducing to humanity so very long ago.

Finally, the limousine pulled into the underground garage of the Hermes Building, Boston's newest, tallest skyscraper and the jewel in Stearns' vast telecommunications network. The building remained primarily empty, except for some rented office space, his own living quarters and the living spaces he'd allowed for his associates, and a state-of-the-art broadcasting studio that was the key to his plan.

The car stopped in front of the doors to a private elevator, and the ever-faithful Aubrey opened the door for him. Stearns pulled a key card from his coat pocket as he exited the limousine and slid it into the illuminated slot to the right of the stainless steel elevator door.

The door slid open with a cheerful ping, and Stearns stepped inside, pushing the button that would take him to his partners' floor. He knew they would be awake in spite of the early-morning hour, standing, as they always did, perfectly still in a row in front of the floor-to-ceiling windows that overlooked a spectacular view of Boston.

He also knew that they were seeing far more than just the city. They were seeing beyond it.

Perhaps to Heaven itself.

The doors slid open and he stepped out. The floor had never been completed even though he had told them he would do so. Bare walls, exposed wiring, and ceiling beams enclosed the spacious area. They had refused anything else.

He found them exactly as he knew he would, dressed in their fine, dark suits, watching over the city on the precipice of waking.

"We might have a problem," Stearns stated, without preamble.

The leader slowly turned, having some difficulty pulling his gaze from the view, but finally focusing on Stearns.

"Problem?"

"I was attacked tonight . . . by one of your kind." Stearns reached up to his left shoulder, rubbing at the hole in his jacket and the healing wound beneath. It itched.

"One of my kind?" the leader asked.

"An angel," Stearns replied. The sorcerer sifted through some of the trace memories he'd acquired while feeding on the being. "His name was Francis . . . or Fraciel. . . . I'm getting both names, and much more."

"Fraciel." The leader slowly nodded.

"I believe he could be dangerous," Stearns said, watching as the angel turned his gaze back to the view beyond the windows. "Dangerous to my . . . *our* plans."

The angel did not respond.

"Did you hear me, Armaros?" Stearns asked, knowing full well that the leader of the Grigori host had. There wasn't much they didn't hear.

"I heard you," Armaros said without turning. "Now leave us. . . . We have much to contemplate."

The sorcerer was about to argue, but who was he to argue with an angel of Heaven?

Especially one who was going to help him feed upon the life force of millions.

Marlowe missed his Remy.

He zigzagged through the grass of Boston Common, taking in all the scents that had found their way there since the last time he'd visited.

"Don't go too far, Marlowe," Linda called after him.

He looked up, making sure she was safe before going back to work sorting out all the amazing smells.

Remy had told him to watch over the female, and that was exactly what he had been doing since Remy left. Marlowe was a good dog, and he would do anything his master—his Remy—asked of him.

And besides, he loved this female. She was quite nice and let him sleep on her pillow, and gave him treats every time he asked—and even sometimes when he didn't.

The smell of squirrel urine was particularly pungent in one area, and the Labrador buried his nose in the spot, sniffing until he was satisfied that he could find that particular squirrel if he had to. He moved on to a much more pleasant scent—crackers left from a family picnic. He could smell the family members, each of them with their own distinct aromas: a female, a male, and a young female. The girl's smell was all over the crackers that he gobbled up with ravenous abandon.

"You better not be eating garbage," Linda warned, and Marlowe ate faster so she would have nothing to take away from him.

After all, he had worked hard to find these crackers.

Linda was getting closer. He could hear the jangle of the metal clip on the leash as she swung it in her hand. He wolfed down the last cracker and quickly darted away.

He wasn't ready to leave.

There had been many people on the grass of the Common since the last time his Remy had brought him here; so many different smells stamped into the ground by the soles of their shoes.

And then he caught it—a whiff of something that made him stop at once.

It was a special smell. It was how his Remy smelled, and Francis, his friend.

An angel smell.

Marlowe looked up, tail wagging, already moving toward the familiar scent, until he saw the man standing there very still. Watching him with unblinking eyes.

The dog froze, head tilted back slightly as he sniffed the air. He did not know this one . . . this angel.

The angel stepped closer, eyes locked on his.

Marlowe began to growl, low and menacing. He quickly looked over his shoulder to see where the female was. She was a ways back, talking on her phone, swinging his leash to and fro.

Baring his fangs, Marlowe warned the unknown angel that smelled of sweat and desperation not to come any closer.

"You are his?" the angel asked in a tongue that the dog could understand. "You belong to the one called Remy Chandler?"

"Back!" Marlowe barked, charging ahead threateningly to drive the angel away.

The angel took two steps backward, holding out his hands to show that he meant no harm. "Answer me, animal," he commanded. "Does Remy Chandler own you?"

"Yes," Marlowe barked.

The angel appeared to grow excited, eyes darting around the park.

"Where is he? Show me. . . . It's very important that I speak with him, or . . ."

"Not here," Marlowe answered with a series of barks.

"Then where?" the angel asked. "Where is he? There isn't time to . . ."

Marlowe saw the angel's eyes suddenly look above his head, and the Lab turned to see the female, Linda, approaching.

"Marlowe?" she questioned, hurrying along. "What are you doing?"

He ignored her, locking his eyes again on the angel, making sure that he did not make a move toward the female.

He felt her hands suddenly on the chain about his thick

neck and heard the sharp click as Linda attached the leash to it.

"I'm so sorry," she apologized to the angel. "He's never done anything like this before." She began to pull the dog away as Marlowe struggled to keep his eyes on the angel.

"Do you know him?" the angel called out.

Linda stopped, turning around. "Excuse me?"

"Do you know him?" he asked again.

"Do I know who?"

"Remy Chandler," the angel said.

Marlowe began to bark wildly as the angel reached into the pocket of his clothing.

"Marlowe, no!" Linda yelled, forcing Marlowe to sit beside her. "Yes," she said to the angel. "I'm his girlfriend."

The angel had removed a pen and a piece of scrap paper from the pocket and quickly wrote something down. He inched closer to the female, and Marlowe growled again.

"When next you see him, and I pray that it is soon, please give him this." The angel handed her the scrap of paper. "Tell him that I must speak to him about a matter of grave importance."

The female took the paper and looked at it.

"He'll know what this is?" she asked. "What's your name? Just in case he doesn't—"

"Tell him that the Watchers are going to do something terrible," the angel interrupted as he turned to walk away. "Tell him that they are going to try to change the whole world. And it's all because of him."

"I don't understand."

"It's not your place to."

Marlowe and Linda watched the angel hurry away until he was lost among a group of tourists taking photographs beside the Soldiers and Sailors Monument.

And even though the female tried to pull him along, Marlowe fought her until he was certain.

Certain that the angel was gone.

CHAPTER FOURTEEN

There were monsters in the darkness.

But as Remy dragged Ashley around Deacon's property, he hoped they would be safe as long as they stayed close to the patches of light thrown from the house. There had been an all-too-familiar flash moments ago that had driven many of the larger beasts back into the depths of the shadows.

Remy was weak. He was amazed that he was actually moving, the need to get Ashley back to her family probably lending him strength, but he knew it wouldn't last. He had remembered that Scrimshaw had driven the old car around to the back of the house and figured there'd be a garage of some sort back there. That was their objective now: get to the car and drive back across the Shadow Lands, hopefully finding some way out.

The mansion was still in turmoil, but at least the alarm had been silenced. Primitive golems rushed about, making repairs and clearing debris. The chaos helped shield Ashley and Remy's movements as they crept around to the back of the house.

And there was the garage. Remy had been right.

They stopped behind the skeletal remains of a bush, backs pressed against the house, and Remy took a moment to check Ashley. The girl was breathing heavily, eyes red from so much more than crying. He could imagine what this was like for her, and that just strengthened his resolve to get her home.

He studied the scene before him. The old vintage car that had brought him to the estate was parked outside the multicar garage. Light from a spotlight over the open door of one of the bays illuminated the area in a green-tinged glow. Two golems stumbled about the vehicle, cleaning it with rags.

Remy turned, leaning in close to Ashley's ear so that she could hear his whisper.

"We're going to take that car," he told her. "Your job is to get inside; that's it. I'll take care of everything else. Do you understand?"

He looked into her eyes, hoping to see some trace of the vibrant young woman he had watched grow up on Beacon Hill, but only a shadow of that person remained.

A shadow would have to do.

"Follow me," he said, still holding tightly to her hand.

There was nothing to hide their approach, so Remy waited until the two golems turned their stone backs. He tugged on Ashley's hand and started across the expanse of driveway, dragging her behind him.

The vehicle was a four-door limousine, and he aimed her toward the driver's-side rear door.

"Get in," he called out.

The golem that had been cleaning the windshield reacted at once, silently charging at him.

Remy met the attack, grabbing hold of the stone man's face and using all the strength he had remaining to shove the creature away. It was like pushing aside a brick wall, but he managed nonetheless, and the golem tumbled backward to the ground.

He turned quickly as Ashley began to scream. The other golem was attempting to drag her from the car. Remy threw an arm around its throat, hauling the stone man away from her. The golem attempted to reach behind itself, stone fingers grabbing hold of Remy's shirt, and with a burst of un-

natural strength, pulled Remy over its shoulder, slamming
him against the side of the car.

Remy dropped headfirst to the ground, vision clearing
just in time to see the golem reaching for him, and the other
that he had knocked to the ground advancing.

Scrambling to get to his feet, he tried with all that he had
remaining inside to stir his angelic nature, but it seemed so
very far away. The closest of the golems grabbed the front
of his shirt, hauling him up from the ground. Remy watched
as it pulled back its ill-defined arm of stone, clenching a fist
with the sound of rock grating against rock. Remy realized
that if he took this hit, it would likely rip his head off.

The creature threw its punch, and Remy reacted, angling his head downward, feeling the breeze of cold stone
as it passed across his cheek. The golem was off-balance.
Remy took a risk, placing his leg between and behind the
golem's pillarlike limbs. He then surged forward, putting
all his weight behind a thrust that drove the stone man
back, making him trip over Remy's leg.

The golem went down on his back, but that still left the
other to grab at him with both hands.

The tire iron connected with the other golem's simple
face, breaking away part of its primitive nose and part of its
cheek. It actually appeared stunned, stumbling back a bit,
hands going to its damaged face. Remy was a little stunned,
as well, turning to see Ashley standing there, ready to swing
the cross-shaped metal tool again.

They were far from out of trouble, but she had bought
them some time.

"Get in," Remy told her, and, still holding the tire iron,
she jumped into the backseat as he climbed behind the
steering wheel.

At least there was a little bit of luck to be had. The keys
were still in the ignition, and Remy turned over the engine
just as the golem began to lumber toward the car. He threw
it in reverse with a grinding of gears and drove the car
backward, away from the stone men. But still they came,
arms outstretched.

Remy put the old car in drive, gunning the engine and driving right at the pair. They showed no signs of moving, and he plowed into them, scattering them like bowling pins as he continued across the yard, taking a sharp turn and driving around to the front of the house.

He kept his eyes on the road before him illuminated in the glow of one headlight. The closed metal gate loomed before him.

"Hang on," Remy told Ashley, quickly glancing at her in the rearview mirror. She sat in the center of the backseat, clutching the tire iron like a crucifix to her chest.

Remy stamped down hard on the gas. Holding tightly to the wheel, he gritted his teeth as the front of the car struck the center of the wrought-iron gate, tearing both sides from their worn hinges.

Driving into the total darkness, away from the estate, Remy chanced a look behind him in the rearview. He saw Scrimshaw standing just beyond the gate.

And the golem with the elaborate facial tattoos was blowing them a kiss good-bye.

Armaros of the angelic host Grigori continued to gaze out the window of the skyscraper overlooking an awakening Boston. But he did not see the city sprawling below him.

Instead he saw another place, another time, when their kind had been sent to the world of man to fulfill the most special of purposes. They were to observe the newly emerging human species, to guide them away from wrong, if sin should entice.

They were to be humanity's watchers, there to prevent the Almighty's favored young race from straying from the path of righteousness.

Armaros remembered how amused they had all been by their mission. These creatures had already defied the Lord of lords, and had been evicted from Paradise, yet still God loved them and wanted them to succeed.

But there was something about this species.

None of them really knew what had happened. Perhaps

the Watchers had felt the same kind of love for them that the Creator had. But whatever it was that had caused it, the Watchers had found themselves enmeshed in the day-to-day lives of the young species, teaching them things that they were not meant to know.

And, in turn, the Grigori were taught the ways of humanity—of desire and the pleasures of the flesh. In a way, the Grigori had become human, and that, in turn, had taken them down a most dangerous path.

They had tutored the humans in the art of weapons making, of astrology and astronomy, of adornment and cosmetics.

And some they taught the ways of magick.

Armaros believed *that* was what had annoyed the Lord God most and was the reason for their punishment.

The Creator had stripped them of their wings and denied them entrance to the Kingdom of Heaven. They were banished to the earth, almost as if to say, "If you love them so much, you will live with them for all eternity."

At first it wasn't so bad, for humanity worshipped them, but then they began to feel the pangs of what they had lost.

If it wasn't for their leader, they would have surely gone mad.

Armaros stepped back from the glass, overwhelmed by a wave of sheer emotion at the memory of his beloved Sariel. He gazed quickly at his brothers, afraid that they might have felt this flagrant example of emotion.

But they just continued to stare as they had done since the loss of their leader, since the one who was going to guide them back to Heaven was taken from them.

Murdered by the Seraphim Remiel.

Armaros always suspected that nothing good would ever come from their relationship with the angel whose ties to this earthly realm were so firm. Here was a being of Heaven on Earth by choice; not banished, not exiled for an offense against the Lord. Remiel was here by choice and could go back anytime.

He chose not to.

And those of the Watchers despised him for that.

It had been Sariel's plan to win back the affections of Heaven by making amends for past wrongdoings. Correcting what they had done in hopes that Heaven . . . that the Lord God Almighty would notice them . . . accept their penitence, and open His loving arms to them once again.

But the earthly angel cared not for their methods, blocking their path to absolution with such vehemence that it resulted in the death of their leader, Armaros' true love.

Love.

Something else he had learned from humanity and wished he could forget. Something else that continued to cause him immeasurable pain.

Perhaps this was just another way that God wished to punish them.

An image of Sariel in death flashed before the Watcher's mind. He saw his love consumed by Heavenly fire, his flesh and bone rendered to ash by the wrath of the warrior angel.

Armaros fixed his stare on an intricately carved wooden box that rested on a tall stack of plasterboard. In the wooden box were the remains of their leader—his love—and, sometimes, if the mood was right, Armaros swore that he could hear him—his Sariel—reassuring him that everything was going to be all right.

Of course, Armaros believed himself going mad; the death of their leader sent all of the Grigori deeper into sadness and further into the embrace of decadence that only humanity could provide. They were lost in their grief, and every waking moment they strayed farther from the path that would return them to Heaven and God's love.

Sariel's voice eventually grew silent.

But then a stranger came.

Armaros recalled emerging from a drug-induced stupor to find a stranger among them. He had sat in the shadows, turning a ring on his finger, the wooden casket that held Sariel's remains resting on his lap.

He told them he had come to save them, and he warned

them that a war was imminent, a war between two powerful forces. Then the stranger, his features still hidden in shadow, had placed his pale hand flat upon the lid of the box that held Sariel's remains and had promised that God would notice them once more.

Armaros recalled the hand resting upon the box, his eyes drawn to the signet ring adorned with a six-pointed star.

"But there will be a price to pay," the stranger had said.

A price to pay in magick and in human life.

And Armaros had said, *"So be it."*

The machinations were set in motion, and now, ever so slowly, they were nearing the end of plans that would free them from their torment and give them the means to soar again.

Armaros thought of Stearns and their last conversation.

Such a selfish little monkey, he thought.

If only he knew what was really going to happen.

The sounds of a struggle drifted out over the Shadow Lands, and the hobgoblin smiled.

Standing atop an outcropping of solidified darkness, the diminutive creature squinted through the gloom at the elaborate estate in the distance, now under siege by some of the more destructive beasts that called this deep section of the endless realms of black their home.

Squire chuckled with each new roar that filled the constant night, and the flashes of gunfire that attempted to drive back the attackers.

"Good luck with that," the hobgoblin said with a laugh.

There had been lots of comings and goings from the estate of late. Squire tried to remember how long it had been since the estate had torn through the darkness to drop down uninvited into his solitude. He couldn't remember, although he also couldn't remember how long it had been since he had been driven from his adopted home world to take up residence in the land of shadows.

This place of perpetual night did things to the memory,

made it hard to recall specifics. All Squire knew was that he'd been there for quite some time. And the invaders of his long-sought-after peace?

They'd been there too fucking long.

Which was why he'd instigated this latest wave of attacks, taunting the monsters of the shadow realm into laying siege to the mansion.

The monsters who called this place home could have the estate and everybody inside it, for all he cared. Squire just wanted to be left alone, without a hint of anything that he had been forced to leave behind.

Or the friends who he had lost.

He was squinting through the darkness again, savoring the sounds of battle, when there came a flash.

Squire was violently knocked from his perch atop a petrified piece of shadow as it was eaten away by the explosion of brilliance. He tumbled to the ground below, where he lay perfectly still for a moment.

"What the fuck was that?" he growled, rising on shaky legs. Strange blossoms of color, like a kaleidoscope, swirled before eyes now accustomed to total darkness. It took a little while, but his vision finally cleared, and he began walking across the darkness, drawn toward the estate.

He had no idea what that light had meant, but he knew that it wasn't good. The goblin had been around power such as that and knew its potential for destruction in the wrong hands. . . . Even in the right, it was a force to be reckoned with.

His thoughts began creeping toward the past, and he quickly pushed them away. They were gone, as was the world he'd called his home. This was his home now, the Shadow Lands, and he needed to find out what that light was all about.

His pointed ears picked up a distinct sound carried on the still air.

The goblin stopped to listen, searching the horizon for the source of the mechanical rumble and finding the shape of a vintage car as it barreled across the expanse of darkness, kicking up clouds of granulized blackness.

It looked as though this time trouble had decided to cut him a little slack. This time he didn't have to go looking for it.

This time it was coming to him.

CHAPTER FIFTEEN

It was like driving blindfolded.

The flickering greenish light thrown by the damaged right headlight only illuminated the darkness so far before being gobbled up by the all-encompassing black in front of them.

Foot pushed down on the gas pedal as far as it would go, Remy attempted to keep the vehicle going straight ahead, reaching out with his limited preternatural senses in the hope of finding the point where he had first entered the world of shadows.

But he could sense nothing, the tracking skills normally exhibited by his kind strangely dormant. Remy felt oddly different, and considered that his encounter with Deacon's life force–draining apparatus might have done even more damage than he had thought.

He started to roll down the window, hoping to pick up a lingering scent in the air of this infernal place, when his eyes caught the shape of the young woman cowering in the backseat.

"Ashley," Remy said over the sound of the buffeting wind as came in through the open window. The unpleasant stink of the atmosphere here, like a wet cave or an old, musty basement, was not the scent he was looking for.

Ashley ignored him, continuing to stare at a spot just

behind the front seat. He imagined that she was probably in some sort of shock. How couldn't she be? This sort of thing wasn't easily processed by the rational human mind.

"Ashley," he said again, a little firmer. His eyes went from the girl in the rearview to the darkness in front of him and then back to the girl. "I'm going to get you out of here. I just need you to hold on. . . . Can you do that for me, Ash?"

She still didn't answer, and gazed unflinchingly ahead.

"I know this is a lot to process," he told her. "But you have to keep it together. . . . You have to be strong.

"You've been given a glimpse of a world that you don't belong in. A world that most people never see, but I'm going to bring you back to what you know. . . . Beyond this darkness"—he nodded toward the windshield—"everything you know is waiting."

He was about to look back at the reflection of the young woman in the mirror when something large ran through the feeble beam of light. Remy jerked the steering wheel quickly to the right, stepping on the brake ever so slightly to keep the car from tipping, but still maintaining their speed.

Ashley yelped from the back, the car's sudden movement breaking her near-catatonic stare.

"Hang on," he told her, as the smell of something unfamiliar wafted in through the car window.

Remy was about to turn the wheel again when the attack came.

A large, black claw lashed out, tearing at the driver's-side window and ripping the door away as Remy struggled to steer the car from their enormous attacker. He remembered the beast that Scrimshaw had taken down with his rifle and wondered if that was what they were now up against.

Or was it something worse?

Ashley wailed from the back as Remy stomped on the gas pedal, holding on to the steering wheel for dear life, so as not to fall from the open car to the ebony elements.

Something huge roared close by. The car shuddered viciously, as if struck by a savage hand—or claw—and lurched to a sudden stop. Remy reached behind the seat and grabbed the tire iron from Ashley.

"Stay in the car," he ordered, jumping out into the darkness. Clutching the tire iron, he willed the fire from inside to infuse the metal with the divine power of Heaven.

But the fire did not come.

Like his tracking senses, he found the power of his unearthly birthright strangely silent. Remy could feel it there, but it was weak, deathly still.

A snuffling from the darkness before him sent him leaping backward toward the front of the car. He stood in the beam of light from the single headlight, tire iron ready, waiting. He could hear the shadow beast growl, the sound of its weighty footfalls from somewhere beyond the headlight.

Something moved in the darkness, and Ashley started to scream again. Bending down in a crouch, muscles tensed, Remy waited for the attack that he was sure would come.

He didn't have long to wait.

The monster lunged into the light with a roar, an enormous piece of darkness dislodging itself from the environment of solid black. It was bearlike in appearance, only twice as large.

Remy swung the iron with all the strength he could muster, connecting with the monster's lower jaw with a sickening thud. The shadow bear cried out, rearing back, surprised by the sudden explosion of pain. It retreated into the concealing dark beyond the car's light to reassess its prey. Remy stayed in a crouch, paying attention to the senses he still had, ready for the next attack.

The beast came at him from the side this time, attempting to evade the headlight's beam. Its jaws were open, showing teeth that looked like jagged pieces of coal as it made a move to grab Remy's leg and drag him into the forever dark.

Instincts honed in battle were not diminished by his

confrontation with Deacon, and Remy jumped back as the monster's jaws snapped shut on the air where his thigh had been. Taking aim where one of the shadow animal's eyes glistened like a tiny pool of oil, the Seraphim drove the tire iron down, plunging the blunted end used to pop off hubcaps into the socket.

The shadow bear screamed, thrashing its big, blocky head from side to side in an attempt to dislodge the protruding metal cross.

Remy ran around to the side of the car, pulling open the door and extending his hand to Ashley. "Come on," he said. "This is our chance."

He hoped he was right, for as he had fought with the beast, he had begun to sense something. There was a tickling at the base of his skull, akin to the sensation he would often feel when traveling in his more angelic guise from one location to another.

Remy hoped that meant the passage to his motel room was close.

Ashley took his hand, bounding from the back of the vehicle. The two ran side by side as the shadow beast roared its fury from somewhere behind them.

There came a smashing sound, and Remy chanced a quick look behind him. It sounded as though the beast was taking out its anger on the automobile, pounding on the vintage vehicle as it roared in the darkness. He watched as the single headlight went out, shattered by a swat from the formidable clawed paws of the monster he had partially blinded.

Ashley turned, as well, a gasp escaping her as the light was extinguished and they were plunged into darkness.

Remy gave her hand a yank, pulling her toward an area where the odd fluttering sensation at the base of his neck seemed to be stronger. He hoped that this was indeed what he thought it might be: his weakened senses attempting to return to strength, and not just the beginning of a migraine.

The shadow beast's roar echoed through the darkness, and now they could hear the sound of its angry pursuit.

"Keep running," Remy ordered, tugging at her hand. He wanted to stop, to feel the air, to see where the weird sensation was the strongest, but there wasn't time. If they stopped, they were most assuredly dead.

All they could do was run; run as fast as they could through the darkness, and hope for that little bit of luck stored up from the last time a heads-up penny had been found on the sidewalk or the break in a wishbone went in his favor.

The sensation was most definitely stronger *this* way.

Remy pulled the girl roughly to the right and almost paid a hefty price. Ashley stumbled, pitching forward, but she managed to catch herself.

The entrance to his hotel was nearby, behind a curtain of shadow. But where, exactly?

The animal roared so close that he felt the air vibrate on the flesh of his neck, but they were close, as well.

But not close enough.

The horror of Ashley's hold on his hand being savagely ripped away was more than he could stand. One second the pressure and comfort of her presence was there, and the next he was left holding nothing as he turned pathetically in the shadows to find her.

"No!" Remy screamed, dredging up what little divine power he could muster. His hands began to glow like the burner on an old electric stove, providing him with just enough light to see what he'd feared.

The great beast made from solid darkness hunched over its prey, clawing and biting at the thrashing figure it had pinned to the ground.

With no thought for his own well-being, Remy sprang across the expanse of shadow, colliding with the monster with enough force to knock it from its perch. The beast's roars joined with a sound that at first he did not recognize, but soon realized came from himself.

Remy was screaming.

Screaming in rage and sadness, screaming for the violence he now intended to inflict and for what he was incapable of doing.

He'd made Ashley's mother a promise, and now he saw through bleary, tear-filled eyes that he was about to be made a liar.

The bear swiped at him with claws of ebony, and he managed to jump back and away, even though he could no longer summon his wings. It was as if the beast could sense something from this adversary, that there might be a chance that this one could be dangerous, and perhaps it should show caution.

It could show all the caution it wanted, but there wasn't anything that could keep the enraged Remy from his foe now.

His hands were glowing a pulsing orange, and he could see the monster averting its single good eye from the burning light. Remy dodged quickly into the beast's blind spot and lunged at the foul animal.

The bear was swinging toward him, turning its good eye to the attack when Remy latched on. With all his might he threw his arms around the beast's thick, muscular neck, shoving his face into the rough, dank-smelling fur. And as the monster began to thrash wildly, Remy pressed his burning hands to the shadow flesh, coaxing the fire within him.

The animal became frantic with pain as its fur and flesh began to burn. Remy continued to hold tight, turning his face away from the noxious smoke.

The shadow beast's cries were pathetic as it spun madly in a circle, attempting to fling away the one that caused it so much pain, but the angel held fast. A small part of him actually felt sorry for the stupid animal, but another, far stronger part wanted nothing more than to revel in its cries and to see this hellish beast vanquished.

To see his enemy dead.

But the fire was suddenly gone; Remy could feel the divine power falling away and dragging behind it into the abyss any strength that he had left.

The shadow beast flailed madly again and Remy was flung through the darkness, waiting for the inevitable impact, which came with bone-jarring intensity as he landed on his back.

He knew he had to rise, but no matter how hard his brain attempted to communicate this, his limbs and muscles failed to respond. Lying on the ground, Remy cursed himself for his failure.

The starless darkness above him was suddenly eclipsed by something even darker, something that loomed above, glaring down at him with a single, malevolent eye, the top of its shaggy head burning with a smoky orange halo of fire.

It opened its mouth slowly, the light thrown from the flame on its head causing the razor-sharp teeth within its fearsome maw to reflect the light and show him what was about to rend his flesh.

And for what he had been responsible for . . . for what he had done to Ashley, Remy believed he truly deserved this fate and worse.

Remy braced himself, his fingers digging deep into the solid darkness beneath him.

But the killing strike did not fall, and he found himself looking up at something hard and glinting, protruding from the beast's thick, muscular neck, something that was quickly pulled away but then driven again into another section of the monster's upper body.

A spear.

The bear left his field of vision with a bellow of rage. Remy tried to turn his head but was too weak to do so. Something huge and heavy ran across his prone form, trampling him, rolling him across the ground until he came to rest on his stomach. He could see better now, his foe facing off against . . .

Remy at once recognized the short, hooded shape he'd glimpsed through the back window of Scrimshaw's vehicle when Remy had first arrived to the shadow realm.

It hadn't been a trick of the darkness; the figure was real.

And for some reason, it was coming to his aid.

Remy watched through eyes fighting to close as the beast and his small savior battled. Finally, the shadow beast fell to its side, and the hooded warrior plunged his spear into its chest to still its heart and end its misery.

Remy's eyes grew increasingly heavy as the mysterious figure slowly approached him.

And the angel wondered if the same mercy was about to be shown to him.

Squire hadn't wanted to get involved, but there was something about this one, something that he recognized from long ago.

He knelt beside the man on the ground. Keeping one hand on his spear, he used the other to feel the prone figure for injuries. Considering what he'd just gone through, he would have imagined worse. Just minor cuts, bumps, and bruises.

Squire looked closely at the man's face, hoping he'd made a mistake.

But there it was, plain as day. There was no doubt about it; he was one of the good guys.

"Fuck me," the goblin grumbled, using the spear to pull himself to his feet. He looked around the landscape, squinting through the darkness, spying the wrecked limousine lying twisted upon its side, knowing exactly where it had come from.

"So, what were you doing out there?" he asked, before he was distracted by a faint moan.

He left the good guy's side to go to the girl, surprised that she was still alive. In rough shape, but still alive.

His pointed ears picked up the sounds of rustling off in the distance as more predators looking for a meal approached, drawn to the scent of death. Part of Squire wanted to say *Fuck it* and head back to his camp, where he could forget he'd ever come across these two out here.

For a second he actually convinced himself that he could do that, but then he had to admit what a big fucking liar he was. He knew that what he intended to do would stir up all kinds of old memories and emotions—all things that he'd rather not remember.

He'd been a good guy, too, not so long ago, but it hadn't done him a bit of good. What he and his friends had been up against . . . what he and the other good guys were fighting. . . .

It ate fucking good guys for breakfast.

He had been lucky to escape with his life.

Squire picked up the girl and slung her over his shoulder with a grunt; then he walked over to the man. He was muttering over and over about the girl and how he had to save her.

"You're not in any shape to do shit," the goblin growled. He plunged the spear into the black ground and reached down to take hold of the good guy's wrist.

He guessed that the guy was probably from some other, alternate world, one that hadn't fallen to the threat that had claimed his own.

Hasn't fallen yet, Squire thought as he started to drag the man across the ground. *In the end, no matter how many there are, they always fall.*

Squire had sensed the opening that had likely brought the good guy here some time ago, but had chosen to ignore it.

Why set himself up for future disappointment? The worlds he'd found on the other side of the shadow were often just like the one he and his friends had fought so hard to protect. Sure, there were differences, but there were similarities, too.

Like the fact that there was always a war of good against evil in various stages of development, and that the worlds always had protectors who believed they would triumph over the seemingly insurmountable obstacles that were set down before them.

Images of the place he had left behind and the number of other worlds that he had stumbled across in the throes of death appeared unwanted inside his skull.

And Squire wondered if he had it in him to see yet another.

He paused for a moment, getting his bearings, before his senses zeroed in on the passage.

Of course I have it in me, he thought, trudging across the shadowscape.

For once upon a time, he had been a good guy, too.

Algernon Stearns knocked lightly on the wooden door as he opened it.

The little girl appeared to be sound asleep, but upon seeing him, her eyes brightened and she smiled.

"Uncle Algernon," she said happily, pushing herself to sit up.

Stearns went to her bed and sat down beside her. She wrapped her spindly arms around him and, feigning affection, he hugged her back.

"How's my little Angelina feeling today?" he asked her.

She released him from her pathetic grip and stared up at him, eyes wide. "The angels came to me, Uncle," she said.

"They did?" Stearns responded earnestly. "How exciting."

"And they told me that it would soon be time for me to tell God's message to the world."

He smiled at her as best he could, the muscles in his face uncomfortable with the expression. "How marvelous that will be."

"Very much so," she agreed, grabbing a nearby doll and clutching it to her chest.

"And when it is time, who will be there to help you deliver this important message?" he asked her slyly.

"You will, Uncle," she said adoringly.

He couldn't help but be impressed with her. Even though he knew the truth, he could still not find a single flaw in her design.

The Watchers had far surpassed anything he could have created on his own.

"Yes," he told her. "Yes, I will."

Angelina crawled out from beneath her heavy covers and maneuvered herself into his lap.

"Tell me again how you will help," she said, throwing her arms around his neck. "Just in case I might have forgot."

He chuckled, feeling a slight revulsion from the contact, but he allowed it to pass so that the charade could go on.

"Let's see," he said. "I hope that *I* haven't forgotten."

The little girl giggled, laying her head upon his shoulder. "You're just being silly, Uncle. You would never forget anything so important."

"You know me too well, my dear. Let's see. . . ." He paused for effect before continuing. "When the angels come to you and tell you that it is time for all the worthy to hear God's special message, I will come for you."

"In a big car—right, Uncle?"

"Exactly," he said with a nod. "I will send my special driver to pick you up and bring you to my building."

"The one that goes way, way up into the sky," she said, lifting one of her arms above her head.

"Almost to the clouds," he told her. "High enough so you can hear the message that you will share coming all the way down from Heaven."

"And you'll help me share that message," little Angelina said, placing a tiny hand lovingly upon his cheek.

"Yes, I will," he told her. "Inside my building there is a special place . . . a studio that has been set up just for you."

She smiled widely, her eyes twinkling, even though she had heard this information countless times before.

"A special place for you, the angels, and your message from God."

Stearns felt the palms of his hands grow itchy as the mouths wanted to manifest. He held them at bay, exerting his will on them.

"And when you receive His special message, I will be there with my television cameras, broadcasting to all who wish to hear it."

"How many do you think will be listening?" the little girl asked.

Stearns smiled not at the question, but at the answer.

Far more than the number killed in Hiroshima in 1945, he thought, the mouths on his hands eagerly appearing before he forced them away again.

"Millions," he said, leaning in close to whisper in the child's ear.

"And I will touch each and every one of them with my message," Angelina said.

"You most assuredly will," Stearns agreed. "Each and every one; they will never be the same after they hear you."

She placed her head upon his shoulder again, snuggling her face into the crook of his neck. "Why me, Uncle?" she asked. "Why did God choose me over so many others?"

"It's quite simple, really," Stearns said. "You are very special, and God would select only a very special someone to deliver His message."

"But I don't feel special." Angelina lifted her head to gaze into his eyes.

"If you only knew how special you really are," he told her, for the first time being completely honest with the child.

"You're special, too," she said then, hugging him tightly in a fragile grip.

Stearns was finished here, and reached up to peel the girl away.

"Uncle needs to go now," he told her as he laid her back down on the bed. "There is still much to do in preparation for the big day."

She crawled beneath the covers, and he pulled them up to her chin.

"Rest now, my special girl." He forced himself to lean forward and kiss the child's damp forehead.

"What do you think it will be?" Angelina asked.

"What will what be?"

"The message," she whispered. "What do you think God's message will be?"

For a brief moment he heard a million voices raised in a scream of terror as their lives were stolen away.

"I have no idea," he said, opening the door. "But I'm sure it will be something wonderful," he added as he closed it behind him.

Stearns turned from the room to view the child's immediate family standing there in the hallway, waiting for him.

"Was she happy to see you?" the child's mother asked, wiping her hands on her apron. Her husband smiled, uneasy in Stearns' presence, which he had every right to be.

Stearns was not used to being questioned by beings such as this; they were normally created only to carry out orders, but there was a charade to maintain.

A story to be played out.

Again, the Watchers had outdone themselves.

"As happy as I was to see her," Stearns told the golem family. It all felt like a game to him, and he did not have the time or the patience for games. But if this plan, conceived in part by the fallen Grigori, was to succeed, he had to partake of this fiction.

The parents of little Angelina Hayward must fully believe in their humanity, just as completely as the little girl must believe that she was chosen by God.

If the life forces of millions were to be his.

CHAPTER SIXTEEN

It was the closest thing the fallen Guardian angel had to dreaming.

Remembering.

Francis remembered how scared he had been . . . how weak he had felt in the presence of God.

Where was the big, bad warrior then? he thought. *Where was the angel that had chosen to fight on the side of Lucifer, just to help the Son of the Morning make his point to the Creator?*

He had been but an insignificant bug kneeling before a force that had shaped the universe from nothing, and even though he had known it would help him naught, he had begged for the Almighty's forgiveness, honestly believing he had learned the error of his ways.

And he'd waited for what seemed like an eternity for his punishment to come, but it never happened.

Instead, the Lord had given him a penance to perform, and that was where he had learned the art of dealing death.

Killing in the name of Heaven.

When he remembered like this, he saw their faces, all those who had somehow offended God or posed some sort of threat to the Golden City.

He saw their faces as they were before they died—before he killed them.

He saw them all now, but this time the expressions they wore were different. No longer did they appear surprised or angry or scared.

They seemed amused.

Smiling as if they knew something that he did not.

Francis opened his eyes.

"Now, that sucked," he said with a grunt, rolling onto his side and attempting to stand.

The motel room where he'd last met with Remy Chandler was completely dark, and he used the side of the small wooden desk to steady himself as he searched the shadows for his companion, worried that he might have gotten lost along the way.

A toilet flushed noisily, and the bathroom door opened, illuminating the room in fluorescent harshness.

"Oh, good. You're awake." Angus stumbled back into the room, looking like death warmed over. "For a minute there I thought I might've killed you."

"You thought you might have killed me?" Francis asked. The room seemed to be moving beneath his feet, and he pulled out the desk chair to sit down and ride out the storm.

Angus dropped down on the room's double bed, mattress coils screaming out in protest. "I would have died if I hadn't fed," the sorcerer explained. "But I took only enough to keep on living."

"So I'm guessing you're not talking about room service or a quick jaunt to the burger joint down the street," Francis said, not the least bit happy about where he knew this was going as he realized how weak he was feeling.

The sorcerer shrugged.

"You're like the asshole that almost killed us in New Orleans," Francis said, his voice becoming louder.

Angus nodded. "Like Stearns . . . yes."

"You fed off me," Francis stated, the words dripping with fury.

"Only a little," Angus defended himself. "Stearns took so much from me that I would have died if I hadn't—"

Francis was up with his gun drawn in a blink.

"If you hadn't had taken a few nibbles from the Francis snack bar," he finished, aiming the pistol at Angus' fat, flushed face.

Angus raised his hands in surrender. "I would have asked if you had been conscious, but I had no idea when you were going to wake up. And this way at least one of us would be able to alert someone to Stearns' plans."

Stearns' plans.

Even though he wanted to perforate the sorcerer's round face, Francis lowered his gun and returned it to the bottomless pocket inside his suit coat.

"Tell me about this Stearns character," he said, sitting on the desk chair before he fell down. "I thought the problem was with somebody named Deacon."

Angus lay on the bed, legs splayed, head back against the headboard. "It appears that I was mistaken. It's not the betrayed reaching out to kill us from beyond the grave at all. . . . It's one of our own."

"And the mouths on his hands?" Francis asked, holding up his own as examples. "What the fuck's up with that?"

"I told you before: The cabal was part of an experiment to use the life force of living things as an energy source, and it achieved everything we had hoped. But there was a price to pay, one that we didn't realize at first."

"It gave you nasty little mouths on your hands," Francis said. He reached into his coat pocket and removed a crumpled pack of cigarettes. If there was ever a time for a smoke, it was now. He offered the pack to Angus.

"Thanks," the sorcerer said, grabbing a cigarette and leaning forward so Francis could light it. "The magick obviously changed some of us more dramatically than others," he continued to explain. "It appears, though, that we all must feed on the life energies of living things in order to survive, but I certainly haven't grown mouths on my hands to do so."

Francis wasn't sure that he wanted to ask the next question, but he did, anyway. "So how do you feed?" he asked, blowing a cloud of smoke into the air.

Angus pointed a chubby finger to his mouth. "This works just fine."

"You put that on me?" Francis felt his ire begin to climb again.

"Just a gentle peck on your cheek," Angus said.

Francis could see that the fat sorcerer was struggling not to laugh. Maybe he would shoot him after all.

"What an interesting existence you've led, Fraciel."

"Don't call me that," Francis warned.

"Aren't you going to ask how I know about you?" the sorcerer teased.

Francis just puffed on his smoke, knowing that Angus would answer his own question.

"When we feed on your energies, we get a good taste of what you are . . . who you are . . . where you've been, what you've been up to . . . Your experiences become ours. . . . We live them as you lived them," Angus explained.

Francis glared across the room.

"No worries," Angus assured him. "Your secrets are safe with me."

"You said something about Stearns being up to something." Francis pinched the still-burning end of the cigarette to extinguish it and dropped the remains into the barrel beside the desk.

"As he fed on me, I tried to feed on him . . . and I saw that he is very hungry."

"Thinking an all-you-can-eat-buffet hungry?" Francis asked to help him gauge the level of importance.

"Hungry for the power that only the deaths of countless people would satisfy." Angus finished his own cigarette, grinding it out on the bedside table and leaving it there.

Francis felt a sudden dip in the temperature of the room and knew it wasn't a chill from Angus' statement. The Pitiless pistol was in his grip once again as he stood, his every sense on full alert.

"What is it?" Angus asked nervously, throwing his tree trunk–sized legs over the side of the bed, ready to flee.

"It feels different in here." Francis carefully stepped

away from the desk, attempting to home in on the cause of the disturbance.

"I feel it, too," Angus said. He extended his arms, fingertips wiggling. "It's as if something is pulling the energy from the room—"

The fluorescents in the bathroom went dark with a hum, plunging the room into darkness.

"Don't move," Francis ordered, blinking to adjust to the sudden loss of light.

The room was awash in shadow, but for some reason he could not take his eyes from the covering of shadow that had appeared on the closet door. There was something about it, blacker than all the other shadows in the room. He moved closer to it, holding out his free hand, and felt an exhalation of cold.

"Got it," he said, raising his gun to the shadow just as a short, stocky, hooded figure began to emerge. He almost began to fire, but quickly removed his finger from the delicate trigger of the Pitiless pistol when he noticed the form of a teenage girl slung over the creature's shoulder, and the body of a man he was dragging from the darkness behind him.

Francis' aim never wavered as the ugly creature let the girl's still body drop to the floor, then turned to haul the man from the passage of shadow into the room. He would have liked to say that he was surprised to see the unconscious form of Remy Chandler lying on the floor before him, but when it came to his Seraphim friend, nothing surprised Francis anymore.

"Why don't you tell me what's going on?" he ordered, aiming at a line of particularly thick wrinkles on the ugly wretch's forehead.

The small creature slowly raised his eyes, as if realizing for the very first time that he wasn't alone.

"Why don't *you* put down that gun before *I* forget I'm on a mission of mercy and shove it up your ass?"

Squire glared at the man still holding the pistol on him.

"Okay, how about this: Why don't you put down that

gun before I forget I'm on a mission of mercy and shove it up your ass, *please*?"

"Well, since you said please," the one with the gun replied, losing the weapon inside his suit jacket. He knelt down beside the man that Squire had dragged from the Shadow Paths. "Is he all right?"

Squire could tell right away that the two shared a special bond, something stronger than mere friendship. He guessed that this one was one of the good guys, too, but he could also sense another vibe from him, one that suggested he could go either way. He was well acquainted with those types, as well, and had put many in the grave for choosing the wrong side.

"Got knocked around pretty good, but he seems to be durable." Squire pointed to the girl. "She's probably going to need some attention."

A fat guy that reeked of magick knelt with a grunt beside the injured girl.

"Wouldn't do anything that might harm her, if I were you," the goblin warned the magick user. "In fact, I'd do everything in my power to see that she makes it. This one seems pretty darn attached," he said, pointing to the still-unconscious Remy. "And something tells me you wouldn't want to get on his bad side."

The one that had held the gun on him lifted the man from the floor. "This one's a pussycat," he said, carrying him to the bed and letting his body fall limply to the mattress.

The magick user carefully picked up the girl and laid her beside the man on the double bed.

"Now, why don't you explain who you are and what you know about these two?" the man with the gun said, coming around the bed toward Squire.

"Nothing much to tell," Squire said. His preternatural senses had already started to fan out, feeling this world for what it was. It wasn't as far along as many of the others he had discovered off the paths that he'd wandered through the years, but he could still sense the potential for disaster.

This world seemed to have a much longer fuse than some of the others, but he imagined it would eventually end up as they had. The hobgoblin suddenly couldn't stand to be there anymore; the temptation to stay was too great.

"My job is done," he said, pulling his hood up over his blocky head and pointed ears. "Make sure they're well taken care of." He nodded toward the two on the bed. "I get a sense they're special, and you don't want to lose special."

"Who are you?" the friend asked the goblin.

"Nobody, really," Squire responded. He wanted to dive into the darkness, to be gone, to return to the Shadow Paths, but something held him there, savoring a world very much like his own.

A world he missed.

"I used to be a lot like you, living in a place a lot like this, but then things got out of hand. . . ."

"And?"

"Let's just say it didn't end well. Take care of this place," the hobgoblin said as he waded into the passage of darkness. "You never really know how much longer it's going to be around."

Even when he'd had the combined life forces of 166,000 Japanese coursing through his body, Konrad Deacon had never felt anything quite like this.

"It's magnificent, Teddy," he told his son, who cowered in a corner of the master bedroom, eyes reflecting the living fire that trailed from Deacon's hand as he waved it in the air before him. "It's like no other power I've ever experienced. . . . It's as if it's alive inside me."

The fire rippled across the smooth muscles of Deacon's newly invigorated flesh like solar flares on the surface of the sun. He admired himself in the reflective surfaces of the room, finding it difficult to tear his gaze away.

"Look at me," he proclaimed to his frightened child. "If I had known it would take the life energies of only one angel to feel this way, I would have hunted one down years ago."

He had always known that the world was a secret place, its many dark corners and angles filled with mysteries not for the common man to fathom, but now—as his mind filled with the knowledge of an angel—a divine light had been shined upon the darkness.

And Konrad Deacon knew so much more.

The world was a far more dangerous place than he had ever thought, and he realized that with this level of power within him, he now had the means to do something about it.

He now had the means to make it safe.

But to be successful, he knew that he must transcend his humanity, giving up all mortal frailties and embracing what he would become.

Deacon smiled, imagining wings of fire erupting from his shoulder blades.

And they did.

"I could become a god," he told his child, whose eyes were wide and wild at the sight of the appendages of flame that gently fanned the stagnant air of the bedroom.

Deacon began to laugh, gently at first, but growing to near hysteria. He was laughing so hard that he was losing control of the divine fire, and burning feathers dropped from his wings, setting the floor and some of the furniture ablaze.

Teddy jumped up with a frightened yelp, running to the closed door, fumbling with the doorknob in an attempt to escape.

"Don't be afraid, son," Deacon called to his child. "It just takes some time to get used to."

He was trying to absorb the holy fire back into his new form, but succeeded only in making it worse. The flames burned furiously, reducing objects in the room to blackened ash in a matter of seconds. Deacon imagined the fire being used on the flesh of his enemies and wondered if there was a way to slow it down.

To prolong the agony.

That would be a wonderful thing.

The bedroom door flew open, slamming against the

plaster wall already cracked by the passage of the home from earth to the shadowy realm. There was no talking to the boy in his current state, and Deacon allowed him to scamper off. There were far more important things to concern himself with at the moment.

He had to start thinking about his future and the future of the world. Not the world outside his window, but the world he had fled to escape his betrayers.

Deacon made his body glow like the sun, casting his holy light from the dingy windows to chase away the darkness—and anything that might be hiding within it.

Someone cleared his throat behind him, and Deacon slowly turned toward the sound.

Scrimshaw stood just inside the doorway.

"Scrimshaw," Deacon said, and thrust out his arms for the golem to admire. "What do you think?"

"Quite impressive, sir," the artificial man said. "I wanted to let you know that we've boarded up just about all of the broken windows, and reset the alarms. I'm waiting for a work crew to let me know how long it will be before the fence is—"

"Don't bother," Deacon interrupted his faithful servant.

"Excuse me, sir?"

"I said, don't bother," Deacon repeated. He slowly turned back to the bedroom window, allowing the fire that radiated from his body to grow all the brighter. "We're not staying here."

"Sir?" Scrimshaw questioned.

"You heard me," Deacon said testily, crimping his annoyance, realizing that he must be above such emotions if he were to attain his new stature. "We're leaving this place."

"Leaving?"

Deacon looked to his servant. "How am I to attain godhood and save humanity from the hidden horrors of the supernatural if I remain in this desolate place?" he asked.

Scrimshaw, smart enough to know that it wasn't a true question, didn't answer.

"And besides," Deacon added with a sly smile. "Now that I have all of this power, I can finally take my revenge on those who wronged me."

"Shall I pack your bags, sir?" Scrimshaw asked, ever the faithful servant.

Deacon began to laugh again, amused by his servant's naïveté.

"No need for that," he said, turning his attention back to the window and the fleeting darkness outside.

"I brought it all here, and I intend to take it all back."

Angus Heath could not sleep, and was tired of hearing about the little miracle girl who was waiting to deliver a message from God to the world.

The sorcerer sneered as he quietly passed the television reporting yet another story of the child and her promise. It was all bullshit as far as he was concerned. The Creator . . . God . . . or whatever it was being called now had lost interest in its earthly creations a long, long time ago, and the only message that Heath could imagine the little girl delivering was that the human race was a total disappointment.

Francis was deep in some sort of trancelike state that was as close to sleep as a fallen angel could manage, while the other—Remy was what Francis had called him—was still recovering from the injuries he had sustained in the place of shadows.

But it was neither of the two divine beings that interested him at the moment; it was the girl.

Angus moved around the bed to where she lay. The bathroom light had been left on, the door partially closed, shedding some light in the rented room.

Light from which he could check on his suspicions.

The girl had been hurt pretty badly, looking as though she had been mauled by some kind of animal. He had cleaned the wounds and bandaged them the best he could while Francis fretted over his unconscious friend.

That had been when he started to suspect that there was more to this young woman than initially met the eye.

Angus hovered over her as she slept, angling his body in such a way so as not to block the light leaking from the bathroom. Carefully, he reached out to peel back the girl's covers. Her shirt was still unbuttoned, exposing her young flesh and the heavy bandages he had placed upon her wounds.

He could not deny the fact that he felt the pangs of hunger emerging, but doubted he would receive much in the way of sustenance from this one if his suspicions were correct.

Angus first pulled away a piece of the tape and, when he saw that his touch did not disturb her slumber, lifted the bandage to get a better look at the wound. It had already started to heal, far faster than it should have been able to. He leaned in closer and stuck his finger into the healing gash, attempting to pull the flesh apart to see what secrets lay beneath.

"What the fuck are you doing?" asked an angry voice, and he felt the cold barrel of a pistol against the back of his head.

Angus pulled his fingers away and froze.

"I'm checking something."

"Looked a little nastier than that to me," Francis said. "Planning an unauthorized midnight snack, perhaps?" the fallen angel suggested.

The sorcerer sighed. "If I'd planned to do that, I could have just kissed her."

"What were you checking?"

Angus felt the pressure on the back of his head ease, and he turned to face Francis. "I was checking to see if she's real."

Francis looked at him, head cocked to one side. "Excuse me?"

"As I tended her wounds, I got a sense that maybe she isn't as human as she appears to be."

"You're talking nonsense."

"Perhaps, but that still doesn't explain the strange aura I'm sensing."

"Strange aura," Francis repeated. "That pretty much says it all."

Angus couldn't stand it any longer; he needed to be vindicated. He turned again to the girl and reached out, plunging his fingers into the exposed stomach wound and ripping a portion of the flesh away.

Francis reacted as Angus thought he might, pistol-whipping him and throwing him to the floor.

"Are you out of your fucking mind?" the angel said, going to the girl's side but stopping cold when he saw what had been revealed.

"Not what you expected to see, is it?" Angus asked, rubbing the sore spot at the back of his head.

"That's not what I think it is . . . is it?" Francis asked, moving in for a closer look.

"All depends on what you thought you might see," Angus said, joining him at the bedside. "If you thought you'd see bloody flesh and exposed muscle, no, not at all." He stared at the open wound and the damp gray material that lay beneath it. "But if you expected to find clay, then we were both right."

"It isn't her," Francis said, eyes darting to the unconscious Remy on the bed.

"No, it isn't," Angus agreed. "She's a golem . . . a very advanced golem, but a golem nonetheless."

"Then where's the real Ashley?" Francis asked, worry in his voice.

Angus looked over to the closet door, remembering the thick wall of shadow that had appeared there.

"Still over there, I'd imagine."

CHAPTER SEVENTEEN

*N*ever talk to strangers.

Ashley heard her mother's voice over and over again, echoing inside her skull, growing louder with every utterance until she felt as though she might scream until her throat bled.

But she had already done that.

When she'd awakened inside the metal cage.

She opened her eyes quickly, hoping that something—anything—might have changed, but she was still there.

Cramped inside a cage, stuck in the corner of a filthy room that had been decorated for a small child a very long time ago.

There was a part of her that still hoped something was wrong with her, that maybe she'd had some sort of horrible illness, a fever so high that it caused her to hallucinate, or maybe she'd been in a car accident and this was some kind of head trauma. She would even accept being drugged at a party, but she couldn't remember the last time she'd even been to a party.

All she could remember was that afternoon, heading downtown and filling out job applications.

And the strange man.

Never talk to strangers.

She almost told her mother to shut up, but just the

thought of her mother made her begin to cry, and she had been crying so often, for so long, that she barely had any tears left.

Ashley had first noticed the man in the antique store, watching her as she had petted the cat. She remembered how she was annoyed at first and then creeped out. She'd been tempted to tell the guy off, but instead she had moved on to the next on her list of potential employers.

Remy would have been proud of her, being aware of her surroundings and who was in them. He'd always drilled that into her: Pay attention to details, no matter how small. All good advice, like . . .

Don't talk to strangers.

As she lay curled up on a dirty blanket draped across the bottom of the cage, Ashley realized that the alarms had stopped. The grating sounds had started suddenly and had seemed to go on and on for a very long time.

But they'd finally been silenced.

She had thought the alarms might have had something to do with her, that maybe somebody—*Remy*—had come to take her home.

But the alarms had stopped, and she was still here.

Remy hadn't come.

She hadn't a clue as to where she was or why she had been taken, so even though she didn't want to relive it, she allowed the scene to replay in her mind. Maybe she had missed something.

She had finished her job search for the day and wanted something to drink. Knowing that there was nothing good back at the apartment, she had stopped at a convenience store not too far from her new home.

It was funny the details that she remembered leading up to . . .

Ashley began to tremble, pulling herself tighter into a ball. It was cold in the little kid's room, and she reached out to pull a corner of the blanket over herself.

The convenience store had been empty. A song had been playing softly over the speakers. She'd recognized the tune but couldn't remember exactly what it was; it had been mangled so badly in this horrible Muzak version.

She recalled wandering the short aisles, considering all kinds of purchases, even though she'd just gone in for a drink. And finally she'd just headed to the refrigerator cases at the back of the store. It hadn't taken her long to make her pick: a cherry-flavored iced tea that she seemed able to buy only around there. She'd shared that information with Remy the last time he'd been up, and he had told her that it probably was because Massachusetts had laws preventing drinks that foul from being sold in the Commonwealth.

Ashley smiled briefly at the memory of her friend; then the reality of her situation again weighed down upon her.

Was anybody looking for her? Was Remy looking for her? Did they even know where to start?

Ashley had paid for her drink and then returned to her car, still trying to figure out what song was playing in the store. It was probably that distraction that had made her less than careful.

"Don't Fear the Reaper" . . . Blue Oyster Cult.

She had remembered the song just as she'd climbed into her car, and placed her drink in the cup holder. She thought she might have been laughing when she'd inserted the key into the ignition, thinking about how cheery a song about not being afraid of death could sound when run through a Muzak filter.

The first person she'd thought to call about it was Remy. The two had had some interesting discussions about death over the years, and she thought he might get a kick out of hearing how the classic rock tune was being mangled.

Never mind the fact that she missed him . . . missed Beacon Hill, missed Marlowe, and missed her parents. This going-off-to-college-to-learn-to-be-an-adult thing wasn't nearly as easy as she had thought it would be.

She'd been reaching for her cell phone when the man had attacked. She knew instantly who it was as his hands came over the front seat from the back to grab her. She saw most of his creepy face reflected in the rearview. She had tried to fight him off, bloodying her nose in the process, but as soon as his hands touched her, her strength had started to fade.

The creepy man just held her tight, an unusually hard hand pressed over her mouth, the other across her neck, waiting until the fight was gone from her.

It hadn't taken long.

She remembered feeling incredibly tired and wanting so desperately to go to sleep as another part of her brain screamed like crazy for her to wake up and run.

But that wasn't going to happen.

The creepy man's touch was like a drug, and before she knew it, she was gone.

Anger quickly replaced the sadness and fear. How pathetic was she to be so easily taken from everyone she loved, to not even put up a fight?

Maybe she deserved this.

A flash of bright light crept into the room from a torn window shade, and for a moment she thought it was lightning.

Ashley waited for the sound of thunder to follow, but it didn't come.

She angled her body in such a way as to keep her eyes on the shade, not remembering a time when she'd seen any light come from outside.

It always seemed to be dark where she was now.

Even something as simple as that flash of light was enough to bolster her hopes for a moment. Thoughts of a rescue played out in her mind.

Remy coming to save her.

She was about to close her eyes again, to try to escape through sleep, when the door into the room swung open. Thoughts of Remy still at the forefront of her mind, she sat up, holding her breath.

Hoping.

But her hopes were quickly suffocated as the strange

little boy ran into the room, slamming the door closed behind him.

She had no idea who he was and didn't know if he could even speak. He seemed more like an animal, grunting and growling.

He glanced at her briefly as he passed her cage. His eyes were wide, wild, and he appeared to be out of breath. The boy went to a cabinet in the corner of the room, pulling open one of the drawers and reaching inside.

Ashley wished herself smaller, pushing herself deeper into the corner of the cage, one of the bars now digging painfully into her back as she watched him.

Praying he would leave her alone.

But the filthy animal child removed the leather collar and leash from the drawer and slowly approached the cage.

It was time for her walk.

Carroll Funeral Home
September 2008

He'd asked for some time alone with her.

Remy stood perfectly still, staring down at the remains of his wife of fifty years lying in the coffin.

But she wasn't really there.

Madeline Chandler had been a loving, vivacious woman who had enjoyed every moment of her life, even as her time on this earth was slowly ticking away, eaten up by cancer.

It wasn't her that he saw lying there. Certainly it looked like her in elder years, but what really made her who she was—his wife, his lover, his friend—had left this shell once it had decided to quit working.

He found this moment alone with her remains similar to looking at a photograph, the image a reminder of what had once been.

And what had been lost.

He could remember every moment that they had spent

with each other, the important to the mundane. There wasn't a single minute that he would have traded away.

Unless it would have given him another minute with her.

As an angel of the Heavenly host Seraphim, he had prepared himself for this.

Not this specifically, but for the pain that he was certain would be part of the human life he had chosen to live. As he lived and loved among them as the centuries passed, he thought he had learned what it was all about.

What it meant to be human.

It had never been clearer than when he had met her and their lives had inexorably become entwined. What he had thought he'd learned from the human species had merely been a scratch on the surface; Madeline had shown him the reality of it.

Her love for him—their love for each other—truly showed him what God had seen in these magnificent creations. After believing that he had read the entire book on humanity, being with Madeline made him realize that he'd read only the prologue to the most wondrous tale still to be experienced.

But now that book was done.

He thought he had prepared himself for the inevitable end to their story, but now realized that nothing could have prepared him for this.

The pain was so bad it made him doubt everything he had done since renouncing Heaven and coming to Earth.

Was it worth it to lose it all?

Death was a sure thing for them, but they still carried on, living their lives to the fullest extent. Once again he thought he'd understood them, but now he saw how strong they actually were.

And he had begun to wonder about his own strength. The skin of humanity that he'd proudly worn for more than a millennium had been damaged by the death of his companion. It was a pain that seemed never to diminish, instead growing more pronounced with the passing of each day that she wasn't there with him.

Remy laid his hand upon hers, remembering all the times that her lovely fingers had been entwined with his, and would never be again.

He was close to shucking it all, abandoning the life he had created for himself and returning to the world he had turned his back on. He had thought that what he'd experienced there during the Great War had been the most painful moments of his existence.

Until now.

He would have gladly endured that pain twofold rather than deal with what he was going through now.

It felt as though he were disintegrating, that if he stared at his hands he would see the skin there slowly beginning to blemish and crack, eventually falling away to reveal what lay beneath.

What he had been before . . .

The hairs on the back of his neck reacted to another presence, and he knew that he was no longer alone. He turned to see Ashley standing there, the once-little girl on the verge of blossoming into a mature young woman.

He forced a smile as he looked at her.

"Hey," Remy said. "Thanks for coming."

She looked incredibly uncomfortable, eyes darting everywhere but to the coffin in back of him.

"Mom said that it went from seven to nine, and I didn't want you to . . . y'know, be alone or anything."

"Thanks."

Ashley looked as though she might jump out of her skin as she stood in the doorway to the viewing room.

"Have you ever been to a wake before?" Remy asked, pretty sure that he knew the answer.

She shook her head. "Does it show?"

Remy shrugged. "I wouldn't worry about it."

"I have no idea what I should be doing," she confessed. "Mom and Dad said that I could wait for them, but then I thought of you here alone, and I knew that I would want somebody here with me if . . ."

Remy went to her and put his arm around her shoulder.

"That means a lot."

She leaned her head against his shoulder, the two of them just standing in the viewing room's doorway.

"I'm really sorry, Remy," she said softly.

"There's nothing to be sorry for," he replied. "These are just the things that happen."

"Doesn't mean we have to like them."

"No, it doesn't."

"How's Marlowe doing?"

Remy thought about his canine friend for a moment. The dog actually seemed to be taking Madeline's death better than he. Maybe it had something to do with an animal's simplicity, more accepting of the natural order of things, or maybe they were just smarter than everybody else.

"He's doing all right."

"And you?"

"Marlowe's doing all right." He answered the previous question again, not wanting to face the pain.

They were quiet for a bit, just standing together. He could tell that she was looking at the casket and its contents, getting used to the image.

"So, what are we supposed to be doing?"

"We're doing it," Remy said. "We're saying good-bye."

"Over here?" she asked him.

"If that's what makes you comfortable."

She looked up at him them, and he saw in her eyes the little girl he'd first met on that hot summer's day. But he also saw a beautiful young woman filled with promise and wisdom. She reminded him more and more of Madeline, and that made him very happy.

This world needed more like her, now that she was gone.

"This is no way to say good-bye," Ashley said, taking his hand.

She led him to the coffin, where they stood in silence hand in hand.

"She looks nice," Ashley said finally.

"Yeah," Remy agreed. "That was her favorite dress. She picked it and the jewelry before . . ." His voice trailed off.

The agony was back.

Remy wanted to shed it all, to return to the simplicity of being one of God's divine creations. It would be so much easier than this.

But he was brought back from the brink by his hand being squeezed tightly, and glanced over to see Ashley's gaze riveted to his deceased wife.

"Was she a good one?" Ashley asked, eyes unwavering.

For a moment he wasn't quite sure he understood the question.

Ashley turned her head to look at him. "A mom . . . was she a good mom?"

"Yeah, she was the best," he said, nodding, remembering that only the very few who knew what he was knew that Madeline was his wife; everyone else thought she was his mother. Madeline had always been amused by the interpretation of their relationship. Remy Chandler, the Mama's Boy, she used to tease him.

He found himself smiling now.

"I always thought she would be," Ashley said. "Just watching her with Marlowe, you could tell."

It was then that Remy realized if he were to return to Heaven, his pain would fade, but so would the memories of what he had created here—what he had had. He wasn't sure that he wanted to give those up, despite the agony of his loss.

He turned his head ever so slightly to look at the young woman who had made it a point to come here tonight and share his sorrow. He thought of how special she was, and how special he felt to have her and other friends like her in his life.

Did he really want to leave all that behind?

"Mr. Chandler?" Someone spoke softly behind him.

He and Ashley turned to see David Carroll standing in the doorway.

"Visitors have started to arrive," the fair-haired man said, motioning toward the funeral home door behind him.

Remy nodded. "Thank you." He looked back to Ashley, who was watching him with a careful eye. "Here we go," he said, taking a deep breath.

"Are you going to be all right?" she asked him.

"Yeah," he said, not yet 100 percent convinced, but on the road to finding out.

"I think I might be."

Remy Chandler awakened to the smell of blood.

Eyes fluttering, he rolled onto his side to see a heavyset man standing over Ashley, his hands stained red. Remy reacted instantly, rising to his knees and reaching across to grab the fat man by the front of his shirt, pulling him down close enough for Remy's fist to connect savagely with his face.

The big man howled in pain, nose gushing blood as he was driven away from the bed. Remy gazed down in horror at Ashley's mangled body. Bloody bandages littered the bed, and his eyes became transfixed by the vision of her gore-stained midriff.

"What have you done?" he screamed at the man, who sat slumped on the floor, chubby hand clutched to a badly bleeding nose.

"It's not what you think," the man cried. "Let me explain."

But Remy heard none of it, his warrior's mind already activated. He bounded from the bed and hauled the blubbering man to his feet. If he had been able, the fires of the Seraphim would have already been flowing, eating the man's flesh inch by inch.

But the fire did not answer his call, so Remy had no choice but to hit the man again and again.

There came a sudden flash, and Remy found himself flying backward over the bed and into the wall beside the door. He lay there breathing heavily, his heart rapidly beating as if shocked by a defibrillator.

"I could cook your flesh to the bone," the fat man snarled, blood running from his nose to drip from his chin. His hand crackled with supernatural energies, and Remy realized that he was dealing with a magick user.

So be it, he thought, springing to his feet again. He would just have to hit the guy that much harder.

The man fired another blast of destructive energy, but Remy managed to avoid it, throwing his shoulder into the man's expansive gut and driving him back toward the closet door. He was atop him in seconds, punching him with both fists, until he heard the sound of a door opening behind him.

He paused and turned to see Francis entering the room, arms loaded with shopping bags.

"Why the fuck are you beating the crap out of Angus?" the former Guardian angel asked, setting the bags down on the floor.

"He didn't give me a chance to explain," the big man gurgled.

Remy pointed to Ashley's body as he stood on shaky legs.

"That," he said, going to the girl who meant so much to him.

"Calm down. It isn't her," Francis told him.

"What do you mean, it isn't her?"

"Look at her," Francis said. He was helping the fat man to get up.

Remy was on the verge of panic, but he did as his friend told him.

"I don't think Ashley was made out of clay," Francis continued. He had given the magick user a handkerchief from his pocket for his bloody face. "But, then again, I didn't know her as well as you did."

Remy looked closely at the gaping wound in Ashley's belly and found himself carefully poking at the damp gray clay.

"She isn't real," he said, looking up.

"That's what I was trying to tell you," the fat man said.

"Who are you?" Remy asked, eyes squinting suspiciously.

"This is Angus Heath," Francis said. "He's the guy I talked to about your golem situation . . . which doesn't seem to be getting any better, by the way."

Remy looked back to the girl on the bed. "Deacon did this," he said.

"Deacon?" Angus asked, stepping forward, bloody handkerchief clutched to his face. "You know that for sure?"

Remy nodded. "He's over there," he said, gesturing to the air. "His whole estate in some shadow world."

"I knew he wasn't dead," Angus said. "He must've transported himself there when we tried to kill him."

Remy stared at the magick user.

"It was a long time ago," Angus said quickly. "Algernon Stearns . . ."

"Stearns," Remy interrupted. "Deacon wants me to kill Stearns. That's why he took Ashley."

Remy stopped short, realization sinking in like a bolt from above.

"If this isn't her, that means the real Ashley is still there," Remy said, looking at Francis and Angus. "I have to go back." He went to the closet. "There was a door here."

"It's gone now," Francis said. "It went away when the goblin left."

Remy looked at him. "Goblin?" he asked as a hazy memory surfaced of the creature that had saved him from the shadow animal.

"Yep, little guy, bad skin, pointy ears," Francis explained. "I know it sounds crazy, but a goblin brought the two of you back. Haven't a clue as to who he was, but he seemed to think there's some serious trouble brewing in the world and didn't want to stick around."

It was a thought that Remy shared—he'd felt that way since he and Francis had helped to avert the Apocalypse.

"It must have something to do with Stearns," Angus

said, looking into his bloody handkerchief as if searching for something he'd lost.

"What about Stearns?" Remy asked.

"You mean besides him trying to kill both of us by sucking out all our life energies?" Francis asked.

That surprised Remy, as well. "Deacon almost did that to me. In fact, it's left me a bit . . . depleted."

The power of Heaven was still somewhere inside of him, but it had gone deep to recover.

To heal.

"I knew there was something different about you," Francis said. "I thought you might've lost some weight."

"I haven't quite sorted it all out yet," Angus started to explain, chubby hand flitting around his head. "But Stearns is up to something . . . and it's something that could prove deadly to millions."

Remy stepped back from the closet door and sat down on the bed. He looked at the body of Ashley's imposter again. "I need to go back there, to bring the real Ashley home."

He looked at Francis and the magick user. "This Stearns, he's a powerful sorcerer?"

"All of the cabal were extremely powerful and—"

"Answer the question," Remy snapped.

"Yes, he was probably the strongest of us," Angus said quickly.

"Good answer." Francis patted the man on the shoulder.

"I think we should pay Algernon Stearns a little visit, then," Remy said. "A sorcerer that powerful will probably have some idea how I can get back to the shadow place, and I'm guessing we'll catch his attention with the news that the man he thought he'd killed is still very much alive and looking for a little revenge. And, oh yeah, now has the power of a Seraphim at his disposal."

"Stearns isn't a trusting man," Angus said. "And if he's in the midst of some master plan, he'll be on full alert for trouble."

"I didn't say it was going to be easy." Remy stood up and looked to his friend. "Think we might need some accessories."

Francis nodded ever so slightly.

"And guess what. I think I know where we might be able to find some."

CHAPTER EIGHTEEN

Armaros stood on the roof of Stearns' office building, admiring the garden of large satellite dishes that had been constructed there. They resembled a cluster of high-tech mushrooms growing up among a forest of steel, glass, and stone.

The thought made the angel smile, knowing that Sariel would have been amused by his blossoming imagination. To be able to see in something more than the reality of it was not a trait normally associated with the minions of God, but the excessive time spent here among them—among humanity—had allowed the Grigori to evolve some.

And Armaros took much pleasure in flexing this new visionary muscle, imagining the kind of world they were about to usher in. There would be panic and chaos for a time, but in the end it would transform the humans, taking them a place closer to where the Lord wanted them to be.

If there was one thing that the Grigori had learned over the countless millennia, it was that the human animals were stubborn beasts and not so easily swayed. They had to be shown the consequences of their actions, and the more gruesome the presentation, the easier it was for them to listen.

Since the Grigori had been partially responsible for the wedge driven between humanity and the Almighty, it seemed only fair that they attempt to make things right.

The Grigori's final penance for the sins they'd committed. But first they needed to capture humanity's attention.

Armaros reached out and placed a hand on the cold metal of one of the satellite dishes, impressed at how far the humans had come with their technology. It was almost like magick. With just these metal dishes, they would be able to reach out to millions of humans all around the world and deliver their message.

It was just a shame that so many of them would have to die.

"Neat trick," Remy said, following Francis and the sorcerer, Angus Heath, through the fissure cut in the fabric of reality in the deserted back parking lot of the Vermont motel.

The magick user had helped them dispose of the golem Ashley, using a spell that caused the clay body to burn from the inside, turning it to crumbling ash that was easily washed down the drain. To say that the sight of his friend's visage, even if it was a magickal doppelganger, crumbling away to nothing in a cheap motel bathtub was mighty disturbing was an understatement.

He'd settled his bill and then met the others in the parking lot, stepping through the passage opened by Francis and exiting in the shadow of a Toys "R" Us.

"It comes in handy," Francis agreed, turning his head slightly to watch the perforation seal close behind them. "One of the perks of a new client."

"Anybody I know?" Remy asked.

Francis ignored the question and turned away.

"Are you sure we're in the right place?" Angus asked. "I thought we were going to get weapons, not a new bike."

"We're not going there." Francis sounded annoyed, and walked away from the toy store. "What we're looking for is this way."

Behind a Dumpster was a fence, and in that fence a hole had been cut. One by one they climbed through the opening, into a lot filled with rows of storage lockers.

"Where are we, anyway?" Remy asked, not recognizing their whereabouts.

"Brockton," Francis answered as he paused, getting his bearings.

"Brockton?"

"Is there a problem with Brockton?"

"No, I'm just a little surprised that you'd keep items of this nature here."

"Let me tell you, Brockton is the perfect place to keep items of this nature." Francis led them to a particular storage shed, number 666.

"Nice," Remy said, shaking his head in amusement.

The hint of a smile tugged at the corners of Francis' mouth as he punched in the code, and the folding door slowly climbed to grant them access.

From where they stood, it looked like the typical storage unit filled with random boxes and old pieces of furniture.

"Is this it?" Remy asked.

"This is it," the fallen angel responded.

Angus started inside, but Francis quickly stopped him.

"Wait a second," he said. "I've installed a few security measures."

Francis looked around to be certain they were alone, then pulled up the sleeve of his suit coat and shirt as far as he could manage and removed the glowing scalpel from an inside pocket of his coat.

Remy felt the hair at the back of his neck stand on end at the sight of the instrument. "Don't tell me that opens doors, too," he commented, watching as Francis brought the thin blade of light toward his exposed wrist.

"You don't know the half of it," he said, making a quick cut in his flesh.

A single drop of blood escaped the gash before it was immediately cauterized. That drop landed on the threshold of the storage place, and the sight of the items stored there began to shimmer and waver out of focus.

Remy and Angus entered the shed as Francis reached

up to pull the door down behind them. As soon as the folding door was closed, the space became illuminated.

Remy turned, not surprised to see that they were now standing in a room at least ten times the size of a normal storage unit; row upon row of metal shelving housed some of the special items that Francis had acquired over the years.

Angus began to laugh, heading down one of the many aisles.

"Very nice, Francis," the sorcerer said. "I like your style."

Remy went in the opposite direction. As he walked among the rows, he found all manner of weaponry, from pistols to rifles, from knives to spears and swords. There were enough arms in this shed alone to fortify an army.

"Find anything you like?" a voice asked from close by.

A box on a shelf in front of him slid aside and Francis peered through from the next aisle.

"Plenty, if I wanted to overthrow a third-world nation," Remy answered.

"Haven't done that in a while," Francis mused.

"How is this stuff categorized?" Remy asked. "Is it even categorized?"

"Kinda sorta," Francis answered. "I hired a high school kid a while back to get it better organized, but . . ."

"A high school kid?" Remy asked, aghast.

"Yeah, didn't work out too well."

"Imagine that."

"Caught her trying to lift a few ounces of my powdered saints' bones." Francis took a box from the shelf. "Can you imagine what a snort of Saint Pelagius would do?" he asked as he peeled back the flaps on the box to look inside. "Hey, I was wondering what happened to my bowling shoes," he said, then placed the box back on the shelf.

"Where's Angus?" Remy questioned.

"He's in the paper-goods section. Found some old scrolls and texts that I bought at an estate sale a few years back. They used to belong to a combat magician I'd had few runins with over the centuries."

Francis disappeared for a few minutes, and then Remy saw him heading toward him down the aisle, carrying a large black gym bag. He stopped and picked up a plastic container. "These are good," he said, pulling off the lid to reveal tiny hand grenades. They were a coppery color and covered with strange, runic designs that made them look almost like Christmas decorations.

"Grenades?" Remy asked, as Francis stuffed the container in the bag.

"Souped up for magickal barriers," the former Guardian angel explained. "Lotsa bang for your buck."

Remy found a black case on a bottom shelf and pulled it off, unlatching the clasps and opening the case to reveal two black service Colt .45s. "These are nice."

"Oh yeah," Francis said. "With the right ammunition, the twins can be killer."

"And do you have the right ammunition for the twins?" Remy asked, closing up the case but deciding to bring it with him.

"In the ammunition aisle. I think they're on special today."

Remy's phone began to vibrate in his pocket, and he removed it to see that Linda was calling. She had already left a couple of voice messages while he had been in the shadow place; this time she was leaving a text.

Please call. Important.

He slipped the phone back into his pocket and found Francis staring at him.

"Same person that called back at the motel?" he asked.

"Yeah," Remy answered.

"Anybody I know?" Francis inquired, and for a moment Remy wasn't sure if his friend knew who it was or not.

Francis had had a crush on Linda Somerset, and although they had never met, the former Guardian had spent many a night watching the pretty waitress at Piazza, fantasizing about a relationship that had never transpired.

It was after Francis had gone missing in Hell that Remy and Linda met and something drew them together.

Francis had yet to be told.

"Nobody that I've talked about," Remy answered.

"I love it when you're coy." Francis headed off down another aisle. "Just as long as she keeps you from moping. . . . I hate it when you mope. Follow me. The bullets for the twins are over here."

They found Angus pushing a battered shopping cart filled with boxes of books and ancient-looking scrolls toward them.

"A shopping cart?" Remy looked at Francis.

"Anything to make your experience at Weapons Mart a pleasant one."

"We just about done here?"

Angus looked into his cart and nodded. "Yeah, I'd say so. Maybe a few more this and thats, but I think we're good."

"Can you open a passage to my house?" Remy asked Francis. "There's something I need to check before we get going."

"I think I could do that," Francis said, putting the gym bag down and rubbing his hands together. "While you're making your booty call, Angus and I'll check out Stearns' place."

Remy made a face, staring at Francis as if he didn't know him.

"Did you just say booty call?" he asked incredulously.

"I did," the former Guardian answered, closing his eyes and taking a deep breath before starting to conjure the passage that Remy would use to get to his car. "It was the word of the day on my calendar," he said, as the air before them grew incredibly thin. He reached out to tear through it, revealing another place on the other side.

"And I swore I'd use it in a sentence."

The little black bugs tasted like peanuts—peanuts boiled in bat piss and then sprinkled with dried shit, but, yeah, he could taste peanuts somewhere in the rancid mix.

Squire took a handful of the squirming insects and

dropped them in the pan of boiling black oil. He'd never get used to the screams the little fuckers let out when they went into the hot drink. This brought a smile to the hobgoblin's face as he squatted before the tiny fire in the shelter he'd made from the skin and bones of one of the shadow region's larger predators.

There's no place like home, he thought, stirring the boiling bugs. The little beasties had already started to break down, releasing their fine, stinking aroma.

He couldn't stop thinking of another home . . . not *his* home, but one that felt like the home he'd lost. All he'd seen was the motel room, but Squire got a sense of the world he'd passed into almost immediately. It wasn't like the one he'd left in ruin, but then again, it was.

Cable television, pork rinds, Internet porn, dollar stores, Doritos; he bet they were all there. He could feel it in the pit of his protruding belly. So much like the one he'd had to abandon.

He poured his steaming bug stew into the open end of a hollowed-out shell and carefully began to eat.

He couldn't stop thinking about that other world, but he had to. There was no sense in getting attached to another, only to have it yanked away like the first. Squire wasn't sure he could survive another loss like that.

He sipped at the edge of the shell bowl, sucking pieces of beetles into his mouth. He chewed them quickly, searching for that peanut taste before the other, less appetizing ones, kicked in.

Nope, this was his home now. And it was just the way he liked it: dark, cold and bleak. Nothing to get attached to.

Through the membranous cover of the shelter he'd erected, Squire thought he saw a flash of something . . . something so bright that it cut through the pervasive shadow like an ax blade through muscle. He sat, sipping his meal, eyes locked to where he thought he'd seen it, waiting in case it happened again.

And it did.

The sudden explosion of light was bright, and it left

dancing snowflakes of color on his eyes, now used to the total darkness of the world of shadow.

Downing the remainder of his bug stew, he placed the empty bowl on the ground at his feet and rose to check out what was happening outside.

Squire pulled aside the flap of skin and stepped out into the harsh environment. His goblin eyes scanned the shadows.

"Big fucking surprise," he grumbled as he caught sight of the mansion that had been nothing but trouble since it had entered his world.

The explosion of light came again, and Squire witnessed firsthand the aftereffects. The air around the mansion pulsated like a long black curtain billowing in the wind. It was as if the very substance of the shadow realm was being tested, reminding him of the time just before the mansion had first appeared.

"That ain't good," Squire muttered. He had a bad feeling about what he was seeing, and as he listened to the wails and moans of the various life-forms of this dark, alternate reality, he knew they could sense it, too. Squire always knew that the residents of the mansion were troublemakers, but now he suspected they were something worse than that.

Another flash erupted from the front of the building and radiated out from all of the windows. A rapidly expanding halo of fluctuating darkness around the home again began to show signs of duress.

Squire had a sudden, sinking feeling in his awesome gut that the shadow realm was being threatened, that whatever was going on inside that house was doing something to the fabric of this world's shadowy existence.

Something that it might not be able to recover from. And then where would that leave Squire?

"Up shit's creek without a paddle." The hobgoblin answered his own question, knowing at that very instant what he had to do.

Squire turned and went back into his shelter. He was

going to need a few things. From the corner he hefted the old leather golf bag into a standing position and reviewed its contents. There were a few swords, a spear, and his personal favorite: a battle-ax. He had made many of those over the years, but these were the last of them. His babies, tools of his violent trade that he had not been able to part with.

Squire figured that this would be more than enough to deal with what he would find inside the mansion. Slinging the bag over his shoulder, he headed out across the sprawling expanse of shadow.

He'd been wanting to have a little chat with his new neighbors. Now seemed as good a time as any.

CHAPTER NINETEEN

The passage that Francis had summoned brought Remy to the small backyard of his Beacon Hill brownstone, giving him enough time to zip into his house for a change of clothes. He doubted it would be wise to show up at his girl-friend's place covered in blood.

He'd already called Linda and found out she and Mar-lowe had returned to her apartment that morning to do some laundry. Remy had sensed a bit of tension in their conversation, and he'd guessed that it had something to do with the mysterious stranger she had met in the Common. When pressed, she had said that the guy had been kind of weird, but when she mentioned something about the Watchers go-ing to do something terrible and that it was all because of him, Remy felt his blood go ice-cold.

In his calmest voice, he'd told her that he would be there in a few minutes and ended the call. A familiar dread gripped him. It was that same horrible feeling he'd experi-enced when he'd realized that Ashley had been taken be-cause of what he was.

Now Linda had been touched, as well.

Remy made amazing time from the Hill to Brighton, taking the first parking space he could find and sprinting to her building. She buzzed him in, and he took the steps two at a time, banging on her door perhaps a little too eagerly, hearing Marlowe's barking response on the other side.

Linda opened the door, an ecstatic Marlowe by her side.

"Hey," she said with a stunning smile, coming into his arms for a hug and kissing him on the neck before planting a noisy one on his lips.

She pulled away, arms still around his neck, and looked at his face.

"What's wrong?" she asked. "Is it Ashley? Is she all right?"

"I don't really know," he answered in all honesty. Linda let him into the apartment, closing the door behind him.

"Still no luck?"

"Some nibbles," he said. He would have loved to explain more but was unable. Marlowe was trying to get his attention, jumping up to lick at his face, flipping his hands to be petted. He could see the dog was eager to communicate with him as he always had, but Remy found that he was now deaf and dumb to his best friend's language.

He looked deeply into Marlowe's eyes, attempting to reach him on an emotional level, but all he could see was panic in the Labrador's gaze.

"What are you going to do?" Linda asked, as they sat side by side on the sofa.

"I haven't a choice, really," he told her. "I'm going to keep flipping over rocks until I find something."

He didn't want to alarm her any more than he already had, so he tried to be casual with his next question. "So, somebody approached you in the Common? I wonder who it could have been."

"I have no idea, but Marlowe certainly didn't care for him," Linda said.

Remy was frustrated that he couldn't talk with Marlowe, but the fact that his friend didn't care for the mystery man was very telling.

"He gave me a piece of paper with a phone number on it and said what I told you on the phone." She stood up. "That he needed to speak with you . . . that it was an emergency and . . ."

"That the Watchers were going to do something terrible," Remy finished.

Linda nodded. "Yeah," she said. "For something that you did. What the hell does that mean?"

He shrugged, trying not to show any emotion, pretending to be as perplexed as she. "Do you have that piece of paper?"

"Sure," she said as she headed for her bedroom. "It was in the pocket of my jeans. I took it out before I put them in the wash."

Marlowe was sitting at Remy's feet, staring up at him with great intensity in his dark brown eyes.

"I know that you can sense something is wrong with me," Remy said softly, taking the dog's blocky head in his hands. "And you're right. Something has happened to the angelic part of me. . . . Something has made it so that I can't talk to you. . . . I can't understand you."

Marlowe barked and then began to whine, shifting himself closer in a panic. Remy could only guess that his basic message was getting through to the Labrador.

He was still holding the dog's heavy face in his hands, and Marlowe leaned his snout over to lovingly kiss his wrist.

"We're going to be okay," Remy tried to reassure him. "I'm going to get better. All right? We'll be able to talk to each other again very soon—I promise."

There was a twinge in his heart then, a feeling that told him that maybe he shouldn't have made such a promise to the dog. He had no idea if what he was experiencing was only temporary.

The dog jumped up, licking his face with his thick pink tongue.

"You're a good boy," Remy told Marlowe, hugging the dog to him. "We'll be chatting up a storm again in no time."

Linda returned from her bedroom, reading the piece of scrap paper, before handing it to Remy. He read, with zero recognition, the phone number that had been scrawled there.

"He said it wasn't my place to understand," Linda said, as Remy read the number again. "But you would. Do you?"

Remy shook his head slowly, not wanting to lie but having no choice. He and the Watchers—the Grigori—had a long, sometimes violent history, and they couldn't have picked a worse time to start something new with him. He got up, slipping the paper into the pocket of his slacks.

"Aren't you going to call?" she asked curiously.

"Not from here," he answered. "I have to get back out there, follow up on a few things about Ashley."

Linda nodded, but he could see that she was disappointed. She was better off in the dark. He just couldn't have anyone else he cared for being dragged into the unusual world he frequently lived in.

"I'll give you a call the next free minute I get," he told her, leaning in for a kiss. "You and Marlowe still getting along?"

She pulled him close for another peck on the lips.

"He's a bed hog, but we're doing all right," she said, eyes shifting to the animal who sat before them, tail wagging.

"Talk soon," he told her, eyes then dropping to Marlowe. He hoped that the statement was true on many levels.

"Hey, Remy," she called out just before he shut the door.

He stuck his head back in.

"You be careful, all right?"

"Only because you asked," he told her with a smile that he tried to make reassuring before closing the door and heading on his way.

Deacon felt as though he could change the world. And wasn't that what he had always wanted?

As a child he had feared the dark—not so much the nighttime environment, but what he feared was lurking there, just beyond his vision.

It was the fear that had fueled his desire to pursue the art of sorcery—that and some gentle urging from a Romanian housekeeper who had looked after him. He had shared his secret with her, how he feared the darkness, and she had shared with him the knowledge that his fears were justified, that there were things out there waiting for the opportunity to claim a life, a soul, a world.

She had shown him real magick, and his world had been changed forever. In the mystical arts he had found a way to beat back the darkness, to protect himself and his loved ones from the sinister forces that lurked in the shadows. He became voracious, using his family's wealth to pursue his hunger for the arcane, but also using that newly found power to increase his fortune exponentially.

The more he learned, the more knowledge he acquired, the safer he could make the world. When he had first met the cabal, he believed that he had found like-minded individuals, that they all shared responsibility for protecting the world from encroaching supernatural threats—from the things in the dark.

But he had been wrong, and the lesson had been a painful one.

What he had learned as a result of his ill-placed trust was now the distant past to him, the power that coursed through him directing him only toward the future.

Spells and incantations that had been fading from his memory as the years raced past during his banishment here in the shadow realm were now ever present at the forefront of his thoughts.

The divine power of the Seraphim had changed him, making him so much better than he had ever hoped to be. Now he had the power not only to continue his prolonged existence, but to at last return to the world of his birth, where those who had betrayed him would pay the cost for their treachery.

Konrad.

Deacon paused in the hallway of his home, listening. Not hearing it again, he continued on his way, preparing himself and his home for the journey they were about to undertake.

Konrad.

He was sure that he'd heard it now.

"Who's there?" he called out. "Scrimshaw, is that you?"

Konrad, it's me, said the voice. And now that he was listening, it seemed so very familiar.

He thought that it might be coming from farther down the hall, and proceeded forward until he reached the dining room, doors still hanging from their hinges.

In here, said the voice.

"Who is it?" Deacon asked, stepping fearlessly inside. For what would dare challenge him now?

The dining room had yet to be cleared. It looked as though a war had been fought there, and in a way it had.

"Hello?" Deacon called out, but found nobody inside.

Deacon, said the voice, and suddenly he knew from where it had come.

"Veronica?" he asked, moving farther into the room. "Is that you?"

Who else would it be? she answered, her voice raspy and dry. *You left me . . . you left me in here alone.*

He found her withered body lying on the floor under broken pieces of the dining room set.

"I'm so sorry, my dear," Deacon apologized, gently picking her up. "Things have become a little crazy." He found an unbroken chair at the back of the room and set his wife down on it. Stepping back, he allowed the divine fire that pulsed through him to light up his new body.

"Things have changed," he told her as he spread his arms to show off his magnificence.

Have they? she questioned, her skeletal form slumped to one side in her seat.

"Look at me," he commanded. "Can't you see how much has changed . . . how much *I've* changed?"

I see the same man that I courted and married, she said. *A man striving to be better for a world that barely realized he existed.*

Deacon was stunned by his wife's hurtful words. Even after all this time, her opinion of him had still not changed.

"But now I can . . ."

You can what? she asked huskily. *Show how powerful*

you are, only to have one more devious than you steal it all away?

"That was then," he muttered. "I would never allow Stearns to . . ."

Stearns will smell your new might like a shark smells blood in the water, Veronica uttered harshly. *And then he will come and he will take it from you.*

The power of the angelic now dwelling inside him surged with his rage, wings of fire unfurling at his back.

"Stearns will do no such thing," Deacon roared, body humming with the power to level cities in the name of God.

I wonder what he will do with all that power, she pondered.

"He will not have it!" Deacon raged.

Perhaps after taking it from you, he will seek out others of a divine nature and take away their power, as well.

"I won't let him!"

Maybe when all the power of Heaven on Earth courses through his veins, he will pay a visit to God.

"He will not have it," Konrad Deacon repeated, tendrils of living fire lashing out, setting the room ablaze . . . setting the corpse of his wife afire.

"That power will be mine," he told the woman he'd loved, whose dry flesh was burning away to reveal a yellowed skeleton beneath. "Algernon Stearns and all the members of the cabal will pay for their crimes. . . .

"And then I will make my way to God."

And even though Veronica's skeleton had become blackened with the intensity of his fire, burning so hotly that the bone was gradually turning to ash, Deacon could still hear her inside his head.

And she would not stop laughing.

Remy called the number on the piece of paper, and the phone was picked up immediately. A voice that sent a slight shiver down his spine quickly asked who it was, and when Remy told him, it gave him an address and abruptly ended the call.

He wished he could have been a little more surprised when he pulled up in front of the former Saint Augustine Church in West Roxbury. Saint Augustine was another one of those churches that everyone in the Commonwealth had read about, closed down by the Archdiocese because of poor attendance and even poorer contributions to the Catholic Church's coffers, despite it having been a fixture in the old neighborhood for well over seventy-five years. The church had been deconsecrated, and now it was just an empty building waiting to be sold.

Remy closed the door of his car and crossed the street to the steps leading up to the old building. There were two older women sitting in collapsible lawn chairs in front of the entrance.

He knew why they were there; many parishioners of the closed churches had been sitting vigil twenty-four/seven, hoping that somebody with some power would take notice of their protest and eventually reopen their place of worship. Their faith in their cause was admirable, but it had all become matters of dollars and cents to the monolithic church; Saint Augustine, he guessed, wasn't even a blip on their radar.

One of the women was knitting furiously and looked up as he approached, reaching out to nudge the other beside her, who had fallen asleep, a hardcover book in her lap.

"Good morning," Remy said, placing a foot on the first step leading up to the entrance of the church.

The one who had been napping eyed him with suspicion. Remy could have sworn that he felt her eyes boring into the top of his shoe.

"Good morning," the old woman who continued to knit said with mock friendliness. "Can I help you? Are you lost?"

"I don't think so," Remy said with a smile and a shake of his head. "I'm supposed to meet somebody."

The old women shared a cautious look.

"I don't know who you'd be meeting here," the knitter said. "There's only us until we're relieved at two thirty."

"There's no one else around?" Remy asked, suspecting that the old girls knew more than they were letting on.

"Just Clara and me," the knitter said, as Clara continued to practice her death stare.

He was about to retreat to his car when he caught the sound of a lock being turned, and one of the large wooden doors opened a crack.

"Let him in," a voice whispered from inside.

"Are you sure?" Clara asked, her beady eyes going from Remy and back to the door.

"I'm sure."

The knitter dropped her needles for a moment and gestured for him to approach. Remy climbed the stairs.

"Can't be too careful," she said, retrieving her needles and picking up where she had left off.

Remy took note of how quickly her hands manipulated the twin needles, and also the fact that they were quite thick and golden in color. He also noticed sigils that he recognized as markings of power etched upon them.

The knitter looked up, realizing that he was staring. She smiled, pulling one of the thick needles from her work in the blink of an eye and pointing its sharp end at him.

"Can't be too careful," she repeated, and, having made her point, returned to the blanket she was making. It was then that he chanced a quick glance over at Clara to see her adjusting her book over the pistol in her lap.

"Are you coming in, or do you plan to sit vigil with the girls?" asked the voice from behind the door.

Remy took the heavy wooden door in hand and opened it enough so that he could enter. It was dark and cool inside, and he had to blink his eyes repeatedly to adjust to the gloom.

"Where the fuck have you been?" an unfamiliar voice asked as the figure hurriedly walked away from the door into the empty church. "We don't have much time."

"I've been on a case," Remy said, following the man. "Would it be too much to ask why you bothered my dog and scared my girlfriend?"

The figure turned and Remy recognized him as one of the Grigori. "Believe me, I didn't want to get you involved. It's just that when I realized how big a cluster fuck this was, and that it likely had something to do with you, I figured you might as well get involved."

"You're one of Sariel's," Remy said, watching a steely reaction come over the fallen angel's face.

"Yeah. I'm surprised you recognized a face in the background. I'm called Garfial." The angel quickly turned around again, motioning for Remy to follow him.

Remy followed Garfial across the deconsecrated church. He was surprised how bare it was; even the wooden pews had been removed, leaving only a large, empty room where the faithful had once communicated with their God. There was a sadness to the space but also something more, and since his senses were still numb, Remy couldn't quite put his finger on what it was.

Garfial climbed the stairs to the altar, disappearing through another doorway and then down a set of stairs to more darkness.

Even though his senses were practically dead, Remy could still feel the preternatural energies that filled the air in the cool chamber below the church altar. It was like some kind of strange laboratory filled with tables upon which beakers and test tubes sat. There were stacks of books everywhere, and a number of jars sweaty with condensation, their contents a mystery.

"What is all this?" Remy asked.

"This is what I do," Garfial said. "I was kind of like the biologist of the Grigori. I was to keep tabs on the various life-forms that the Almighty had seeded the planet with, making sure that everything was going along as planned." The angel paused, looking around his makeshift lab.

"Which it was. Which is why I became bored and . . ."

"You did something stupid," Remy finished.

Garfial snarled. "You should talk. I'm not the one who killed Sariel and got us into the mess we're currently in."

Remy leaned against a table.

"Why don't you fill me in on what my stupidity has supposedly done," he said.

Garfial was staring at him now.

"There's something off about you," the angel said. "You're different. . . . There's usually a scary vibe that isn't there now."

"Let's just say I'm a bit under the weather."

"Well, let's just hope you're functioning with all cylinders firing by the time things hit the proverbial fan," Garfial retorted. He went to one of the steamed jars and carefully picked it up.

Remy watched as the fallen angel unscrewed the top of the jar and reached inside.

"I should have known killing Sariel would come back to bite me," Remy said.

"And then some," Garfial agreed, pulling something from the jar between his fingers. Whatever it was hung limply for a moment, dripping with a slimy substance, and then it began to move.

"This is one of the stupid things that I did when I got bored with the world of man," the fallen said. "I learned how to create life." The object dangling from Garfial's fingers started to struggle, tiny arms and legs thrashing about, a faint squeal drifting in the air as the life-form showed its displeasure. "And then teaching humans how to do it was my next big mistake."

Garfial placed the squirming, artificial life-form back inside the jar and screwed on the lid. "That one isn't even remotely ready," he stated. Setting the jar back down beside at least ten others, he wiped his hands on his black pants.

"You're losing me," Remy said.

"Believe it or not, this all has something to do with what's going on," Garfial said. "I learn how to produce artificial life, I teach some humans, the Lord gets pissed about that and some of our other dalliances, and the Grigori are condemned to Earth. And here we've been ever since."

Remy had started to walk around the lab, only half listening as the Grigori continued to speak, until he noticed a large pile of damp-looking clay on a nearby table, and something clicked into place.

"Artificial life," Remy said aloud, looking at him.

"You're gonna have to keep up with me," Garfial chided.

"You showed them how to make golems."

"I did at that." Garfial nodded. "And they got pretty good at it, too. . . . Not as good as me, but still not so bad. Many human magick users put their own spin on these creatures."

"Life-energy collectors," Remy stated flatly.

Garfial smiled. "Now you're catching up. So here the Grigori are, living among the humanity they corrupted, trying to make amends for what they did so they could someday go home."

Remy would have smiled at the perversion of the facts, but he just couldn't bring himself to do it.

"We were doing everything we could to get Heaven to notice us again, trying to make things right," Garfial went on. "Sariel promised us that one day God would see us and how sorry we were, and welcome us back through the pearly gates with open arms."

Remy couldn't hold it back any longer.

"You guys worked with widows and orphans, right? Helped the homeless and unwed mothers? You make it sound like you were all playing on Mother Teresa's team. I've seen some of the parties you guys threw."

Garfial chuckled. "They were pretty intense, weren't they?" He smiled at the memory. "Some of us really did believe that we were going to be forgiven. . . . Personally, I like it here and couldn't care less if I ever see the Golden City again. The Golden Banana on Route One was just as good to me, if you know what I mean."

Sadly enough, Remy did. Living among humanity had done pretty much the same thing to him, minus the perversity and decadence.

"But like I said," Garfial continued. "Some of us were

actually working toward going home, but all that got thrown into the wood chipper when Sariel was killed."

"He murdered Noah," Remy said.

"Yeah, I know," Garfial said. "But he was still our leader, and without him, many of us were lost."

The fallen angel grew quiet, starting to move beakers of strangely colored fluid around, seemingly neatening up the space.

"After Sariel's death, I kind of lost track of you guys," Remy said.

"We became lost," the fallen said. "More lost than we had ever been. You thought the parties we had before were wild. . . . Days blended into weeks, into months. . . . Without Sariel, we lost our purpose . . . our direction."

"I'm guessing that didn't last," Remy said.

"No, it didn't," Garfial agreed. "A new leader rose in our ranks, and his name was Armaros . . . Sariel's lover."

Remy sighed, crossing his arms as he leaned against a table.

"And let me guess: He wants revenge."

Garfial brushed off his table with the side of his hand. "You killed our shining star . . . our guiding light . . ."

"He was a murderer," Remy stated.

"And Armaros loved him."

"So now he wants the world to suffer for what I did?"

"Armaros wouldn't admit that, but I'm sure it's there, writhing beneath the surface," Garfial said. "What he's telling us is that he wants to make God notice the Grigori again . . . to really recognize how sorry we are."

"And how does he intend to do that?" Remy asked.

Garfial's eyes drifted to the television in the corner of the room, distracted by the frantic movement of what appeared to be *The Price Is Right*.

"I love this show," the fallen angel said dreamily.

Remy waved a hand in the air. "Hello? World on the brink of something disastrous?"

"Sorry," Garfial apologized, collecting his thoughts once more. "Sariel always believed that humanity was in such a state because of the path we led them down, and Armaros shared that belief."

Remy waited for all the pieces to present themselves, forming an image he could understand.

"He believes that most of humanity has become godless, forgetting who's responsible for their very existence. Armaros has concocted a plan to make humanity remember God . . . to fear Him as we know He should be feared."

Tension started to form across Remy's brow and at the back of his neck; a sign that he was about to learn something that wasn't going to make him the least bit happy.

"This is where I come in to the picture," Garfial said. "Even though I gave them the knowledge, it was the human magick users that perfected the artificial-life process, nudging and tweaking their creations to a whole new level."

Remy waited silently for the head butt he was sure was coming.

"Armaros wanted me to join with one of these sorcerers, the most powerful of them all, to design and create a flawless piece of work—a tool to drive the faithless back into the Lord God's arms."

"A tool," Remy repeated, confused.

Garfial snatched up a leather-bound journal, opening it and holding it out toward Remy. He saw exquisite drawings of two human figures, older women, and recognized them as the knitter and Clara.

"Golems."

"Tools," Garfial corrected. "Like the ladies upstairs who protect my workshop from prying eyes. Tools with a specific purpose and function."

Remy felt the band of tension across his forehead grow so tight that he imagined his skull imploding.

"This wouldn't happen to have anything to do with Algernon Stearns?" Remy asked, a piece of the puzzle looking to be placed.

"Very good, Remy," Garfial applauded. "You must be a detective."

"Yeah, I've heard that before."

Remy had a terrible feeling that he knew exactly where this was going. Francis and Angus had both talked about Stearns' plans that could harm millions, and Remy dreaded this connection.

"This golem . . . this special tool," Remy fished. "What was it created to do?"

Garfial grabbed the notebook and flipped to another page. He was about to show it to Remy when the fallen angel froze, his eyes on the television again. "Oh, shit," the Grigori said.

"What?" Remy asked, turning around to see that *The Price Is Right* had been replaced by a special news report.

The anchors seemed to be very serious as they talked, the image of a smiling little girl projected behind them. A little girl that Remy recognized as Angelina Hayward.

Confused, he looked back to Garfial. "What's going on?"

"You wanted to know what the special golem was created for?" Garfial asked. "I think the world is about to find out."

"Who does this car belong to again?" Angus, sitting beside Francis in the front seat of the pristine 1960 Lincoln Continental, asked.

"A friend," Francis answered, cruising along Boylston Street, searching for a place to park.

"It smells like blood," the sorcerer said, moving his large bulk uneasily in the passenger's seat as he tried to get comfortable.

"Yeah, I know," Francis said casually. "But beggars can't be choosers. My friend Richard agreed to do us a solid as long as we didn't take her out of the city. Right, girl?"

Angus could have sworn that the vehicle responded, the low murmur of a talk show on the radio suddenly changing to a syrupy pop song from the seventies.

"That a girl," Francis said, still looking for the perfect

space as he reached a hand out and rubbed the black leather dashboard affectionately.

Angus could not get comfortable. The tangy, metallic odor of the car and the warm, almost fleshlike feeling of the leather beneath his ass made him feel as though he were inside the mouth of some large predatory beast.

"There's something wrong about this vehicle," Angus flatly stated.

"You might want to keep your opinions to yourself," Francis warned. "You don't want to hurt her feelings."

"Then you admit this ride is . . . different?"

"She's different, all right," the former Guardian agreed.

The steering wheel suddenly jerked roughly to the right, startling Francis as the car pulled itself into a space just vacated by a UPS truck.

"Good one," he said. "I would have driven right past it. Thanks, Leona."

"Is that its name?" Angus asked.

"That's *her* name," Francis quickly corrected as the engine turned off without his hand being anywhere near the crowded key chain that dangled from the ignition. "Relax. She has this kinda effect on a lot of people," Francis explained. "Actually, you should be honored that she's letting you ride inside her."

"I feel like Jonah in the belly of the whale," Angus stated, every instinct that he had on full alert.

"Look, we needed a ride to check out Stearns' headquarters, and my business associate was nice enough to allow Leona to take us," Francis said. "So, let's do what we came here to do."

Francis got out of the car.

Angus pulled on the door handle, but the door would not open. He was about to motion to Francis for assistance when the handle suddenly functioned again and the door swung wide.

For a moment he could have sworn that he heard a sinister chuckling over the car's speakers, but he decided that it was likely only the pinging sounds made by the car's engine as it started to cool.

"Will this be all right here?" Angus asked Francis.

"She'll be fine," Francis said crossing Boylston Street. "Richard fed her just before we called."

Angus followed the fallen angel to the small plaza and the eighty-story skyscraper that he recognized from his contact with Algernon Stearns. A large sign read HERMES TELEVISION NETWORK.

Angus stared up at the impressive building of smoked glass and polished steel, feeling a queasy uneasiness pass over him. He turned to speak to his partner, but the angel was gone. Looking around the crowded street, he found Francis at a food truck.

"What are you doing?" Angus asked, walking over.

"Getting a bite. Want something?"

"No, I do not want something. We need to report back to—"

"They have American chop suey."

"They do?"

"Two American chop sueys," Francis told the man behind the counter.

"The building is quite fortified against the likes of us," Angus said, looking back to the front entrance.

"Figured as much," Francis answered, going through his wallet. "Gonna need to come up with a way of getting inside without making too much of a ruckus."

"I'm sure the magickal barriers are only the first line of defense," Angus stated, watching the building. He caught sight of multiple security officers, and from the vibe they were giving off, he doubted very much that they were human.

"Here," Francis said, handing Angus a heaping Styrofoam container. "What do you want to drink?"

"Water's fine."

"Two waters," Francis added, as the counter person brought the remainder of his order and he paid.

"Let's sit over here," Francis said, leading Angus to the short concrete wall that bordered the plaza.

It was lunchtime in Back Bay on a beautiful fall day, and the area was humming with activity. *A perfect time to go unnoticed,* Angus thought as he enjoyed his meal.

"So, what do you think?" Angus asked after a while.

Francis had eaten in silence, staring at the formidable skyscraper before him, as if committing every detail to memory.

"I think we have a problem," the angel assassin said. "There are wards scrawled everywhere. Every brick fifty feet or less from the main entrance has been scrawled with some mystical hoodoo to keep the likes of us from passing through the front doors."

He took a bite of chop suey and slowly chewed.

"I hate it when somebody tries to keep me out," Francis stated. "It makes me feel so unloved."

"There will be even less in the world to love you if Stearns succeeds," Angus reminded the angel. "And by feeding on that level of death energy, I hate to think how powerful he might become."

They had finished their lunches and stood to throw away their trash in a nearby barrel when there was a flurry of activity from the building. Security guards—large, powerful-looking men that probably weren't men at all—spilled from the building and took up positions around the entrance.

"Something is happening," Angus said, as they made their way back to the waiting Leona.

"I'm guessing somebody caught wind of our visit," Francis said.

"Or whatever it is that Stearns is up to," Angus added, "is about to begin."

CHAPTER TWENTY

Scrimshaw squatted down beside his threadbare bed, going through the wooden chest that he had hidden beneath it.

Mr. Deacon wanted them to be ready for what was about to happen; now infused with the power of the Seraphim, his master was about to attempt something that Scrimshaw had never believed possible.

Mr. Deacon was going to attempt to bring them home.

His pale hands rummaged through the contents of the chest, old yellowed photographs, Social Security cards, driver's licenses—anything that could define someone as who they were.

Scrimshaw hungered for such an identity, and if he could not have one of his own, then he would covet the lives of others.

He was afraid that something might happen to his treasures and decided that he would carry some of them with him, just in case. A photo of a family picnic; three smiling children standing before a man and woman. He could see such love in their eyes, so much life that had already been lived and so much to come.

There was no denying what he truly was: an artificial life molded from clay infused with magick in his master's lab, sculpted to look human for the sole purpose of carrying out his master's wishes no matter what they would be. He should have been just like all the other golems that populated the Deacon estate, but from the first day he'd come to life, he knew that he was different.

He yearned for an identity, something to set him apart from all the others. His master was amused by this odd, independent thought, and encouraged him to grow, even allowing him the unique tattoos that he'd etched upon the pale, artificial skin of his face that had become his namesake.

Scrimshaw.

He hungered not only for the life he would create for himself, but for the lives of others—looking upon their life experiences like multifaceted jewels, bounty for the taking.

Selecting a few of the driver's licenses and a pretty red bow he had claimed from a child on her sixth birthday, Scrimshaw placed the cover back on the box and slid it beneath his cot. Then he put his prizes into the top front pocket of the heavy denim shirt he wore, close to where his artificial heart pulsed with magickal life.

He remembered how he had acquired each of them on his occasional visits back to the earthly realm to check up on the golem vessels that Mr. Deacon had sent out to collect the life energies he needed for his continued survival. As Mr. Deacon needed those energies, so did Scrimshaw grow hungry for the life experiences of others. Life experiences that he took as his own. Images of murder flashed in his mind, but he was not bothered by them.

Killing was all part of the process, the final step to claiming what he needed to be his.

Scrimshaw looked forward to acquiring even more keepsakes, knowing that being back on Earth permanently would make his access to the thriving populace even more bountiful.

Standing up beside his bed, he felt the house begin to shake. It was a strange sensation but not unfamiliar, recalling when the Deacon estate had first been transported from the Catskills to the world of shadows.

His master was already at work, manipulating the

magicks necessary to transport the entire estate back to where it had originated. Scrimshaw hadn't a moment to spare. He left his room in search of the master's son. Mr. Deacon wanted the boy prepared for the journey they were about to undertake.

Scrimshaw walked the tilted hallway to the wing where Teddy kept his room. The house shook again, the lights in the wall sconces flickering to darkness, before illuminating again, but this time at only half their brilliance. The passage was deep with black shadows now, and Scrimshaw grew cautious, taking a knife from his pocket.

Just in case.

Something moved in the deep darkness ahead of him, and Scrimshaw stopped, squinting his eyes to try to pierce the shadows. The sound of grunts and gurgles reached his ears as bounding feet drew closer.

Scrimshaw tensed the muscles in his legs, preparing to lunge and gut whatever it was that was about to pounce. It was almost upon him, and he brought his arm back, ready to drive the point of his blade up into the torso of his attacker, when he saw that it was Teddy.

The feral child scampered from the dark, dragging the angel's little girlfriend on a leash behind him.

"That's a good way to get yourself killed," Scrimshaw grumbled, dropping the blade to his side.

Teddy grunted, rubbing his running nose with the back of his hand. He looked behind him and gave the leash a violent tug, causing the girl to stumble forward, tripping over her own feet and falling to the floor.

Having gotten more from the angel than they'd even anticipated, the girl was really no longer needed and had obviously been forgotten by his master. Scrimshaw stared at the young woman, who struggled to keep from crying as she slowly climbed to her feet on the uneven floor. He wondered about her life and what had made her so strong. He couldn't imagine that an average girl of her age, taken from the world and brought to this place, wouldn't have lost her mind.

Scrimshaw admired her and wished that there was time to speak with her about her life and its defining moments. He would have loved to have them as his own.

"Your father is taking us home," Scrimshaw told the wild child.

Teddy just looked at him, head cocked, and then gestured to all around him.

"Yes," Scrimshaw said. "All of it. He's going to use his new power to take us back."

Scrimshaw caught something from the corner of his eye and looked to the girl. One of her hands had shot to her neck and appeared to be undoing the leather collar.

"Don't you . . . ," he began, but before he could get the remainder of his warning out, she was gone, running off in the opposite direction.

Scrimshaw couldn't help but smile. Sure, he was frustrated, he didn't have time for such things, but then again, this might give him the opportunity that he'd been hoping for.

A chance to spend a little quality time with a girl named Ashley.

Algernon Stearns entered the darkened television studio where history was about to take place.

He flipped on the lights, taking in all the sights that he had grown accustomed to over the past year as the place where little Angelina Hayward's special message would be broadcast to an eager faithful.

And, in so doing, satisfy his hunger for ultimate power.

The center of the studio had been set up like a little girl's bedroom: a fancy pink bed with fancy pink bedding, stuffed animals, and baby dolls yearning for a child's attention. Everything that his little messenger would need to feel comfortable.

He still found it hard to believe that Armaros—a supposed creature of Heaven—had come to him, helping him to formulate this plan, helping him to refine his ideas for the largest yield. It had been the angel who had come up with the idea of a sick little girl with a message from Heaven. All Stearns had to do was assist in her creation and provide the means for distributing the message.

He quietly thanked any and all who had suggested he invest heavily in television during its golden years, and, more recently, the Internet. He could not have asked for better delivery systems.

Stearns' thoughts started to wander to unknown territories again. He had no real idea why the angels were so keen on helping him achieve such a level of sorcerous power, although they had indicated that they were somehow attempting to reconnect humanity with its God.

Personally, he felt the killing of millions to be a bit dramatic, but, then again, he was dealing with a species that thought nothing of flooding the world in order to make a point about sin.

And besides, who was he to judge? Stearns was about to become one of the most powerful beings on the planet. He wondered, as he wandered about the empty studio, if having that much magickal power might put him at odds with his angelic comrades. It would be something he'd have to consider once he had his power. He might have to do some extensive research on the best way to kill angels.

Stearns' phone beeped, interrupting his thoughts, and he snatched it from his pocket.

"Speak," he commanded.

"She's here," said one of his golem security officers.

"Excellent." Stearns was unable to keep the smile from twisting his features. "Bring her right up to the studio. . . . I'm sure she's eager to get started."

Armaros remembered that the party had gone on for days.

Even though they were sorry for all the sins that the Grigori had committed in embracing the ways of humanity, it did not stop them from committing more.

It was like a sickness. The more they tried to distance themselves from the decadent ways of the human animals, the more they were drawn to them, eager to participate.

Armaros had tried to be good, but it never seemed to be enough. The longer they were here in exile, the harder it was to remain pure.

The party at one of the isolated French villas that the Grigori had acquired throughout the centuries was moving into its third day; every conceivable vice concocted by mortal man and woman was on display, and the fallen angels were more than happy to indulge.

Armaros, high on multiple drugs and alcohol, had become lucid enough to realize that Sariel was nowhere to be found; in fact, Armaros could not remember the last time that he had seen his leader. Shaking off the effects of the party, he had gone in search of Sariel, curious if perhaps their leader had found a vice so special that he did not wish to share.

He'd left the party, descending into the deeper levels of the villa, toward where he remembered seeing an ancient, secret chapel. As he had journeyed deeper into the winding stone passages tunneling beneath the estate, he'd heard the sound of a plaintive voice. At first he did not recognize it, but as he stepped from the passage into the chapel, he found Sariel slumped upon the altar before a great stone cross.

And the leader of the Grigori was crying.

Armaros was stunned, any residual effects of the party's concoctions now completely gone from his body as he stood there watching.

His leader continued to kneel, raising his head to speak aloud in the tongue of the messenger—the language of the angels.

Sariel was praying, begging God to listen to him.

"Sariel?" Armaros had called out, moving farther into the church.

The leader of the Grigori had risen suddenly, an expression of surprise on his tear-streaked face.

"What are you doing here?" Armaros had asked as he approached him, placing a gentle hand on his cheek. "Alone."

Sariel moved his face from the comforting hand, turning his gaze to the cross. "Sometimes I come down here to listen."

Armaros did not understand. "Listen?" he asked.

Sariel looked at him again. "The prayers of the faithful and those who have lost their way and have nowhere else to turn."

Armaros was quiet for a moment, listening, but heard nothing.

"I don't . . ."

"Listen," Sariel commanded forcefully.

Armaros tried again, this time his acute senses reaching out beyond the confines of the underground church to the festivities above. He was about to confess that he still did not hear them when he heard the first fragment of prayer.

"I hear them," he had told his master, focusing on the prayer and hearing all the more in a cacophony of sound. "I hear them all."

"No matter the time, there is always someone calling out to Him, begging for His help . . . for His guidance."

Sariel looked back to the cross.

"When I entered the church . . . it sounded as though *you* were praying," Armaros said to his leader, a part of him hoping he had been mistaken.

It looked as though Sariel was about to object. "I was listening to the prayers of the faithful and those who had lost their way with nowhere else to turn," he began, then paused. "Listening, but also praying, hoping that maybe if He was listening to them, He might be listening to me," he finished.

Armaros could hear the pain in his leader's voice—see it in his eyes.

"We're lost, Armaros," Sariel told him. "For what we have done to this world, we are damned . . . no matter how much penance we do or how loudly we beg—"

There was a quiver in Sariel's voice, a moment of weakness that Armaros had never seen. And it chilled him.

"We are lost," Sariel finished, the sadness in his tone suddenly replaced with anger.

And with those words, the fallen angel sprang atop the

stone altar, grabbing hold of the cross, and with a show of inhuman strength, tore it from its perch, allowing it to tumble forward and smash upon the ground.

Sariel and Armaros stood together, staring at the rubble that had once been humanity's symbol of their faith.

Of their God.

And then, after some time, Sariel spoke.

"Do you still hear it, Armaros?" the leader of the Grigori asked, brushing the dust of many years past from his silk shirt.

"The prayers?"

"Oh, dear no," Sariel scoffed. "Upstairs . . . in the villa."

And Sariel put his arm lovingly around Armaros, leading him from the church and into the labyrinth.

"We're missing the party."

Was that when our leader truly died? Armaros mused, leaving the memory of that day in the hidden church.

His eyes focused out the window again, but instead of the same Boston he and his brethren had pondered over for years, he saw something entirely new.

Armaros saw a world on the cusp of change.

He closed his eyes, reaching out with his mind, searching for the ones he was sure would come; the fallen Guardian and the Seraphim who wished so much to be human. The Guardian he had sensed earlier, sniffing around what was to be ground zero.

It was the sign he had been waiting for.

Now was the time to begin things anew, to awaken the world and show God that they were still here.

The Almighty may have turned a deaf ear to Sariel's prayers, but that would no longer be the case once their message was broadcast through the golem child.

As the Grigori and all angels had the power to hear the world's prayers, so did they have the ability to respond.

And that was what the Grigori intended to do.

When the time was right, the child would speak to the faithful, and she would deliver a message.

Their message.

That the Lord of lords was unhappy with humanity and was about to show His displeasure.

And those who heard would be struck down by death, but their passing would not be in vain, for it would show the unbelievers—the sinners—that the divine *did* exist.

And was watching.

The sacrifice of the faithful would lead to the conversion of an even greater number. Like a prescribed fire in a forest, the burning of trees and vegetation so that it may grow back all the stronger.

He thought about his love again—the leader no longer beside him—and felt his anger grow. Sariel should have been here. But, then, would they have gone this far if he had still been alive?

Sariel's death had been the fire that burned what they used to be away, allowing what they were now to grow.

Making them stronger, as the human species would soon be.

For they would need to be strong. . . . They would all need to be strong.

Armaros remembered the figure sitting in the shadows, the promises that he made.

He said that God would hear them but that there would also be a war.

Armaros pondered if what they were about to do might be an aspect of the coming conflict. That the potential death of millions could be the catalyst that triggered the start of war.

If that was what it would take to again gain the attention of their Creator, then so be it. He was willing to take that chance.

He reached out with his mind to his brethren, stirring them to attention. The Grigori turned from their view of the world to stare at him.

Armaros clutched the wooden box that contained the ashes of his leader and lover to his chest. Their eyes bored into his, and he felt himself touched by their familiar stares.

He knew each and every one, for they had endured this world, its pleasures and its torments, together.

Reaching out to them, to their minds, he told them that it was time.

And they would be either praised and welcomed back to the bosom of the Lord God Almighty . . .

Or they would be damned.

But, really, they had already been damned once. How much more damned could they be?

CHAPTER TWENTY-ONE

Garfial pushed past Remy, grabbing the remote from what looked to be a pile of bones, and turned up the television's volume.

The newscasters were still talking, going over again the history of little Angelina Hayward.

"Okay, this is good," Garfial stated, staring at the screen. "It hasn't happened yet. . . . There's still time."

"I need to know what's going on," Remy told him, not really sure how much help he would be in his current state.

The Grigori looked away from the television screen but his eyes kept darting back, afraid that he might be missing something.

"They had me create a golem in the form of a little girl," Garfial started to explain.

"That little girl." Remy pointed to the TV.

"Yeah," Garfial said. "She's pretty complicated . . . has no idea what she really is . . . believes one hundred percent in the history that we created for her."

"As does everybody who is hearing about her," Remy added.

The fallen angel nodded. "And that's where the fun begins. How many people do you think are watching this now? How many other channels are picking up on the story about the little girl who came out of a coma, promising a message from God and is now about to deliver?

"This is probably reaching all over the world. . . . Right this minute, millions of people are waiting to hear little Angelina's message. And that doesn't even count the people on the Internet."

Remy looked to the television to see that they were showing footage of Angelina when she first awoke from her coma. The little girl was pale and quite sick-looking, an oxygen mask clamped onto her tiny face. She was clutching a pink teddy bear to her chest as her mother stroked her sweaty head.

"What was she created to do?" Remy asked, not really wanting to know.

"Think of her as both a transmitter and receiver."

"And what is she transmitting and receiving?"

"Armaros and the other Grigori are going to provide her with the message that will go out to everybody who's listening," Garfial said. He seemed to be growing more agitated.

"As soon as she begins to speak, she will create a psychic rapport with her listeners, and then the Grigori will provide their message to the faithful."

Remy stared, waiting. "Which is?" he prodded.

"They're going to project all the pain and suffering they've endured since being exiled to Earth, and kill everyone who's listening," Garfial said.

Remy felt the world go out from beneath him. It was worse than he suspected.

"Then the girl will act as a receiver, and the sorcerer—Stearns—will reap the benefit of the megadeaths. She'll collect all their energies and transmit them to him."

"Making him incredibly powerful," Remy finished.

Garfial's eyes had drifted back to the television. They had gone to a commercial break. "I'd say the most powerful magick user on the planet," he confirmed.

And that didn't make sense to Remy. "Why would Armaros want to kill millions and then hand over all that power to somebody like Stearns?"

The reporters were back, announcing yet again that little Angelina Hayward was close to delivering the message she'd received from God.

"That's something you'll have to ask him about," Garfial announced. "All I can tell you is that I like it here. Any desire I had to return to . . . Him"—he pointed to the ceiling—"went away a very long time ago. This can't be allowed to happen," he said, indicating the television, then looking at Remy. "You have to stop them."

Remy remained silent, knowing Garfial was right, but having no idea how he was going to accomplish it.

"Hell, you're part of the reason this is happening in the first place," Garfial added with a disturbed laugh.

The news program was showing the little girl and her family as they were assisted from their home to a waiting van. Throngs of onlookers waving signs and holding banners lined the street.

As soon as Angelina was safely inside the van, the cameras cut to a live shot on the plaza in front of the Hermes Building in the Back Bay, where reporters began to explain how Algernon Stearns, multimillionaire philanthropist, had been so touched by the little girl's amazing story. . . .

"I need to get in there," Remy said, pointing to a splendid aerial shot of the skyscraper and the Boston skyline.

The Grigori nodded. "Uh-huh. And then what?"

Remy didn't have an answer.

"Look at you," Garfial said. "Here I am sneaking around the city, trying to find you, and when I do, you're nothing but a shadow of yourself.

"This is going to happen," he said, a look of resignation on his pale features. "Millions will die, and we'll be responsible."

"Can you get me inside?" Remy asked, ignoring the Grigori.

"Sure," Garfial said with a nod. "But Armaros will smell the Seraphim on you like . . ."

Remy slowly shook his head. "Maybe not."

It was Garfial's turn to be silent.

"You said it," Remy continued. "I'm a shadow of myself. If I can get in there and do some damage before the broadcast . . ."

Garfial was gnawing on a fingernail like it was his last meal.

"We're going to have to leave, like, right now," he said, a spark of hope now burning in eyes that moments ago were filled with dread.

On the television, a large black van turned from Boylston Street into the parking garage beneath the Hermes Building.

"I need to make a call first," Remy said, taking his cell phone from his pocket. He didn't mention that he also had to force Stearns into getting him back to the shadow realm so he could find Ashley and bring her home.

"Make it quick," the fallen angel said nervously.

Remy punched in the number and waited.

"Yeah," the Guardian angel answered on the first ring.

"It's worse than we thought."

There was a slight pause, and then Francis' voice.

"Isn't it always?"

As she ran for her life through the twisted house, all Ashley could think of was *The Wizard of Oz.*

She would have preferred to be thinking of how to escape the monsters chasing her and how to survive, but the favorite film from her childhood had decided to take up residence in the forefront of her brain.

Maybe it had to do with the story: young girl swept up from her home to awaken in a strange place filled with incredible sights. Or maybe it was the question of whether or not Dorothy was dreaming, for Ashley wanted so desperately to wake and find that this was really a horrible nightmare.

The floor beneath her feet suddenly heaved upward, followed by the moan and snapping of wood, and she was pitched to one side, bouncing off a wall and falling to her knees. She stayed there for a moment, stunned, as the walls and the floor around her faded in and out of focus.

At first she thought that maybe she had hit her head, but then she realized that everything around her—a vase on the table at the end of the hall, a painting hanging crookedly on the wall—seemed to be vibrating, becoming blurry. And then she felt the tingling in her body and looked down at her hands to find that they too were becoming hazy, prickling as if she were receiving a mild electric shock.

What's happening now? she asked herself, wishing there was a wizard who could give her the answer.

The vibrations through the corridor were growing more and more powerful—more intense—and she watched as jagged cracks appeared on the walls. Until the thumping sound of running feet and the grunts of a little boy more animal than child spurred her to move.

"I'm off to see the Wizard . . . ," she began to sing aloud, holding back a near-hysterical giggle, afraid that if she allowed it out, she might never be able to stop.

She started to run again, imagining the awful, pale-faced man with the black, spiraling tattoos all over his face and the wild boy looming up behind her.

"The wonderful Wizard of Oz . . ." Ashley muttered and sang beneath her breath, squinting into the oncoming darkness in the hallway ahead.

"Ashley!" bellowed a voice from behind her, and she partially turned, dreading to see how close her pursuers actually were. "You don't want to get lost in this house, Ashley!"

He was right: She didn't want to get lost in this house. But she didn't want to end up with him or the boy, Teddy, either, so she kept running, focusing on her song.

"I hear he is a whiz of a wiz if ever there was a wiz . . ."

Something lurched up from the darkness before her and she wasn't quick enough to avoid it, colliding full force and sending both of them to the ground. She got back on her feet as the figure she'd hit also rose with a grunt.

The shadow's head was partially covered by a hood, but

his eyes—yellow eyes—the way they looked at her, it was almost as if he knew her.

"I thought I brought you back to the motel," the figure growled, reaching up to pull the hood from his oddly shaped head.

And that was when Ashley realized that this wasn't a guy at all, but all she could think of was a twisted mash-up of a munchkin and a flying monkey.

That laugh was upon her again, creeping up from the back of her throat, and this time there was no way she could keep it in. Her sanity began to crumble.

And it was the craziest sound she'd ever heard in her life.

Squire had been drawn to the old house as if his goblin body had been caught in some powerful current.

Whatever was going on there wasn't good.

Cloaked in shadow, he had watched the sprawling estate vibrate and blur, like he was looking through a pair of unfocused binoculars.

Nope, this wasn't good at all.

Squire moved closer, and the closer he got, the worse he felt. Whatever was going on there was affecting the whole environment of the shadow realm.

He'd repositioned the golf bag of weapons on his shoulder and searched out a particularly deep path of shadow that would lead him inside the mansion. It had taken him three tries—some of the paths actually collapsed and dispersed—but he'd eventually found one that worked and entered the house.

To find the girl.

What the fuck's up with this? the goblin thought as he got back on his feet. He could see a look that he'd grown familiar with over the years beginning to appear in her eyes. It was the look of someone about to go over the deep end, and it wasn't a pretty sight.

She started to laugh hysterically, and Squire, feeling bad for her, decided to throw her a line.

"What's your name, kid?" he asked in his friendliest tone.

Her body did a little twitch then, eyes temporarily blinking back the madness.

"Ashley," she said.

A voice cried out from somewhere down the hall, and Squire could hear the sounds of footsteps approaching. Ashley looked over her shoulder, fear creeping back into her gaze.

"Hey, Ashley," Squire said, emerging fully from the darkness. "Do you need some help?"

"Who are you?" she asked. The fear was still there, but now it seemed to be tempered with curiosity.

"Someone who can get you out of here, if you want," he told her. The footsteps were closer now, and the structure began to shake and fade again.

She looked at the darkness of the hallway behind her and then back to him. "How—how do I kn-know that . . . ?" she stammered.

"That you can trust me? Just look at this face." Squire pointed to his goblin mug. "It's got *trustworthy* written all over it." He held out his hand, sensing that their time was running out. "C'mon, take my hand. I'll get us both out of here."

Ashley hesitated as the pale-skinned man and a kid running on all fours came upon them. Squire was familiar with the tattooed dude; he'd tried to kill him a few times out on the paths.

"What do we have here?" the man asked, sizing up the situation. The little kid simply growled.

A gun appeared in the man's hand, and Squire decided that it was time to go.

He reached out and grabbed Ashley's hand. "This is gonna feel a little weird," he said to her; then he yanked her toward a shadow passage that had been opened by whatever was going on in the house. Ashley's surprised squeal was cut off as Squire pushed her through the opening and into the passage.

The tattooed man immediately began to fire, bullets punching deep holes into the plaster walls as Squire dove to join Ashley in the open path.

He found her frozen in the total darkness.

"Crawl!" he yelled, pushing her forward. "There should be an opening up ahead."

Squire turned to close the passage behind him, but the shadows in this place had gone wild and would not obey him. The rules were breaking down, and he suddenly realized how dangerous the situation truly was.

"I see you," said the tattooed man, his white skin practically glowing as he held up a lighter, illuminating the confined space just inside the passage. He extended his arm and fired the gun.

Deacon was bending the world to his whim.

He stood in the open foyer of his home, calling on ancient spells that until now were too powerful for him to manipulate.

Sparks of fire leapt from his outstretched hands, sizzling on the marble floor, providing the only sustained light as the chandelier and the supernaturally powered bulbs in the wall sconces flickered in and out, the greenish glow growing fainter by the seconds.

"Do you see?" Deacon asked the golem staff that watched him from a safe distance. "Do you see what I can do?"

He was also addressing his wife. Even though her body had burned with the dining room, he knew that she was still with him.

Expecting him to fail.

But he was beyond failure now, or would be as soon as he had his revenge.

The shadow realm was fighting him, not wanting to give up the stately home that had been part of its inky environment for so many years.

How dared it think that it could keep him there?

Deacon again flexed magickal muscles that grew stron-

ger and stronger every time he exerted them. The home
around him began to violently vibrate, straining against the
reality of the shadow place, as he attempted to take it from
here to there.

In his mind he pictured it as it was, the Catskill Mountains, where his family had used their substantial wealth
to build what was to be their castle, a place were American royalty went to escape the day-to-day stresses of the
world. Deacon saw the home as it had been: a vast section
of barren woods followed by the wooden skeletal structure that would soon grow its epidermis of wood, plaster,
stone, and glass.

He felt a sense of calm pass through his energized form,
recalling the joy he'd experienced in the home and what he
yearned for again.

Going home to hide.

He heard the voice and whirled around, distracted.

"Veronica?" he called out, half expecting to see her
burning form behind him, but there was nothing except the
entrance to the parlor. He was about to resume his casting
when he heard her again.

At least Stearns will know where to find you.

"What are you going on about?" Deacon demanded,
spinning again, his body throwing off sparks of divine fire.
He looked to his staff to see if they were hearing it, as well.

"Where is she?" he asked them.

They did not respond, probably fearing that they might
anger him.

"I *will* bring the estate back," he called out to Veronica.
"And then I will deal with Stearns."

Veronica chuckled, and Deacon felt his anger growing.
It was not a healthy thing to anger one with the power of
the Seraphim coursing through his veins.

"Did I say something humorous, my love?" he asked as
he strode across the marble floor.

The golems scattered, revealing nothing. She was nowhere to be found.

Stearns will sense your return, and he will come for you.

Deacon was about to object, but knew that there was some truth to his wife's taunting words. Since that morning in 1945 when he and the cabal were transformed by the death energies of Hiroshima, he could sense the others, as if they had somehow been joined—connected—by their experience.

Even in the shadow realm, he could feel them. . . .

And if he could feel them, then they . . . *Stearns* . . . was indeed aware of him.

Sense you . . . find you . . . take what is yours . . .

"Never again," Deacon growled, his anger stirring the power of an angel.

You need to . . .

"Go to him," Deacon finished.

Before he can . . .

"Try to take what is mine."

Yesssssssssssssssssssssssssssssssss.

Deacon closed his eyes, wiping his mind clear, and focusing on another thing entirely. He reached out across the veil of darkness to find the one who had taken so much from him. He found Heath right away, but only lingering traces of the others, clinging to one powerful scent.

Stearns.

Deacon smiled. *Won't it be something,* he thought as he fixed a new location inside his head, *killing all those birds with one very large stone?*

"I'm coming for you, Algernon," he said, flexing his magickal muscles once again, feeling the fabric of the shadow realm stretching tighter against his onslaught.

And then it began to tear, the darkness ready to escape from one realm to fill another.

CHAPTER TWENTY-TWO

Though he hadn't been without them for long, Remy missed his wings and the ability to get to where he needed to be in no time at all.

He knew that he could drive, but Boston traffic was always iffy and time was of the essence.

Isn't it always?

Fearing that they might be too late, Garfial risked using angel magick to open a passage from the basement of the church to a room in the practically empty Hermes building. The doorway opened with an electric hum, and Garfial dove through, motioning wildly for Remy to follow. On the other side, they stepped into what looked to be an office space. The air was heavy with the smell of paint and a newly laid rug. Boxes of unassembled office furniture were piled in the corner.

Remy felt a bit queasy from the trip, but took a deep breath before getting down to the brass tacks.

"Where's the studio?" he asked, already looking for the exit.

"It's on the eightieth floor," Garfial told him. "Why? What do you have in mind?"

"Disrupt the broadcast, and we're almost out of the woods," Remy told him.

"And your friends?" Garfial asked.

"Get them inside and they'll take it from there," Remy told him, seeing the red exit sign at the back of the darkened office space. "They should provide just the right amount of distraction."

Garfial began to conjure another portal to retrieve Francis and Angus.

"You never said what you wanted with Stearns," the fallen angel commented as a tiny hole in the fabric of time and space appeared, growing steadily larger.

"He might have some information I need," Remy said, thinking of Ashley trapped in the land of shadows, and of Deacon now filled with the power of the Seraphim.

One thing at a time, he thought. First he had to save the lives of millions, and then he would go after Ashley.

"Good luck with that," Garfial said. "You're probably going to need it."

Remy turned to thank the angel, and gasped at the sight.

"Watch out!" he screamed, running toward Garfial, who was just about to step through the crackling passage as a darkly clad angel of the Grigori struck.

Garfial couldn't have even known what hit him. An anguished grunt was all he could muster as the sword buried itself deep in the thick muscle of his neck. The Grigori attacker pulled back on the blade, watching as Garfial pitched forward and fell through the conjured doorway that disappeared with a sound very much like that of an electrical transformer blowing.

Remy froze, watching as the shapes of other Grigori all holding ancient-looking blades appeared alongside their murderous leader.

"Remy Chandler," the fallen angel that had to be Armaros snarled. "I was hoping that you'd join us."

Remy knew that his chances against them were nil, so he turned and sprinted for the door, the red of the Exit sign his inspiration.

But he wasn't fast enough. The Grigori brought him down roughly, the stink of newly laid carpet nearly choking him, as they bounced his face off the floor again and again, until he finally gave them what they wanted and blacked out.

In an anteroom off the studio, Algernon Stearns prepared for the next-best thing to godhood.

He stood perfectly still as his golem servants dressed him in the elaborate armor and harness that would allow him to feed on the life forces of more than a million faithful viewers.

The unnatural hunger that had been his constant companion these many years was like a wild animal now, as if sensing the meal that was about to come. He could feel on his palms the movement of multiple tiny, eager mouths opening and closing in anticipation.

"Please lift your arms, sir," one of the golems asked.

He did, raising his arms, turning his hungry palms outward, and imagining the entirety of the world laid out before him.

For the taking.

With the kind of power he would soon possess, there would be very little he couldn't do. A tremble of fear and anticipation raced up and down his spine as the workers continued to strap him into the exoskeleton. He thought of what the power had done to him the last time and was both eager and terrified.

He hoped that this time, it would take him that much closer to God.

That much closer to *being* a god.

Movement in the studio caught his attention, and he saw that Angelina had arrived. Her parents accompanied the frail child, her father pushing the wheelchair into the studio.

"Are we almost finished here?" Stearns asked those attending him.

He was answered with a few grunts as some final pieces of the harness were attached.

"We're done, sir," said one of the golems, and they all stepped back as if to admire him.

"Well?" Stearns asked, spreading his arms and turning in a semicircle.

The golems looked at one another, unsure of what was expected of them.

"How do I look?" Stearns finally asked.

"Magnificent, sir," one of them said.

"A sight to behold," said another.

"I don't know why I bother," Stearns snarled, moving toward the door to the studio. "Perhaps when this is done I'll have the power to create a staff that truly understands my needs."

He replaced the snarl of displeasure on his face with his best facsimile of a smile as he entered the studio. "Angelina," he said, the exoskeleton clanking like armor as he approached.

Her father was helping her from the wheelchair.

"Allow me," Stearns said, taking the child into his arms and carrying her to the fancy bed in the center of the room.

"There you are." He set her down and pulled the covers over her scrawny legs.

"You look like a knight in shining armor," Angelina said, eyes wide with wonder.

Stearns chuckled, looking down at himself. "I guess I do," he agreed.

"Why are you dressed that way?" she asked, as her mother brought a few toys to place around her.

"So I can help you," he said. "We want to make sure that each and every person out there hears your message."

His eyes traveled up to the glass window of the control booth. More of his golem staff stared down at him, and he raised his hand to signal that it was time for them to get ready. The golems went to work, and Stearns watched as multiple, automated television cameras emerged, tracking along the floor to encircle the bed.

Angelina's eyes were filled with fear. "They scare me," she said, clutching a pink teddy bear to her chest.

"There's no reason to be afraid," Stearns soothed. "This is how the people will hear your message."

He thought of all the programming that would be interrupted to broadcast this historic event, all the eyes that would be fixed on television screens and computer monitors. If he remembered correctly, there had even been a few stadiums that had licensed the rights to display the little girl's message.

Oh, what a glorious event this will be.

More of his artificial staff emerged from the side room to make certain that the child would be ready.

"Who are they?" Angelina asked, her voice tinged with panic.

"They are my helpers," Stearns told her. "No need to concern yourself."

One of the golems approached the bed, attaching what looked like high-tech handcuffs to each of the girl's tiny wrists.

"What are these?" she asked, on the brink of tears. "I don't want to wear them."

"Don't you want to look pretty for the world?" Stearns responded, thinking quickly. "Those are special bracelets worn only by those important enough to hear a message from God."

His staff then attached leads from the special bracelets to components hidden beneath the mattress, which would eventually be connected by cable to the exoskeleton he wore.

Angelina was in tears, slumping farther down in the bed, clutching all her toys.

"Why are you sad, sweetie?" Stearns asked, feigning compassion. He stood beside her, reaching out with a metal gloved hand to stroke her cheek.

"I'm scared," the child spoke, eyes darting fearfully about the room. "And the angels haven't come to—"

As if on cue, the door to the studio swung wide, and a man was violently tossed from the entryway onto the floor. The Grigori, Armaros in the lead, followed.

"What is the meaning of this?" Stearns demanded.

"This is our very special friend, Remy Chandler," Armaros said.

The man, bloodied and beaten, moaned as he struggled to regain consciousness.

"And we thought it only fair that he have a front-row seat to the events that are about to transpire."

"You . . . you can't do this," the man called Remy Chandler mumbled through swollen lips as blood dribbled from his injured mouth.

"And that is where you are wrong," Armaros said as he and the other Grigori gathered around the little girl's bed. "We can, and we are."

Francis sipped his Starbucks coffee and waited.

The call from Remy had come fifteen minutes ago, but so far nothing had happened.

"What, exactly, are we waiting for?" Angus asked, nervously watching the traffic and people going by. "Maybe we're just missing it."

"Hasn't happened yet," Francis said between sips of his scalding drink.

"What should we do?"

Francis didn't answer the sorcerer, choosing instead to think this through. He wasn't the most patient of beings. There was a part of him, one that really didn't get to come out all that often, that wanted to be patient—to do exactly what Remy had asked of him. But there was another side of him, one that often seemed to get its way, that thought they should be doing something right now.

"Maybe he took care of the situation himself," he said finally, turning to look at the sorcerer sitting beside him. "Maybe the problem wasn't all that big and he didn't need to call in the big guns."

"Big guns?" Angus asked, confusion written all over his fat face. "Who . . . ?"

"Us," Francis explained. "The big guns . . . the heavy hitters. Maybe there wasn't any need to—"

The sound like an angry swarm of hornets filled the backseat of their borrowed vehicle, tickling the insides of their brains.

Francis spun around in his seat, pistol pointed and ready to fire, without spilling a single drop of his coffee. He recognized the shape of an angelic portal opening and guessed that this was the sign Remy had told him was coming. The pinprick hole grew, and with a rush of air unleashed its contents into the backseat.

A fallen angel's body spilled out, pitching forward, crimson gore spewing from an angry neck wound.

"Holy fuck," Francis screamed, tossing aside his coffee and jumping into the backseat, forcing his hand against the bleeding gash in the traveler's throat.

"Get me something to stop the bleeding," he yelled at Angus.

The angel thrashed wildly as warm blood flowed out from between Francis' fingers. Angus handed him a small stack of napkins, and he jammed them against the gushing wound, hoping it would be enough but knowing otherwise.

Francis noticed that the blood was being quickly absorbed by the upholstery of the car's backseat, not even leaving a stain. Leona may have been fed earlier, but she obviously wasn't above having an unexpected snack.

"Remy," Francis said, leaning down to look into the dying Grigori's eyes. "Where is he? Is he inside?"

The angel's eyes were growing dimmer, but he struggled to respond.

"Yes . . . ," he gurgled. "Taken . . ."

"He was taken," Francis repeated. "Taken by Stearns? Your boss . . . Who took him?"

"Maybe a spell of healing?" Angus suggested, and the tips of his fingers started to grow a fiery red.

"Too late for that," Francis replied.

"Stop . . . them . . . ," the fallen angel managed, reaching up to take hold of Francis' shoulder in a weakening grip.

"Yeah," Francis said, watching as the life went out of the angel's eyes. "That's what we're trying to do."

The part of Francis that liked to act first and think later was in full control now as he climbed back into the driver's seat.

"What are we going to do now?" Angus asked, movement in the backseat capturing his attention. Now it wasn't only blood that was being absorbed by the upholstery.

"We're getting inside," Francis said, turning over the engine.

"But there are wards in place and golem guards . . ."

"And they'll be dealt with." Francis put the car in drive and leaned closer to the steering wheel. "Leona, I know Richard said you'd only give us a ride, but I was wondering—especially since I just gave you that nifty angel snack—if you'd be willing to get us inside that building across the street."

The car didn't respond, as if considering his request.

"I happen to know that there are magickal wards in place to keep people like us from entering and there are probably armed guards, but a really good friend of mine is trapped inside, and a lot of people are going to die if we don't help him."

"Correct me if I'm wrong, but you're reasoning with a car?" Angus asked, horrified.

Francis held up a finger, signaling for him to be quiet.

"What do you say, Leona? Can you get us inside?"

The radio that had been playing softly in the background went to static, before Wagner's *Ride of the Valkyries* was suddenly blaring from the speakers.

"Oh, God," Angus screamed, fumbling to get his seat belt on.

"That a girl," Francis said, grabbing hold of the wooden steering wheel. He let the car do what it did best, what it had been created to do.

Drive.

Effortlessly and with great speed, Leona freed herself from the parking space, driving down Boylston Street, accelerating by the second. Just as she was about to pass the building, she slammed on her brakes, spinning around so that she faced the sidewalk in front of Hermes Plaza.

"Dear God in Heaven!" Angus wailed, grabbing for anything that might give him purchase.

"Hold on," Francis cried, as the Lincoln jumped the curb, barely missing gaggles of screaming pedestrians, and sped toward the front entrance of the building.

Leona's engine roared like some great jungle cat about to take down its prey.

Something was wrong with the shadow path.

Squire could feel it deep in his rounded gut, the quill-like hair on the back of his thick neck standing at attention.

The first rule any hobgoblin learned about traveling the paths was to pay attention to location and the stability of the path. That very rule suddenly came to mind when he felt the darkness beneath his feet grow soft, and watched as Ashley stumbled in front of him, falling to her knees.

"Get up," Squire ordered, fearing the worst. "Get up, get up . . ."

A gunshot rang out from behind them.

They had to get to the other end, and fast.

There were more gunshots, but the bullets were absorbed into the substance of shadow, likely coming out in some other dark place. Squire pictured some poor schmuck getting in some quality porn time when a bullet found its way out from a patch of black behind the La-Z-Boy. Could seriously ruin a guy's evening.

The passage was breaking down, and that could mean only one thing was happening: The environment in which the path had originally existed was now different.

Squire came up close to Ashley, who was still struggling to regain her footing in the mudlike substance that was now the floor of the tunnel. He wrapped his arms around her tiny waist and hauled her back onto her feet, practically dragging her through the sucking surface.

The passage was closing in on them, growing smaller, narrower. If they didn't find an exit soon, it would collapse in on itself and they would drown in this shit. Not a bad fate for the jerk-offs that were chasing them, but it wasn't something that Squire was looking forward to.

More gunshots rang out, and he felt a bullet whiz past his face. The assholes were getting closer.

"We gotta move faster," he urged Ashley. He did have to hand it to the kid: She was hanging in there pretty well. Most couldn't handle five minutes in a shadow path, never mind being in one on the verge of collapse.

"I can't go any farther," Ashley screamed, pressing herself against a solid wall of shadow.

"Outta the way." Squire pushed her aside. He placed his hands against the cold, sticky surface and closed his eyes. It was just as he thought: This had been the exit a few minutes ago, but since something was happening to the environment outside, it had almost healed over.

Almost.

Squire could still sense a place on the other side, and since he had no desire to suffocate within the stinking bowels of a shadow path, he decided to do something about it.

He swung the golf bag from his shoulder and rummaged through it, pulling out a battle-ax.

No need for anything dainty here.

"Get behind me," he told the girl, as more gunshots rang out.

Squire raised the ax above his head, chancing a quick look behind him. The path was constricting faster, squeezing Tattoo Man and Dog Boy in its shrinking grip, buying him just enough time.

The goblin let out a scream, putting everything he had behind the strike as he brought the blade down on the hardening wall of shadow before them.

The blade buried itself deep within the solidified midnight, but he believed he could see a hint of light from the world that still existed behind it. Yanking the blade back, he hefted the mighty ax, striking the wall again and again.

"We ain't got much time," he said to Ashley, hacking at the wall once more and then grabbing the edges of the cut and pulling.

Ashley hesitated at first but then joined Squire with

gusto, sinking her fingers into the gelatinous dark and ripping away chunks to open the passage.

A sickly light leaked from the opening they'd torn, and it appeared large enough for them to get through, but the way the wall was healing up, it wouldn't be for long.

"Now," Squire ordered, pushing Ashley toward the hole.

She started to protest, fear creeping into her eyes, but he insisted, shoving her into the gradually diminishing crack and forcing her through to the other side.

He was about to follow her when he felt a powerful grip clamp down on his ankle.

"Going somewhere?" the tattooed man asked as he slithered on his belly through the intestine-like passage that was collapsing all around them. The schnauzer boy had managed to make it past his partner, crab walking toward him, mouth open to bite.

A quick backhand across the face was enough to discourage the youngster, but then Squire watched as Tattoo Man, who was still holding him with one hand, pulled his gun up in the other and prepared to fire.

Squire knew he had only seconds before the passage he'd cut healed up twice as thick as before, trapping him here, and he didn't cotton to that at all. He glanced down, seeing the hilt of his ax sticking up from the softening surface beneath his feet, and yanked it free with a moist sucking sound. He managed to bring the ax down on the wrist of the hand that held his ankle, just as the tattooed man fired his gun with the other.

Yanking his foot back, Squire found that he was free, but he'd also been shot, the bullet punching its way into his shoulder, forcing him to drop his battle-ax.

But things weren't any better for Tattoo Man.

He was screaming, clutching the stump of his hand, as Squire pushed himself backward toward the fissure—less than half the size it had been mere moments before.

Sensing that it was now or never, Squire dove headfirst into the passage, forcing his way through the tight squeeze of the wound he'd cut in the hardening blackness. It wasn't easy; the walls of the passage attempted to crush him as he wiggled his way through. He'd always been curious as to what it would feel like to be born, and figured that this was probably the closest he'd ever get to having the experience again.

The passage was closing behind him, but he could see a hint of soft light ahead. His shoulder screamed in protest, but Squire didn't listen. There'd be time for pain later, when he was still alive and on the other side with the time to bitch about it.

He clawed at the membranous caul that had formed over the exit, pulling himself through, out into the light with a series of grunts and a scream of freedom.

Out of the frying pan.

"Don't want to be doing that again anytime soon," he said, rolling on his stomach and starting to stand. He saw that Ashley was there, but her stare was fixed on something he had not yet noticed.

And then he saw that she was staring at a naked and perfectly muscled human figure standing with arms outstretched. Wings of fire grew from his back, and the words of some ancient magickal spell spilled from his mouth to seed the air.

Squire knew where they were, and they hadn't gotten very far. They were back inside the old mansion, but he could feel that something wasn't right. It was moving. . . . The magick spell that the man was casting was taking the entire estate to someplace else.

Out of the frying pan, he thought, feeling reality whizzing past him.

And into the fire.

CHAPTER TWENTY-THREE

They were going to make him watch.

Remy was hauled to his feet by two of Stearns' goons, as the deaths of more than a million people were set in motion.

There was a flurry of activity in the television studio. Technicians moved about a glass control room above the main studio while more of Stearns' techs were attaching thick cables to the external skeleton of metal that the sorcerer wore, cables that trailed across the floor to the strange machinery that was part of the little girl's bed.

"Quickly now. Quickly," Stearns bellowed.

Remy could not take his eyes from the Grigori calmly standing beside the child's bed, waiting to do their part.

He was disgusted, nauseated by the idea that they and he were actually of the same species. He'd suspected that the Watchers—the Grigori—had been driven insane by their banishment to the world they had helped to corrupt, but he never imagined how truly crazy they had become.

Or how far they'd go to show it.

"I get it," Remy yelled over the voices raised in preparation, temporarily bringing silence to the studio.

Armaros was looking at him now with cold, dead eyes.

"I get it," Remy said again. "You're pissed . . . pissed at

God for forgetting you, pissed at yourselves for being so damn weak, and pissed at me for killing your leader."

He could feel the fury radiating from them in waves; it was like static electricity, charging the very air. It made the hair on his arms stand on end.

"But don't do this," Remy begged. "Take your anger out on someone who deserves it. . . . Take it out on me, if you have to."

Armaros drifted closer.

"The great angel Remiel," the new Grigori leader scoffed. "You actually believe this is all about you? Such arrogance. But then again, what would we expect from one of the Almighty's elite?"

The fallen angel moved to stand before Remy.

"This isn't about past angers and sorrows," Armaros said. "This is about the future of this world . . . of humanity and of Heaven itself."

Remy wasn't sure he understood. "How can the killing of a million of His flock be seen as a positive move toward the future?"

"Are you so blind?" Armaros asked. "Can you not see the signs? There's a war coming . . . and the world of man will become a battleground."

"It'll never come to that," Remy said, trying to hide his uncertainty.

"The signs are there, Remiel, whether you choose to ignore them or not. What we are doing today is preparing the world . . . preparing the people for what is to be a time of great loss."

"You keep talking, but I still don't see how killing a million people and giving a sorcerer this kind of power is preparing the world for anything."

"We did this to them, Remiel," Armaros said. "We steered them down this road to decadence. This will be our chance to make things right, to set them on the path to believing again."

Armaros turned to his brethren, Stearns, and the little girl cowering in her princess bed.

"They will believe in their Creator again, and they shall fear Him as they should. And then they will be prepared for the troubled times to come."

Remy had no idea what to say; it was all so insane. He knew that there were changes in the wind. . . .

But war?

Could he have been so blind?

Stearns cleared his throat, and Remy looked over to see the sorcerer fully adorned in the armored apparatus that would feed him the death energies of those cut down by the Grigori's message. He was tapping a watch on his wrist, urging them to proceed.

"Of course, Algernon Stearns," Armaros said, returning to stand with the other Grigori.

The fallen angel turned his attentions to the little girl partially hidden beneath her covers.

"Are we ready, my child?" he asked her.

"Is God gonna tell you His message?" she asked, peeking out.

The angel nodded and smiled. "He is, and then we are going to tell you . . . and then you will tell the world."

"Armaros," Remy cried out again, hoping that this time . . . maybe.

But he succeeded only in annoying Stearns, who gestured to his security guards, and Remy was forced to his knees, his arms bent unnaturally behind him.

"Make him watch," the sorcerer ordered before turning his attention back to Armaros and the other Grigori.

"Are we ready?" Stearns asked.

"We are," Armaros answered.

The world went deathly quiet. Armaros leaned in toward the small child, his lips dangerously close to her ear, as the remaining Grigori joined hands.

And suddenly all Remy could hear was the whine of the television cameras' auto focus as they fixed the child in their robotic sights.

And the Grigori leader's whispering voice . . .

"Hear the words of the Lord."

*   *   *

The wards of protection cast around the plaza were doing their job.

The vintage car, engine racing like a turbulent ocean surf as it drove at the Hermes Building in a breakneck pace, felt as though it had struck an invisible wall.

The Lincoln came to a screaming halt, the shining chrome bumper and front end of the awesome car buckling. Francis and Angus were like rag dolls in the front seat, whipped viciously forward but prevented from continuing their journey through the broad expanse of windshield by their straining seat belts.

Leona was angry. The living car did not stop for long, its thick tires digging into the brick and spinning wildly, filling the air with the acrid smoke of burning rubber as she moved inexorably forward toward the building.

It was one supernatural force against the other.

The air was filled with so much smoke and noise that Francis had no idea what was truly happening. Angus sat perfectly still, holding on to his seat for dear life as the car bucked and bounced, the sounds of twisting metal like a symphony of destruction in their ears.

This can go one of three ways, Francis thought as he continued to grip the warm wooden steering wheel. Leona could be totally decimated, or the living car could show the wards who was truly queen shit by getting them inside the building, or the two unmovable forces could cause one helluva explosion, leaving Hermes Plaza with a decent-sized crater that could be used as a swimming pool in the summer.

The car began to thrash like a Jack Russell with its fangs buried deep in a rat, giving it that special shake to snap its neck.

There were bursts of fire and the smell of brimstone and the sounds of screaming somewhere off in the distance. For a second Francis believed that the wards had won, that Leona just didn't have what it took to beat the protective spells.

But then her engine began to roar and the tires spun even faster, and Leona lurched forward, seemingly shucking off the destructive effects of the sorcerous handiwork that should have been strong enough to keep them out.

But never underestimate the craftsmanship of demonic ingenuity.

Leona's cries were deafening; it sounded like all the engines of every NASCAR race ever run had been spooled together to create one horrendous clamor. Her spinning tires were finally able to gain purchase, and the vehicle leapt forward, battering through the revolving doors in an explosion of metal and glass.

And as soon as she was inside, her engine died, cutting out with a sputter.

Francis knew that the car had done the nearly impossible and that was all they could expect from her.

"We're in," he said, already swinging open the driver's-side door. Angus moved as he did, extracting his bulk from the vehicle.

Alarms wailed and an artificial rain from the sprinklers fell upon them. Francis could hear scuffling in the smoke and dust and saw movement toward them.

"Trunk!" he yelled, slamming his hand down on the back of the vehicle, and Leona managed one more act for them, popping the trunk and allowing them access to their gear.

Shots rang out, pinging off the open trunk as both Francis and Angus reached inside and readied themselves for the task ahead.

Francis tossed a handful of the walnut-sized grenades first, the explosions of magick canceling out any sorcery that was being used in the lobby. Then he moved around the car, pistol in hand, firing one shot after another, taking out the stunned golem sentries. Angus backed him up, handgun firing from one hand while the other wove powerful new magicks to repel their attackers.

"Do you think the elevators are still working?" Angus asked, waving his hand in a circle and creating a mini twister that spun four of the guards in the air before slamming them into the gray marble wall beside the reception desk.

"Can't see why not," Francis said, firing into the face of a golem whose body exploded in a cloud of dirt.

An engine roar captured his attention, and Francis turned to see Leona, battered and broken, backing out of the lobby.

"Thanks, sweetie!" he called after her. He could see the flashing of police lights outside and hear the sounds of angry voices screaming for the car to stop, but Leona didn't listen. A distraction; something else he'd have to thank her for later.

"Shall we go find Remy?" Francis asked, throwing the weapons-filled duffel bag over his shoulder as he stepped through the open doors of the elevator. He stabbed at the button that would take them up to the studio level, but the door refused to close.

He looked at the pained expression on the sorcerer's face.

"Sorry, Chubs," the former Guardian angel said, leaving the elevator with the dejected Angus in tow.

"Looks like we're using the stairs."

The scared little girl had been replaced.

No longer was a sickly child hiding beneath the covers; now an almost-regal figure sat, back perfectly straight, and spoke directly to the cameras that were pointed at her.

"Hello, my name is Angelina Hayward," she began, a slight distortion to her voice, evidence that the power wielded by the Grigori was flowing through her. "And I am about to deliver unto you a message from the Heavenly Father."

Remy struggled fruitlessly in the grip of the golem sentries, fighting to get to his feet, attempting to find and rekindle even the slightest bit of angelic fire that might have been left by the sorcerer Deacon.

"No!" he screamed, fighting and thrashing, even though

it felt as if his limbs might snap like twigs. "No . . . you can't do this!"

The child was distracted by his outburst, turning her gaze from the camera to him.

"Don't let them make you do this," Remy implored her. "It isn't a message from God; it's something else entirely."

A silent nod from Stearns was all the sentries needed to begin punching Remy with their flesh-covered fists of stone. But over the sounds of his vicious beating, he could hear the child questioning his outburst.

"What does he mean that it isn't a message from God?" she asked.

"Hush, child," Armaros soothed. "Prepare yourself for . . ."

"Hurry!" Stearns bellowed. "We can't afford this distraction. . . . We can't afford to lose any eyes."

"She will speak the words when it is time," the Grigori leader responded in a calm yet threatening tone.

Remy tried to remain conscious, tried to cry out, but the fists were like hammers and he found it harder and harder to keep the darkness at bay.

Maybe oblivion was best right now.

But the thought just enraged him.

The blows continued to fall and suddenly he welcomed them, taking each hurtful strike and using the pain as fuel for his rage. He may not have the divine fire at his beck and call, but it did not change what he was.

Seraphim.

He'd tried to hide it for so very long, so it would not remind him of what he had lost.

Heaven.

Yet it was always there, waiting beneath the veneer of humanity that he had constructed. It had always known what he truly was, even though Remy had liked to think otherwise.

Seraphim.

And of late he had come to accept this, finally understanding that there was no way to ignore his divine nature, no way to ignore the soldier of Heaven that lived beneath his skin.

We are one and the same.

Sometimes he needed a little reminder of that, something to stir the memories of where he'd been . . . where he'd come from . . .

And what I've done.

Remy was a warrior, and he could not even count the number of lives he had extinguished on the battlefields of Heaven in his Creator's name.

Remy remembered who he was—*what I was*—

Warrior. Killer. Murderer of my own kind.

No matter how painful.

He remembered the long-ago past with a surge of anger, the memory of the horrors committed in the name of his master inflaming his blood and summoning a fury that could not be bridled.

In the here and now, he surged to his feet, an inhuman bellow of rage escaping from a place deep within him. He yanked his arm away from one of his attackers, bringing his elbow up into its face before it could grab him again. The force of the blow was tremendous, caving in the artificial man's face and revealing the inhumanity beneath. But the warrior was already on to the next, taking hold of his front, lifting him up from the floor, and hurling his great weight across the room with ease.

The cries of his foes were frantic, the Grigori, clutching their tarnished blades, already on their way to him. The warrior's nature was still in full control, and he searched for a way to defend himself. His eyes fell on the weapon holstered at the waist of a fallen golem guard. Remy dove for the gun, yanking it from its resting place, and started to fire.

Bullets connected with the fallen angels' flesh, driving them back, injuring but not killing the creatures.

Finally he saw the opportunity that he was waiting for, a way to stop this insanity. He saw the little girl sitting up in her princess bed.

Remy aimed the gun . . .

But hesitated.

He knew she wasn't real, nothing more than magick and clay, but at the moment, he saw a little girl. . . .

The magickal blast struck him square, enveloping him in a cocoon of electrical agony. Remy screamed, his body experiencing pain down to a cellular level.

Stearns stood there, arm outstretched, magick streaming from his fingertips.

"I've had just about enough of you," the sorcerer said, casting him off to float above the room in a bubble of torment. What made it all the worse was that Remy could still see, watching it all through tears of agony.

And there wasn't a goddamn thing he could do about it.

Stearns felt himself growing weaker as the terrible hunger intensified. It was as if his altered body knew of the coming feast and was purposely expending vast amounts of magickal energy so that it would be fed all the quicker.

Holding the troublesome spectator aloft, Stearns decided he must take the bull by the horns if this procedure was to commence in a timely fashion.

"Armaros," he bellowed, while motioning to those who served him in the control room above the studio. "If you would be so kind as to continue."

The injured Grigori, clutching their bleeding wounds, returned to their master's side. Armaros glared at him, but returned to the child, who appeared to be in shock, cowering on the bed. He stroked her hair, whispering something that Stearns could not quite hear, but her back straightened and her eyes suddenly stared straight ahead as the cameras came to life, ready to capture the message she was about to herald.

Stearns saw that it was actually about to happen, and double-checked the attachments that would bring him the power he so desperately craved.

And then his eyes went to the man held within a sphere of magickal power, hanging above the studio floor, his body racked with pain that should have rendered him lifeless, but somehow he remained conscious, staring with eyes absent of hope.

"Hear the words of the Lord," Angelina Hayward proclaimed as the angels of the Grigori leaned toward her, filling her ears with their message.

The child grew suddenly statue tense and her eyes began to glow as if an inner light had come alive. She opened her mouth and light streamed out, but there was also a sound the likes of which Algernon Stearns had never before heard.

It was the saddest of songs.

A lament of the past, but also of the future.

And as the first notes of the song began—the first words of a divine message whose meaning meant only death, the first strains of power began to flow into the child and into the machines beneath the bed.

And Algernon Stearns truly understood the meaning of the word *God*.

If only for an instant.

Steven Mulvehill had been raised Roman Catholic.

As a child, and even into his late teens, he had attended Mass every Sunday, had gone to Sunday school, had received all the blessed sacraments, and had even been married in the Catholic Church.

But he'd never really thought of himself as a believer. He went through all the motions but could never truly commit to the idea of a guiding force in the universe, especially since he was a homicide cop, especially after all the badness he had seen.

How could there be any supernatural guidance with the kinds of things he saw going on every hour of the day, and not even just in his city, but all over the world?

It all seemed so terrible . . . so cruel.

So the older he got, the less he went through the motions, and the further he drifted away from the faith he had practiced since childhood.

Then he met Remy Chandler and he learned that there actually *was* a powerful force out there in the universe, a Creator of all things; that there really were such things as angels and devils, Heaven and Hell. And one would think that after all those years of wondering—questioning a faith that had been part of his life since he was old enough to walk—that would have meant something special to him.

It's true. It's all true.

Yet all it did was make him afraid.

Steven had been enticed by the world that Remy Chandler had hinted at, but he'd managed to keep it at arm's length. He didn't want to know because he wasn't sure he could handle the truth.

And the verdict was in: He couldn't. It was too much for his little human mind to wrap itself around.

Now he couldn't even bring himself to talk to his friend or go out into a world that he now knew was vastly different and far more dangerous than he could ever hope to realize.

It terrified him, and that fear made him angry.

It made him angry that he had not yet gone back to work, that he had sustained injuries in his confrontation with something not of this world, something from a world that Remy Chandler, up until then, had kept him safe from, something that had almost killed him.

Something that had pulled back the curtain and forced him to look at a world that he did not want to know about.

And now he hid, locked inside his apartment, venturing outside only to buy the bare essentials—cigarettes, whiskey, microwave dinners—dreading when he would run out of something and have to venture into the world again.

Mulvehill was disgusted with himself, but it did not make the fear go away.

He guessed he was looking for some sort of answer, something that would tell him that everything was going to be all right, which explained why he found himself sitting in front of the television set in the middle of the afternoon, waiting to hear a little girl speak a message that she was supposedly getting from the Big Guy Upstairs.

There had been some sort of technical difficulties and the newscasters were wasting time until things were up and running again. He'd heard all about the little girl and how she'd been in a coma for years, until a few weeks ago when she unexpectedly awoke and started talking about how God was going to speak through her.

He remembered the Steven Mulvehill of a few months back, and how he would have scoffed at something like this, but after seeing what he'd seen—experiencing what he had—maybe God really did have something to say to the world.

And maybe it would be enough to give him the courage to leave the house again and get on with his life.

He'd gone to the kitchen to get some more ice for his second whiskey of the afternoon when he heard one of the newscasters say that they were returning to little Angelina. Mulvehill plucked three cubes from the tray in the freezer and hurried back to the living room.

Sitting down on his sofa, he reached for the bottle of Seagram's and was just about to pour two fingers into the glass when his eyes touched on the screen.

The little girl's face filled the television, and he was nearly brought to tears by the beauty of her. He couldn't have pulled his eyes from her even if he had wanted to; it was almost as if she had gone inside his head, the message she was about to speak spoken only to him.

One after another, the Grigori drew their weapons.

The receiver was ready, open to broadcast her message—*their message*—to the waiting faithful.

Armaros gazed around the studio one final time, taking in the last sights he would see before his tortured existence was finally brought to a close.

The sorcerer stood ready, a look of euphoria on his face as he awaited the flow of death energy. And the pained expression of the Seraphim, Remy Chandler, imprisoned within a sphere of magick—he could see the terror in the angel's eyes.

"It is for the good of them all," Armaros proclaimed, positioning the tarnished blade above his heart.

"Don't do it!" Remy managed, but it was too late for Armaros and his followers to be persuaded otherwise.

Now the Grigori would deliver their message. *The Lord God is watching and He is very disappointed in what humans have become.* But with their sacrifice, the human race still had a chance to reach its full potential.

"Brothers," Armaros said, addressing the others of his host. They, too, held their blades, poised to strike, ready to end their lives in a flash of brilliance—a flash that would touch those who were watching and listening.

A flash that would end the Grigori's lives and the lives of those waiting to hear Heaven's message.

"The curtain falls."

And with those words, the Grigori plunged the knives into their chests, piercing their hearts.

Their final message, their final cries flowing into the child, and from her . . .

Out into the world.

Rita Dollans moved her wheelchair closer to the television screen so that she could see. Her body had been racked with rheumatoid arthritis for years and she had great difficulty getting the chair precisely where she wanted it, but she managed.

And now she eagerly waited to hear what the Lord had to say.

Denise Kelleher cradled her crying infant in her arms, rocking him ever so gently. She wanted to hear the message, and as she bent forward to pick up the remote from the coffee table, as the little girl's face filled the screen, and the child prepared to speak . . .

Her baby went quiet.

Almost as if he wanted to hear the message, too.

Dillon Ratner looked at his watch as he sat in the waiting room of the Toyota dealership. He'd been there for well over two hours. He'd brought a book and had read several chapters, but was now tired of reading and tired of waiting.

He was about to get up and check on the progress of his Camry when he noticed how quiet it had become in the dealership, everyone around him transfixed to the image of a little girl on the sixty-inch flat screen that hung on the wall.

Curious, he reached up, pulling the headphones that were attached to his iPhone from his ears.

And was assailed by the message.

The message had started to crawl into Peter Vestmore's mind. He hadn't any intention of even listening to the sickly looking kid, wanting instead to check on an eBay bid he'd made for an original *The Good, the Bad and the Ugly* movie poster, but there was something in the little girl's eyes, something in the strange, foreign words that she was speaking.

Something that made him start to scream and the blood begin to gush from his nose, now that he had looked.

Unable to look away.

And the message of the dying Grigori poured out over the ether, transmitted through the child and into a digital signal picked up by Algernon Stearns' cameras, broadcast to a waiting world.

The message reached out to those who were watching and listening, grabbing them in a steely grip, as it started to fill their brains with the sad lament of the Grigori's passing.

And all who saw and heard this mournful dirge were touched as they had never been touched before.

CHAPTER TWENTY-FOUR

Even trapped within the sphere of magickal energy, Remy could feel what was happening.

He could feel the Grigori dying, their life energies leaking out of their bodies, their psychic communication—their terrorist act against an unsuspecting public—flowing from their dying minds and into the child-shaped golem and out across the ether.

It was the most horrible thing that he had ever seen, and he had seen much on this world since he'd decided to walk it.

The child had begun to speak. . . .

The machines beneath her bed had started to hum ominously, gauges and dials illuminated as the first inklings of death energy began to flow.

The sorcerer gasped at his first taste, face twisted in ecstasy as the trickle of accumulated life force was delivered. His exoskeleton sparked and glowed with unearthly power, the hum of the great machines growing louder and louder, like a hive of angry bees.

Remy again attempted to summon what strength that he could, pushing against his magickal confines in the hopes that he might free himself to do something—*anything*—to prevent this travesty.

The magick struck him down once more, like the crack

of a million whips on his nervous system. The pain was everywhere, and he dropped back to the floor of the energy sphere that held him aloft.

He lay on his stomach, too weak to rise, waiting, when he noticed something.

It was the flicker of lights that caught his attention.

Remy watched the figures in the control booth start to scramble. He perked up, watching, waiting for what could be an opportunity.

The lights went dim again, the hum and pulse of the machinery beneath the child's bed sounding a bit strained as its flow of power began to be tested.

It's the power, Remy thought, pushing himself up into a sitting position. Something was straining the electricity to the building—to the studio.

The look on Stearns' face was priceless: ecstasy replaced with shocked surprise, blending into absolute rage. If Remy hadn't felt like a hundred miles of bad road, he would have laughed.

"What's happening?" Stearns screamed over the labored hum of the infernal machines. He looked to the control room. The PA crackled that the entire building was experiencing some weird power fluctuations and that they were looking to fixing it.

"Fix it now!" Stearns shrieked, as the lights grew dim and the robotic cameras ceased to function.

And when the cameras stopped, so did the deadly Grigori transmission and so did death.

The room went completely dark and stayed that way, a sudden silence like a death pall falling over the room. Something was happening, more than just a power failure, and Remy hadn't a clue as to what it was. And from the looks of it, neither did Stearns.

"What is this?" Stearns demanded. He lumbered over to the Grigori, who had dropped to their knees, blood pooling beneath them. Remy could see that they were somehow still alive, but just barely.

"What is happening?" Stearns screeched, reaching out

with a gauntleted hand to grip the shoulder of Armaros. The angel was too weak to speak, tumbling onto his side as the room began to quake.

Dust rained down from above; loose tiles dropped from the ceiling. Remy could feel a change in the air, a sudden drop in the temperature and air pressure that made his ears ache.

"You!" Stearns screamed, pointing one of his armored fingers at him. "This has something to do with you. Doesn't it?"

Remy wished that he could take the credit, but he barely had the strength to stand, never mind being behind whatever this was. Stearns reached up with his other hand, manipulating the sorcerous energies that surrounded Remy, shattering the sphere and letting him drop to the floor.

"You will stop it this instant," Stearns warned, his metal-clad feet stomping across the floor toward him. He grabbed Remy by the front of his shirt and hauled him to his feet. "Do you realize how much is at stake?" Stearns bellowed, shaking him.

Remy couldn't help but smile. "Was at stake," he corrected.

He watched Stearns' face twist with rage and he figured that he just might not survive what was sure to follow when the building around them shook with so much force that the sound of shattering glass could be heard drifting inside the soundproof room from outside.

Stearns lost his balance, releasing Remy as he fell.

Remy landed atop some broken ceiling tiles; the room continued to shimmy and shake beneath him. If they were in Los Angeles, he might have believed that the big one had finally arrived, but this was Boston.

Stearns lurched around the studio, desperate to salvage something from the events that were unfolding. He went to the child sitting on the bed. It was as if she had been frozen in time, her body rigid, eyes fixed to where the cameras had been focused on her.

Stearns started to disconnect himself from the machines, attempting to detach the cables that would have fed him the precious life energies as they'd flowed through the child.

Remy managed to rise to his knees, his body now more numb than pained, fooling him into thinking that he was better off than he actually was. Holding on to the corner of a small desk, he stood, swaying from side to side as the building did the same.

Glancing up, he saw that Stearns' technicians were still running about, trying to fix the situation, but Remy doubted a solution was forthcoming.

At first he thought it was a trick of his eyes, a lingering effect of Stearns' sorcery, but he soon came to realize it was more than that. There was something wrong with the shadows in the room, puddles of darkness expanding like liquid as the building violently shook again.

Stearns had frozen as he knelt before his damnable machine, and that was when Remy began to feel it.

This was more than a mere temperature shift or a change in air pressure. The air had become incredibly heavy as the darkness became even thicker, darker even than darkness should be. . . .

And Remy found himself thinking of a world composed entirely of shadow, a world he had visited not too long ago, a world that still held a dear friend.

A world he had every intention of returning to once he was able.

The darkness had become all-encompassing, every existing speck of light swallowed up by the hungry dark. It was even getting difficult to breathe. An attempt to summon even the slightest hint of angelic fire, to throw some light within the studio, met with total failure as the air grew heavier.

The silence had become almost deafening. And then the room seemed to explode, the very structure of the place tearing itself apart as Remy was thrown into the air by the disintegrating environment.

The atmosphere of the room felt suddenly different, and

as he again attempted to get back on his feet he found that the floor of the studio had become dramatically uneven, with what appeared to be metal girders rising through the floor. It was almost as if the building had been twisted by the hands of some unspeakable force.

Through the thick clouds of swirling dust, Remy saw the hint of light, an unearthly glow that drew him toward it. The unknown source illuminated the twisted remains of the studio, showing a place that no longer resembled the room it had been mere minutes ago. Remy wasn't quite sure what he was bearing witness to, but it was as if another space—another room entirely—had somehow been crammed into the studio.

The little girl's bed had been mercilessly tossed across the room by the traumatic upheaval, and Remy found the golem child curled in a ball on the floor. He knelt down beside her, pulling her into his arms. She was crying, as a small child would, and he could not help but comfort her.

"I don't understand," she kept repeating over and over, and Remy shared her confusion.

Kneeling on the floor, he saw now that the glow was coming from beneath a set of double doors that hung strangely askew at the top of a set of broken stone steps. Stearns stood at the bottom of those steps and started to climb.

It was when the doors came suddenly open, flying from their hinges in an explosion of light and sound, that Remy realized what he was looking at. He knew these doors and the broken stone steps that led up to them.

A striking figure stood just inside the doorway, his body glowing in its efforts to contain the power that was now housed within it, a power that Remy had known intimately, for it had belonged to him for many millennia.

Konrad Deacon stood in the entryway to his home, glaring at Algernon Stearns, who lay upon his armored back like a turtle unable to right himself.

"Hello, Algernon," Deacon said, wings of fire unfurling. "It's been a long, long time."

*   *   *

They had temporarily stopped in the stairway, Angus needing a quick breather, before continuing on up to the television studio, when the building started to shake.

"Okay," Francis said as the lighting flickered.

The temperature dramatically plummeted, and Francis was nearly overwhelmed with an odd sensation reminiscent of dropping down in an elevator.

"Did you feel that?" Francis asked.

"Yes," Angus said, in between heavy breaths as the hallway went entirely to darkness. "And it isn't anything normal."

A dancing orange flame suddenly appeared, hovering above Angus' outstretched palm, shedding some light in the stairway.

The building was rocking, a powerful vibration moving through the stairs and the metal handrail beneath their grips.

"Earthquake?" Francis suggested.

"Worse," Angus answered, as cracks began to appear in the wall. "Much worse."

And then they heard it from somewhere in the stairwell below them: a horrible roar unrecognizable to anything that existed in this world.

"I'm guessing that's part of the problem you're talking about?"

"A part," Angus said. "We might want to get out of this stairwell as quickly as possible," the sorcerer suggested as they listened to the new sounds of something large and growling dragging its considerable weight up the concrete stairs.

The light from the hovering flame showed them that they were near an entrance to one of the upper floors, and Francis darted toward it, pulling open the door.

What they found on that particular floor was not at all what they had expected.

"What the fuck is this?" Francis asked, totally taken aback. It looked as though they were in the hallway of some great old mansion run through a fun-house mirror. Everything was skewed to a bizarre angle.

"It's what I suspected," Angus said, moving the flame around to pierce the darkness so that they could better see their environment.

"Which is?"

"We're no longer in Stearns' building," the sorcerer said.

"What the fuck are you talking about, we're no longer in the building?"

"Right now we're no longer inside the building," the sorcerer repeated. "Outside that door, yes, we're in the building. . . . Down the staircase a floor, where we heard the unnatural sounds . . . probably not."

"You've fucking lost me," Francis said.

"Don't ask me how," Angus started to explain. "But I believe that Konrad Deacon has returned, and in doing so has somehow transferred his estate back to this realm, occupying the same space as Stearns' office building."

"So the two are sort of smooshed together," Francis asked, eyes darting around the corridor. He slowly removed the Pitiless pistol from within his jacket.

"If you want to be scientific," Angus responded.

The shadows in the hall appeared to be moving, shifting, flowing along the walls and floor. There were sounds coming from the ever-expanding pools of blackness.

"Anything to say about that?" Francis asked, watching the flowing darkness.

"Nothing other than it appears as though some of the shadow world where Deacon has been living seems to have leaked through along with his house."

"That can't be good," Francis said, watching something large and covered with black spines erupt from the shadow pool, leaping from one body of darkness to disappear into another.

"It's not good at all," Angus agreed, his fingers beginning to crackle with defensive magick. "Especially if it's still leaking."

"Leaking is never good."

"No."

Francis felt what little hair he had left on the back of his neck suddenly stand straight on end. He didn't have time to utter a warning or to tell Angus to get away; the former Guardian angel just reacted, spinning around and firing at the large, serpentine shape that had silently risen from a body of shadow that had formed behind them.

The pistol roared angrily, a seemingly endless supply of bullets entering the thick, trunklike body of the snakelike thing that appeared to be molded from tar. Seemingly unfazed by the gunshots, the creature lunged, its cavernous maw open to consume at least one, or maybe even both, if it were lucky. Francis dove from its path, continuing to fire into the serpent's shiny black face.

Angus clothed himself in a shield of crackling blue energy. The monster's snout struck the obstruction violently and made its already sunny disposition all the more pleasant. Frustrated, the serpent reared back, opening its mouth wider, its jaws unhinging as if getting ready to swallow an egg.

The gunshots weren't helping matters, and Francis slipped the pistol back inside his jacket and went through his duffel bag of weapons in the hopes of finding something that could damage the beast of shadow.

The serpent clamped down upon Angus' bubble, its curved obsidian fangs actually penetrating the energy sphere. It pulled back savagely, dragging the bubble, and Angus with it, toward the body of liquid darkness from where it had originated.

Francis found an ornate short sword and lunged at the beast. It was probably only supposed to be used for special rituals, but beggars couldn't be choosers, and he swung the sword with all his might. The razor's edge bit deeply into the oily black flesh of the monster, but it failed to slow its progress. With horror, Francis watched as the serpent disappeared back into the bubbling liquid pitch, dragging the energy sphere, with the screaming Angus inside, down beneath the shadow.

At the edge, Francis looked down into the still surface, not a ripple showing what had just transpired. He considered diving into the pool in search of the sorcerer, but decided against it. He didn't like the sorcerer that much, and, besides, he suspected that Angus had already met a nasty fate.

He stepped away from the edge, not wanting any surprises. There were strange noises coming from other patches of expanding shadow all around him, and he figured it would probably be in his best interest to get the fuck out of there and try to find another section of the office building that didn't have a leaking problem.

Turning his back, he returned to the duffel, tossing the short sword back inside, and was just about to take hold of the handles when he again sensed something happening behind him.

Francis barely had time to turn as the great serpent surged up from the lake of darkness, a shriek of ferocity escaping from its cavernous mouth. Leaving the duffel, Francis leapt toward the corridor in front of him, evading puddles of darkness that littered the floor as he ran. He chanced a quick glance over his shoulder and was shocked to see the upper trunk of the shadow beast pitch forward, landing heavily on the floor outside the pool to lie perfectly still.

Hesitating, he watched the thing. The serpent appeared dead, and Francis had to wonder if eating Angus had somehow poisoned it. He stepped closer to the dead monster to retrieve his bag of weapons when he saw movement ahead—not from the shadow beast, but from the now bubbling pool.

What the fuck now? the Guardian angel wondered, dashing ahead to quickly snatch up his bag and get as far away as he could before some other nightmare emerged.

And something did rise from the tarlike body of liquid, coughing and sputtering as it reached to grab hold of the edge of the floor. It was Angus, but there was something bubbling up from below behind him.

"Angus!" Francis cried out, pulling his pistol as the

other shape and another behind that one swam up behind the sorcerer, helping to push him from the pool.

"Put that fucking thing away," said a voice that was vaguely familiar to him.

Francis came forward and bent down to grab hold of Angus' arm and pull him from the sucking blackness, careful not to fall in himself.

"Nice to see you again," Francis said. "Didn't think you'd made it."

The sorcerer coughed, spitting filth from his mouth. "Wouldn't have . . . if . . . if it wasn't for them."

Two more figures had crawled out of the black lake, a smaller, stockier form helping the thinner, more petite.

It didn't take Francis long to recognize the goblin that had brought Remy back from the shadow realm and the teenage girl that Remy had been so desperate to save.

"Are you responsible for that?" Francis asked, as the goblin walked over to the dead serpent, brushing off the clinging remnants of liquid shadow from his clothes. The goblin squatted down and with a grunt rolled the massive body of the snake over. There was a nasty-looking knife blade protruding from its lower body.

"Yep," the goblin said, removing the blade and letting the body flop back heavily to the floor. He wiped the thing's black blood on the leg of his pants.

"Impressive," Francis said.

"Thanks."

The goblin went to stand beside the girl, who was peeling away the darkness that clung to her, flicking it onto the floor. There was a look in her eyes, something that probably hadn't been there before all this, when she was just Remy's neighbor, looking after his dog.

"You all right?" Francis asked her.

She just stared at him with those intense eyes. Eyes that had seen so much in such a short period of time.

"Ashley, right?" Francis said, positive that this time she was the real thing and not some artificial life-form created from magick and clay.

She nodded quickly. "Do I know you?"

"No, but you know my friend . . . Remy."

"Remy," she said.

"Yeah. I'm going to take you to him, all right?" Francis said.

Ashley nodded again. "Remy will take me home," she said, a hint of hope in her voice.

"That's the plan," Francis said, his mind already on to the next obstacle.

It wasn't going to be easy.

The two sorcerers stared at each other for what seemed like an eternity, but it was Stearns who blinked first.

Remy watched as the exoskeletoned Stearns uttered some guttural spell, casting a wave of destructive power toward his opponent. Reacting instinctively, Remy threw his body over that of the little girl, shielding her from the devastating repercussions that were sure to follow.

From the corner of his eye, Remy watched as Deacon cast his own spell, a shield of protection that deflected the magickal outburst from Stearns toward the ceiling with catastrophic results.

There was a cacophonous rush of air as the ceiling of the skyscraper exploded in a shower of rubble, glass, and steel. Remy could not help but turn his gaze to the nightmare unfolding above him, coming to the sickening realization that things were even worse than he suspected.

He'd pictured the wreckage of the skyscraper rooftop plummeting to the streets of Boston below, never imagining that the rubble wouldn't get the chance to fall. In the dark and tempestuous sky above him, there was a black and swirling whirlpool; a spinning hole in the fabric of reality, sucking up the pieces of refuse blown into the air by the deflection of Stearns' magickal attack.

"Dear God," Remy uttered. He could feel the pull of the vortex, and knew without a doubt where it had originated. Somehow by coming here, Deacon had created some sort of opening—a breach between the shadow realm and the world outside it.

It was Deacon's turn to attack now, the fires of the divine flowing from his outstretched hands to incinerate Stearns below. Remy could feel the power move as it flowed from the air, hungry to consume its adversary, a familiar tugging at the core of his being for the divine might that once was his.

Stearns awkwardly leapt from the path of the hungry fire, already unleashing another magickal attack on his adversary. Explosions of supernatural energies were decimating what remained of the television studio, and Remy knew that it wouldn't be long until he and the child were left exposed and helpless.

"We have to get out of here," he told her over the near-deafening sounds of a sorcerers' duel. The child began to protest as Remy bent down to lift her, and he was startled by what he saw. A section of wall had fallen on the child's lower body, the injuries exposing the truth about her.

"Leave me here," she said, attempting to push him away.

Though her lower body was revealed to be made from clay, Remy saw genuine pain in the artificial child's eyes then, and it moved him to not even consider her request.

He tossed the section of wall away and lifted her up from the ground, the pull on him from the swirling maelstrom in the sky above becoming stronger. It was something he didn't even want to consider, but he could feel the dark dimension tugging on his clothes as he made his way across the pieces of rubble, toward where he remembered the door leading into the studio had been.

"I'm going to take you someplace safe and . . ."

"And then?" Angelina asked, her voice frightfully soft over the sounds of magickal conflict going on behind them.

"Don't you worry about that," Remy said, finding the twisted remains of the staircase that would bring them down to the level below the studio.

"I would have killed them," Angelina said into his ear as he carefully descended the broken steps.

On the next level, he found a safe place to set her down beneath a section of ceiling that still appeared relatively intact.

"Don't think of that now," he said, gently leaning her back against a section of wall.

"If the attack hadn't come, I would have killed everyone who was watching and listening to me," she said.

He didn't argue, knowing that what she said was indeed the truth.

"I knew that something was wrong when I felt them—the angels—inside my head." The little child paused, eyes welling with tears. "They were hurting so bad," she said. "And they actually believed that their hurt could make things better."

Something exploded above them, plaster dust raining down on them like a fog.

"But we don't have to worry about that now," Remy told her. "I have to go," he started to explain. "But I want you to stay here and be safe until . . ."

"Until," she said.

"I have to try to do something," he told her.

She smiled at him, tears running down her filthy cheeks. She lifted a hand and placed it on his face.

"You're special, aren't you?" she said. "You're like them . . . the angels. But instead of sadness, you're filled with hope."

He tried to leave her, but for some reason couldn't.

"I can feel something inside you," she said, still touching him. "Something buried so very deep . . . It wants to come out, but it's hurt . . . weak."

The entire building was shaking again, the fight above intensifying. He had no idea what the two sorcerers were capable of; it was a distinct possibility that the city could be destroyed as a result of their confrontation.

He took her hand and started to pull it away.

"I need to go, Angelina," he told her.

"I have some of their life still inside me," she said.

Remy didn't understand.

"When I began the angels' message, some of those who were listening passed away, and their life energies were passed into me," the golem child said.

"Didn't Stearns . . ."

"He received some, but not all. When the power went out, for a little bit, there was still energy flowing into me."

"I don't understand what that has to do with me," Remy told her.

"I can use that power. . . . I can wake it up," she said.

Remy cocked his head, still unsure where this was going.

"The thing inside you," the child said. She pulled her hand from his, laying it flat against his chest. "I can give it the strength it needs . . . the strength *you* need . . ."

"What are you . . ." Remy started to ask, as a surge of something entered his chest.

He cried out, falling backward as something exploded inside him. He lay in the rubble-strewn hallway, the sound of magickal conflagration happening all around, and felt the fires surge inside him.

"What did you do?" he croaked, his body now racked with incredible pain as the spark of the Seraphim surged hungrily to life.

"I've given it what it needs," the child said, barely able to keep her eyes open, her head lolling to one side. Her skin had taken on a sickly gray pallor, more like cold stone—or wet clay—than flesh.

Fire trailed from Remy's fingertips, but it was a fire the likes of which he had never known. It was a fire fed by life, and it burned hotter and faster than the divine fire that had been stolen from him. It filled his mind with the experiences of thousands, pieces of their lives; moments of tenderness, joy, hope, fear, misery, and sadness. All these were now his, part of the fire that fed his angelic nature, making it drunk on the life forces of thousands.

It took everything that Remy still had to keep his power

in check; it wanted to explode from him, to wreak vengeance on those who had humbled it so. It wanted to make them all pay.

And while it was at it, it would make the world pay.

"No," Remy roared, flexing the muscle of his will. He had finally unified his dual natures and was not about to let that of the Seraphim rip free now, no matter how much this new power desired to do so.

Remy had fought too hard to make this so.

Angelina looked even worse than she had before, her once-beautiful dark hair now dried and brittle like straw and falling from her head as the life left her.

"It will soon be dark for me again," she said, withered hands playing feebly with a clump of hair that had fallen into her lap.

Remy breathed in and out, holding on to the power—to the myriad emotions that threatened to push him over the edge.

"But that's all right," she told him. "As long as we were able to stop this. . . ."

The building violently shook, dust and pieces of ceiling raining down, as the shadows around them unnaturally started to expand.

"As long as *you* are able to stop this."

He felt compelled to hold her as life ran out, and he knelt down amid the rubble and put his arms around her.

"The angels' message was a lie," she told him sleepily. "But I heard another."

Remy looked down at the artificial child, startled to see that her childlike features were now completely gone. It was like he was looking at the beginning of a clay sculpture, the rudimentary shape implying that it would soon resemble the human form.

"There was another message," Angelina said, a blocky hand of clay now reaching up to rest on his shoulder. "And I think it really was from Him . . . from God."

Remy was silent, feeling nothing but sadness as this special life-form readied to leave the world.

"And He told me what to do," she whispered softly. Eyes that were little more than dark impressions in the clay but still somehow able to convey emotion gazed up at him.

"He told me to give it to you," she said. "To give you the power . . . that you would know . . ."

The child went quiet then, and he knew that she was no longer with him. Gently he set the primitive clay shape dressed in a little girl's pajamas down on the ground, showing as much tenderness as he would have shown any once-living thing that had just sacrificed so very much.

The battle continued to rage on the floor above as well as inside him. The Seraphim inebriated on the sustenance of life wanted to join the fray, to smite the wicked for what they had done.

But the Seraphim was blind to the true strength of the power it would be up against, power that easily rivaled its own. He needed to be careful in how he dealt with this.

Leaving the child's body to the encroaching shadows, he climbed the broken steps toward the battlefield, Angelina's final words echoing at the forefront of his mind.

He told me to give it to you . . . that you would know.

As Remy reached the studio floor and witnessed the terror that was unfolding there, he hoped that the child's faith in him . . . that *His* faith in him was not in vain.

CHAPTER TWENTY-FIVE

He hadn't expected to wake up facedown on his living room floor, the droning sound of a television test signal buzzing in his ears.

Steven Mulvehill rolled onto his back and sat up, a wave of dizziness and intense nausea almost putting him down again. As he sat there, he felt a tightness on the skin beneath his nose and carefully brought his fingers there to find a wet, tacky substance that was revealed to be drying blood.

"What the fuck?" he muttered. Sure that the swimming in his head had passed, he attempted to stand. Swaying slightly, he stared at the television screen and at the message displayed there: *We are temporarily experiencing technical difficulties. Thank you for your patience!*

He remembered the child on the TV and how she had begun to speak, and then he remembered nothing. In his gut he knew that she—the child—had something to do with what had happened.

Mulvehill walked drunkenly from the living room into the kitchen, tearing off a sheet of paper towel and sticking it beneath the faucet to wet it. He wiped the drying blood from beneath his nose. The droning alarm of technical difficulties was replaced with the sound of voices, and he returned to the living room to see if there was any explanation for what had just occurred.

There was only one anchorperson now, and she looked a little worse for wear, her blouse and normally perfectly coiffed hair disheveled. He had to wonder if the same thing that had happened to him, had happened there in the studio. In the back of his mind he remembered a story about a Japanese television broadcast of some cartoon show that had triggered seizures in many of those who had been watching.

Has something like that happened here? he wondered.

He caught the tail end of the anchor's explanation about losing the signal from Angelina's broadcast, but she then began to talk about breaking news: There was an emergency being reported at the Hermes Plaza, where the child had been delivering her message.

Mulvehill was riveted in place, standing in the center of the living room as a live shot filled the screen. It was an aerial view of the Plaza, the focus on the smoldering upper floor of the Hermes office building. Mulvehill gasped at the sight, his mind already trying to fill in all the gaps of what could possibly have happened. Through the smoke he could see the twisted wreckage of the rooftop, girders bent by some powerful force sticking up through the thick, billowing smoke. Mulvehill found himself moving closer to the television screen, trying to make out what was happening through the smoke. There was a sudden flash behind a billowing gray cloud and the rumble of what could have been an explosion. The picture suddenly went to hissing static, the signal from the helicopter's camera failing.

But not before he saw something that turned his blood to ice.

Smoke was pouring out from many of the Hermes Building's shattered windows, but there was also something else. At first glance it could have been mistaken as smoke, thick and black, but Mulvehill noticed that it hadn't moved the way it should have. Just as the image had gone to static, Steven Mulvehill saw the strange blackness flow out from one of the windows, dripping down the front almost like wax from a melting candle.

It wasn't natural, and he felt that familiar surge of panic come upon him as he remembered his experiences of late. He looked toward his living room windows at the sun shining outside his Somerville apartment, and he could have sworn that he heard screaming.

Mulvehill closed his eyes and saw the darkness running down from the skyscraper, slithering like a thing alive.

The disheveled anchor had returned, talking about what they believed was happening down in the Copley Square area, that the Hermes Plaza had been cordoned off by the fire department and police, and that they were still trying to determine whether this was an accident or something of a more malicious nature.

He had turned off the TV before he even realized that he was doing it. His hands were shaking, and he craved a drink like never before.

It would be so easy to put a stop to these feelings, he thought. A few quick gulps of whiskey would do the trick nicely. He already imagined the warm sensation in his belly as the booze took effect.

But it didn't change the fact of what was happening at the Hermes Plaza.

He'd seen it on the television, and now, as much as he'd like to, he couldn't un-see it.

What happened to me is now going to happen to others, he thought, imagining the darkness as it spread down Boylston Street, doing God knew what to whoever it encountered.

Mulvehill was terrified, but he had been terrified since his collision with the supernatural more than two weeks ago.

There was a moment of temptation where he almost picked up the phone to call his friend, to call Remy Chandler to ask him if he'd seen the news, but he managed to stop himself.

As far as he knew, this wasn't about Remy. It was about him and the world he lived in, a once-secret world that from what he had just seen on the television was no longer hiding.

Hiding.

Mulvehill knew that this was what he had been doing: hiding himself away from the reality of it all, hoping that it wouldn't come for him again.

He was still scared but he was also angry, which was a good thing, because he was finally feeling something more than overwhelming fear. Mulvehill embraced the anger, fueling it with the shame he felt over hiding away in his apartment.

He knew the fear would kill him if he let it, slowly eating him away, making it so that he would be forced to leave the job that he loved. For how could he be a cop if he was afraid of what could be around every corner, hiding in every shadow?

The image of the darkness as it poured from the sky-scraper came into his thoughts again, followed by a surge of panic, but he pushed it down beneath the fire of anger he continued to stoke.

What's happening at Hermes Plaza? he wondered with equal parts fear and intense curiosity. He thought of others like him, before he'd learned the truth about the world— *the real world*—and experienced a surprising urge.

Mulvehill left the living room, entering his bedroom and going to the dresser in the far corner. Pulling open the bottom drawer, he rooted around beneath a stack of old sweatshirts for the cigar box he kept there. Opening the lid, he looked at the old service revolver, something he had kept as a backup weapon since first making detective. In the drawer there was also a box of ammunition, and he loaded the gun.

For what he was about to do, he thought that he might need some protection, and hoped that bullets fired from a gun would be enough.

He grabbed his jacket from the back of his closet door, shoved the loaded handgun into his pocket, and headed for the door.

Before he lost his courage.

*   *   *

Algernon Stearns wasn't quite sure, but didn't think he had ever seen anything so magnificent that filled him with so much rage.

A blast of fire so hot that it started to melt the metal of the apparatus he wore sprang from the fingertips of his foe. A quickly erected spell of shielding was the only thing that prevented him from becoming nothing more than smoldering ash on the studio floor.

He conjured his own offense, casting the spell at the sorcerer who appeared to be wielding power of some divine origin.

There had always been a part of him that suspected that Konrad Deacon had survived the cabal's betrayal of him, that the sorcerer had gone off someplace to hide and lick his wounds, but Stearns never imagined him returning in such a way.

Commanding a level of power that practically made Stearns' mouth—*mouths*—water.

He felt the hungry orifices on his hands open up, eager to feed upon the unimaginable power now in the control of his enemy.

Where did he go? And how did he come to possess a power this great? Stearns wanted to know as he evaded another rush of unearthly flame that scoured the rubble-strewn ground where he'd been standing.

The exoskeleton was still functioning on a reserve-battery charge, a precaution that he'd enacted when considering how important this operation was and how many things could possibly go wrong. Hiding behind a crumpled section of soundproofed wall, the sorcerer adjusted the suit's functions to allow him to collect and utilize some of the energies that were now being cast at him.

"Are you hiding from me, Algernon?" Deacon asked, a sickening tone of superiority dripping from his words.

Stearns waited, wanting to be certain that the suit was functioning properly before reentering the fray. Seeing that everything appeared to be in working order, he uttered a spell of destruction, felt the magick of murder collect in his hands, and emerged from hiding, throwing the death spell with the controlled precision of the murderer he was.

"Hiding, Konrad?" Stearns asked, the magick leaving his possession in the form of a humming ball of roiling energy. "It appears your time away has certainly bolstered your confidence."

One of Deacon's fiery wings folded down to block the spell. The magick detonated just in front of its target, but its effect was still devastating, shrapnel of pure magickal force peppering the air and slicing into his body.

"What was that, Konrad?" Stearns asked, striking while the iron was hot. He unleashed another blast of concentrated magick, blowing away part of the floor beneath Deacon's feet, causing him to stumble. Stearns watched as Deacon attempted to recover, imagining the death magick from the shards protruding from his foe's skin already starting to permeate his blood, weakening him from within.

"Was that a scream? Don't tell me that even with all that power you've managed to acquire, you're still no more of a threat than a child."

Stearns came in closer, a corruption spell now encircling his fist. He brought that fist down, connecting with Deacon's face and driving him to his knees.

He was stepping in for another strike when Deacon retaliated. His wings of fire exploded to life, flapping wildly and flicking globules of divine fire.

Stearns was driven back, wiping frantically at the flashes of fire that clung to the armored skeleton he wore.

"Impressive," he sneered. "But still not enough."

Deacon's body had begun to radiate an insane amount of heat, the air warping around his form as he readied himself for what was to happen next.

"It was my biggest fault, you know," Deacon said, stalking toward Stearns.

Stearns was ready, hundreds of different spells floating around in his mind, just waiting to be used.

"No matter how powerful I became, or how much knowledge I acquired, I always felt myself second to you," Deacon continued.

Stearns erected a shield of magickal protection while propelling another wave of pure, undiluted malice at his foe. Deacon responded effortlessly, catching the spell in his hand and allowing it to fizzle into nothing.

"Even when I knew that I was better, there was still that nagging voice at the back of my mind," Deacon explained.

"A voice to trust," Stearns said with a sneer, unleashing a barrage of destruction to attempt to drive his enemy back.

But Deacon kept coming.

"Now there's a new voice speaking inside my head," he said, a hint of a smile on his lips. "Whispering that the old Konrad Deacon is gone."

A rush of hurricane-force wind swirled from Stearns' fingertips; he hoped it would give him the time he required to consider his situation. He needed Deacon to be unprepared for what was to happen, unable to fight back when he began to feed on the energy he so coveted.

"But there was still something that nagged at me, that I couldn't quite put my finger on."

The wind drove Deacon back, but only by inches. The sorcerer planted his feet, the ground crumbling into dust as he held his place and started to advance again.

"And then I realized what it was," Deacon said. He flapped his wings of fire and propelled himself across the brief expanse.

Stearns would be a liar if he said that he wasn't afraid. But, as is often the case, from great fear comes great reward.

Deacon pounced on him, driving him back to the floor with inhuman strength.

"I realized that it was still you, Algernon," Deacon said, looming over him. "No matter how powerful I felt or how powerful the new voice inside told me that I was, I knew that you were still out there."

Lying on his back, Stearns looked up at Konrad Deacon. There was a fire in his eyes and something else—something that hadn't been there seventy years ago.

It was madness.

"You were still out there, ready to take what belonged to me."

Stearns watched as Deacon raised a hand that started to burn like a miniature sun.

Oh, how he coveted that power.

"So the only way that I could truly be at peace was to find and deal with you," Deacon said. "To finally take something away from you . . . your life."

"You're quite the prophet," Stearns spoke, focusing not on the idea that his own death was merely moments away, but that he would soon have his latest desire.

The mouths beneath his metal gauntlets were dripping in anticipation as Stearns raised his hand to Deacon's face, grabbing hold of the magician's cheek in a steely grip.

At first Deacon was smiling, amused by his enemy's struggles, but that look quickly turned to unease and then to pain as the mouths, aided by the sorcerous mechanics of the exoskeleton, proceeded to feed.

"You should have heeded that voice, Konrad," Stearns said gleefully. "For there is nothing that you can possess that I am not strong enough to take away."

There's no place like home. . . . There's no place like home. . . .

The line from her favorite movie echoed over and over inside Ashley's head as she and the others made their way slowly down the hallway.

Just seconds ago, they had passed a wicked old library, its high wooden bookcases stacked from floor to ceiling with books, and now they were in the corridor of one of those fancy office buildings. Ashley wondered what awaited them in the shadows up ahead and where they might be after they passed through them.

She pictured them all entering the cool shadow and

emerging in the crowded and damp-smelling basement of her Beacon Hill home. The thought caused the corners of her mouth to tick upward as she imagined them all climbing the stairs up from the basement, she leading the way, eager to introduce her new friends to her parents.

My parents.

How long have I been missing? They must be worried sick.

Squire's hand reached out, snagging her arm and violently yanking her back and from her thoughts.

"Pay the fuck attention!" the goblin screamed at her.

She was startled, and at first didn't know what he was talking about, until she saw that she had been on the verge of treading across a circular patch of shadow. She stared into the blackness, witnessing a ripple of distortion across the liquidlike surface as something moved beneath it.

"Sorry," she said. They were all stopped now, watching her. The building moaned like some kind of haunted house, and it sounded as if something big might be moving around behind them, where they'd just come from.

"I think there's a stairwell up here," the guy Francis said, taking all the attention from her.

He'd turned with the fat guy, and they were moving again.

"Here, take this," Squire said beside her. She looked down to see that he was trying to force some sort of small sword into her hand. Ashley hesitated, slipping her hands into the back pockets of her jeans.

"No, that's okay . . . I'm good."

"Take it!" the goblin demanded, roughly pulling at her arm and shoving the cool grip of the weapon into her hand. It was heavier than she imagined it would be, and it served as yet another reminder of how absolutely insane this all was.

"I don't want this," she then said, letting the sword drop on the carpeted floor. "I can't . . ."

"You can and you will," Squire said angrily, picking up

the sword and shoving it right back into her hand. "If you don't, you're gonna die."

She was suddenly back in her senior college-placement biology class with Mr. Harpin. *Adapt or die,* she heard the old man with the extremely large Adam's apple proclaim as they discussed evolution.

"Adapt or die," she said aloud, clutching the sword's hilt.

"Yeah, something like that," Squire agreed. "Now, let's keep an eye on where we're walking or . . ."

"Where are they?" Ashley asked.

Squire followed her gaze and saw that Angus and Francis were gone.

"Son of a bitch," the goblin hissed. "Whatever the fuck is going on in this building must've caused shit to shift again. Who knows where those two are now? There goes our safety in numbers."

She felt bad for slowing them down, causing them to lose their numbers.

"Yeah, but now I got this," she said, waving the short sword around.

"Be careful you don't poke your eye out," the goblin grumbled. He grabbed her elbow more gently this time and urged her to start moving.

"Let's go. Maybe we can catch up to them."

They started down the hallway again, careful to avoid any puddles of shadow spreading across the red-carpeted floor. She was being extra careful now, hefting her sword, ready.

Ready for what?

Ashley didn't know . . . didn't want to know . . . She just wanted to get home and see her parents.

There's no place like home. . . . There's no place like home. . . . There's no . . .

It was as if a curtain of solid black material had dropped down in front of them. Squire's arm shot out to prevent her from going any farther, but she had already come to a complete stop.

"This is what I'm talking about," the goblin muttered. "Everything's shifting around."

She could see that he was leaning forward slightly now, like he was sniffing the air in the darkness.

And then they heard the sounds.

"Hey, there you are," said a voice from behind the curtain, and at first she thought that it sounded like Francis. But she realized that it was too happy-sounding for the balding man with the golden pistol, and before she could say something there was a flash, followed by a crack of thunder, and Squire went flying backward.

The white-skinned man with the tattooed face slithered out from behind the curtain of shadow, smoldering pistol in one hand, the stump of the other pressed to his chest, a length of leash leading to a collar around the creepy little boy, Teddy's, scrawny neck, wrapped tightly around it.

"Thought we'd lost you," the pale man said with an unnerving smile.

Squire lay on his side, clutching a bloody leg, weapons from his golf bag strewn about the hall.

"Get out of here Ashley. Run!" he roared.

There was a moment's hesitation, as she didn't want to leave her friend, but there was also something in the pale man's eyes, something that told her that he was even more dangerous than the things that swam in the shadows. Ashley turned and started to run down the corridor. She had no idea where she was running or even what she might run into, but she knew that she had to do this if she was going to survive.

Running as fast as she could, avoiding the puddles of shadow on the floor around her, she heard the ominous words of the tattooed man following her.

"Go get her, Teddy. . . . Bring your toy back to me."

CHAPTER TWENTY-SIX

"Never let them take anything away from you," Konrad Deacon remembered his dementia-racked grandfather saying to him. *"And if they do . . . make them pay dearly for taking it."*

Even as he experienced the excruciating pain of Algernon Stearns attempting to steal away his divine power, Deacon could still remember the old man's urgings and the disturbing smile that adorned his ancient face as he spoke them.

"Make them pay dearly for taking it."

As soon as Stearns laid his hands upon him, he'd felt his strength, his angelic power, gradually being drained away.

How is he doing this? Deacon wondered, always questioning, always the seeker of knowledge. He could see that his rival was adorned in complex mechanics—something akin to the exoskeleton he himself had worn to siphon the collected life energies from his golem receptacles.

But there was something different about Stearns, something that went beyond the special suit.

Deacon struggled in the sorcerer's grasp, reaching up to pull away the hand that was pressed against his face. And that was when he saw how much Stearns had been changed by that experiment so many years ago.

That was when he saw the mouths.

"They're hungry, Konrad," Stearns said, "And now that they've gotten a taste of you, they're absolutely ravenous."

For a brief instant, Deacon had to wonder how drastically the others of the cabal had been altered by his experiment, but his thoughts were replaced by agony as Stearns laid his hungry hands on him and resumed his feeding.

From the corner of his eye, Deacon saw his wife. Of course she would be here to see this.

It's exactly as I told you, she chided, never lifting a finger to help. *Stearns is going to take it all away.*

"No," he screamed aloud, but that just made Stearns laugh, and he felt himself growing weaker all the faster.

A supernatural halo of fire had started to burn around his enemy's head, and that infuriated him to the brink of madness.

This was his power . . . *his* . . . He had taken it from one of Heaven's soldiers himself . . . not Algernon Stearns . . . *Konrad Deacon.*

He had taken it. . . . *He* was the master.

Deacon looked up into Stearns' smiling face and smiled back. He watched as his rival's expression went from one of joy to confusion . . .

And then to concern.

This was his power . . . and he would control it.

Deacon reached within himself, stopping the flow of divine energy into Stearns' body.

His wife's nagging voice was replaced by that of his grandfather, urging him to make his enemy pay. Flashes of a moment from his past exploded within his memory as he took control of the power. He recalled the first time he had truly listened to his grandfather's words.

When he was just a boy of six or seven, the family's driver was a man named Keady, a cruel man who resented young Konrad and the life of wealth and privilege into which he'd been born. And on one particular day, when Mr. Keady was supposed to be driving Konrad to a child's birthday party at the home of another family of wealth and privilege, that resentment reared its ugly head. Young Konrad was enjoying a lollipop—cherry flavored; he'd always loved cherries—when Mr. Keady ordered him to throw it away, or he wouldn't be allowed in the car. Of course, he had protested, and the driver took full advantage of the authority he had been given when it came to the car, citing rules laid down by Konrad's father himself that there would be no food or drink allowed in the vehicle.

And still Konrad had refused, attempting to climb into the back of the limousine with his cherry treat, which was when Mr. Keady happily acted, tearing the lolli from his mouth and tossing it to the ground.

Konrad remembered crying as if he'd lost a loved one, but he also remembered Mr. Keady laughing, as if this act of cruelty was one of the funniest things he had ever seen.

Konrad remembered.

The recollection of his past trauma now gave him the strength to stand. Stearns fought him, fought to feed, but Deacon had stopped the flow of power, keeping it all to himself.

Make them pay for taking it.

After he had gone to the birthday party, where treats of every conceivable imagining had been available to him, but not his cherry lollipop, he had gone to see his grandfather, to tell the old man what Mr. Keady had done.

Never mind the fact that he had already told his mother and father, who had ignored his indignant ravings; if there was anybody in his home that would understand, it would be his grandfather.

And his grandfather had understood perfectly well, and told him what he needed to do.

"Make them pay for taking it."

Some of his mother's special sleeping medicine crushed up and slipped into Mr. Keady's nightly coffee was how he set his revenge in motion. He had been so careful and quiet that night—invisible. The driver knew nothing of his drugged drink, downing the coffee and preparing a bath. The cruel man had collapsed on the bed in his bathrobe as the water had run, filling the tub.

Konrad didn't know if he would be strong enough at that young age to do what he needed to. It had taken him close to two hours but he had done it, dragging the unconscious man to the now-filled tub and, with great effort, putting him into the bath.

One of the maids had found him the next morning, screaming at the discovery that Mr. Keady had drowned in the bath.

Konrad remembered how he had smiled when he heard the commotion caused by the discovery, and relived the satisfaction he had felt as he watched the man sink beneath the bath waters, the last of the bubbles from his mouth and nose popping to the surface.

It was similar to what he was feeling now as he watched his enemy struggle to regain control.

Veronica was there again, dancing at the corner of his vision. He could sense that she was about to tell him yet again what Stearns would do, and he didn't want to hear it.

"Shut up," Deacon snarled, letting the divine power that he had been holding back flow into his enemy's body unabated.

For a moment, as the heavenly energy surged into his body, Stearns actually believed that he had won. *Foolish man.*

Remy Chandler was drunk on the life forces of thousands.

He could feel energy coursing through his veins like blood, sparks of memories, not his own, exploding in his mind in a cacophony of emotion, sight, and sounds.

He had never experienced anything so wonderful and yet terrifying. It was like he was being hit by tsunami-force waves, one right after the next.

Waves of people's life experiences.

Births, deaths, celebrations of every conceivable kind; one tumbling into another, his every sense on fire with the phenomena. He felt himself starting to slow, being driven to the ground by the perpetual onslaught, but he knew that he couldn't falter.

The fate of so many more were depending on him.

As he used to do with the power of the Seraphim, he forced the bombardment down, pushing it deep within, where it threatened to explode from its confines. But he could not think of that.

Remy found the broken stairway and made his way upward to where the television studio had once been, but now was nothing more than rubble open to the world.

His attention was immediately drawn to the struggle going on across the expanse of wreckage: Deacon versus Stearns. The energy that radiated from the battling pair was incredible; he could feel its intensity on his face from where he stood.

And then his eyes turned skyward, and he gazed in awe and horror at the swirling maelstrom of darkness that had opened there. It had grown larger in the short time since he'd last laid eyes on it, and it made the current situation all the more dire.

Remy moved from the ruined doorway, up farther into the demolished studio. He found himself drawn to the sorcerers' struggle, sensing that the fight was over the power that once belonged to him.

The power of the Seraphim.

A power that he would need if he had any hopes of stopping this madness.

He gazed at the magick users in mortal combat through flying rubble and smoke, and had no idea what he should do.

But he had to do something.

His gaze dropped down to see the body of the Grigori Armaros slumped back against a section of broken wall. The other Watchers lay around him, all of them with the hilts of daggers protruding from their chests.

A surge of memory like a bolt of lightning caused him to gasp aloud as it filled his mind. He was about to wrestle

it, to shove it back away with the others, when something
made him pause.

And remember.

Remy experienced the memory of the Grigori leader as
he was given his gift of death. Hands from an impenetrable
wall of shadow reached out to present the Watcher leader
with something rolled in ancient sackcloth.

"To still the heart of Heaven's own," said a silken voice
as Armaros took the gift. "And create believers of us all."

The memory seemed to fast-forward as Armaros held
the ancient dagger poised above his heart, and the explosion of pain and joy that was experienced as his life—and
those of his brethren—came to an end.

Their life energies surging outward into the golem child,
and then out into the world.

Remy gasped for breath as the memory released him,
and he found his eyes locked on the hilt of the mystical
blade protruding from the dead, fallen angel's chest.

To still the heart of Heaven's own, he heard the mysterious voice echo within the halls of his thoughts, as he turned
his gaze to the spectacle of battle still going on across from
him.

It appeared now that Deacon was winning.

He squatted down, hand temporarily hovering over the
hilt of the blade, before taking it in his hand.

And pulling it from the angel's stilled heart.

Francis stopped at the stairwell door and turned.

"Where the fuck are Squire and Ashley?" he asked.

Angus turned to the corridor and the darkness that
eventually swallowed it.

"They were right here a minute ago," the sorcerer said.

"Damn it," Francis snarled.

"Should we go back for them?" Angus asked.

The building trembled violently again, helping to shake
loose his decision.

"No," the former Guardian answered. "We've got to
reach Chandler if we don't want this all going to shit," he

said, hand on the doorknob. "That Squire is one tough puke. I don't think he'll have any problems holding his own."

Francis pushed open the door, and they found themselves in a stairwell untouched by hungry shadows.

"Isn't this nice?" Francis commented, already moving toward the stairs that would take them higher. "Too bad we couldn't hang for a bit. Have some lunch; maybe take a nap."

"I would love a nap right about now," Angus said.

"You and me both, but we've got some shit going on up above that's going to need our attention."

On the next level they found another door, and another stairway that led up into a wall of solid shadow.

"Something tells me I don't want to go to the next floor," Francis said.

Angus had already pulled open the door, holding it for his companion.

"After you," the sorcerer said.

"I would think you were being nice if it wasn't for the fact that there could be some shadow beast just inside, waiting to eat my ass."

"You wound me, sir," Angus said, as Francis passed through.

"Looks pretty clear," he said.

The office space was obviously a prime location, the walls of one entire side of the expanse covered in floor-to-ceiling windows. Francis found himself drawn to them, curious as to what might be happening outside the building.

"Holy crap," the angel assassin gasped.

The streets below them were filled with chaos, crowds of people surging away across the expanse of plaza. He could see the flashing lights of emergency vehicles, as well as some that may have had a connection to the military.

A tendril of darkness flowed down from above, past the window, slithering to the streets below.

"What the fuck was that?" Francis asked, pressing his

face against the cold glass to see what was happening directly below.

"The same thing that's happening in here," Angus answered. "The shadow realm is flowing into this world. By coming back here, Deacon must've somehow punctured a hole between realities."

"And that's bad because . . . ," Francis urged.

"That's bad because the shadow realm could easily continue to flow into this one, eventually breaking down all barriers and flooding this world with total darkness."

Francis watched through the window as more and more streams of slithering black rolled down the front of the skyscraper to the streets below.

"We've got to plug that hole," he said finally.

"Is that all?" Angus answered.

Francis couldn't stand to see anymore, leaving the window to find the next set of stairs that would take them closer to where they needed to be.

Just another thing added to his to-do list.

CHAPTER TWENTY-SEVEN

Squire didn't care to be shot again; he was funny like that. His shoulder already hurt like hell, and now his upper thigh felt like shit.

The hobgoblin surged up onto his stubby legs, ignoring the pain, running to where he saw a particularly inviting patch of shadow.

"Where are you going?" the tattooed man asked, firing his weapon wildly.

How many fucking bullets does this guy have? Squire asked himself as he dove, his injured body hitting the pool of darkness, the substance of darkness swallowing him whole.

He emerged on the other side of this particular path. It looked as though he was in some kind of warehouse, the smell of the ocean close by making the hairs in his pronounced nose tingle. It had been a long time since he'd smelled a living ocean.

Squire crawled from the passage, using the moment of calm to check out his wound. The tattooed man's bullet had hit him in the meaty part of his leg, but it looked as though it had passed through. He was lucky; if it had hit bone, he would have been a sitting duck. He would heal, but it would take a little time.

His attacker surged up from the pool of black.

"Bet you didn't think I could follow you," he said, aiming his weapon as Squire scrambled to his feet. "But it seems I've developed a knack."

He got off one shot, and then the gun clicked once, twice, three times on an empty chamber.

About fucking time.

"Huh. Outta bullets," the pale assassin said as he tossed the gun aside and pulled a nasty-looking hunting knife from his side. "Guess we're gonna have to do this up close and personal . . . which is fine by me."

Squire had lost his golf bag along the way, but he still had a few tricks up his sleeve. His eyes scanned the warehouse, and he sniffed at the air, getting past the salty goodness of the thriving ocean. What he was looking for . . . what he needed wasn't to be found here.

He would have to take this conflict elsewhere.

"Up close and personal is good," Squire said, limping on the injured leg, making it seem as though Paleface might actually have the upper hand. "Why don't you start without me, and I'll get back to you as soon as I can."

The goblin was running again, eyes scanning the various shadows, searching out one that could give him what he needed, a nice, ripe patch, one with real potential.

The tattooed man was running full tilt, knife by his side.

"I can follow you wherever you go," he growled. "And as soon as you get tired . . . oh man, the fun will start."

The guy was a complete asshole, and Squire couldn't wait until his piehole was shut for good, but he was gonna need to be very careful and play this just right, or he'd wind up with the shitty end of the stick.

The stink of a ripe passage was close by, and Squire stopped momentarily to tilt his head back. Down an aisle of shelves, behind a wooden crate spray-painted with the words MACHINE PARTS, he found what he'd been searching for.

"You mean the fun hasn't started already?" Squire called out. "Thought we'd reached our full fun potential when I cut off your hand. Don't know if my poor old constitution can take anymore."

He dove at the shadow, waiting for the cold, enveloping sensation as he entered the passage to another place but feeling only the viselike grip close around his ankle.

Squire thudded to the floor of the warehouse with a grunt, the shadow path just beyond his reach. He flipped over to see that the tattooed man was on his belly, holding on to him with his one good hand.

"Look at that," the pale man growled. "You made me drop my knife."

Squire struggled to squirm free, but the man's hold on him was ferocious.

"Guess I'm just gonna have to use my teeth," the tattooed man said, smiling like a great white, beginning to drag his weightier bulk up Squire's body.

Squire lashed out, bringing one of his legs up and kicking the pale man squarely in the face. He felt the sensation of something breaking through the sole of his boot.

"You fucking monkey," the tattooed man groaned, letting go of Squire to clutch at his own broken face. He picked at some loose pieces of white skin, revealing what looked like some sort of wet stone beneath.

"Wonder how long I can keep you alive," the pale man growled, then lunged for Squire.

Squire did a tumble, rolling away into the embrace of a shadow passage. He felt himself falling, then landed unceremoniously on something soft and rubbery.

The killer landed atop him with a grunt, and Squire took full advantage of the fact that his adversary was stunned by the landing. The goblin dug his stubby fingers into the man's face and pulled wet chunks away.

The tattooed man screamed like a banshee, arms flailing wildly. There was a glint of something in the dark, and Squire realized that his foe had managed to find his knife again. Reaching down to the floor of their confined space, Squire grabbed at something—anything—that he could use to block the blade.

The sneaker he brought up from the floor was just the thing.

Sneaker?

The killer was going wild, slashing out with his blade. Squire tried to stay low, reaching up to find what he suspected he would find: hands wrapping around the cool, metal knob and giving it a twist.

The two tumbled from the closet into a child's bedroom.

The little boy sat up in his bed, screaming that the monsters were coming out of his closet. *If only you knew how right you are,* Squire thought as he tried to get away.

In the faint glow of a night-light, he could see the damage he had done to the pale man's face. It looked as though most of his nose and even more of one of his cheeks were gone. The tattoos didn't look half as impressive anymore.

"Shut your fucking mouth, brat!" the pale man roared at the child, as he surged after Squire.

Squire had found an aluminum bat on the bedroom floor and used it to his fullest advantage. Swinging with all his might, he connected with his attacker's leg, driving him to his knees.

"Are we having fun yet?" Squire asked, hitting him again across the back.

The pale man dropped to the floor, and Squire felt as though his arm was going to fall off.

He glanced at the child, staring wide-eyed from the bed, and was about to tell him that everything was going to be all right when the tattooed man unexpectedly struck.

What is he, the Energizer Bunny, for fuck's sake?

The knife blade slashed across Squire's chest, cutting at least a five-inch-long gash.

"Son of a bitch!" Squire hissed, jumping back and away before any more damage could be wrought.

His attacker was already standing. It looked as though he was having difficulty with one leg, but he still seemed like he could do some serious damage.

Squire decided to get the fuck outta Dodge. He turned his back on the man, already searching for an exit, and found it beneath the kid's dresser. Not wanting to waste any time, he reached the piece of furniture, flipped it over, and dove inside.

He didn't even have to look to know that Paleface was following. Exploding out the other end of the path, he hit the ground at a run. His chest felt as though it were on fire, the pain blending with the pain of his shoulder and leg wound; one big, happy fucking pain family. He could feel the blood running from the wound beneath his shirt, which wasn't necessarily a bad thing, considering the situation he hoped to create.

He knew immediately when he was in the right place. His balls grew incredibly tight, disappearing up inside him, and if he could've disappeared inside himself, he would have, too.

"Where are you, you ugly fuck?" the pale assassin screamed as he emerged from the path, gunning for bear.

"Look who's talking," Squire goaded, sensing where he needed to be. "Think there might be some difficulty in the A Face Only a Mother Could Love competition."

The pale man stalked toward him, knife blade still clutched in his hand.

"Wait a minute," Squire said, backpedaling. "Did you even have a mother? From the looks of it, I'm going to be taking home first prize."

"Gonna cut your face off and wear it like a mask," the assassin said as he lunged.

Squire managed to avoid the attack, but barely. He was starting to slow down, the loss of blood and the accumulated pain of his injuries getting to be too much.

But if he did this right, it wouldn't take much longer. . . . And if he didn't do it right, nothing would really matter anymore.

An icy tendril of fear ran down the goblin's spine. Squire stopped, remaining perfectly still as the pale man limped closer.

"What's the matter—too tired to run?"

"No, I could probably keep this going quite a bit longer, but I really don't see the need."

"The first rational thing you've said so far," the killer said, a glint of madness in his cruel, dark eyes.

"Yeah, I figure we've come full circle, and we might as well end this here and now."

The tattooed man started, looking around, for the first time taking note of where they were. "We're back where we started?" he asked, sounding somewhat uncertain.

"Yeah, back in the Shadow Lands, minus the ugly house, of course."

"Fitting," the pale man said with finality. "This is where I became obsessed with you, and this is where it all comes to an end."

The killer lurched forward.

Squire was looking off into a particularly deep patch of gloom, searching . . . searching . . . and felt the hair on his entire body jump to attention.

"Yeah, it pretty much ends now."

He pulled up his shirt, revealing his bleeding wound. He placed his hand beneath the gash, wetting his fingers, and then flicking the blood into the darkness.

"Shouldn't pick at that," the pale man said with a hiss. "It's gonna get infected."

And then he lunged, knife blade ready to take another bite out of Squire. . . .

Just as something struck from the expanse of darkness.

It was large, probably one of the bigger shadow serpents that existed in the Shadow Lands. Squire had always been lucky enough to avoid it, but he knew that it had been aware of him. They'd both gotten each other's scent.

The goblin dove back as the serpent hit the pale man's side, flinging him violently across the blackened landscape. He must've lashed out with the knife as he was struck, because the serpent had reared back, away from its prey.

Squire managed to find an outcropping of solidified darkness to hide behind and watch the horror unfold.

The pale man was hurt pretty badly, what passed as blood oozing from his side, but he didn't seem to be concerned with protecting himself from the inevitable second strike. He seemed concerned with something else entirely.

The serpent's strike had torn away a section of the killer's shirt, and something had spilled from the top pocket.

Through squinted eyes, Squire watched as the killer dropped to his knees to collect what had fallen to the ground. They looked like photographs, and he crawled across the frozen darkness, desperately snatching them up and clutching them lovingly to his chest.

He had grabbed the last of the objects; his gaze had just found Squire's when the shadow serpent struck again.

The great beast latched onto the pale man, his precious objects flying into the air as the serpent yanked him back toward the darkness of its lair.

Squire tentatively emerged from his hiding place, the curiosity of what had been so important to his attacker drawing him like a beacon. They were exactly what he thought they might be: photographs. Squire looked at each of them, frozen moments in time with no rhyme or reason, until the last image.

It was a driver's license, and it belonged to the girl, Ashley. Squire slipped the plastic identification into a pocket, just in case, before starting to search for a passage to take him back.

Ashley ran until she couldn't run anymore.

It looked as though she'd made it inside a company lounge of some kind, big, overstuffed couches and chairs positioned around modern-looking coffee tables covered with magazines. One entire wall was nothing but large, tinted windows looking out over the city.

She came to a stumbling stop at the windows, peering out through the smoky glass at the spectacular view below, but the view was the least of her concerns.

The short sword still in hand, she spun around to face her pursuer.

"Stay back, Teddy!" she warned, but she couldn't see the youth.

Her eyes scanned the darkened room as she stepped away from the floor-to-ceiling glass. With Squire's warnings to avoid puddles of darkness prevalent in her thoughts, she was careful where she stepped as she looked for the wild boy.

Heart hammering in her chest so hard that she thought it might bust a rib, she moved toward the chairs but still could find no sign of the youth that had tried to keep her as a pet. She had no idea what was wrong with the boy, only that she'd heard his father say something about magick having killed his humanity, leaving only the beast behind.

It sounded right to her.

Ashley stood in the middle of the lounge, eyes darting about, searching for any sign of movement. There still was nothing, and she began to wonder if he had fallen victim to one of those shadow pools.

The back of her leg bumped up against the edge of the glass coffee table, and she stumbled back ever so slightly, her gaze falling to the clear surface of the table, reflexively reading the titles of the magazines lying there.

It was to the left of *Cooking Light* that she saw the grinning face peering up at her through the glass.

Ashley let out a scream, jumping away as Teddy surged up from where he had hidden beneath the coffee table. He was growling like a mad dog as he came at her.

She tried running again, her panic making her blind, and she ran head-on into the sofa, falling up against it as Teddy pounced.

Ashley cried out as the boy landed atop her, his jagged fingernails scratching her skin as he attempted to restrain her.

"Teddy, no!" she cried out, hoping to reach what little humanity might still exist.

The wild boy tried to pin her against the couch, but she continued to thrash. She felt his groping hands on her body and felt another piece of her sanity snap off and drift away. It was then that she realized she was still holding the sword and lashed out with it, hoping to drive her attacker away.

"Stop it!" she cried out, the flat of the sword connecting with the boy and actually knocking him back to land on the coffee table, shattering the top into what appeared to be a million pieces.

Ashley didn't waste any time, climbing over the back of the overstuffed sofa onto the other side. The sound of something thrashing among pieces of broken glass could be heard behind her, but she didn't want to turn around.

Teddy tackled her, his limbs entwining with her legs and bringing her hard to the lounge floor.

The air punched from her lungs, Ashley lay there stunned, the boy straddling her, as she rolled onto her back. In a flash of panic, she realized that she had dropped her sword and tried to find it, but the wild child appeared to sense this and bore down on her.

Ashley was wild, fighting beneath the boy's weight, but he kept her pinned, leering down at her, his lips pulling back to reveal sharp, yellowed teeth. Her panic set in as he leaned toward her, his mouth opening as he got closer to the soft flesh of her throat.

Close enough to bite.

I'm going to die, was the first thought that shot through her mind as she watched the animal child's open mouth come closer. After all that she had been through, this was the way that she was going to go out.

She imagined what it would feel like when the boy bit into her flesh, the popping of her skin as the teeth broke through, the ripping sensation as he tore away the first bite.

Ashley didn't want to feel it, but if that was the case, then she had to live.

She had to survive.

Adapt or die. She heard Mr. Harpin's nasty old voice echo through her mind, and Ashley knew what she had to do.

Teddy's breath was hot on her throat when she lost it, screaming like a madwoman and bucking her body so violently that she flipped the boy off her.

She knew that she couldn't hesitate, not one little bit, or

he would be back at her. Teddy was getting to his feet and coming at her just as she found her sword. Without a moment's pause, she snatched it up from the carpeted floor and spun to face her attacker.

"Get the fuck away, or I'll kill you!" she screamed, but it didn't slow the boy down. He came at her full force, and there was only one thing she could do.

Ashley brought the sword down with all her might, the blade striking off the top of his shaggy head and continuing down across his shocked face.

The wild child cried out in pain and backed quickly away. His trembling, clawed hands went to his wounds and came away covered in scarlet.

Teddy stared at her with eyes that said, *How could you do this to me?*

Ashley remained perfectly still, blade ready to strike again, if necessary.

"I warned you," she said, the sound of her voice scaring her with its ferocity.

Teddy whined, rubbing at the blood that now flowed freely down his face, but the whine quickly turned to a growl as he tensed to come at her yet again.

"Teddy . . . ," she started to warn, but he was already hurling himself at her.

Ashley struck him again, this time sinking the sword blade deeply into the fleshy area between shoulder and neck. Blood was now squirting from the wound, as he stumbled back and away from her.

The air was filled with a strangely metallic odor that she guessed was fresh blood, and would have likely gotten sick from the stink if she hadn't been preoccupied with the wild child's next attack.

Bleeding profusely, Teddy lunged, and Ashley defended herself. She swung the blade with excellent precision, cutting into the boy again and again, feeling the arterial spray of his blood hitting her face as she finally cut him down.

Teddy at last dropped to the floor, his lifeblood seeping

from multiple wounds into the carpet, as he lay there for a moment longer before expiring.

Ashley stood over him, sword still poised, waiting for him to rise, waiting for him to come at her again.

But he didn't.

It took a little bit longer for it to sink in—what she had done.

She didn't know how long she had been standing there, staring at the boy's dead body, when Squire found her.

"Hey, Ashley. You all right?" she heard the goblin ask her as he emerged from a particularly dark section of shadow near a tall potted plant.

She would forever remember the look on his face as she turned toward him, bloodstained sword in hand.

"It was just like Mr. Harpin said," she told him. "Adapt or die.

"I adapted."

Mulvehill could drive only as far as Mass Ave. before the traffic came to a complete standstill. Waiting for the traffic to move just far enough, he found an alleyway with No Parking signs posted and pulled his car down to do just that. He had a Police Business placard in his glove compartment and placed it in his window as he climbed from the car.

There was a constant, hurried flow of foot traffic coming down Boylston Street, and he moved against the current, going toward where they were coming from. He knew that he had to go there; it was practically calling to him, even though he had no clue as to what he would find.

And the unknown was terrifying.

His hand drifted down to the weapon inside his coat and he felt a surge of courage flow through him, giving him that extra bit more to continue on.

The street was blocked off at Fairfield, two uniformed officers nervously standing on one side of the yellow wooden horses, occasionally calling out to the people who flowed passed them to keep moving.

Mulvehill recognized one of the young officers, having worked with his father, and approached. At first the police officer didn't recognize him and was preparing to keep him from passing, but Mulvehill already had his badge out to flash at the man.

"Sorry, Detective Mulvehill," the officer said. "Didn't recognize you."

"That's all right, DeWitt," Steven said, looking past the man, up the street to where he needed to go. "What's the story?"

The young cop looked over as the other officer approached.

"We're really not sure. . . . We're hearing all kinds of shit," DeWitt said, a twinkle of fear in his dark brown eyes.

"Heard it might be a terrorist act," said the other cop. "Or maybe just an electrical fire. They got the whole plaza cordoned off, and we've been told to keep the foot traffic moving and the curious away."

"Interesting," Mulvehill said, moving past the young officer and behind the barrier.

"Are you going in, Detective?" DeWitt asked.

Mulvehill took his eyes off his destination for just a moment.

"Duty calls," he said with a chuckle. "And on my fucking day off, too."

Both of the officers laughed nervously.

A woman approached them with a panicked expression, asking how she was going to get home if her car was parked in the garage below the plaza.

"I'll catch you two when I'm coming out," Mulvehill told them with a wave. "See if I can't get you a better handle on what's going on."

They both waved, appreciative of his offer, as they began talking to the panicked woman.

Mulvehill continued up Boylston. One more block and he saw it: the Hermes Building, looming off in the distance, towering above many of the other buildings surrounding it. It looked as though there was a thick black cloud surrounding the top of the skyscraper. . . . *And what's that swirling around in the sky above it?* he wondered. It looked like a whirlpool in the sky.

The crowds and emergency personnel in front of him appeared impenetrable, so he headed back down Exeter Street, hoping to cut through on St. James Ave. and approach the building from the other side. He was still moving against the flow of traffic, the looks in people's eyes reminiscent of the news reports he had seen on 9/11. *What did they experience?* he wondered, fear whirling like the thing in the sky, but in the pit of his stomach. Then he was reminded of the weight of his gun by his side, and it allowed him to go on.

Mulvehill found it odd that the closer he got to the location, the darker it seemed to be getting. It was almost as if he were entering a different time zone or something, the shadows of dusk crawling across the faces of businesses and brownstones, but in all reality it would be hours before the sun started to set.

The fear churned, almost as if he could sense the unnaturalness of it all. *Maybe I've developed some kind of weird shit detector,* he considered, still moving forward.

The crowds were becoming more sparse, and when he did see anyone coming from that area, they were running . . . running as if the Devil himself were chasing them.

Or something worse.

Images of the things he had faced while helping Remy Chandler flashed before his mind's eye, and he actually found himself flinching. Mulvehill slowed slightly, blinking his eyes repeatedly as he tried to force the terrifying recollection to pass.

There was a through alley on his left that would take him that much closer to the Hermes, and he decided that he would cut through to see how close he could actually get. There was a woman, a cute blonde, in jogging shorts and a T-shirt coming down the opposite side. A little bit of a thing, no more than five-one, she must've been out for an afternoon run when the shit hit the fan.

He wasn't exactly sure why, but he wanted to tell her to hurry it up, to move as quickly as she could through the dark, shadow-filled alley to get to someplace safe.

Where there were lights and others.

He was just noticing that she was wearing earbuds, an iPod attached by a band around her biceps, and that she wouldn't have heard his urgings, anyway, when the shadow on the brick wall to her left seemed to explode.

It didn't make a sound as something long and snakelike shot out from the dark patch on the wall, wrapped itself around the woman's bare legs, and yanked her violently to the filthy ground.

The woman had no idea what had happened as she went down and was dragged across the alley toward the area of shadow that undulated and moved like the surface of a lake on a windswept day.

Mulvehill did not hesitate; he did not question what he was about to do, even though fear had grasped his heart in an ever-tightening grip and he thought that he might actually be having a heart attack.

But he wasn't listening to the pain or the panic; all he saw was the look of fear on the jogger's face as she was dragged toward the shadow moving on the wall.

"Hold on!" Steven cried, taking his gun from his jacket pocket. He doubted that she could even hear him, deafened by the iPod and her terror. He ran to her side, holding his pistol at the ready, and she began to scream as she saw him.

His gaze fell on the pool of darkness from where the limb—the tentacle?—originated. He didn't want to fire the weapon too close to the woman, so he decided to shoot where the limb came from.

Taking aim, he fired at the base of the black arm, one shot right after another hitting his target.

And the terrible limb reacted.

The tentacle recoiled, releasing the woman from its grasp and withdrawing into the pool of shadow on the wall.

The woman lay on the floor of the alley, hysterical, and he went to her, helping her to rise.

"Thank you. Thank you so much," she said over and over again between gasping sobs.

Mulvehill checked her out to be sure she was okay. She had circular bruises along both shapely legs but otherwise seemed unscathed.

There was a sudden explosion of some kind from close by, and he could feel it in the air, a vibration that made the skin of his face tingle and itch. That was followed by screams off in the distance.

"Get out of here," Mulvehill told the woman, waving his gun around as he turned his attention to the other end of the alley.

He did not watch her leave, feeling the pull of his destination at the end of the alley.

There was no stopping him now; Mulvehill knew exactly where he needed to go.

Where he needed to be.

CHAPTER TWENTY-EIGHT

Like a faithful dog, the power of the divine was coming back to him.

Deacon could not help but smile as he was filled again with the energy Stearns had so desperately coveted. He held Stearns tightly by the shoulders, watching as the divine force the sorcerer had tried to rip from him flowed back into his own body.

He allowed wings of flame to unfurl, reveling in the rush of cosmic energies that made him feel like the next-best thing to the Creator Himself.

"What was that, Algernon?" Deacon asked the man who had started to wither and age in his grasp. "What was that about taking away what's mine?"

"Please," Stearns gasped as a bloody tooth fell from blackened gums to dribble on a string of spit to the floor. "Leave me with something . . . just a taste."

Deacon threw his head back and laughed, catching sight of the rip in the fabric of reality swirling above his head. *Is that getting larger?* he wondered offhandedly.

"I gave the power to you, Algernon." Deacon turned his attention back to what was left of the sorcerer. "A gift . . . but you were too weak to contain it."

"Please," the old man begged, the flesh on his face sagging.

Deacon had never felt so strong.

"Please?" Deacon repeated, giving the man a violent shake. "If I had begged for my wife's life . . . or mercy for my little boy, would you and your cabal have granted it?"

Stearns looked away, his eyes closing.

"I thought not," Deacon said. "All those years I spent in the shadow place . . . all those lonely, lonely years . . . it led me here . . . led me to this very special moment." He gave Stearns another shake.

"Do you hear me . . . old man?" he asked with joy.

Stearns' eyes flickered open, hooded at first but growing wider by the second.

"Yes, that's it," Deacon urged. "Wake up for me . . . wake up for that special moment when I take it all from you."

He was about to flex the full extent of his power, to allow the fires of the Seraphim to surge through his body, down into his hands, to incinerate the sorcerer to cinder and ash. Until he realized that Stearns' milky gaze was focused not on him, but on something somewhere beyond him.

And his mortal enemy was smiling.

Deacon began to turn but was not fast enough.

Two daggers of metal entered the resurrected flesh of his back, just below his beautiful wings of fire.

There was a whisper in his ear.

"I believe you have something that belongs to me."

And the fires of the Seraphim surged to greet Remy Chandler.

The power of Heaven flowed through Remy's hands as he gripped the hilts of the murderous blades.

He screamed as the power entered him, its home for countless centuries.

But its dwelling had changed, and the divine fire of Heaven wondered if this receptacle for its glory would be strong enough to contain it.

Remy sensed its hesitation and urged it forward, even though his body burned with its heat and the scent of his singed flesh filled the air.

"Come into me," Remy cried out, his voice rough and choked with smoke. "Come into me and be at home."

And the power did, rushing in to fill the void that had been left by its passing.

Filling Remy close to bursting.

Deacon felt his body grow weaker.

The muscles in his back shriveled and he slid off the dagger's blades, dropping to his knees on the broken ground. Then he pitched forward, lying on his belly, desperately holding on to what little life energies he had remaining, and was shocked to find himself staring into the equally desiccated face of his rival.

Deacon did not know if his adversary was dead or alive until he saw the sorcerer's shoulder twitch and his arm begin to move. Fingers splayed, Stearns weakly extended his arm, reaching for Deacon.

Reaching for his face.

Too weak to move, Deacon could only watch in horror as his enemy's hand grew closer, horrible puckered mouths, like multiple versions of his grandfather's toothless mouth, hungrily descending.

Deacon wanted to scream but he did not have it within him to do so.

Stearns' hand fell upon him and the mouths greedily began to feed on what precious little he had left.

And suddenly Deacon found himself transported to another place.

It took him but a second to realize when and where he was.

It was August 6, 1945, and he was standing in the center of a road that led to Hiroshima.

He looked up to the sky, closing his eyes, waiting.

There came a flash so bright that he could see it, even though his eyes were still closed.

And a sound followed that could have been the sound of Creation.

But he knew, in fact, it was the sound of the end.

*　　*　　*

Remy felt as though he'd been born again.

The Seraphim was whole once more—*he* was whole once more.

But something was wrong.

Remy's body swelled with power, his every muscle burning, throwing off waves of intense heat. He tried to rein it in, to calm its fury, but something stirred it to action, and suddenly he knew the cause.

The golem child—Angelina—had filled him with the power of life, and this was what the holy fire was feeding on. The fires were stoked too high.

The sustenance of life was the most splendid and delicious of energies, and he was drunk on its potential. Remy struggled to focus, but he was high on the power that coursed through him.

He needed to do something, to find a way to alleviate this dangerous overflow. His gaze moved across the blighted rooftop before him, falling on the most horrific of sights.

The nearly skeletal Algernon Stearns lay atop the body of Konrad Deacon, feeding on what residual life force still remained within his enemy's withered corpse.

As if sensing the power in Remy's stare, Stearns raised his gaze to him.

There was hunger in the old sorcerer's eyes.

And this time, Remy was happy to oblige him.

He surged upward with a single flap of his powerful wings, dropping down in front of the cadaverous figure. Fear had momentarily surpassed hunger as Stearns looked at him, but that was quickly dispersed as Remy moved closer and extended his hand.

It was like dangling a bloody piece of meat before a hungry dog. At first there was some wariness, and then all sense of caution was jettisoned as the hunger got the better of him and Stearns reached up, wrapping his fingers around Remy's hand.

The sensation was nauseating, and Remy had to make a conscious effort not to yank his hand away in utter disgust.

He could feel the mouths moving against his flesh, sucking away the excessive energies that threatened to overtake him. The intensity of the power that rushed through his body was beginning to diminish, and he could at last begin to focus.

Finally feeling a sense of calm, a sense of peace, Remy tried to take his hand away from the energy vampire, but was met with considerable resistance, the eager mouths on Stearns' hands sucking all the faster, attempting to take even more than what was being offered.

It was exactly what Remy would have expected from such a creature, and why he had decided to do what he was about to.

Stearns brought his other hand around for even more of the angel's power, but Remy was faster, snatching the sorcerer's wrist before he could take hold.

The sorcerer grew frantic, desperate to partake of that much more of the Seraphim's precious life energies.

But Remy had decided that he had had enough.

Stearns must have seen something in Remy's eyes, something that told him that he had fed for the last time. In a last-ditch effort, magick exploded from his fingertips, bolts of crisscrossing energy causing the ground before him to detonate explosively as he attempted to flee.

But the Seraphim was not hindered by the magickal display, soaring up and over the mystical conflagration to descend behind the sorcerer.

"Please," was the last word to escape his mouth, as Remy reached out for him. He grabbed Stearns by the head, and violently snapped his neck like a dry twig.

Remy felt little remorse for the magick user as he released his twitching body, letting it drop limply to the broken ground. There were other, more pressing matters that required his—

"Remy?"

He heard his name carried across the rooftop and turned, in all his angelic glory, toward the sound. He was stunned by what he saw.

At first he thought it some kind of trick, some last bit of

magickal mischief perpetrated by the sorcerers that had turned his life around of late, but soon came to realize that she was real.

Ashley.

He was overjoyed to see her and about to approach when he saw the expression on her face.

How long has she been standing there? What did she see me do?

It was an expression of fear.

CHAPTER TWENTY-NINE

Ashley felt something inside her brain let go.

It wasn't that she had been kidnapped and taken away from everything she loved. . . . It wasn't that she had just killed someone, hacking him with a sword until he was bloody and unmoving. . . .

It was stepping from the shadows, Squire by her side, to see him.

Him. My Remy.

At least, she thought it was him, but why did he look that way? Why was he glowing as if he were blazing hot, and wearing armor, and . . .

Are those wings?

She was still overjoyed to see him, and was about to cry out when she saw—*heard*—what he did to the person he was struggling with.

As the muffled snap of the person's neck filled her ears, something went inside her as well, and she knew that nothing—no matter how hard she wanted it to be—would ever be the same again.

"Remy."

She hadn't even known that she had spoken; his name was just suddenly there, dropping from her lips like the twitching body that fell from her friend's grasp.

He had been looking toward the open sky at the swirling black whirlpool.

Here was something else that had changed: She'd never seen a whirlpool in the sky before, and she had to wonder what else had changed in the world since she had been gone. . . .

Or have these things always been here and I just couldn't see them? It was something to think about.

As a little girl, she had always wondered about the life Dorothy had led after coming back from Oz. . . . How had it changed her? She couldn't be the same old Dorothy anymore.

Remy was looking at her now, and he seemed happy to see her, but the way he looked . . . and what he had done . . .

Ashley could see it on his face. He was actually coming toward her when he stopped.

She'd never been very good at hiding how she was feeling, and right now she was terrified of him . . . of what he was.

Maybe it was just like in the movie, and the scarecrow was Hunk the farmhand, and the Wicked Witch was actually Miss Gulch.

Remy Chandler was actually . . .

What is he?

The word was suddenly there, and there was no doubting it was right.

Angel.

But she'd never seen an angel so . . .

Scary.

She was going to try to speak to him when something happened to stop her. The thing in the sky—that swirling, whirlpool thing—it was getting bigger.

And she thought that it might be trying to swallow the world.

The thing in the sky screamed and swirled in all its fury, bringing darkness as it grew, blotting out the sun.

And with the darkness there came shadow.

More and more shadows.

It was not hard for Remy to look away from the girl. The look of fear in her eyes was enough to dissuade him as he turned his gaze to something not as troubling: the rupture that had been created between two realities. The pull of the maelstrom was getting stronger, the hole tearing larger with the passing minutes. He could hear panic in the streets below, imagining the horrors that might be emerging from the darkness spawned by Deacon's return to his world of birth.

But it was not only the people on the streets who faced danger from the shadows.

A beast of black flowed out from beneath a section of rubble, hungry for the taste of angel. Surprised by the attack, Remy fell backward to the ground as the shadow monster pounced on him. Its claws were like ice, sinking into the exposed flesh of his arms. He saw from the right corner of his vision the hobgoblin coming to his aid, leaving Ashley alone.

"No," he cried out, attempting to heave the thrashing animal from atop him. "I've got this. . . . Don't leave her side."

The goblin warrior obliged him, backing away to stand before his charge, as Remy attempted to thwart this latest attack on him from the realm of shadows.

And if something was not done about the opening in the sky above, it would be far from the last.

He got the flat of his forearm beneath the slathering animal's throat, holding its snapping, black jaws at bay, and was forcing it from him when there came an explosion of gunfire, and its head temporarily transformed into a Rorschach pattern before rolling off of him to the ground, where its mass was swallowed up by yet another bottomless pool of darkness.

Remy jumped to his feet in time to see Francis and Angus coming across the wreckage of the rooftop toward him. The passage above their heads had grown larger still, expanding across the sky, the shadow realm now pouring into this reality.

"You know that isn't good, right?" Angus said to him, pointing up into the sky. Francis and the sorcerer had now joined the hobgoblin and Ashley.

"Is there anything you can do?" Remy asked the sorcerer, hoping for a quick fix but already knowing the answer.

"I've got nothing," Angus said grimly over the sound of the shrieking anomaly in the sky above.

Remy peered up into the eye of the unnatural storm, shielding his vision from the flying dust and debris, and looked into the heart of darkness.

He felt a stirring at the center of his being, the reality of what he was—where he had come from—roused to act.

He was the embodiment of God's light—which drove away the darkness—and he knew what he must do.

As if sensing the realization he had come to, the center of the vortex grew suddenly larger. With an ear-piercing cry like a living thing, the whorl of the gyre became faster.

Larger pieces of stone and glass were now being sucked up from the rooftop, and he could see that his friends were having difficulty staying on their feet.

There was no more time for hesitation.

"It's time for you all to go," Remy yelled over the storm.

They all began to balk, and he spread his wings and began to flap them furiously, adding to the winds and driving them back.

Francis was the only one who did not move, standing his ground, gun still in hand.

"What do you think you're doing?" he asked Remy.

"I'm ending this before it's too late."

"Is there anything that I can do?"

"Get them out of here," Remy said. "Keep them safe until it's over."

Francis knew what he had to do; they'd always had an understanding about these things. Remy turned away from his friend, knowing full well that he would do what Remy had asked of him.

Remy couldn't think of them anymore, only of what needed to be done. Springing off the rooftop, his wings beat the air, propelling him skyward, fighting the insane winds as he allowed himself to be sucked up into the cyclonic force.

He did not fight it as he was spun around and around, inexorably pulled toward the center of the widening gyre. This was what his life had felt like of late—slowly being pulled toward the eye of storm, no matter how much he fought, inevitably being dragged toward the center.

But he wasn't going to fight it anymore.

For at the center was solution.

Remy felt the cold of the mouth as it yawned wider to accept him, and for the first time in a long while, he was completely at peace. His natures—his human and angelic—were as one, knowing what needed to be done.

What the Almighty would want them to do.

And as the darkness took him, he heard the words so often attributed to his Heavenly Father.

Let there be light.

And there was light.

An old woman pushing a shopping cart filled with bottles and cans was coming toward him, terror in her eyes. Something was after her, something that jumped from one patch of shadow to the next as it stalked its prey.

Mulvehill saw this and acted, guessing where the beast would next appear and aiming his pistol accordingly. He smiled at the fact that he had been right as the lionlike monster sprang out of a shadow cast by the overhanging sign of an Indian restaurant that he frequented.

His pistol barked twice, the shots hitting the unearthly animal in its muscular side, sending it thrashing to the ground in death. Mulvehill ran to the old woman, who had fallen. Her brimming cart had tipped over, spilling its contents onto the sidewalk.

The shadow beast had crawled onto its feet, considering them with hungry eyes as it bled darkness onto the sidewalk.

"C'mon, then," Mulvehill said in defiance of the monster. "I'm not afraid of you."

As if accepting his challenge, the monstrous thing sprang across the expanse of sidewalk, as Mulvehill raised his weapon once more to fire.

And that was when the sky became filled with a sudden brilliance and the threat of the beast was gone like the passing of a nightmare with the coming of dawn.

The light was like nothing he had ever experienced before, permeating every crack, crevice, and corner of the city where the darkness could hide.

He could feel it even inside himself, burning away any despair and fear that still remained and filling him up with fire.

Filling him up with hope.

Eyes watering from the intensity of the flare, Mulvehill's vision cleared and he found himself making his way into the center of the street across from Hermes Plaza, where he gazed up to the desolated top floor of the building.

But the sky above it was as blue as the sea and twice as calm, and the shadows around him were just shadows.

He didn't know where the words came from. They just came, bubbling up from one of those places locked inside the brain where things like that were stored away.

And God saw the light, and it was good. And God divided the light from the darkness.

CHAPTER THIRTY

Remy knew where he was even before he opened his eyes.

He could hear the sound of the crashing surf, the smell of the ocean invigorating him as it came into his lungs.

It was a Cape Cod beach that didn't really exist, an amalgam of many of the Cape beaches and other seaside places that he and Madeline had enjoyed in her lifetime.

He had created this place in his mind as a kind of tribute to her after she had died, and would come here often when things were tough and he wanted—*needed*—to see her again.

It was foggy here today, heavy, moist air cutting visibility down to mere feet. Despite the gloominess of it all, Madeline and he had always loved these days, walking for hours hand in hand, never knowing what was in front of them in the shifting haze.

Never knowing what was ahead.

Now he walked the shore alone, searching for the one that would make this piece of life he had carved away for himself complete.

A cool gust blew off the water, stirring the miasma of gray that filled the air, and he could just about make out a shape there in the distance, and moved toward it.

He found it a little strange that she hadn't been there waiting for him when he'd first arrived, but really didn't think all that much about it. When they finally found each other, he would ask where she had been, and she would likely say something fresh, like it was good that he had to wait until he found her, that absence makes the heart grow fonder, or one of those things she liked to say.

And he would tell her that he had no patience when it came to things involving her, and he would take her into his arms, remembering all the times he had done just that.

Holding on and never wanting to let go.

The shape was becoming more defined and Remy was just about to call out to her when he came to a most startling realization.

It wasn't Madeline.

A spark of anger flared within him as he approached the male figure standing with his back to him in the rolling surf. The man was dressed in a dark suit, his slacks rolled up to his knees as the water surged up to greet him like an excited dog before receding in play. This was his special place, his and Madeline's; there shouldn't have been anybody else here.

He didn't want anybody else here.

"What are you doing here?" Remy asked the man's back.

"Which name do you prefer?" the man spoke over the roar of the tumbling waves.

Remy was confused by the question.

"What? What do you mean?"

"Which do you prefer, Remiel or Remy?" the man asked, slowly turning his back on the ocean to face him. "I think I'd like to call you Remy," he said, and smiled.

There was no mistaking who this man was, and Remy felt the air sucked from his lungs as he dropped to one knee in the sand, head bowed, eyes averted.

"Oh, stop that," the man said. "Stand up and look at me. I didn't come here to make you grovel."

But why did you come? Remy thought, his mind in turmoil. *Why did* He *come?*

Remy rose ever so slowly, eyes gradually drifting to the

older gentleman's kindly visage, wondering if there was any reason why He had chosen to appear like this . . . as if *He* needed a reason.

"You'd once seen this man walking the boardwalk of Coney Island with his wife, his grown children and their wives, and their children," *He* said, answering Remy's question before it was asked. "Then you believed him to be the embodiment of a happy existence—everything that you wished for yourself, the things that you would strive for."

Remy recalled the moment suddenly; it had happened not too long after he'd decided to live among humanity—to live as one of them.

"I thought it might make it easier for you to accept why I have come to you," *He* said.

The implication hit Remy like a sledge to the heart.

"Am I dead?"

The man turned His gaze back to the fog-enshrouded sea.

"You could have been," *He* said. "But I preferred that you were not."

As did Remy.

"Why are you . . ." Remy began, stopping as *He* again turned His attention to him.

"I need your help, Remy," *He* said. "The Kingdom of Heaven needs your help." The surf grew suddenly angry as winds began to howl off the restless water. "The world of man needs your help."

Particles of sand hurled by the wind stung his face, and he raised a hand to shield himself from the onslaught.

The man had again turned away from him, gazing out into the fog and the unknown that existed beyond it. There came a low rumble of thunder; the ominous growl of uncertainty.

"There is a war coming, Remy Chandler," *He* said. "And I need you to stop it."

The smell of coffee had replaced that of the sea.

Remy groaned as he opened his eyes, looking up at the

white tin ceiling. It took only a few seconds to figure out where he was; coffee beans grown and harvested in Hell had a very specific aroma when brewed.

He was reclining upon the leather sofa, covered with a heavy afghan, in Francis' basement apartment. Remy sat up, peering across the living room into the kitchen, where Francis, the hobgoblin, and Angus were sitting around the kitchen table, having coffee.

"How did I end up here?" Remy asked, pulling the afghan off.

"Hey, look who's awake," Francis said. He rose from his chair, going to the cabinet and reaching for a mug. "Coffee?"

"Sure," Remy said, noticing that he was wearing a turquoise sweat suit. "What the fuck am I wearing?"

"Your clothes were pretty much nonexistent after you fell from the sky," Francis said as he poured a steaming cup from the carafe. He crossed the room and handed Remy the cup.

"How did you all get in here?" Remy asked, ready to take a sip, desperate for the taste and the jolt the Hell-grown beans would bring. "Thought I had the only keys."

When Francis had disappeared and was believed dead, Remy had been left the Newbury Street brownstone. He thought he was the only one who could get inside.

"I left a key under the mat," Francis said, returning to the kitchen.

"What mat?" Remy asked after his first sip of the rejuvenating brew.

"There's got to be a mat around here somewhere," the former Guardian said, filling his own cup again.

"There's always a mat," Angus agreed with a nod.

"A dime a dozen," the hobgoblin added.

Remy left the living room and approached them, coffee in hand.

"Anybody care to fill me in on what happened out there?" he asked. "I'm guessing that the outcome was favorable?"

Francis shrugged. "All depends on how you define *favorable*."

"The shadow realm didn't flood the earth, so that's good," the hobgoblin stated.

Remy eyed the small, ugly creature.

"You dragged me out of there—the shadow realm—with Ashley," Remy said.

"Yeah," the hobgoblin said, rising from his chair with a wince. He was wearing a yellowed wifebeater stained with blood, and Remy could see that his shoulder was heavily bandaged.

"The name's Squire," the goblin said, reaching across the table to take Remy's hand in a powerful grip. "Sorry that I didn't bring back the real girl on the first try."

Remy shook Squire's hand. "Thank you," he said. "I didn't even know."

"Golems can be tricky," the sorcerer Angus added, chubby hands wrapped around his coffee mug.

"Where is she?" Remy then asked. "Is she all right?"

Francis lowered his mug, silent for longer than Remy cared for.

"She's up in one of the apartments on the first floor," Francis answered. "I said that she could use it to get herself cleaned up. Get her shit together."

"Is she all right?" Remy asked again.

"Yeah, I guess," he said. The others were nodding in agreement. "She's been through a lot . . . seen some things that somebody like her . . ."

Francis seemed as if he wanted to say something else, but stopped and had some more to drink.

"Not just her," Angus spoke up, turning his coffee mug in his hands. "As of tonight, the entire world has seen things the likes of which have never been witnessed on such a grand scale." The sorcerer got up from his chair, going to the coffeepot for a refill. "Little girls promising a message from God, things emerging from the shadows, a swirling black hole in the sky . . ."

Angus looked directly at him as he poured.

"An angel flying into that hole and exploding in a flash of heavenly light."

He set the carafe back down and took a quick sip from his cup as he returned to his seat.

"As of tonight . . . I would say the whole goddamned planet has changed."

Remy had hoped that maybe, somehow, the rational, thinking minds of the world would have explained it all away as some sort of mass hallucination brought on by . . . he didn't know exactly. He expected those same rational brains to fill in the blanks.

Didn't sound like that was in the cards this time.

"That bad?" Remy asked.

"Pretty bad," Francis said. "More than two thousand dead, and that was just a result of the television broadcast. We haven't even gotten a number yet on how many as a result of what happened on the plaza."

Remy felt the weight of the world push down even further on his shoulders as he remembered the message given to him in his subconscious.

There's a war coming.

"Did Ashley get in touch with her folks?" Remy asked, needing to change the subject.

"I gave her my phone," Francis said. "But she said that she wanted to wait until you woke up . . . to talk with you before . . ."

Remy understood what he needed to do. Nodding, he finished his cup and set it down on the table. As much as he'd rather not, he needed to speak with Ashley, to explain to her how sorry he was for getting her involved in his insane world.

"I guess I should get up there," Remy said, motioning toward the door. "What room is she in?"

"Maybe you should take it easy for a little while longer," Francis suggested. "Give her some more time to wrap her brain around everything that she's gone through."

"I think she needs an explanation now," Remy said.

"Angus and Squire are going to be hanging out for a while. Why don't we get some Chinese and . . ."

"What room?"

"Gave her the key to 1G," Francis said, resigned to the fact that he was going.

Remy headed toward the stairs that would take him up to the lobby and was halfway up when Francis called up to him from below.

Standing on the stairs, Remy turned to see what he wanted.

"Can I talk to you about something?" Francis asked.

"Can it wait until . . ."

"It's about Ashley," Francis spoke out, his features frighteningly still. "And what I could do to help her."

The discussion he'd had with Francis lingered like a bad smell in his thoughts as he stopped before the door to apartment 1G.

He looked toward the stairs to see Francis reach the first floor.

"I'll wait out here," he said. "If she says yes."

Remy nodded, chilled by Francis' suggestion, but also feeling a twisted sort of relief that the option he was going to present to her even existed.

It would be up to her to decide.

Remy knocked lightly upon the door and waited.

"Yeah?" called a tiny voice from behind the door.

"It's me," Remy answered.

"Come in."

Remy opened the door and stepped into the apartment, closing the door gently behind him. He noticed that every bit of lighting had been turned on, making the barren walls of the empty apartment seem to glow. Ashley was sitting at the far end of the living room, up against the wall, beneath the open window. It was raining softly outside, and a gentle breeze that carried the smell of fire and magick wafted into the apartment.

He left the door to stand on the border of the hallway and living room, not wanting to get any closer to her. Ashley tensed as he stood there, pulling her legs up closer to her body and refusing to look at him.

"Are you all right?" he asked her. "Do you need to see a doctor?"

She shook her head no, sniffling, a wad of toilet paper appearing in her hand to wipe at swollen, teary eyes and a running nose.

"The first thing I want to say to you is how sorry I am," Remy told her.

"For what?" she asked, still refusing to look at him.

"This never would have happened if it wasn't for me and what I am."

"What are you?" The question was quick, harsh, as if she'd been waiting for the opportunity to present itself.

"I'm an angel . . . a Seraphim."

"Like, from Heaven and stuff?" Ashley asked, sniffing again.

"Yeah, like that."

"That's pretty nuts," she said, and started to laugh, but she was soon crying again.

"It is pretty nuts, and it's why I've kept it a secret from you all these years."

"Does anybody know?"

"Mulvehill found out by accident. Francis, who's got issues of his own. Marlowe . . ."

"Marlowe understands that you're an angel?" she asked. It was the first time she'd looked at him.

"Yeah, I can talk to him just like I'm talking to you. I can speak and understand any language. It's one of the angel perks."

"You can speak dog?"

"Dog . . . cat . . . wombat . . . yeah, anything that has any kind of language."

"Did Madeline know?" Ashley asked.

"Yeah, about that—"

"Wait—if you're an angel, how could you have a mother?" she wanted to know.

"She wasn't my mother," Remy admitted with a sigh. "She was my wife."

There was silence as the answer slowly permeated.

"I knew it," Ashley said finally. "I knew there was something different about you guys . . . about your relationship. Mom said that she thought you might be one of those gay guys who's really close to their mothers, but I knew you weren't gay."

"Your mother thinks I'm gay?" Remy asked, finding out more than he cared to.

"Yeah, she did at first," Ashley said. "Now she doesn't know what you are."

"I can't believe your mother thought I was gay," he said.

"What would you think?" she asked. "Good-looking guy, lived with his mother, now lives alone with his dog."

"You think I'm good-looking?"

She laughed softly. "Is also very neat and tidy."

"Neat and tidy? I'm a slob."

"I've never seen a dirty dish in your sink . . . ever, and I've known you for, like, a hundred years."

"That's because I seldom eat at home."

"Not even a dirty glass or cup. It's freaky."

"But you didn't think I was gay," he said to her.

She shook her head. "I just thought you were . . . eccentric."

"You and your mother didn't have any kind of bet, did you?" Remy asked, trying not to smile but completely powerless not to.

Ashley was smiling back, and he saw her old self finally breaking through the darkness he had caused.

"With my dad," she said, and started to laugh. She looked at him then and the fear was gone.

"Your dad? I think I need to sit down."

Remy came into the room, lowered himself to the floor, and leaned back against the living room wall, no more than three feet from her.

"So no money has exchanged hands yet, I gather?"

"Nope," Ashley said. "There's been nothing definitive yet to say who's won."

"How's it feel to be right?" Remy asked.

A shadow passed over her pretty face, and she studied something underneath one of her fingernails.

"You're probably wishing I was gay."

"That would have been normal," she said. "Easier to understand."

"Is there anything that I can say or do to make it easier for you?" he asked.

He could see her thinking. It looked as though it might've hurt.

"There's still a part of me that hopes I'm having hallucinations or something, that the crap I've just gone through has all been in my head."

She looked at him, eyes hard.

"It's all been real, hasn't it?"

Remy just nodded, feeling ashamed. He was about to tell her how sorry he was again, but knew that it would have little impact.

"You have no idea how hard it is for me to be sitting here and not crying or screaming or curled into a ball with my eyes closed, but no matter what I do I can't escape what I've seen . . . what I've done."

The fear was back, swirling behind her eyes, and he could see that she was doing everything in her power to hold it together.

"The world isn't the same anymore, Remy," she said, looking at him, swollen tears dribbling from her eyes, down a face that somehow appeared older to him.

"No," he agreed. "It isn't."

"I'm not the same anymore," she added.

It was then that he remembered that Francis was standing outside in the hallway, and what they had discussed.

"What if there was a way that I could make you the same?" Remy asked.

Ashley looked at him. "What are you talking about?"

"I'm just saying, how would you feel if there was a way that you could be made to . . . forget."

He wasn't sure if it was more fear or excitement he saw in her gaze then.

"That isn't possible," she said in a whisper.

"Do you remember that you're talking to an angel?"

"How? How could you make me forget?"

"Francis . . ."

"Francis can make me forget?"

"He's acquired this . . . instrument," Remy started to explain. "It's a scalpel of supernatural origin."

Ashley was just staring at him.

"A scalpel so precise that . . ." Remy paused, even the thought of using the instrument on the girl making him feel sick to his stomach.

"A scalpel to cut out my memory?" Ashley finished for him.

"Yeah, that's about right."

"How could . . . How would you . . . ?"

"Francis would go in and cut the bad stuff away," Remy explained. "Like cutting away an infection. He'd likely start just before you were taken and stop not too long after now . . . just before you get home."

"And I wouldn't remember any of it?" she asked.

"It would be gone," Remy said.

He could see that she was thinking . . . thinking hard.

"It would be so easy to say yes," she said to him. "To let Francis take away all the scary stuff, but that's the stuff that has changed me. . . . And no matter what I can and can't remember, I'm still changed. I'm still that new person now, whether I can remember what happened or not."

She paused for a second.

"Does that make any sense at all?" she asked.

"Yeah, it does," he told her. "It would be like having a scar and having no idea where it came from."

"The experience, no matter how bad or painful, it teaches you something . . . forces you to grow."

Remy nodded, understanding exactly where her head was. He could not help but be pleased at her decision.

"So I'm guessing that Francis and his scalpel will not be required," Remy said.

"No," she said firmly. "I think I need to remember what's happened."

"You're sure that you can live with that?" he asked, just to be sure.

"Yeah," Ashley said. "I don't think it's going to be easy at first, and will probably take a while . . . but I think I'm going to be all right."

It was good to know.

"And us?" Remy asked.

She stared at him intensely, studying his face as if seeing him for the very first time.

"I think we're going to be okay, too," she told him, a sly smile starting to form before disappearing entirely. "Especially after I collect my winnings."

They had a good laugh then, until Remy remembered her parents. They were probably still worried sick.

"Have you been in touch with your mother and father yet?" he asked.

"Not yet," she said. "I wanted to talk to you first."

"Do you think they could handle the truth?" Remy asked.

She shook her head vigorously. "No way," she said. "I think they both have a difficult time with the way the world is currently, never mind adding this other business."

"What are you going to tell them?"

"How about that I freaked out . . . that I needed to get away . . . that I wasn't ready for the whole college-and-adulthood thing."

Remy made a face. What Ashley was planning on selling to her folks and the authorities that were looking for her was ridiculously thin.

"They found blood in your car," he said.

She shrugged. "I cut myself."

"Do you seriously think they're going to buy it?" Remy asked.

"I'm not going to give them a choice," Ashley said firmly, rising to her feet as she took Francis' phone from her pocket.

"And, besides, what I'm giving them is more believable than the truth."

The city was still pretty much in turmoil, even spreading as far as West Roxbury, where Remy had gone to pick up his car from where he'd left it in front of Saint Augustine's Church.

He didn't see the old ladies there holding vigil, and he wondered if maybe they'd somehow ceased to be with the death of the Grigori Garfial. It might be something he should look into at a later date, just to be sure. He didn't want the angel scientist's lab falling into the wrong hands.

The ride home was a little hairy, lots of streets still closed off, but he managed to get to the Hill in a round-about way and had even managed to find parking on Pinckney Street.

He'd used Francis' phone to call Linda before leaving, his phone having been incinerated when he'd gone nova in the expanding eye of the shadow storm. She was excited to hear from him and equally excited to hear that Ashley was safe and sound. Before hanging up, she'd asked him if he'd seen the news, if he knew what had gone on in the city to-day, and he told her that he'd caught it in bits and pieces and that it all sounded pretty crazy.

Linda said that it was beyond scary, and for him to hurry home, that she would be waiting for him at his place.

Remy let himself into his building, stepping into the foyer to find his door wide open.

"Hello?" he called out, moving toward the opening cautiously. After what he'd just gone through in the past twenty-four hours, cautiously was just the way to go.

From inside he heard the sound of toenails scrabbling across the hardwood floor, and Marlowe bounded out to greet him.

"Hey, buddy," Remy said, bending down to wrap his arms around the dog's thick Labrador neck. "How's my good boy?"

"Talk again?" Marlowe asked, between furious licks of his face.

"Yeah, I can talk to you again," Remy answered him. "And it feels good."

"Missed talking," Marlowe said, giving him his paw.

"And I missed talking to you," Remy said, giving it a shake. "This is a new trick. Who taught you this?" As if he didn't know.

"Linda," the dog barked.

"Thought so. What else has she taught you?"

The dog then proceeded to get down on the floor and place his face between his paws, looking up at him pathetically.

"What's that?" Remy asked.

"Sad face," Marlowe answered, springing to his feet, tail wagging.

"And what does that get you?" Remy asked him.

"Treats!" the black Labrador barked happily.

"I think you're also learning to play Linda like a fiddle," he said, sticking his head into the apartment to see if she was inside. Finding it empty, he figured she must've been up on the roof.

"No fiddle," Marlowe explained. *"Shake and sad face. No fiddle."*

"Got it," Remy said. "Is Linda on the roof?" he asked the dog, already starting up.

The dog told him she was and joined him on the stairs, practically running him off the steps in order to get up to the rooftop of the brownstone first.

The dog barked his excitement as he bounded out onto the top floor of the building, announcing his and Remy's arrival. He could hear Linda telling him to calm down, and smell what he believed to be swordfish steaks wafting from the grill.

"Hey," she said, putting the grill cover back down and

coming to greet him in the entryway with a kiss. "It's good to have you back."

"It's good to be back," he told her, returning her kiss and putting his arms around her thin waist to hug her. Touching her, he realized how much he needed this at the moment and didn't want to let her go, fearing that he might be pulled from the rooftop, sucked up into a swirling vortex that had appeared in the sky.

"Hungry?"

Remy looked from the nighttime sky, where a swirling hole between dimensions had not appeared, and turned his attention to Linda.

"Starved," he told her.

"Excellent," she said, pulling from his embrace to return to the grill. "The swordfish should just about be done. Why don't you open that bottle of Chardonnay for me and pour yourself a whiskey, and we should be ready to eat."

He heard a crunching sound and looked to see that Marlowe was lying down and happily gnawing on a giant-sized pig's ear; the ultimate treat when it came to the Labrador.

"Seems as though everybody is eating good tonight," he said, opening the bottle of wine as he watched Linda take the steaks from the grill and place them on a plate.

All so perfectly normal.

They sat down and ate their meal at the patio table, enjoying each other's company.

All so perfectly normal.

After they had finished, they took their drinks to the rooftop's edge, looking out over the sparkling city, the shape of the darkened Hermes Building sticking up among the lights like a jagged spike of darkness.

All so perfectly normal.

And, in reality, as far from the truth as it could possibly be.

"It feels different now," Linda said as he held her.

She had told him everything that had happened in the city as they ate, about the little girl's message and how some of the people who had been listening had somehow been stricken dead, about the explosion on the rooftop of the

Hermes Building, and the strange atmospheric phenomenon that nobody could explain that had appeared in the sky.

And of the sighting of what some people were saying was an angel just before the thing in the sky disappeared in a flash of light.

He remained silent as she told him everything, holding her tighter as he felt her shiver in his arms.

"Some people are saying that it's the beginning of the end of the world," she told him, and he was certain that she wanted to be reassured by him that this was all crazy talk, that there was a rational explanation for every one of the strange incidents that had happened today.

But Remy said nothing, choosing instead to continue to hold her, hoping that this gave her some sense of security.

"Just tell me that everything is going to be all right," she asked of him then.

And he told her, "Everything is going to be all right." But Remy knew otherwise.

For this, too, was as far from the truth as it could actually be.

EPILOGUE

Steven Mulvehill awoke feeling . . . different.

Reborn.

He smiled at how stupid and over-the-top the thought was as he left his apartment building on his way to the grocery store, but there was a certain truth to it. The heavy cloud of dread that he had worn as a cape since the events connected to Remy's case was apparently gone, and he no longer felt paralyzed by the fear that had been his constant companion since that day.

He closed the door behind him and started down the steps.

He'd had his first really good night of sleep in close to a month and actually was feeling terrific.

The events of the previous day flashed before him: the jogger he had saved in the alleyway and the old woman—and the things he had confronted to rescue them. Mulvehill felt himself immediately start to react, his heartbeat quicken, the itchy sensation of cold sweat prickling on his neck and back, but then he remembered what had come from the top of the Hermes Building.

And then he remembered the light.

The light from atop the building had given him something. *Courage? Is that the appropriate word?* he wondered as he left his apartment building and headed for his car.

Whatever it was, it made him want to go back out into the world, despite the shadows and the things that lurked inside them. It hadn't taken away his fear, for only very stupid people weren't afraid, but now he understood his fear, and, in understanding it, he could confront it and shoot it in the fucking face, if necessary.

He'd reached his car and was taking his keys from his pocket when he saw the man approaching from the corner of his eye.

"Steven Mulvehill?" the man asked, stepping out from between two parked cars to address him.

"Who wants to know?" Steven answered, giving the man the once-over as he looked up and then back to his keys. The man was dressed in a dark suit—expensive-looking—and white shirt, black-striped red tie, black shoes. He wore his blond hair cut short, and Mulvehill thought that he might have heard the hint of an accent, but would need to hear him speak again to be positive.

"My name is Malatesta," the man said, reaching inside his suit jacket pocket and removing his identification.

Mulvehill took the offered leather folder and flipped it open to read. "That you are," he said, eyes scanning the information presented. "What can I do for you, Mr. Malatesta?"

Mulvehill's eyes came to an abrupt stop, the sound of cartoon brakes slamming down in a screech inside his head as he read where the man was from. He looked up from the identification, unsure of what to think.

"I'm from the Vatican, Mr. Mulvehill," Malatesta said, taking his identification from him and placing it back inside his coat.

"I see that," Mulvehill responded, still in shock. Why would somebody from the Vatican be speaking to . . .

"What can you tell me about a man named Remy Chandler?" Malatesta asked.

And suddenly, it all made a terrible kind of sense.

He was not certain at first, but the stranger decided that he would indeed miss the sad Grigori.

He stood inside the Boston skyscraper they had called home and stared out the very windows that had once captivated them, twirling the star signet ring upon his finger. The glass was stained and cracked, but the stranger saw as the Grigori did, and so much more than that.

Turning away from window, he scanned the empty space, searching for anything of theirs that might be salvaged, anything that could be put to use in the coming days. The wooden box that contained the ashes of their beloved leader caught his attention, and he glided to it, taking it from its place of honor atop a stack of wallboard.

The stranger carefully opened the lid, turning his dark gaze to the powdery contents.

"Hello, Sariel," he said softly. He poked a finger into the ashes, looking for any fragments of bone that might not have been devoured by the Seraphim's flames.

Armaros and the others had certainly loved their leader, and their sadness had provided the perfect incentive for them to follow the stranger's . . .

Suggestions.

From amidst the ash, he found a fragment of bone—something that perhaps had once been part of the angel leader's finger—and carefully took it from the box and slid it into a pants pocket.

One never knew when something like this might prove of use.

His search exhausted, the stranger callously tipped the box over, allowing the ashes to join the layers of dust and plaster residue that were already there. He then tossed the empty casket over his shoulder to land among the other pieces of refuse that had been left behind when the construction of the office space had halted.

Scanning the remainder of the room, the stranger found nothing of importance and decided that his time there was at an end. One of the angels—the Grigori—had practiced the art of creating life. The stranger decided that he would have to see about finding that one's workplace.

Who knew what treasures might be found there?

Sensing that the stranger was ready to depart, a sphere of light ignited in the center of the room, allowing the demons to emerge.

He could sense them behind him, waiting, but he did not acknowledge their presence. They were always in such a hurry—so impatient—and he found it good for them to have to wait.

Waiting was what it was all about.

"Sir?" one of the three demons called.

He was going to ignore the request, but decided that since he'd pretty much found everything that he was going to find, he'd respond.

"Yes?" the stranger answered, still not looking at them.

"We felt that you were ready and . . ."

"You sensed correctly," he said, turning to face them.

They hated him—he could feel it in their horrible gazes—but they could do nothing about it. He reached over and casually twirled the ring on his right ring finger.

All they could do was obey.

They had no choice.

The stranger stepped toward the foul, pale-skinned creatures and entered the glowing circle on the floor.

"Take me home," he commanded, his thoughts already racing. He had to find another sorcerer to serve him, seeing as neither of the two that he had been considering had worked out. If he'd been a betting man, he would have thought Stearns to be the victor, but Deacon had managed to prove himself quite the surprise.

If only one of them had survived.

It was just one more detail to be added to his list of chores for the coming days. *There is still so much to do,* he thought as he gave the demons a barely perceptible nod to activate the sphere of transference to take them from this place.

So much to do to start a war.

And bring the dominions of Heaven crashing down.

R0013